"Just one more question. Tell me how your art career happened to pick up so quickly after your two roommates were murdered? One day you were teaching school and saving your pennies, and a few days later you were suddenly supporting yourself on your painting."

There was a moment of silence, and then Jill Wilkes snarled, "A few days! It took months of hard, hard work!"

"Months is still a few days in my world. I coached football for nearly ten years before I was even close to moving off square one."

"Maybe you just weren't any good, parole officer."

"Or maybe," Reppa countered, "I didn't have a sugar daddy to pay my bills so I could stay home and paint. Or maybe I didn't need a sugar daddy because a certain gallery owner decided to have a show of my work. For a reason, let's say, that had very little to do with art."

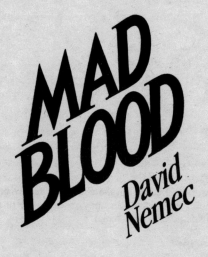

MAD BLOOD

David Nemec

A TOM DOHERTY ASSOCIATES BOOK

MAD BLOOD

Copyright © 1982 by David Nemec

Reprinted by arrangement with Doubleday & Company, Inc.

A TOR Book

Published by Tom Doherty Associates,
8-10 West 36 Street,
New York, N.Y. 10018

First TOR printing: October 1984

ISBN: 0-812-50704-5
CAN. ED.: 0-812-50705-3

Printed in the United States of America

To Beth

ACKNOWLEDGMENTS

I would like to express my gratitude to fellow
writers George Blecher, Tom Engelhardt,
Beverly Gologorsky, Steven Kroll, and Nancy
Newman for their helpful reading of this book
in manuscript form. Thanks are also due to
Paul Sweda for his technical eye and to the
MacDowell Colony for providing the
atmosphere and work space where parts of this
book were written. A special gratitude is owed
to my editor, Rick Kot, whose contributions
were immeasurable, and once again
to my agent, Felicia Eth.

"Now, these hot days, is the mad blood stirring."
—William Shakespeare,
Romeo and Juliet,
Act III, Scene i

PROLOGUE

JUNE 5, 1968

A long shadow slanted across the bare wood floor to the metal bridge chair where the young woman sat. She was naked. Her arms and legs were bound to the chair with belts and sashes. She watched the man approach her. His pallid, hairless body was clad only in a pair of blue cotton briefs. In his right hand was a bone knife. Yet the look in the woman's eyes was more curious than frightened, and her mouth held a slight smile.

"What are you going to do?" she asked.

The man raised the knife as if the gesture were answer enough.

"Tell me," the woman persisted. "It makes it easier for both of us if you tell me."

He stared at her a moment and then shook his head almost sadly. "How quickly you've learned."

"I had a good teacher," she said, still smiling carefully.

"Had?"

She gave him a speculative look. "Don't think it means I'm getting bored because I need you to talk to me about what we're doing.

"What does it mean?"

The woman was silent. Then, coaxing him with her smile, she said, "Take off your panties."

"When I'm ready."

"To fuck me? How are you going to fuck me today? Tell me."

The man winced. Less firmly he repeated, "When I'm ready."

"What are you going to fuck me with?" she said, ignoring that his head was shaking in a plea for silence. "The knife? How are you going to do it? *Tell* me."

He stood immobile in front of her.

Again she said, "Take your clothes off."

"I have."

"Everything."

The man took a step toward her. "I'm not ready. Can't you understand . . . ?"

The woman stopped smiling for a moment. She raised soft, somber eyes to the man.

"Let me help."

His head shook rapidly.

"Why not? Why are you always so . . . ?" She paused to hunt for a word that was gentler than the one she'd almost spoken. "When are you going to stop being so self-conscious? I mean, look at me. I'm not exactly Jayne Mansfield myself."

Her eyes lowered to her small breasts, skimmed over her slim hips and thighs, and then raised again to engage those of the man. He glanced swiftly away at her bed, where her clothes were laid out beneath his on a colorful patchwork quilt. Beside her bed, separated from it by a maplewood dressing table, was a second bed, belonging to one of her roommates. Her other roommate occupied a smaller bedroom down the hall. Since it was a weekday, both women were at work this morning. But for the events of last night the woman in the chair would not have been home either. When the man had arrived, she'd been listening to the radio. "They don't think he's going to make it." He had just shrugged and begun tying her to the chair. California was a continent away; everything he cared about was here on West Ninety-fourth Street. Himself, of course, and more and more this woman who seemed to understand so much about him. Still, when she'd called to tell him she'd been given the day off unexpectedly, he hadn't wanted to come here. His place was much safer. But the sunlight in her room was so fantastic this morning, she'd said. And besides, she was already naked. . . .

"Be glad you're at least normal," he said to her now.

For an instant her smile turned ironic. "Then what am I doing here with you?"

"As far as your body goes. You don't have anything wrong."

"Neither do you."

He gave a bitter, contradictory laugh.

"I wish . . ." Once more the woman struggled to find gentle words. "You're too critical of yourself. You have no reason to be. You're a fine-looking man."

"You don't really believe that."

"But I do. Right from the first I was very attracted to you."

"Hardly from the first. Considering how surprised you were when you found out about me."

"Not all that surprised. I think I knew almost right away that you weren't—"

"You're the only one now," the man cut in quickly. "The only one who knows the truth about me."

"Don't be so sure. Others sense it, too."

"Never. I've been very careful."

"What about Jill? She knows there's something going on between us."

"You've *told* her?"

"No! But I can tell from the looks she's been giving me—"

"Stay away from Jill," he said savagely. "She's a viper."

"A viper? What do you mean?"

The man shook his head. "You're so innocent underneath it all. Still such an innocent."

"I know." The woman was smiling again. "I need you to teach me. Come now, teacher of mine. Take off your panties and teach me. Teach me everything."

For a final second or two the man hesitated, staring down at the hand that held the knife. Then he turned his back to the woman and removed the blue cotton briefs. As he tossed them on the patchwork quilt, his eyes grazed the window. Although it faced a blank wall on the building across the alleyway, he was compelled to draw the blind. Even then he still could not turn around and face the woman. He stood in front of the window, silent and tense.

The woman called to him. Her voice was soft, almost a croon, but he heard it as teasing, even mocking.

"Come to me. Tell me what you're going to do with the knife. Come, my teacher."

"Close your eyes."

"Why?"

"Because," the man said impatiently. "I want you to."

"But really, you don't have anything to be ashamed—"

He craned his neck and looked over his shoulder.

"I said, *close* them!"

The woman recoiled, and then obediently her eyes closed. The man approached her slowly until he was standing over her, so close that his knees brushed against hers. He slid the knife under his penis and raised it with the edge of the blade. It hung limp for a moment and then, very slowly, began to stiffen.

"Now," he said quietly. "Now put me in your mouth."

Without opening her eyes the woman brought her head forward. Her lips found his penis and drew it eagerly into her mouth. Sitting rigidly upright, bound to the chair, she began making slow rhythmic thrusts with her head and shoulders while he spoke to her. His voice altered now. Not only did it become louder, but it took on a singsong quality that made his words sound more soothing than menacing.

"Harder, pet. Do it fast and hard, or I'll cut off your tongue. Harder, I said. Bite. Use your teeth. Better, pet. That's much . . . *much* . . . better . . ."

Neither of them heard the front door of the apartment open.

The man was the first to realize they were no longer alone. Throwing his head back to give himself completely to the woman's mouth, he saw one of her roommates standing in the bedroom doorway. He had no idea how long she had been there, but he knew instantly that she had already seen too much. Her eyes were wide with shock. They took in the knife in his hand, his penis in the woman's mouth. She stood there, face frozen, arms straight down at her sides.

He had no choice. He could not risk that look in her eyes. That look that would at any moment change to revulsion. Disbelief. *Recognition*. He lurched against the woman in the chair and bowled her over backward, sending her and the chair crashing to the floor.

"What are you . . . ?" the roommate began. But then he was upon her. He struck at her mouth with one hand, swinging the knife with the other. The blade plunged into

15

her chest. Was withdrawn and plunged again. And again. And again. She sagged to the floor, the front of her blouse crimson, blood darkening the waist of her cotton skirt. She sprawled on her side, arms limp, eyes sightless.

He whirled on the other woman. She lay dazed, still bound to the chair, shaken by the fall but more by what she had seen.

"Why?" she murmured dully, too stunned to react physically or scream.

"You know why."

The trouble was she only knew part of it. The part she knew was bad enough, but the part she didn't know was even more awful. She must never know the rest; no one must.

Step one was clear. To gain time to think he lifted the woman in the chair by the shoulders and slammed the back of her head against the floor. Did it a second time. A third. Until she was unconscious.

Then he ran to the bed and wrapped the blue cotton briefs, the shoes, all the clothes he had worn to her apartment that morning in a plastic dry-cleaning bag so they would not get stained. . . .

CHAPTER ONE

DROP A DIME
ON DANNY

Women were an intrusion on all the things that brought order to his world, but Frank Reppa could not live without them. If he was out of their company for so much as a single day, he grew irritable and depressed. During his four football seasons at Ohio State he had never drunk a beer, smoked a joint, or stayed up past midnight, yet evenings after practice he could not settle down to study until he had snuck out of the team dormitory to spend at least an hour or two with his girl friend of the moment. In the army he had breezed through all the grueling hours of training and reveled in the harassment dealt him by the officers and NCO's, but he found the nights in the barracks without women unbearable. It was not entirely sexual; not anymore it wasn't. In recent years he had begun learning he needed women for other purposes, too. They might not have the scope or intelligence of men; they almost never wanted to talk about the same topics he did (mainly sports and crime); but they made better friends, sometimes, than men. And, my God, they made sleeping and life in general easier when they were around.

Which was why he had more or less moved into Leilah Sturm's ground-floor apartment on Bank Street last December and was reluctant to stop occupying her bed even though sex between them had become difficult if not downright impossible. For the last three months, whenever he reached out dreamily for Leilah during the night, he encountered not a warm healthy buttock but the cold metal guardrail that separated them; and his first vision each morning upon awakening was no longer of her dark-brown eyes impatiently waiting to resume whatever argument they had gone to sleep on. Instead he saw what seemed to be a huge bug with a shiny thorax—for Leilah lay encapsulated in a steel upper-body brace under a cobweblike network of pulleys. Reppa shook his head, wryly thinking that any sane woman would have convalesced in the hospital, just as any sane man would have moved out long ago, forcing her to hire a full-time nurse. That he hadn't moved out told him he must feel guilty about what had happened to her. To prove to himself that, whatever he was feeling, he could still escape, he'd tried sleeping at his place on East Ninth Street one night but given up after several hours of staring at the ceiling when he realized that he had grown terribly accustomed to Leilah's bed, metal railing and all, and frighteningly unaccustomed to having only his own noises and smells for company.

He raised himself up on his elbows, observing that she was still asleep. Eyes closed, mouth slightly ajar, a small bubble of saliva occupying one corner. It all felt very domestic. His wife, Irene, had slept with her nose wrinkled up like a rabbit's. Ex-wife actually, though he would never be comfortable about applying that term to her unless he married again. Even then it would go against his grain. If he one day had more kids by another woman, would he be obliged to call his three girls his ex-daughters? Perhaps Leilah had the right idea about him after all. She maintained he was gripped by more conventions than any

18

man she'd ever known, and at one and the same time was gripped by a sleeping worm of rebellion that would, if it were ever stirred awake, be all his own.

Sunlight spilled in through the window at the east end of the bedroom. It was too late to go back to sleep, but Reppa couldn't make himself get up yet either. His body was bursting with energy, but it wasn't energy for shaving and going to work.

He lay back, wondering once again how his ambitions had come to the impasse they had. Growing up in Cleveland, all he had wanted was to play middle linebacker for the Browns. When, by his senior year at Ohio State, he was still no better than third string, he had revised his goal and decided to become head coach of the Browns. For nearly a decade, with two years out for the army, everything had gone smoothly. Steadily, one rung at a time, he'd climbed the ladder toward an assistant's job at a major college. He was just one step away, needing only a conference championship to culminate the massive rebuilding program he'd undertaken at Riverside High the year after the school had lost every game, for the feelers from Notre Dame and Penn State to become firm offers. But it rained heavily the night of the title game against Tylers Landing, forcing both teams to keep the ball on the ground. And then his fullback, Zinser boy, had to go and get himself kicked in the head in a pileup. Zinser boy hadn't even seemed hurt at first; a hulking rhino of a kid, over two hundred and forty pounds, he'd carried the ball six more times (as the game film they showed at the inquest attested) before collapsing in the huddle. Some vein or other had hemorrhaged in his brain with the ball on the four-yard line . . . four meager yards short of the conference championship. Of course that had all suddenly become meaningless to Reppa, even though he couldn't convince anyone in Riverside of that. The town drew back from accusing him of outright murder, but there were too many parents who were ready to lynch the superintendent if Reppa's contract was renewed. From that of a hard-nosed Bear Bryant type, his image swiftly altered to that of a mad bull. Since none of the other high schools in Ohio would hire him either, he had no option but to move on.

In a way, the course events subsequently took could have turned out to be a break. He had signed on as a linebacker coach with the New York Stars of the ill-fated World Football League, but the franchise moved, leaving him behind. For a while he assisted the coach of the New York Fillies, the women's professional team; but that club folded, too. Nobody in New York, it seemed, wanted to pay to see a troupe of women bounce one another around like jacks. Reppa's secret hunch was that if the Fillies had played the Jets or the Giants, all the seats in the stadium would have been sold out five minutes after the game was scheduled. The classic battle of the sexes.

Meanwhile, until the Stars or the Fillies or some other off-brand team resurfaced and went shopping for a maverick coach, he had to find a way to make ends meet. Staying in New York didn't make much sense, but neither did returning to Ohio; and the only other place he'd ever called home was Fort Knox, where he'd done his basic training followed by twenty months as a company clerk and a linebacker on the post football team. Briefly and self-punitively Reppa really did consider reupping in the army, but then an opportunity came along to join another kind of service. Civil. The results of the parole officer's exam he'd taken when he saw the Fillies were futureless ranked him third in the New York City area, and within a few months an offer of an appointment had appeared in his mailbox.

So now he was Parole Officer Reppa, working out of the Fortieth Street office across from Port Authority. Being a comparative newcomer, with barely three years in an outfit that went strictly by seniority, he had something less than a plum for a case load—central Harlem. He lived in dread of field days, like today, when he was expected to visit the homes of a dozen or so men on his case load, mostly just to make sure they were still living where they said they were and not dealing heroin or bimbos out of their living rooms. Well, maybe not actual dread, but close. Even though he was over six feet tall, still had the frame of a college linebacker, and carried a Colt .38, state issue, he knew he was little match for the rage on the streets he walked. Cops had the asset of traveling in pairs and the support of the whole police department only a radio call away if they ran into trouble; a parole officer, especially if he was white, was usually all on his own— and God help him if the corner junkies decided to clean his clock. A parole officer's shield could pass from a distance for a cop's, but up close it had about the same clout as a toy in a Cracker Jack box.

Reppa sighed with a sense of his imprisonment. He turned over on his right side, away from Leilah, and let the sheet slide off his bare flank. It was getting on toward seven thirty. In another half hour his car had to be moved, or it would be towed away. All over the country it was late April, the heart of spring, a reprieve, but in New York spring meant the traffic patrol came out of the woodwork, making up with a vengeance for the revenue the city had lost over the winter to snow days, when alternate-side parking rules had had to be suspended.

April. In just a few more days May! Central Park. The outdoor cafés in the Village. Weekends at the beach ahead of the summer crowds.

The previous October, on their very first full day together, he and Leilah had journeyed to a secluded lake she knew about in Harriman State Park. Although the temperature had only been in the sixties, she had stripped and plunged into the water, calling him a candy-ass for not joining her. What else had they done that day? Hid each other's clothes. Eaten a can of smoked oysters with their fingers. Made love behind some blackberry bushes along the Appalachian Trail, and again in his car on the drive back to the city, pulling off the road onto an observation promontory high above the George Washington Bridge—and finally in her apartment, which by then he'd already foreseen he would be spending a lot of time in. Leilah was desperate that they get in as much as they could before the romance ended or winter overtook them. He wasn't in quite as much of a hurry—he just wanted the day to last. This October, barring a miracle, there would be no such outings. As for the rest of the spring, if all went perfectly, about the best he could hope for was that Leilah would be able to sit up in bed without having to hang on to any pulleys.

Such was the situation. The first real tomboy he'd met as an adult, and instead of a mate (in the British sense) with whom he could share all the things he enjoyed, he had a near basket case. If only she hadn't been so competitive with him. But if she hadn't been so competitive, would he be here now? The world was full of women who would play gin rummy or tennis with you if no score was kept. There were very few, though, who insisted on winning all the time, or at least admitted they couldn't stand losing. Competition. In Leilah he had at last found a woman who would make any kid with aspirations of playing pro ball a good mother. Maybe even his own next kid, assuming it was only a dreadful fluke his first three issues had all been girls. ''Sons are better,'' Leilah had agreed the one time she'd had anything to say on the subject. "They don't spend as much time in the can." He knew what she was really trying to tell him, and she might well have forced him to revise his view of the place women occupied in the scheme of things had she stayed healthy just a little longer. He was only a beat or two away from bringing up the possibility of another kind of living arrangement when their present one was ruined. Once a near Amazon, all five feet of her in sweat socks, she had become as helpless as an infant, barely able to manage a knife and fork. Though of course it hadn't diminished her appetite in the least. It just meant that along with everything else he had to feed her, meanwhile suppressing his own appetite, of a different nature.

It was present in him now.

All it took was a few seconds of thinking about their first day together last October. He had never gotten off to a faster start with a woman, or a more erotic one. Heaving himself out of bed, he did ten quick push-ups on the floor, still cluttered with last night's dinner dishes. Then five more, until his arms were aching pleasantly. After the last push-up he rested on the floor, his chin pressed against the rough wood. He could smell, coming faintly from the dishes, the wine sauce in which he'd simmered the chicken. Under the bed he saw an empty beer bottle. Where had that come from? One of her friends? The woman upstairs who played nursemaid to her while he was at work? Most people who were bedridden demanded that their visitors bring them news of the outside world, but Leilah yearned only for food. Eerily she never gained an ounce. He could almost believe she was hiding a secret boarder if he hadn't watched her pack it away so many times all by herself.

He got up and glanced at her again. She was wide awake now, fingers scrabbling irritably over her brace.

Over the last few weeks he had learned to read even her minutest signal, and this one was fairly obvious. She wanted the bedpan. As with so many things, though, she still resented the need for it too much to ask for it.

He lugged it in to her from the bathroom. Then began the struggle to get it under her. It was probably just as well she had him there. A nurse might have had better technique but would have lacked his strength. Leilah's one hundred and two pounds, although almost completely immobilized, still had the feline combativeness of an animal twice her weight. She looked at him while he maneuvered her legs and hips as if she were competing to keep him from lifting her. His cock swung into her field of vision, and he remembered too late that he ought to put a pair of pants on before he undertook this task.

She seized him while his hands were defenselessly removing the bedpan. The tips of her fingers. Tweaking teasingly. He stood precariously holding the bedpan.

"If I spill this . . ."

Leilah laughed. He remembered when he had found it a wildly exciting sound. It was still a little like being cheered on from the sidelines.

The alarm clock said seven forty-three. *Two more minutes;* he made it a vow. Her fingers would tire by then anyway. Once indefatigable from years of pounding a typewriter, they now wore down quickly from their recent months of inactivity. Still Leilah wouldn't let him leave without a valiant effort to make sure he wasn't in a state of even mild horniness. She imagined that inside every home in Harlem he visited there lurked a cunningly molten woman who would have liked nothing better than to seduce her husband's parole officer, and it was a fact that when he'd first started this job, he'd imagined something very similar. In three years, though, he had yet to do anything sexier during a home visit than change a light bulb.

*   *   *

Ten twenty-five. He was working his way downtown from 148th Street, aiming to knock off for the day around two o'clock. The lunch-hour crowd at the McBurney YMCA would have begun to thin out by then, freeing the paddle-ball courts for an hour or two of good hard uninterrupted play. Lidsky, his supervisor, expected him to call the office at four, maintaining the pretense that he was working that late, but there were pay phones at the Y he could use to carry off the sham. ("Hello. Mel. It's Reppa. Up on a Hundred Sixteenth Street and about to pack it in for the day. Any late-breaking developments at your end?") It was part of the game. You seldom put in more than four hours of actual work on a field day, but you claimed double that on your activity sheet. Most supervisors went along with it routinely. Lidsky did, too, but he had to be made to feel that you weren't aware he did.

Civil Service. The State of New York. You gave them about three days work for every five for which you were paid. The equalizer. They were only paying you roughly three fifths of what the job was worth anyway. Coaching in high school had given him the same feeling, but there he'd put in around triple the time that he'd had to. And he would have put in the whole of next year for free, at the smallest and lowliest high school in the country, just to have a crack at getting back in the saddle again. Every time he remembered the flutter in his stomach before the opening kickoff of a game, his eyes swam and his throat ached. It was getting further and further behind him. By now he was almost used to the grinding activity his stomach underwent prowling the streets of Harlem. In the winter it wasn't so bad. There were few people abroad, and no one paid too much attention to a white man in a sheepskin jacket, thinking he had tools under it to do some repair job for Con Ed or Ma Bell. But as the temperatures climbed, so did traffic on the streets and interest in him. Coatless, he was clearly not carrying an array of tools. Just one that made a bulge under the shirttail he wore out over his belt, if you looked closely. Many unfortunately did, and it wasn't only paranoia that made him glance dartingly behind him every fifth step or so.

Carrying a gun. Very close to the feeling he used to have on guard duty. *I will walk my post in a military manner, keeping always on the alert and observing everything within sight or hearing.* Good training, now that he could look back on it from a distance of eleven years, and it astonished him how much of what he'd been taught had stuck. But it was that way with football, too. Every coach he'd played under had contributed a phrase or two to his education. Most of all his last coach.

Avoid getting in a bind.

He was wondering how he could do that as he went down 123rd Street, heading for Jimmy Wallace's building. Wallace, who had missed two office reports in a row, should have been his first visit of the morning instead of his fifth, but he hadn't wanted to get to Wallace's place too early for fear he'd find him still in the sack and have to ream his ass for not being out looking for a job. It was a crock: the parolees knew it, and they knew you knew it. There weren't any jobs around now for nineteen-year-old junkies who hadn't finished eighth grade, and meanwhile Wallace wasn't the only one with an aunt who had some sort of cozy deal worked out with the Welfare Department, which gave her a special allowance each month for having a parolee living with her. Reppa didn't even mind that Wallace's aunt probably wasn't his aunt at all but just a family friend that Wallace had written to while in prison and somehow conned into letting him live with her so he'd have a residence program when he went in front of the parole board. Of all the men on Reppa's case load, perhaps only half lived with legitimate relatives. The rule had once been that there had to be a blood connection between a parolee and anyone of the opposite sex he lived with, but that was no longer true. Quite a few of the rules had been relaxed in recent years. With all the court decisions lately that limited the right to revoke parole, it had become pretty much policy not to take anybody off the street for anything less than committing a new crime.

Wallace and his aunt lived on the fifth floor of a walk-up. The breeze coming out the front door of the building smelled of stale urine, damp plaster, and rat droppings. It was a smell worse than usual. The evacuation had begun; the place was on its way to joining the vast legion of deserted buildings that littered the city. Already all the doors on the first and second floors were covered with lead plating. Reppa couldn't fault anyone for wanting to get out of here as fast as possible. He had a hunch that if he'd had to grow up in a place like this, there would be a parole officer coming to visit him every month now. Climbing the stairs, he kicked a brown clump that looked like a dog turd out of his path and realized when a residue clung to his shoe that that was what it had been. Only a day or so old. His first sign here of habitation.

Broken glass crumbled underfoot on the next landing. The light socket above his head was empty. Craning to peer up the air shaft, he saw a pale, watery beam of light two flights up. They were still up there. Wallace and his aunt, who leastways was old enough to be somebody's aunt. For Lidsky's sake Reppa had listed her on Wallace's personal data sheet as the sister of Wallace's father. That Lidsky would see, if he read Wallace's case folder, that Wallace's father had been a siblingless orphan wasn't even a risk. Lidsky never read case folders. There was too much in them that reminded him of the tricks he'd used in his own days as a parole officer to hide how much dirt there was under the rug. With upwards of fifty cases you knew you were never really on top of any of them. By the time you became a supervisor, you understood it wasn't necessary to stay on top of very much in order to do the job. You merely had to keep your own ass covered.

Reppa listened to distinguish the sex of the footsteps coming to answer his knock. Definitely there was a difference between the way men and women walked, and knowing that difference told you in advance what expression your face should have when the door opened. If it had been Wallace coming to let him in, Reppa would have looked pissed at finding him home this late. Since it was the aunt, he forced a smile to hide his fear that there would be yet another discussion of all the ailments that plagued her. Among other things she suffered from so severe a case of pyorrhea that she customarily sat with a saucepan in her lap, spitting blood into it while she filled Reppa in on her latest crossed condition and strange sickness. On winter days she'd also had a tendency to rub her crotch and complain that there was just no way with the little bit of heat they gave her to keep the juices flowing. "Call me Della," she said once after Reppa called her Mrs. Wallace. "I been married, you could say, but I ain't never been missus nobody." She was too old for even Leilah to have worried, but those crotch rubs still gave Reppa some eerie tingles.

There was another sort of tingle today. Upon seeing him at the door Wallace's aunt drew a sharp breath. Since her usual reaction to him was a studied lack of reaction, he knew immediately that something was wrong.

"You lookin' for Jimmy, he in the bed."

28

At ten thirty? "Sick?"

"Sick with waitin'. He knowed you's comin'. Sooner or later."

Reppa watched her various small signals closely. "What's the matter?"

She answered with a question of her own. "You people gonna take him back to the prison?" He saw her take a backward step, then come forward again and squint into the hall. She looked almost disappointed to discover he was there alone.

He went down a long hallway, stepping around an ancient cardboard trunk, shelves of knickknacks, and piles of newspapers en route to the back room where Wallace resided. The aunt had used it as a storeroom while Wallace was in prison, and there was still so much junk in it that only an armless rocking chair and a lumpy cot could be accommodated.

Wallace lay on the cot staring at the ceiling. He was wearing a blue sweatshirt, the sleeves of which covered his arms. Reppa supposed at some point he would have to tell him to roll them up so he could check for needle marks. The last time Wallace had reported to the parole office, his arms had been clean, but that had been over two weeks ago, and if Reppa was getting the signs right, the aunt had been telling him drugs had become a problem again.

"What's going on, Jimmy?" Reppa stood beside the cot, waiting for Wallace's eyes to come down from the ceiling. Often you could spot it in the pupils; dilation if a hit had been recent, a glazed restlessness if it was overdue.

Without shifting his gaze Wallace held out his right arm. Reppa was about to tell him to roll up the sleeve when he realized Wallace was sitting up and holding his other arm out, too. He had misread the gesture. Wallace expected to have handcuffs put on his wrists.

29

Now Reppa understood why the aunt had been so rattled. Wallace hadn't gone back on the needle. It was even worse.

"When did it happen?"

"When what happen?"

"When did you get busted?"

Wallace was silent awhile. Finally he murmured, "Last Monday."

"Monday a week ago? Is that why you haven't been in to report?"

Wallace's eyes still hadn't left the ceiling, but his shoulders were twitching now in a series of little shrugs.

"Come on, Jimmy. Tell me about it."

"Why don't you just lock me up and get it over with?"

Reppa started to explain that just because a man was arrested didn't necessarily mean he'd blown his parole. Before any decisions were made, he would have to interview the arresting officer and see how serious the beef really was. To most men this news would have been consoling, but Wallace just looked more dismal. He squinched his eyes, pulling the skin tighter across the high cheekbones. Reppa was reminded that there had been a mother with French blood. Martinique, he seemed to recall having read in the case folder.

"Don't care no more about parole," Wallace said. "I mean, after what I done, there ain't no more hope."

It had to be exaggerated. Anything that bad and Wallace wouldn't have been allowed back on the street.

"What did you do? Tell me."

"Ain't nothing I did. It's what I *said*."

"You're talking in circles, Jimmy."

"Circles." Wallace at last yanked his eyes down from the ceiling and turned them on Reppa. They were nakedly pleading for—for what? "Man, the circle's got me in the

30

middle. They put me in the middle and made me drop a dime to get out.''

"Drop a dime on who?''

"Danny.''

"Who's Danny?''

"Danny his brother. Half brother.''

The aunt was standing in the doorway. It startled Reppa. Good as he was at listening outside of doors, he hadn't heard her follow him down the hall.

"Tell Mr. Reppa what you say about Danny,'' she ordered Wallace. "You just tell him.''

Wallace made an anguished face. "What they made me say. What they tell me they gonna lock me up for twenty years if I don't.''

"What who made you say?''

"Cops.''

"What cops? Which precinct?''

"Man.'' Wallace fell back on his elbows.

Reppa gnawed his lower lip, wanting to hurry things along, never very good at pulling out of people stories that were impacted like stubborn teeth.

"Look—let's start at the beginning. What were you arrested for?''

"Nothing.''

"Come on, come on—it couldn't have been nothing.''

"Yeah?'' Wallace's voice was as defeated now as Reppa's was impatient. "Man, you don't know. I was walking, just on the street, and they throwed me upside their car. Next thing I look down, and there's all these little bags on the ground they're saying fell outa my pocket. 'What we got here, Jimmy?' they say. 'We got a A felony.' ''

"Bags of heroin?''

"What else you think, man?''

Reppa had heard this same tale with only a minor

31

variation or two from a dozen parolees, and it exasperated him that he still didn't know how to respond. If you were gullible, you could believe the cops went around planting drugs on innocent people all the time, but he was just cynical enough to be fairly sure it happened at least some of the time.

He made a neutral grunt. "All right. You're saying they faked a possession bust. Why?"

"To make me scared not to tell them what they wanna hear about Danny."

"Which is what?"

But Wallace was going to tell the story in his own way. "Like the judge, he tell me I really can get twenty years, just like they say."

"What judge?"

"Where they take me."

"Criminal Court, down on Centre Street?"

"No court. This little room someplace upstairs in the precinct."

Reppa frowned. "They don't have judges in precincts."

"Ain't true, because this dude was a judge. With the robe on and everything. He listen to them, and then he say I can get twenty years if I don't do like they telling me."

"Was there a lawyer in there with you?"

"No lawyer. They say I don't need no lawyer unless it gets to court, and it ain't ever gonna if I tell them what they wanna hear."

Reppa nodded somberly. It was a new one on him. He was also beginning to suspect it might be true. Wallace wasn't overly shrewd and would be an easy prey for the kind of charade he was describing. You grabbed a kid off the street, scared him shitless, and then dragged him in front of a phony judge who threatened to throw the book at him. Any case against Wallace would fall apart once he

32

got into a real courtroom and told what had been done to him, but that hadn't been the point. What was the point, though? He asked.

"Like I said. Make me drop a dime on Danny."

"And did you?"

"Twenty years. I couldn't go back in there for no twenty years."

Wallace's eyes lost their grip on the ceiling, changed to liquid.

Reppa felt his own eyes beginning to sting a little: bastards. "And after you told them what they wanted to hear, they let you go?"

"Just for now. They can pick me up again anytime, they say, and they will if I don't cooperate."

"Did they also tell you not to tell anyone what happened? Is that why you haven't come downtown to report to me?"

"Twenty years," Wallace repeated. He lifted his hands to cover his eyes. The fingers were clenched.

"I told him to go see you," the aunt intervened. " 'Talk to your parole officer, maybe he can help,' I told him. But he wouldn't. He just wanna lay up here in the bed and hope it go away."

"Ain't gonna go away," Wallace said. "I know that. Gonna be a trial, and then I'm gonna have to say all those lies I told the judge in front of everybody."

"What kind of trial?"

"Danny." The aunt paused to duck into the hall and clear her gums noisily into some unseen object before explaining. "They puttin' him on trial again, and this time they afraid he gonna win. So they got this poor boy scared and make him say he saw Danny when he didn't. Couldn't of, because he was in the school. Seven-year-old boy, I remember his mother tellin' me what a good thing he was so little or they'd of had him up against Danny along with

33

everybody else. They didn't stop at nobody until they got what they wanted to hear, and now they're startin' all over again. Only being as it's so long ago, people's gone, and Jimmy's the only one they can find.''

Seven from nineteen, Wallace's present age, was twelve. So whatever Danny had done, it had happened in 1968. But what was it? Reppa asked.

Wallace turned his back to the room and spoke to the wall. "Don't let's talk no more. Please, Mr. Reppa, just take me in. Lock me up and throw the key away."

His whole body started shaking. It wasn't an act. Wallace had been badly scared by the cops, and now he was sick over what they'd made him do. Sick, and still very scared. Undoubtedly of his half brother now as well.

"Does Danny know what you did yet?"

Wallace's shoulders made another small shrug. The aunt said, "Not unless they told him, and I don't think they gonna do that until they have to—in the court."

"Where is Danny now?"

"Where he been all the time. In the prison."

"All the time since when?"

The aunt looked around as if she had to empty her mouth somewhere again. "Them murders. Them two murders he didn't do. They sent him away for the rest of his life, but now he gonna get a new trial, they afraid, and they got this poor child to tell lies against him."

"Lies of what sort? Where did he say he'd seen Danny?"

"Outside them two girls' building. Jimmy seven years old in the school, but they made him say he play hooky and see Danny go in that building to rob them two girls and stab them all up."

"Twelve years ago . . ." Then it began to dawn: the memory. Even though he hadn't been in New York at the time, it was still vivid. Behrman-Moffett . . . ! Chilled,

Reppa said, "Danny—is Jimmy's half brother Danny de Spirit?"

When the aunt nodded, he steered her into the hallway and closed the door of Wallace's room so Wallace couldn't overhear them. Ten minutes later he left, retrieved his car from its parking spot at a broken meter, and went to the 26th Precinct, where he spoke briefly to a Detective Graham. Then he hurried downtown to the Criminal Court building and spent half an hour in the main record room with the arraignment books, combing through all the arrests in Manhattan a week ago Monday whose last names began with W. Finally he called Lidsky from a pay phone.

"Graham claims they didn't actually arrest him?" Lidsky said after listening awhile. "And there's no record of his being arrested? Yet Wallace insists they took him to court."

"Some kind of mock job they put together in the precinct."

"Does Graham admit they picked him up?"

"Just to talk to."

"About what?"

"Keep him on his toes. Graham wouldn't be specific."

"Typical. Most of the time they don't even tell each other what they're doing." Lidsky grunted. "Meanwhile Wallace claims they tricked him into making a false statement against de Spirit? Sworn? A deposition?"

"Graham wouldn't admit to anything, and Wallace stopped talking to me before I could get the full story of what went on in the precinct. His aunt says he told her they made him sign something and threatened to charge him with perjury if he tried to deny it later."

"Want some advice, Reppa?"

"I know. Stay out of it."

"Way the fuck out. We received a memo from Albany on de Spirit just this morning. The governor is requesting

35

us to do an investigation to determine what the attitude is now toward the Behrman-Moffett case. It appears he's considering giving de Spirit an executive pardon. There's liable not to even be a new trial.''

"Then what was the purpose in jerking Wallace around?"

"Assuming they did."

"You think he's lying? He's not clever enough to make up a story like that."

There was a short silence, and then Lidsky said, "Did Wallace testify against de Spirit at the original trial?"

"No. According to his aunt, nobody even questioned him."

"And now, twelve years after the fact, they're making him a key witness. It sounds fishy, Reppa. It sounds like a snow job he's giving you."

"It could also sound like they've got a few holes in their case to plug up in the event there is a new trial. I seem to remember there wasn't any real evidence against de Spirit except the testimony of a junkie and an oral confession he insisted he didn't make."

"Reppa, you want a crusade, I've got one for you right here in the office. A memo explaining where your monthly report is. It's later than a nun's period. It was supposed to be on my desk two weeks ago."

Lidsky's social and political views were as elusive as his metaphors. Reppa never knew where Lidsky stood on anything. If Reppa sided with the police against a parolee, Lidsky accused him of being a red-neck reactionary. But let him take a parolee's side, and Lidsky called him a bleeding heart. Lidsky was the perfect supervisor. If you were around him long enough, you too stopped taking sides.

Reppa called the public library information number to get the exact date of the Behrman-Moffett murders,

June 5, 1968. There was something else that had happened around then. An antiwar riot? Another murder? He had been at Fort Knox that summer, and it had been a gruesome one. The perfect prelude to Nixon. And like a lightning bolt it struck him. June 5. Awakening that morning in Echo Company and turning on the radio and hearing . . . Bobby Kennedy shot, on the verge of death. No reason, Reppa thought, to connect the two events, no reason at all. And yet . . .

Lidsky had told him to stay out of it, but if he did, Lidsky would ask him what was wrong with him. Didn't he recognize it was his duty to make a complete investigation? A no-win situation, so he went with his own instincts, which were mostly an outraged curiosity. What the hell had really happened a week ago Monday in the 26th Precinct? Jimmy Wallace was his, his case, for better or worse. Parole was like a marriage in that sense; when one of your men got into trouble, you followed through.

Wallace's aunt had told Reppa that the elementary school Wallace had gone to at the time of the murders was somewhere in the high nineties, but she couldn't remember the name of it. The telephone book had only one school that fit the description: PS 163 on West Ninety-seventh Street. It was three twenty, past regular school hours, by the time Reppa got there, but by showing his parole officer's shield he inveigled an assistant principal into going down in the vault and looking up Wallace's records for 1968. The AP wouldn't let him see the records for himself, however, or give him any information from them without a court order.

Not even whether Wallace was in school on a particular day?

Not even that. Eventually, perhaps because the AP was

a woman and Reppa was not without charm, or perhaps because she was somewhat unsure of the legal ramifications here and there was no one around to ask, she told Reppa the name of Wallace's official teacher in 1968: Sara Wallrapp. Reppa, after asking whether Wallrapp still taught at the school, was disappointed to learn she'd retired several years ago. He didn't really expect to be lucky enough to find her in the phone book, but it was worth a try.

There were no Sara Wallrapps listed, but he did find an S. Wallrapp on West End Avenue.

He called the number. A woman answered. Sara Wallrapp, formerly of PS 163? Yes; why? Yes, when he explained, she would, for a few minutes. Yes; now. Why not?

The elevator in her building was temporarily out of service. He trudged up nine flights and was greeted at the door of her apartment by a young man with long blond hair who left him standing in the foyer.

In a few moments a gray-blond woman in jeans appeared in a doorway down the hall and beckoned to him.

"May I see some identification, please?"

While she examined the case that held his parole officer's shield and laminated ID card, Reppa inquired out of politeness if the young man was her son.

Very evenly she said, "Grandson."

She led Reppa into a small library and shut the door. When they were seated, she smiled warmly at him, and he began to understand that although she'd retired from teaching, she was not retired.

Owlish brown eyes, but the rest of her resembled an egret. Tall, long legs, a lightening agent in her hair. S. Wallrapp. Divorced? A widow? Reppa had to think a moment before he remembered what he was there for.

"The student I mentioned over the phone. You don't remember him probably, but I was hoping you might have kept some sort of records that you'd still have access to. Specifically, attendance records."

"My Delaney books."

"Delaney?"

"The name of the man who originated them, I suppose. Anyway, they have everything in them. Every name, birth date, and locker number. What was the name again?"

She didn't remember Wallace, but she asked if Reppa could give her a few minutes, and left the room. She returned with a thin green book, *1968* embossed on the cover.

"I have my personal copies of them all, 1941 through 1975. Missing only the four years I went on leave after my daughter was born. I always intended to do a book on my experiences one day. A novel. There was a woman in the middle sixties, Kaufman, something Kaufman. *Up the Down Staircase*. Nice title, nice job. But the definitive book remains to be done . . . Jimmy Wallace. Wallace, James?"

Reppa watched her slim fingers glide down the outside of the lefthand page to which she'd opened the book. Near the bottom they stopped and flipped forward several pages. To June, he guessed.

"Find him?"

"Well, there was a James Wallace, but I still don't . . . Ah, wait a minute. A thin little boy who used to say *'Voulez-vous coucher avec moi?'* He knew a few other phrases, too, and they were all . . ." She withdrew her fingers from the book, and Reppa waited for her to say "dirty." But she gave him a wry smile and said, "A rather delightful contrast to always hearing 'fuck you.' "

For a moment her candor kept him from speaking.

39

"Thin little boy. He probably would have been on the thin side. His mother was from Martinique, I think."

"Imaginative, but something a little sad about him," Sara Wallrapp recalled as her fingers went back to the book. When they reached the end of the page, they started tapping a little beat. "Oh, I can't get around it. I'm going to need my glasses."

Reppa helped her find them. They were in the kitchen, where she'd been making cookies when he arrived.

"Chocolate chip," she said, offering him one. "For my grandson. Chocolate still gives me zits, even now, as a grandmother. Great-grandmother one of these days soon if he doesn't stop zapping everything at Walden. Walden's where he's going until his mother gets her head together on the Coast and sends for him. What's so important, by the way, about whether little Jimmy Wallace was in school one day twelve years ago?"

"I can't tell you. Just that someone's freedom might someday depend on it."

"His?"

"That's possible, too."

She lifted a chocolate chip cookie nervously toward her mouth. "What's he done? Something terrible obviously, or you wouldn't be here. Drugs?"

Reppa again evaded her. "Whether he was in school on June 5, 1968, won't affect his parole, if that's what you're worried about."

"Truly, won't it?"

Her doubt forced him to make a slight adjustment. "It shouldn't."

"June . . ." She looked around for the Delaney book, but she'd left it in the other room. Back there she discovered she'd brought the wrong glasses: her TV ones. "Here," she said despairingly. "Look for yourself."

He took the book from her. It was right there. Wallace had even gotten a gold star for something or other on June 5.

"It was the day Bobby Kennedy died. Any chance the school might have been dismissed early?"

She distinctly remembered it hadn't been. Everyone had pleaded for an early dismissal, but the principal had insisted on waiting for an official order to close, which never came.

"What was the gold star for?"

"I've no idea. It could have been for something he said in French."

"You gave them for things like that?"

"By the late sixties I was giving them for remembering your lunch money."

"Even though you marked Wallace present, can you say for sure that he was actually in school all day? He didn't cut?"

"He couldn't have."

"Why not?"

"The gold stars were given out at the end of the day. It was a control device. You had to be present and in your seat or you forfeited your gold star."

"But he could have skipped out at some point for a couple of hours, couldn't he?"

"Impossible. I was a good teacher. I ran a very tight classroom."

"How impossible? Would you be willing to swear to it?"

"Why are you hammering at me like this? I feel as if I'm in court."

Reppa thought it was too soon to tell her she one day might be.

* * *

41

The office Graham shared at the 26th Precinct looked like a college dean's that Reppa had once been summoned to after a dormitory prank went awry. There had been nothing on the walls or left out on the desk. It looked more like a cell than most cells did.

"Back again," Graham said, not bothering to close the door after he'd ushered Reppa through it. He sat on top of his desk and motioned to the lone chair beside it, which looked as if it had last been occupied by someone with a bladder problem. Reppa opted to stand.

Graham was small, mousy, hollow-cheeked. He was either a very light-skinned black man or a swart white man, and his voice sounded like a windowpane that had been struck by a fist and was about to shatter.

"We've got a conflict of interests," Reppa began.

"Brother Wallace?"

"You got him to say he saw de Spirit outside the Behrman-Moffett building the morning they were murdered. I happen to know positively that he couldn't have."

"Positively? That's a heavy word."

"Ninety-nine and forty-four one hundredths percent sure, then."

Graham responded to the joke by winking off to his left. Reppa looked that way and caught a black man in a red beret eyeing him from behind a corner desk. A small gold earring twinkled in his nose.

"Evidently you've been doing a little spade work since we saw you this morning," Graham said. He winked again.

"How long you been Wallace's PO?" the man with the earring asked him.

"About five months."

"And in all that time you ain't come around here once until today. Check me if I'm wrong, but ain't it part of a

PO's job to drop by the precincts his case load covers now and then? If you had, you might've learned that we've had our eye on Brother Wallace for quite a while.''

"Drugs?"

"Not only. We see around other corners, too." Which implied the man with the earring was working undercover. Reppa didn't expect to be introduced to him by Graham. He'd had enough experiences of this type to know that parole officers were rated in the law enforcement caste system only a notch above meter maids.

"From now on," he promised, "I'll make it a point to show my face here at least once a week."

"We'll look forward to it," Graham said and left the room.

The man with the earring rose and stiff-armed the door shut. "Danny de Spirit was a very wrong boy," he said. "A lot of people spent a lot of time putting him where he is."

"That I don't doubt."

"But you seem to doubt the necessity of the effort to keep him there."

"When it's based on false testimony. Wallace couldn't have seen de Spirit on the murder morning. He was in school."

"Did he say that?"

"So do his attendance records."

"Those things," the man said, disposing of the matter as he would a doctored expense account.

"I'm just letting you know. As Wallace's parole officer I have a duty to look out for his interests."

"Another very heavy word. We don't use it too often anymore. But Parole has always been slightly behind. You people still speak of rehabilitation, don't you?"

"The more current term is *reintegration*."

43

"Reintegration?" For a moment the man's eyes shone more brightly than the earring. "Do you think Danny de Spirit has been *re-in-te-grated?* Even after twelve years would you want to trust him in a room alone with your daughter? Have you seen the medical examiner's pictures, my friend, of Andrea Behrman and Elizabeth Moffett?"

Reppa shook his head. Usually it was hard not to seem scornful of invectives like this, but now he had to fight not to seem impressed. The man genuinely seemed to believe de Spirit had killed the two girls.

I wouldn't recommend you do. You wouldn't like your job anymore. You'd never again believe anybody who committed a violent crime should be allowed out on parole."

"People change."

"Not people like Danny de Spirit."

"You're trying to convince me to let you use Wallace against his own half brother. Even if you have to make Wallace lie."

"We're trying to do a little more than convince you."

"Warn me off?"

The man shrugged in annoyance. "You just don't know. We've got the biggest, most complex city in the world to protect. The governor's trying to nail down the minority vote by making us look bad for having put de Spirit away. There's your real conflict of interest."

Reppa flared. It was one thing to be called a bleeding heart, but no one was going to call him a babe in the woods. "Well, I think there's another element to the conflict. A number of cops, as I remember, made their reputations by cracking the Behrman-Moffett case. One in particular. I don't recall his name, but when they made that movie of the case a few years ago, didn't he star in it, playing himself?"

"Cupach."

44

"Right. Big Steve Cupach. And what's your name?"

The man's hand strayed to the red beret as if to make sure it was on straight. "Sweet."

"I'm Reppa, Sweet."

"It promises to be a difficult acquaintance."

"Where is Cupach now?"

"Beats me. He resigned, man, years ago."

"But not so long ago, I'm betting, that he doesn't still have a heavy interest in seeing that de Spirit isn't pardoned. Or worse, found innocent at a new trial."

"No heavier than a lot of other people's."

"His partner and all the other detectives on the case?"

"Plus every uniform in the city who wouldn't be too happy seeing a convicted killer back on the street," Sweet said.

His tongue stuck out and touched the earring in his nose, but it wasn't, even in a symbolic sense, a threatening gesture. A statement, rather, of the immense distance between them.

The public library was never an easy place to find anything in. Despite having a list of call numbers that filled an entire note card, Reppa managed to unearth only one book on the Behrman-Moffett case, the others being temporarily lost or, more probably, permanently stolen. He tried to check the book out with his parole officer's shield but was told the library didn't honor such things and wound up having to fill out an application for a temporary card before they would let him take it home.

A somber-looking item with a gray cover entitled *Andrea and Elizabeth*.

The woman on the third floor who attended to Leilah while he was at work was with her when he got home. Since Leilah owned the building, having bought it with the money she got for the film rights to her novel, the woman's payment was free rent until Leilah no longer needed her. She had a long Russian name that had been shortened to Gore. Reppa's contribution to the arrangement was a gadget that enabled Mrs. Gore to stay upstairs in her apartment and wait for Leilah to pull the cord beside the bed that rang a buzzer in the Gore kitchen. Leilah never pulled the cord unless her bladder was about to burst or she finished a book she was reading and wanted another from the pile beside the bed. Since her accident she had read over a hundred books. But she wasn't familiar with the one Reppa was lugging.

"*Andrea and Elizabeth?* The story of two hurricanes?"

"In a way."

He didn't want to have to talk to her just yet about his day. So he busied himself with Mrs. Gore, pretending he was talking to her in the kitchen even after she'd left. Listening in the bedroom, Leilah might wonder why the woman never answered him; but meanwhile she might also fall asleep. She often lost altitude around this time of day, mostly so it wouldn't seem that she had nothing to do while he made dinner, but she always revived the moment the Mets' game came on TV. They were going to have to get two sets if Reppa was going to last out the summer here. He despised baseball, believing it the only sport duller than archery; Leilah despised everything on TV but baseball.

46

CHAPTER TWO

ANDREA AND ELIZABETH

The Mets were playing those loathsome traitors, the Dodgers. Leilah, who'd grown up in Bensonhurst and been the only girl in her third-grade class in the Knothole Gang, screamed and swore at the TV for over two hours. Meanwhile Reppa holed up in the kitchen with his book.

He was surprised by much of what he read. His recollection was that Andrea Behrman and Elizabeth Moffett had come home while a burglar was in their apartment, and he'd panicked and killed them. But the real events were quite different. As best as the cops were able to reconstruct it, Andrea arrived home first; Elizabeth not until some while later. What apparently went on during the time Andrea and the killer were alone wandered pretty far afield from a standard burglary. The physical evidence at the scene of the crime left considerable room for the warped imagination to roam. S&M. Rape. Knives galore. A dilly of a case, in all. A detective's dream.

The bodies had been discovered by the third roommate, who was given a fictitious name (as were several other principals in the case) to spare her any notoriety. "We will call her Jane Walker," the author said, leading Reppa, an avid reader of these books, to conclude her true initials were probably J. W. In any event Walker had come home around five o'clock on the afternoon of June 5, 1968. Her first inkling that something might be wrong came when she found the front door of the apartment unlocked. She entered cautiously. Seeing nothing amiss in the living room or her bedroom, she assumed one of the other women had just gotten home and carelessly neglected to lock the door behind her. She called out. Receiving no answer, she went into the kitchen, where she found a window open and several knives scattered about, one with a broken blade. Alarmed, she raced to the bathroom and there encountered a watery trail of bloodstains that led down the hall to the bedroom her two roommates occupied. After a single glance inside she called the police.

Andrea Behrman and Elizabeth Moffett had died of multiple stab wounds sometime between eleven and eleven thirty, as near as the medical examiner could determine. Andrea was found naked, tied to a metal bridge chair with belts and sashes from dresses belonging to both women. Elizabeth lay fully clothed upon her bed, stabbed repeatedly but with her arms folded so peacefully over her wounds it almost looked as if she had died in her sleep.

Autopsies revealed both women had also sustained cranial contusions, suggesting the killer had beaten them in addition to stabbing them. Because of the open window in the kitchen and the unlocked front door, the natural supposition was that the killer was a burglar who had entered through the first and exited through the latter. It was theorized that Andrea had arrived home while he was assembling his loot. He had overpowered her and in the process decided to add rape to his game plan. Hence Andrea had been stripped and bound naked to the chair. In all likelihood the burglar had been on the verge of ravaging her when Elizabeth walked in. It was the wrong morning for a burglary, the one weekday morning in a hundred when both women were home; the burglar hadn't taken into account that the Kennedy assassination would disrupt a lot of routines, among them Elizabeth's. Around ten o'clock the storefront on Amsterdam Avenue where she did draft counseling had been closed for the day when it became clear Kennedy was going to die, and she'd gone home. Once there, Elizabeth (so the theory went) reacted in such a way that the burglar was compelled to kill both women.

There was a second theory that the killer was not a burglar but someone known to one or the other of the women, most probably Andrea. Supporting this was Andrea's behavior on the morning of the crime. She had gone to the *Vogue* offices, where she was an assistant to the art editor, stayed at her desk only about ten minutes, and then left after announcing she was too upset by the Kennedy shooting to do any work. Several friends were callous enough to suggest she had used the assassination as an opportunity to take a self-declared holiday and arrange a tryst with her subsequent killer. For Andrea was something of a sexual adventuress. Even her nearest friends couldn't deny she slept around a bit, and those less sanguinely disposed toward her claimed that some of her bedmates were, to say the least, dubious choices. She had seemingly settled down when she became engaged to a Wall Street lawyer (called simply ''Jay'' in the book), but the engagement had been broken off a few weeks before the murders, and there were rumors that she had then taken up with a circle of people who were involved in group sex and even outright orgies.

Elizabeth Moffett, on the other hand, had no ostensible love life. The two women were, in truth, a study in opposites. Andrea had grown up in New York and majored in painting at Cooper Union; Elizabeth was from South

49

Carolina and had gone to a small Catholic girls' school in Charleston. Andrea's mother had been a well-known patroness of the arts before her death in December of 1967; her stepfather was a wealthy fur dealer, and her aunt was a famous sculptor, the legendary enfant terrible of the art world, Annabelle. Elizabeth's genealogy was drab in the extreme: her father managed a hardware store, her mother was a kindergarten teacher. The contrasts didn't end there. Andrea worked on a fashion magazine, surrounded by glamor; most of the young men Elizabeth counseled on their draft options were semiliterate ghetto products. Andrea was tall and willowy and had the same large, haunting eyes as her mother and her aunt. Elizabeth, unfortunately, was somewhat dowdy; reports were that she was, if not a prude, certainly very reserved on the sexual front. The view of one detective working on the case was that her repressed sexuality had been the motive for the murders. "Southern girl, Catholic, say she comes home and finds her roommate tied up by this guy, maybe even a guy she knows as a beau of her roommate's. They're just doing a little bondage number, but it's too much for her. She flips out. Could be she even grabs the knife and starts cutting the roommate loose. It sets off the guy, he's highly charged up sexually, and she's in the way. He wrestles her for the knife and winds up stabbing her. Now he has to ice the roommate, too—she's a witness. When he calms down a little, he realizes the only way he can save his ass is to make it look like a burglary."

A few pages farther on in *Andrea and Elizabeth* Reppa learned this detective had been removed from the case after he made the mistake of airing his notions in the presence of Andrea's stepfather.

He started to fold the corner of the page for future reference, then remembered Leilah's admonition that books were national treasures and got up to find a sheet of paper so he could make notes. On the way back to the kitchen he looked in on her. Lee Mazzilli was at bat, her hero. The Wop Fop. With a sigh he returned to his book.

Yet a third hypothesis, he learned, was that the killings were premeditated. In support of this was the absence of fingerprints in the murder room, as if the killer had arranged it so he'd have plenty of time. Then, too, the open window in the kitchen began to seem more and more like a red herring. It had at first been assumed the killer had leaped onto the window ledge from a nearby fire escape, but the detectives soon realized it would have taken Wilt Chamberlain to make such a jump, for the span was some ten feet wide. Consequently most men assigned to the case scrapped the burglary theory and started devoting their efforts to people who knew the women, following the golden rule that most killers are known to their victims.

But after a lengthy investigation no serious suspects emerged. No friends or relatives, no psychos or second-story men. One detective team painstakingly checked out "Jane Walker" on the off chance that she might somehow have been the motive for the murders. Another team flew to South Carolina and spent several days probing Elizabeth's background for a secret high school or college sweetheart.

Zero.

Six weeks went by. Then six months. By December 1968 there were no longer any detectives assigned full time to the case. Overshadowed initially by the Kennedy assassination, it had lingered in the public eye throughout the summer because of the particularly brutal nature of the murders and the vulnerability of all young career women in Manhattan in the event the killer was some sort of maniac. Sirhan Sirhan was under restraint; whoever had killed Andrea and Elizabeth very obviously was still out there somewhere. But as the fall wore on and no other young women were murdered in a similar fashion, the odds lengthened that the case would go unsolved. The work of a very clever or a very lucky killer.

And then one slab-gray morning just before Christmas a detective who had been part of the Behrman-Moffett case from the very start picked up a pimp named Ax who had cut the throat of one of his bimbos with a razor and thrown her body down a dumbwaiter shaft in an abandoned building. The detective's name was Steve Cupach. Because his hair had gone prematurely gray, he was known among his peers as the Silver Serb, and it was always a surprise to people when they discovered he was still only in his late twenties. One of the youngest men in the department ever to be made a homicide detective, Cupach was also the youngest assigned to the Behrman-Moffett case. And the most relentless. Long after most of his colleagues had despaired of finding the killer, Cupach had pursued even the most tenuous leads to the exclusion of all else. Dogged determination, or an instinct that the case had a pot of gold awaiting its unraveler at the end of it? All that was known for sure about Cupach's motivations was that patience paid off. For on the ride to the station that December morning Ax offered Cupach a trade: the Behrman-Moffett killer in return for a quashed indictment on the bimbo slaying. Cupach judiciously feigned only mild interest. Behrman-Moffett, the two girls on Ninety-fourth Street? Ax smiled his affirmation. One of his bimbos had had a john in her crib the morning of the murders; "I just stuck two twitches," the john had threatened, "and you could be next." When he pulled a knife, the bimbo ran ass-naked all the way down the street, where Ax was sitting in his car. He saw the john leave and recognized him. A junkie burglar he'd used to fence for before he became a pimp. Cupach first said no deal, but then he said maybe, just maybe the ADA who was handling the bimbo case would settle for manslaughter. To which Ax agreed. Reppa could too easily visualize them shaking hands on it like two business rivals who'd just completed a verbal merger. "Now give," Cupach said. Ax gave. A kid they called Frenchy on the street. Real name Danny something.

Reppa squirmed. Inside him the gnat of anger, hatched that morning in Wallace's bedroom, had grown to the size of a wasp. The stench surrounding de Spirit's conviction was even ranker than he'd remembered.

He raced through the rest of the book in something of a blur. Ax's pad on Tiemann Place had been rigged with hidden microphones, and Ax was told to invite de Spirit to come live with him. De Spirit was in no position to refuse. He was strung out by then, living in abandoned buildings, an absconder from parole (a fact Reppa hadn't known; and why, now that he thought about it, hadn't Wallace's case folder mentioned that he had a half brother in prison?). As an added lure Ax was supplied with all the heroin that de Spirit could possibly want. Ax's instructions were to entice de Spirit to talk about the Behrman-Moffett murders.

Weeks passed. Cupach had hundreds of feet of tape of Ax and de Spirit talking but nothing that could be used in court. Ax would bring up Behrman-Moffett; de Spirit would say, "The walls're waiting for me to say I sliced them two twitches. Maybe I did, maybe I didn't." Cupach began to suspect he was being had. That Ax had told de Spirit his pad was bugged and the two of them were doing a number, Ax lazily coaxing, de Spirit stopping teasingly short of saying anything incriminating. Meanwhile the department was supporting a hundred-dollar-a-day habit, and a lot of people were beginning to question the expense involved, not to mention the ethics.

Then one night de Spirit said, "Think I sliced them two twitches, Ax?" "I really think you probably did," said Ax. *"Probably?"* De Spirit laughed. "Yeah, probably I did. But probably ain't gonna make it. Probably's only a little better than maybe."

Both were higher than kites. The tape was fuzzy. But Cupach was inflamed enough to haul de Spirit in and try for a confession. First he cut off de Spirit's heroin and sat him in a cell overnight. In the morning de Spirit was in bad shape, shaking and dry-heaving, but he was still together enough to demand a lawyer. One was sent in to visit him. The lawyer advised de Spirit not to talk about the case, then went to the can for a minute. While he was gone, de Spirit orally admitted to both murders. At arraignment de Spirit tried to repudiate the confession, claiming it had come while he was undergoing heroin withdrawal, but the judge allowed it to stand. De Spirit continued to proclaim his innocence at his trial, bringing in his mother and several other people as character witnesses, but countering their effect on the jury was the roommate "Jane Walker," who identified de Spirit as someone she had once seen loitering outside her building. After trial he was found guilty and sentenced to life.

Andrea and Elizabeth had been published three years after the murders. By that time de Spirit was in Auburn state prison, and Cupach had been promoted to detective second grade.

That was as of 1971. Now, nine years later, de Spirit was fighting for a new trial. And Cupach? Where was *he* now? There had been that fat movie role in the early seventies, and then? A house in Malibu surrounded by nubile sycophants, the prematurely silver hair as familiar at openings as Robert Redford's blond locks and Kirk Douglas's dimple?

54

Reppa knew little about how Hollywood operated, but he did know about Auburn and its like. He clamped his knees together and tried to put himself in de Spirit's place for a moment, staring out at the world from a narrow cell. In Leilah's kitchen, under a bare ceiling bulb, it was absurdly easy.

"Even after twelve years would you want to trust him in a room alone with your daughter?" Sweet had asked. Sweet himself wasn't someone you'd want for a tent partner on your next army bivouac, but that was sort of beside the point. So were Cupach's motives and methods, really. Despite it all, it was entirely possible, wasn't it, that Cupach had got the right man? Really, now, did cops make their reps by going around pinning murders on innocent men?

When you stop at nothing, nothing stops you: if there were such a thing as a universal truth about successful men, that was it. Whenever Reppa was confronted, like this, with the depths of his own cynicism, his immediate impulse was to get a second opinion.

Leilah. But consulting her on the topic of cynicism was like a man afraid he was losing his hearing going to a doctor who was a mute. For a while she played with the remote-control channel selector, alternating between games from Atlanta and Boston on the cable stations. Finally, to get her attention, he pulled the TV cord out of its socket. Still, it was not undivided. She had stashed a jar of olives, probably from the lunch Mrs. Gore had prepared for her today.

"Good on pizza," she coaxed, pulling her pillow back to show him the jar.

"Only I don't feel like making a pizza right now."

"Or using your imagination. Those two girls really were burglarized. They called the cops, and two macho types came and tried to get a little nookie. When Andy and Lizzie refused to come across, they were snuffed."

"You don't really believe that," he said, knowing she undoubtedly believed far worse. Her novel had been called *The King of Garbage*. For a while she had introduced him to her friends as "the pig from the provinces." She still refused to accept that everything west of New Jersey wasn't west of the Mississippi, and parole officers, to her, were no better than truant officers for grownups.

"It's coming back to me. Andrea's aunt was that beatnik sculptor, the one with only one name who went around making life-size voodoo dolls."

"Annabelle."

"With the big spacy eyes. And her parents were hot *scheiss*, too. Whereas the other girl was pretty much of a cipher. Which is, of course, what's begun spinning your wheels. You see little Lizzie as a tragic victim. The poor little mouse from North Carolina who achieved immortality only because she came home at the wrong moment."

"She was from *South* Carolina."

"Little Miss Moffett. That was Billie Jean King's maiden name, wasn't it?"

"Billie Jean spells it with an *i*."

"What's the plan, Reppa? We could be a great team. You'd do all the legwork like Archie Goodwin, and I'd lie here flat on my back even more sedentary than Nero. Sturm and Reppa. I'll call my printer and get cards printed up tomorrow."

He looked down at her lean face. The tops of her breasts burst out of the steel brace as they would out of a corset. She seemed, in the same intriguing way as a homecoming queen in a consumptive ward, sexier in sickness than in health.

"I'm not going to do any more than I've already done.

56

I'm a parole officer, and my duty here stops at protecting the rights of one of my own men."

"That why you went to see his old teacher?" He pretended not to hear the arch note in her voice. "And made a second trip to the precinct? Face it. That second time you weren't wearing your parole officer's hat. You've been gripped, Reppa. The cops locked up the wrong dude, you think, for killing those two girls."

"Go on. What else is gripping me?"

"I don't know, but sitting there, you're putting a few grips on me, too. Oh, it's not only you. Watching the game tonight, I think it hit me for the first time that I'm not going to get out to Shea at all this year. Maybe not even next year or ever again."

"You will. Of course you will."

"I'm not being morbid. It's just that summer is such a physical time for me. I look forward to it all year—three little months. I hate to lose even a single minute, and now—oh, shit! Come to bed, Frank, and give me something to hold on to besides this damn metal rail."

He was happier being Reppa. Whenever she called him Frank, it reminded him that they were meant to be something more than adversaries.

From the window in Senior Parole Officer Melvin Lidsky's office Reppa could watch them putting the finishing touches on the new Port Authority building. Lidsky meanwhile was rocked back in his swivel chair, hands clasped behind his head, pipe in mouth. The pipe hadn't been lit in a month. Lidsky was trying to quit. Accustomed to having to speak here through thick clouds of smoke, Reppa didn't know how to begin.

"You want a warrant for this guy Wallace?" Lidsky prompted.

"No, I don't want a warrant."

"Why not? There are plenty of charges. He missed two reports. He didn't tell you he'd been picked up by the cops until you came looking for him. He's not working."

If Reppa had asked for a warrant, Lidsky would have argued that the arrest was Mickey Mouse and the missed reports and lack of employment weren't anything to get excited about.

Among the men he supervised, Lidsky was known as the Great Equivocator. Those above him in the parole hierarchy reckoned him a good frontline commander. He seldom made a decision that got anyone in trouble. Not everyone perceived that he rarely made any decisions at all. Parole officers who sought warrants usually had to go over his head to get them; those who preferred to string along with troublesome cases had to submit memos to the commissioners defending their resistance to getting warrants.

Lidsky's professional stance with Reppa was to play an out-and-out devil's advocate. His eyes would roll back in his head and, "You did *what?*" or, fatherly, "Now I'm not telling you how to run a case load, but when are you going to get your head out of your ass?" It was incredible how adroit he was at keeping his own ass out of a sling—though actually it wasn't incredible. He never gave anyone a target to aim at. He had no profile. At most he was a shadow.

And a supervisor who's a shadow doesn't like hearing that one of his men crossed swords with the cops.

Originally Reppa hadn't been going to tell Lidsky what he'd done the previous afternoon after speaking to him, but then he decided to face up to it squarely. Instead of sneaking his activity sheet under the pile of papers in Lidsky's In basket and hoping Lidsky would record the hours of work he'd claimed without really looking at it, he handed it to him.

Horror froze up Lidsky's eyes as he read down the list of people and places Reppa had visited. They blinked shut, but he gradually forced them open again.

"You went back to the precinct a second time? Why? Who's Sweet? And this woman on West End Avenue, this Sara something—and the public *library*! Reppa, there are people up in Albany who read these sheets. How can I approve a visit to the library?"

"Easy. I was doing research on the Behrman-Moffett case. I took out a book, which I read last night. Were you aware de Spirit was on parole at the time of the murders? This morning I went down to the record room and got his case folder out of the closed file."

"Oh, you did." Lidsky's eyes thawed, and his face wrinkled into an impish expression. "Fine, but any reading you do in it will be on your own time, not the state's."

Folding the activity sheet as he would a paper airplane, he tossed it to Reppa.

"Make up a new one and cut out everything after your visit to the Criminal Court. The rest you did on your own. Wallace is your case. You had no authorization to make any visits on behalf of Danny de Spirit."

"Then give me the authorization. That investigation you told me about yesterday? The one the governor wants us to make?"

Lidsky mustered a minuscule smile. "What about it?"

"I want the assignment."

"Can't be done. You know those are given out in the Assignment Control Center. I've got nothing to do with it."

"But McCreary does."

Lidsky made as if to get up from his desk and go in

search of a match for his pipe, so Reppa had to speak quickly, to hold him there.

"I don't know if you're aware that McCreary was de Spirit's parole officer."

"I'm aware."

"Have you ever read de Spirit's case folder? McCreary put in a lot of work on Behrman-Moffett."

"Like you, without authorization. And you see the results."

Lidsky's voice let it hang in the air. Several years ago McCreary had been relieved of a supervision case load and given a desk job that called for him to do nothing but dole out investigation assignments. It was a career cul-de-sac, lethally dull, usually reserved for men recovering from coronaries or nervous breakdowns; and the hope had been that McCreary, too solidly entrenched ever to be brought up on charges and fired, would quit the agency in disgust. But McCreary was not to be gotten rid of so easily. He had a name that might have been Irish and the temperament to match. He was not Irish, though, or even remotely Anglo-Saxon. In terms of service John Jacob McCreary was one of the oldest blacks in the agency, even though he was still only fifty and looked ten years younger since he had eliminated the gray in his hair by shaving his head. Like Sweet, McCreary had in effect gone undercover. Stalking the halls of the Parole building, he was frequently mistaken for a parolee. In a denim jacket, a gold chain around his neck, wearing wraparound sunglasses, he could have just gotten off the bus from Attica or Clinton. Twelve years ago, however, he had been one of the few parole officers who always wore a suit and tie, even to the field. A new image? Or the manifestation of a severe personality disorder?

Reppa sometimes nodded to McCreary when they passed

each other in the halls, but they had never spoken. Lidsky seemed to take it for granted they soon would.

"Be my guest. Investigation assignments are given out strictly by rotation. Alphabetical order. But anyone can ask," he said.

"I intend to. If this job is anything, it's being able to poke under a rock now and then."

"This one's not a rock. It's a box. Pandora's box. The cops know what they're doing. It isn't always necessary for us to know."

"If I hadn't checked out whether Wallace was lying when he said he saw de Spirit, you'd say I was a border-line incompetent."

Lidsky didn't deny it. His hand strayed yearningly to his pipe, wobbled the empty bowl. "You still should have cleared it with me before you started flashing your tin all over town. The public library! Who ever heard of a parole officer claiming a field visit to the library? Not even in the old days, when guys used to put all sorts of things on their activity sheets just to see if anyone read them. Grant's Tomb. I once slipped that one by Unverferth. You wouldn't remember Unverferth. He was before your time. How long have you been here now?"

"Three years in March."

Lidsky leaned over and patted the back of Reppa's hand earnestly. "Only three, and you're not so young. If you're going to go anywhere in this agency, it's got to be soon. Once you hit forty, about all you can expect is your two-hundred-dollar increment for passing go at the beginning of each fiscal year."

"It's more than two hundred dollars."

"I was making a point." Lidsky sat back with a frown, as if he had forgotten what it was. Then he leaned forward again and said confidingly, "By the way, they know

61

upstairs that you're shacking up with that little college teacher. If you were still doing your six months probation, I don't have to tell you there'd be flak. They might even can you. Fornication. The law is still on the books in this state."

"So is the law against perjury. One of my men committed it when he said he saw something he didn't."

Lidsky rapidly nodded agreement. "As I said, you've got more than enough to lock him up. At least until the dust clears on this de Spirit thing. For the kid's own protection. If the cops are going to phony up a drug bust every time they want to put leverage on him, we owe it to him to get him off the street."

"Then you admit they're capable of planting a few bags on Wallace in order to fake the grounds for an arrest."

"They have their methods," Lidsky acknowledged. "Meanwhile we're all on the same side of the fence: keeping the bad people away from the good people. Sometimes you have to accept on faith that the end justifies the means."

There, he had done the dreaded thing—taken a philosophical position. As if belatedly realizing it, he narrowed one eye in a wince.

"Getting back to my living situation," Reppa said and watched the other eye hastily try to look paternal.

"A word to the wise. It may be 1980, but some of the agency thinking is still back in 1950. Myself, I don't care who you live with. I believe in the nuclear family, but I also believe in freedom. Still, if you're going to pursue a hippie life-style in your private life, it only makes good sense to wear a clean shirt in public. Right?"

Reppa frowned. "Who's said what to you about me?"

"Nothing—nothing's been said. But before you run and

tie your can to McCreary's tail, just remember you don't have the privileged position here that he does.''

''Because I'm not black?''

Lidsky ruefully stroked the bowl of his pipe, distressed that Reppa had felt driven to state what wiser men only implied.

Reppa sat for half an hour by himself when he returned to his office, feet up on his desk, pondering. In his lap was Danny de Spirit's case folder. Stamped across the front of it was RETURNED TO INSTITUTION/ NEW SENTENCE, and a date: 9/4/69. McCreary had dictated his closing chronos on the case a few weeks later, and there had been no new entries since.

Inside its skin of cardboard was the anatomy of a defective human being. The inexorable progression from truant to thief to drug addict to convict to parolee to . . . Reppa's mind still drew back from completing the journey to murderer, although the probation report made it abundantly clear that Danny de Spirit had a long history of violent acts going all the way back to early puberty. At eleven he set a derelict on fire; a year later he stabbed a woman during a purse snatch; on and on it went, suspended sentences, short reformatory stints, until he reached eighteen and was caught breaking into an apartment on Columbus Avenue. His Legal Aid lawyer had requested that since he was still under twenty-one, he be adjudicated a youthful offender, but the court had refused and sentenced him to three years for attempted burglary. It was his first adult conviction; he served nineteen months at Greenhaven before being paroled in February 1968. At the time of the Behrman-Moffett murders he was working in a shoe-repair shop, living with his mother in a basement apartment on West 105th Street, and seemingly doing all right. But shortly thereafter he began using drugs again and absconded from parole.

For several months McCreary had visited the mother regularly to see if she'd heard from de Spirit. He had also filed a wanted card with the Interstate Bureau, with a notation that de Spirit might have fled to Canada. Unlikely, but it had to be considered, because de Spirit's putative father was reportedly somewhere in the eastern provinces. A white Canadian soldier, he had met de Spirit's mother while on furlough in Martinique. The two had married and lived in Quebec after he completed his service tour. Within a year of de Spirit's birth, however, his father deserted them. A black woman who spoke very little English, his mother remained in Quebec and worked as a maid until she met a black American truck driver named Rodney Wallace. In the course of time she divorced de Spirit's father, married Wallace, and went to New York with him. As did her son, who was legally adopted by Wallace but retained his father's name.

The probation report, strangely, said nothing of Jimmy Wallace. Reppa had to read over the report in Wallace's folder before he understood the omission. Wallace, it developed, was not in fact a product of the union between his father and de Spirit's mother. His true mother was a woman his father had lived with but never married before meeting Mrs. de Spirit. It explained why there was no notation in Wallace's folder that he had a half brother in prison. Wallace and de Spirit weren't related at all; they had been stepbrothers and at that only for a very short time. Wallace's father had died of pneumonia less than a year after he and de Spirit's mother were married, and Wallace had been sent to live in the first of a long line of foster homes. No one seemed to know where his true mother was. It was quite understandable that Wallace would claim now that de Spirit was his half brother and the woman he lived with was his aunt. They were the nearest thing he had to relatives.

Nevertheless Reppa was upset with himself for not having paid closer attention the first time he'd read Wallace's probation report. It was all there—the early years of Wallace's childhood that had been spent with a French stepmother and her son—but he'd skimmed it, registering only the exoticism of Martinique. With over fifty cases he could successfully argue with himself that he didn't have time to soak up every word in every probation report, but the reality was that delving into the childhood stuff invariably wound up only confusing him. Bloodlines. Who could untangle all the racial and cultural cross-stitches that comprised a Jimmy Wallace or a Danny de Spirit? Half of this and a quarter of that.

Stapled inside the front cover of de Spirit's folder was a photograph of him standing beside a measuring rod. Taken fourteen years ago while he was still at Greenhaven, it showed a slenderish, good-looking kid in his late teens. Reppa held the photograph in Wallace's folder up beside it. The resemblance dismayed him. The two really did look as if they could have been brothers. Not only were both slim and around the same height, but they had the same high cheekbones and thin, rather delicate features.

The more Reppa thought about Danny de Spirit, the angrier he got—and the more regretful that he'd read de Spirit's case folder. If it had been possible to get a grip on the belief that de Spirit had been a decent kid who'd been railroaded, it would have been easier.

He took the elevator to McCreary's office on the first floor. The stairs would have been faster, but the last thing he was, was in a hurry.

*   *   *

"Know what I hate?" McCreary said, interrupting him. "People who call me Mac. Anybody ever call you Rep?"

As a matter of fact, many had. One of them being, years ago at Ohio State, none other than Woody Hayes. He stood in the doorway of McCreary's office, the question he had posed still unanswered: whether or not McCreary had a few minutes to see him. McCreary, for his part, pushed papers around his desk as if to conceal under them the fact that he had nothing but time to see people. In the room's indirect lighting the top of his skull shone as if it had been waxed. Conscious that he was staring at it, Reppa lowered his gaze a few inches.

There he encountered the ubiquitous sunglasses. Under them McCreary was displaying a set of very white and very even teeth.

"Well?"

McCreary really expected an answer to his question, but Reppa misunderstood and repeated his own.

"What is it now, Rep? The union? The answer is I don't pay anybody dues until they've paid me mine. If you're here to get me to join the Parole Officers Association, ditto."

Here McCreary stopped and clutched his shoulders with his hands, as if pantomiming that he was bound to the desk. Reppa noticed that two fingers on his left hand ended at the first knuckle. One of the stories he'd heard when he first started working for Parole was that McCreary had put his hand over the muzzle of his partner's gun as he tried to shoot an absconder who was attempting to flee up a fire escape. Supposedly the bullet had been deflected, but the tip of one of McCreary's fingers had hit the absconder in the back of the head with force enough to stagger him so that he could be captured unharmed. A terrific story, but Reppa had never bought it. Now, seeing

66

the hand and listening to its owner, he could feel himself beginning to.

"I'm not here to ask you to join anything." He talked fast, leaping into the silence while McCreary was busy demonstrating his bondage, and his words came out stumbling. "But I do want something, a favor, you'd have to say. . . . What I mean is—you're in charge of assigning investigations."

"And you want me to overlook your name next time it comes up on rotation."

"The opposite. I want you to see that I get a certain assignment."

"Where? Brooklyn? You got some broad you're poking in Brooklyn, and you want a way to see her a couple of afternoons and charge the mileage to the state?"

"Actually, it's Danny de Spirit."

Which brought such a look of suspicion to McCreary's face it was as if Reppa had dropped a raw egg on top of the waxed head.

"Man, who told you to come up here?"

"Nobody. In fact, someone has already told me not to. My senior—Lidsky."

Offered as proof to McCreary that he was something of a rebel in his own right. But McCreary's forehead was still furrowed as if he were looking for a trick.

"You happen to know who de Spirit's PO was while he was on parole?"

Reppa nodded.

"It occur to you, man, the irony that I'm going to have to sit here behind this desk while some other cat does his investigation isn't entirely accidental? These people knew when they stuck me here something like this would happen one day. Now you no doubt think I'm just a bitter paranoid nigger—what's the matter, you never heard a nigger call himself a nigger?''

It was true: Reppa had blinked. But then he realized it was his next reaction that McCreary was really watching for.

"I didn't come up here to listen to you bitch. You don't like what you see happening around you. All right. I don't like everything I see either. But the difference is I'm where I can maybe do something about it.''

"Maybe?"

"Can I sit down?''

"And close the door.''

When Reppa had done both, McCreary tipped his chair back and put his maimed hand down flat on the desk as would an old gunfighter. A truce, for the moment.

"You're a new face around here, Rep. Comparatively. Anyhow, I know you don't go back far enough to have any personal connection to Behrman-Moffett. Unless it was before you came to the agency. What'd you do before you became a PO?''

"Coached football.''

"High school?''

"And some pro. I was with the New York Stars before they folded.''

"You know Joe Gilliam?''

"No, but I know people who do.''

"He would have been the greatest NFL quarterback ever if they hadn't fucked him over because he was black.''

"Nobody fucked him over. He blew it. The same as Duane Thomas. In my opinion coaches bent over backward to give them extra chances *because* they were black.''

McCreary made a slight smile acknowledging Reppa's triumph. A test had been given and passed.

"Coach. You like it?''

68

"More than anything."

"Yeah, but." McCreary massaged his smooth brown scalp, as if squeezing a thought out of it. "You ain't doing it anymore."

Reppa squirmed. The next test would not be so easy. "The last year I was a head coach—the last game, when you come right down to it—one of my kids was killed. Kicked in the head. They blamed me for keeping him in the game after it happened, but the truth is I didn't even know he was hurt. Until I saw the game films afterward—"

"Shit," McCreary cut in remorselessly. "They talk like that even in high school, coaches? I thought it was only in the pros they said, 'I really won't be able to say what went wrong until I've seen the films.' "

"In this instance it was true. He just keeled over all of a sudden in the huddle, and the school needed a scapegoat. When the shit hit the fan, the only one who stood behind me was good old Woody."

"Woody?"

"Wayne Woodrow Hayes. He couldn't get me another high school job, but he did the next best thing. Every coach owes a few favors. Woody collected from someone who owed him, and that was how I managed to hook on with the Stars."

"Never saw them play," McCreary muttered.

"Few did. Or the Fillies. I moved over to the Fillies when the Stars went under. The women's team," Reppa added when McCreary looked perplexed. "They folded, too."

"A long association with losing outfits. And now you're with another one."

Reppa shrugged resignedly, as if he couldn't understand how it kept happening to him. But McCreary had no time for method actors. McCreary, McCreary pointed out, was still waiting to learn what had brought him here.

The maverick in him that could not tolerate unfair play? The sense that McCreary was a kindred spirit? Yes, that; all that was obvious. But he had a feeling there was more, something hidden, that must not be admitted to. It was like examining himself in the mirror, seeing no grotesqueries, knowing he looked more or less normal, but afraid nevertheless to go out in public. "I have a man on my case load named Jimmy Wallace," he began, "and yesterday when I made a home visit—"

"Graham," McCreary said in a tone of disgust once he'd gotten the gist.

"You know him?"

"We've had dealings. Go on. You went back to the precinct and told them Wallace had been in school that day. What happened then?"

"Graham sort of disappeared, and a cat named Sweet took over. He made it clear the entire NYPD thought de Spirit was a very wrong guy, and they weren't about to let him out of the slam without an all-out fight."

"Sweet? Big nigger with a ring in his nose?"

Reppa nodded after narrowly checking himself from saying "Big nigger, right." McCreary could mouth it all he wanted, but let him say it just once, and he had an idea the maimed hand would fly up off the desk like a hawk whose nest had been invaded.

"You've got to dig where they're coming from. From where they're looking, de Spirit was guilty of so much other stuff they never nailed him for that they're just trying to get even."

"Including murder?"

"Murder," McCreary insisted, "was on his calendar. If not in the past or present then in the very near future. I

70

don't know what your boy Wallace is like, but de Spirit was not a particularly nice kid."

"Yet you did a lot of work on his behalf."

"Not for him. I wasn't working for him. Not for one minute. No, I was working for something much more important."

Reppa waited. When he saw McCreary meant to wait longer, he said, "What?"

"Myself, man. My eternal lust for truth."

"You mean justice?"

"I said truth, friend. Do a little reading sometime on the case. It was solved—or more like it, *dissolved*—by a born liar."

"Cupach?"

"He lied, Rep. He lied most of all to himself. He got convinced he had his big score when he picked up on de Spirit, and it blinded him to everything else."

"My impression is there wasn't anything else. By the time he ran across de Spirit, he and the rest of the cops on the case were at a total dead end."

"And what got him dead-ended? How do you suppose he wound up with a dime-store junkie burglar when the case was crawling with cats who didn't have to come in no back window to get into that Behrman broad's bedroom?"

"Like who?"

"Hey, I don't know anything for sure, Rep. That's the problem. All I know is Cupach had access to everything and everyone. He could have gone places I couldn't begin to go and asked all the questions I could only ask myself."

McCreary touched the tips of his fingers—the tips that were left to him—to his face in a gesture that did not allow for misinterpretation: a matter of color. Doors opening freely to white Steve Cupach while black John Jacob McCreary was restricted to peering through keyholes. Reppa

71

remembered suddenly that in a staff meeting once the area director had addressed McCreary as J.J.

"What makes you think he didn't go those places and ask those questions? Everything I've read about the case, J.J., suggests that he did."

Conjectured so he could slip the nickname in, for the effect. At first it didn't seem to have one. McCreary just sat with his hands folded under his jaw, motionless. Then he smiled a swift lupine smile and said, "Familiarity breeds contemplation. What's the gimmick, Rep? Lay it on me. How much is the de Spirit investigation worth, assuming I could arrange for it to fall your way?"

A bribe? Not money, hardly money, but what? "A lot," he said, at a venture.

"A simple investigation. Cut and dried. Talking to relatives of the victim—in this case, victims—maybe a few cops who worked on the case, so as to get a sense of who'll jump down the governor's throat if he coughs up a pardon. Then putting it all in a report, one that's definitely going to be read, that a lot of people are going to read. Does that *really* sound like something you'd dig?"

"If the conditions are right," Reppa hedged.

"Such as if upstairs relieved you of your regular caseload responsibilities until the investigation is completed?"

"They'd do that for this investigation? I hadn't realized."

"Everybody else who's been in here this morning has."

When Reppa looked blank, McCreary nodded, politely informing him there was a long line ahead of him. Then, subtly, he started homing in on what Reppa knew was the critical issue. "They'll lean on me heavy if I don't go straight by rotation in making this assignment. Next man up alphabetically gets it. But you and I both know, seniority, sex discrimination, whatever, there isn't a rule in this agency that can't be gotten around if the price is made right for the right people."

Had he been wrong after all? "Money?"

"Christ, not money. Never money. Money carries a price of its own. You don't know, do you? You've still got footballs in front of your eyes, Rep. It's fear. Everybody's got to believe if you get this assignment out of rotation it's because you know something about somebody. Get it? Not that you know somebody in the right place but that you know something *about* somebody in the right place."

Reppa frowned.

"You don't follow? Dirt, man. Everybody who climbs in this agency wears thick socks so you can't see the color of their feet from what they've had to step in to move up. Yet and still, all those socks have a hole or two, and ain't nobody so secure you can't shake them up by staring down around their ankles."

"It won't work," Reppa said. "I've got a reputation for staying out of the politics around here. Nobody's going to believe that I've suddenly out of nowhere got the drop on them."

"Leave it to me," McCreary said quietly, fiddling with his gold chain, the stubbed knuckles polishing two of the links. "I know where the holes are. You just make sure there aren't any in your own socks."

What the hell, Reppa thought. Was it really going to be this easy?

"All this socks and holes stuff, does it mean you're going to give me the assignment?"

"Well, Rep, since you clearly want it very badly, how can a charitable man such as myself deny you?"

Something in McCreary's tone suddenly made him feel uncomfortably obligated.

"And the price?"

"Now that you ask." At the far edge of McCreary's sunglasses he saw, for the barest instant, the ghastly smile of the high school principal who had told him his first coaching job would come with only one very small string attached: The principal had a friend in the sporting goods business, and each time the team needed new uniforms . . . "I have this insatiable appetite for truth. The others who came up here asking for this assignment ran a lie on me when I asked them why they wanted it. You can lie, too, but I'll know. If that sounds to you like a nigger egomaniac bragging he's got the power to read men's minds, go fuck yourself. I don't need you, man. You need me. So why are you here, Rep?"

For over a decade the seeds planted by the brain behind those impenetrable sunglasses had lain dormant in the folder of a closed case. McCreary either didn't credit him with the ability to read between the lines, or McCreary thought him another kind of fool.

Still he stalled, unsure whether it was out of stubbornness or something deeper. "Why? Any number of reasons—"

"Spare me the preamble. Just the bottom line."

The desire to explain himself was suddenly a physical need, but, as in a nightmare when the monster looms at the foot of your bed and you are powerless to scream, there were no words to express it.

"Come on, Rep. Is it curiosity? A couple of weeks of relief from your regular caseload? You don't like thinking a murderer may still be wandering around loose?"

He accepted the coaching. "I'd say all of those."

"I'd say all those and at least one more you ain't saying. But if you'll admit it, I'll content my appetite for the time being with that one little kernel of truth. Besides, I'd rather see this assignment go to a man with a football background. You look like a lineman. Were you?"

"Linebacker."

"Same difference. A lot of slugging away in the trenches,

74

unseen. The last thing this investigation needs is a glory hound looking for his name in lights."

There it was then, if you listened beneath what was being said. Somehow McCreary expected to reap any harvest that grew out of the investigation for himself. Reppa was a moron if he thought otherwise.

And he didn't believe for a minute his football experience had been the main selling point. He debated whether to say so, then decided McCreary would think him all the more a fool if he didn't.

"Listen, J.J., bullshit aside . . ."

"Nobody who calls me J.J. really means that."

"But I do. What's the real reason you're willing to feed me the de Spirit investigation?"

McCreary waited till Reppa was looking at him again. Then, very deliberately, he peeled off the sunglasses like a surgeon peeling away his mask after an operation, to unveil for an imaginary public.

"The real reason," McCreary repeated, leaning across the desk and enunciating each syllable so that there could be no misunderstanding, "is Joe Led-dy."

Reppa had been a parole officer less than two months when it happened. As the newest man in his unit he was assigned to share an office with Joe Leddy. Reppa thought at first that he was being given Leddy as a partner because Leddy was an old-timer who could show him the ropes. Consequently he tried to be tolerant of Leddy's heavy-handed ethnic jokes and crude personal habits. Jowly, potbellied, Leddy ate his lunch each day at his desk— generally a meatball hero drooling with garlic, followed by a full thermos of coffee. The office reeked for hours afterward. On the days he and Reppa took reports and had to stay at their desks till eight in the evening, he would snack on another enormous "sangie" late in the afternoon and then go out for something to wash it down. Usually he did not return for at least an hour; occasionally he failed to return altogether. As Leddy's partner Reppa had to do double coverage during his absences. For several weeks he took Leddy's reports as well as his own without complaint, but gradually he came to understand he had not been paired up with Leddy so he would have a mentor. Rather he had been stuck with a man no one else could abide. That Leddy had a drinking problem on top of everything else eluded him at first. But once he started settling in to the routine of the job and having more time to observe the way Leddy approached his workday, he wondered how he could have been so naïve. Leddy did all his case-load dictation and paperwork before lunch, hastily, feverishly, sweating through the armpits of his shirt; in the afternoon he told his ponderous jokes awhile, read the sports page, and then eventually lapsed into a semicomatose state at his desk. Worn out, was Reppa's erroneous initial assumption. *Guy doesn't work much, but when he does, he works hard. Amazing, though, how he can sleep after all that coffee.*

One morning Reppa picked up the thermos and examined it while Leddy was out of the office. It was empty. But when Leddy sat down to his sangie an hour or so later, he punctuated each bite from it with a long gurgling pull at the thermos. *Must get it filled at the same place he gets those filthy sandwiches*, Reppa figured. Later he noticed Leddy always thoroughly washed out the thermos before sinking into his nap. Still, Reppa did not wake up fully to what was going on until a parole officer named Sadowski drifted into his office one afternoon and took a whiff of the air.

"Smells like a Turkish sewer," Sadowski said.

"Garlic," Reppa informed him. They both paused to

76

look at Leddy, whose head was down on his chest, eyelids adroop. "Cast-iron stomach."

"Covers the breath. But good thing you're not a smoker. Man, light a match after one of his farts, and the whole place'll go up."

"You think he drinks—on the job?"

Sadowski met his gaze reluctantly, as though he saw no way to avoid being introduced to the host of a dull party.

But if Reppa was left to discover Leddy's clandestine love affair with the bottle for himself, he was furious that no one had warned him what Leddy was like while doing delinquency work. Chasing absconders, rousting parole violators, transporting prisoners were necessary parts of the job. Some parole officers enjoyed these activities; others loathed them; a few dreaded them—but all had a healthy respect for the dangers inherent in pursuing a man who had been to prison and who knew when you appeared at the foot of his bed in the middle of the night that you were there to take him back. During his two weeks of training at the Parole Academy in Albany and later, when he'd had to qualify with his .38 at the Lexington Avenue armory, Reppa had sought ways of dodging the admission to himself that the job he was about to embark on was the equivalent of combat in wartime. As in combat, all the training in the world couldn't really prepare you for your first encounter with an actual live enemy, and also as in combat, you usually found yourself alongside some hoople rather than John Wayne.

Leddy was the worst combination possible, a hoople who imagined himself John Wayne. The Tuesday of Reppa's seventh week on the job Leddy suddenly announced, "Well, son, tomorrow you're gonna get your feet wet."

Until noon or so Leddy called everyone under fifty (his own age) son; once he'd plowed through his lunch, that

77

altered to good buddy. If stirred prematurely out of one of his naps, it was just plain bud.

What's he, going to invite me to hit one of his watering holes with him? Reppa wondered. Aloud he wondered, "What's up?"

"A little bread run. Got a guy hasn't reported now in over a month, and it's time to drop iron on him. Pick you up at your place seven sharp. I got blue wheels, Plymouth Fury. Where d'you live?"

"Ninth Street. Near Second Avenue. Why don't we just meet on the corner of Second?"

Leddy scowled. "Corner? What's the matter? You don't want me to see your crib?"

Precisely, but he couldn't say that, of course, any more than he could offer a palatable excuse for not going out with Leddy. If it didn't happen tomorrow, it had to happen sooner or later. They were partners, and partners were expected to team up on delinquency work unless there was a strong reason not to. Thus far Reppa didn't have one. A bread run at night was one thing, but at seven o'clock in the morning Leddy would leastways still be sober.

"What's black with a white ring around it?" Leddy started in as he climbed into the blue Fury the following morning.

"The beach at Coney Island."

"Why'd the Polack girl say she couldn't play with herself?"

"Where're we going?"

"The Bronx. Walton Avenue. Girl friend's crib. She claims when I talked to her on the phone she hasn't seen him in weeks, but I'll lay you two-to-one when we pull the blanket off her, we'll find four legs under it."

And so forth until they crossed the 145th Street bridge. The Yankees were home tonight against the Mariners, the sign on the stadium said. Leddy was still bitching about dumb-dago Billy Martin as they mounted the front steps of the building on Walton Avenue.

Once inside, however, he grabbed Reppa abruptly by both shoulders and expelled a breath that carried the aroma of rancid petroleum. "Here's the plan. When we go in, you take the window in case he's there and makes a break for the fire escape. Big mother, built like you, so don't hesitate to go for your heat. Meanwhile I'm in the bedroom. Say he's there. We drop iron on him right away, nude, sitting on the can, I don't care parapalegic. The guys that get burned, they're the ones that think it's a coffee klatch. Sit around on the couch, 'Why'd you stop reporting, Mr. Jones?' While they're playing social worker, Jones is working his fingers between the cushions for the shiv he's got hidden."

Leddy went ahead of him up the stairs. They stopped in front of a door at the end of the second-floor hallway. "Knock," Leddy growled, ducking out of range of the peephole. "Tell 'em you're here to read the meter or some shit."

Reppa knocked. A woman's voice called out, "Who?"

"Meterman." He felt an eye watching him through the peephole.

Then bolts were thrown, the knob was turned. Leddy pushed him through the door before it was completely open, and he collided with a terrified black woman in a green cotton robe. The blinds were drawn in the apartment, but there were so many holes in them that he could not avoid noticing the conditions here. Broken chairs, water stains on the walls, a gummy substance underfoot that was someone's meager attempt at a carpet.

Leddy went crashing toward the rear of the place, leaving him alone with the woman. When he followed, he

79

found Leddy in a bleak bedroom holding a black man clad only in a tank top at gunpoint.

"Drop iron," Leddy ordered, chidingly adding, "behind his back, good buddy," when the man held his wrists out to Reppa accommodatingly.

It was his first tangible inkling that Leddy'd had a few beforehand to fortify himself.

Once the cuffs were on, Leddy holstered his gun and told the man to face the wall, bend over, and spread those chocolate buns. Behind him Reppa heard a sharp breath being drawn. When he glanced over his shoulder, the woman gave him a piteous look, as if she knew Leddy as only someone in her circumstances could. Still he tried to persuade himself that as the low man here, the rookie, he could not reasonably interfere.

This conviction lasted until Leddy said, "Now your pecker. I know you been going in on yourself. It's just a matter of where."

"He don't use no drugs," the woman shouted. She shouted again, more a shriek, when Leddy seized the man's cock and flung it from side to side.

"Show me a hard-on. Get a hard-on, and I'll believe you're not on junk."

Reppa intercepted another look from the woman that said, *You gonna just stand there?* To Leddy she said, "Cocksucker."

"Up yours, twitch," Leddy retorted. "Reppa, cover me. I'm giving this bugger a total going over, asshole to elbows. If there's so much as a single needle mark anywhere, I'll find it."

"What difference does it make if he's been using? You've got him. Let's get him dressed and get out of here."

Leddy ignored his smoldering unease. "You'll learn, good buddy. When you nail a man, you go for every charge you can get on him."

Reppa gnawed his lower lip, his disgust too self-directed to bear further argument. Around then it struck him how curiously silent the parolee had been throughout. The man had yet to utter a single word or make even the slightest sound of protest. But his eyes said much. When Reppa's own eyes went in search of them across the room, they became very calm, as if awaiting a message. Upon receiving one, they appeared for an instant to smile.

Meanwhile Leddy, afloat in his own form of amusement, didn't notice Reppa take the woman's elbow and quietly accompany her out the door. "What's the matter, good buddy? You can't get it up? I tell your old lady to lie on the bed and open her legs, that push your button? Or are you so far gone on stuff Elizabeth Taylor couldn't put you back in commission? Or how about Dorothy Dandridge or whoever you guys cream for now . . . Hey, bud, whattaya doing—get off my foot!"

Leddy suddenly discovered that he was the only parole officer in the room. "Reppa, where the fuck . . . ?" he inquired just before he suffered a violent butt in the chest that caromed him off the wall.

Still in handcuffs, the parolee had later gone compliantly with Reppa to the Bronx House of Detention, but not until Reppa had made another stop: Jacoby Hospital, where Leddy'd had to be helped out of the car and into the emergency room, murmuring threats against Reppa's hunky life every step of the way. Reppa's story to the area director was that Leddy had fallen down a flight of stairs as they were escorting the parolee out of the building; drunk, not drunk, who was Reppa to judge? When Leddy heard this, he swallowed his own version of events so he

81

could collect disability without a battle while he recuperated. Two cracked ribs, a broken collarbone, and some damage to his testicles befuddled doctors who'd been told he was the victim of a fall. It was a long while before Leddy was fit to return to duty. By then Reppa had been assigned another partner. He had also learned more about the circumstances under which he had been assigned his first partner. A new parole officer, who for one reason or another was not welcomed by the agency but whose test scores were so high there could be no cogent reason for not hiring him, was traditionally paired with men like Leddy. Rummies, creeps, racists that were impossible to work with. The agency, so Reppa heard through the grapevine, didn't look fondly on his coaching record or the wife and three daughters he'd left behind in Ohio. That Irene had remarried, the girls were well provided for, and he had been, at bottom, a winner as a coach were somehow irrelevant. A good parole officer was one who made few waves, and everything in Reppa's background pointed to his being a tempest.

After the Leddy incident his reputation was elevated to that of a full-blown hurricane. Though neither he nor Leddy ever told anyone what had really happened in that apartment on Walton Avenue, the true story still filtered quickly through the agency. Reppa's surmise was the parolee had talked, and word had come down from the institution where he'd been sent. Regardless, no one ever exactly came forward to commend Reppa for the manner in which he'd handled Leddy, but he noticed that many of the black parole officers began nodding arcanely to him when they passed him in the halls, and several even murmured, "Smooth, good buddy, real smooth." He refused to feel affirmed by anything he heard or take bows or hold a grudge against the Powers-That-Be that had teamed him up with Leddy in the hope that he would be gobbled up and washed down the tube like one of those soggy sangies. If some people wanted to think him a hero, let them. If others wanted to think him something else, that was fine, too. He wasn't there to win friends or influence people. The cardinal rule, the way you won football games, Woody Hayes had drummed into his head, was to avoid getting in a bind. That was really what was behind "Three yards and a cloud of dust." As long as you had the ball, the other team couldn't score. The ball, after the Leddy episode, was clearly in his possession.

Now he sat watching McCreary's eyes smile at him. "You know the protocol you have to follow on investigations like this?"

"Track down all the principals in the case and make appointments to see them?"

"One interview to a customer. Those you can't find after a reasonable search or those who refuse to see you, you have to write off. Just remember you're only a parole officer. Even an insurance agent has more investigative power than you're going to have. Anybody who feels you're twisting his arm just has to give one whimper upstairs, and they'll make me yank you off the assignment and put someone else on in your place. About the only asset you have going for you is . . ." McCreary withdrew what he was going to say and counseled in its place, "Don't hesitate to let everybody know you're an ex-football player. They'll be looking for you to drive a shoulder into them. They won't know you know how to bring somebody down without being physical yourself."

That had been the lesson for McCreary in Leddy. A jock with moxie.

Football. Baseball. Even tiddlywinks. Sports and games.

Somewhere in them, Reppa had always felt, there was a teleology for everything. If you knew how to look, it could all be made to fit together. It wasn't just a lot of arbitrary rules.

He got up, but it didn't help. Even when he was on his feet, contrapuntal thoughts kept running between his ears. One moment, looking at McCreary's clubbed fingers, he could see high potential for being dealt a wicked curve. The next moment, remembering the voices that had said, "Smooth, good buddy, real smooth," he could believe he was being given a reward.

He borrowed one of Leilah's favorite tacks: When confused or pressed, wisecrack. "Any other tips, coach?"

"Who're you going to see first?"

"No idea. I was going to reread your chronos in de Spirit's folder for leads."

"Don't rely too heavy on those chronos, Rep. There was plenty I had to leave out. Like with the third roommate, the one who found the bodies. Jill Wilkerson."

Good old Jane Walker. "What about her?"

"I described her as uncommunicative. I couldn't use the word I really wanted or I would've had to spell it out."

"It?"

"You form your own conclusions, good buddy. That goes for everybody else you're going to interview, too. I don't want to prejudice you. Small p."

Reppa didn't know whether he was meant to, but he got a small chuckle out of that.

CHAPTER THREE

STANLEY BEHRMAN

The following Monday morning both Lidsky and Reppa received copies of an interoffice memo from the area director informing them that Reppa was being temporarily relieved of his regular case-load responsibilities pending his completion of the de Spirit investigation.

"When your name's called, you've got to go," Lidsky said, as though oblivious that there might be anything more at work than random chance.

Following the last piece of advice McCreary had given him ("Hit quick, before the cops get wind you're making the rounds and tell everybody they're within their legal rights refusing to talk to you"), Reppa immediately called Andrea's stepfather and her aunt. A young woman answered Stanley Behrman's phone; Annabelle's was answered by a man who identified himself as her secretary. Both were cool when they learned his purpose. "Stanley's very tired this week," the woman said. Annabelle's secretary said she saw no one these days. Marveling at the smoothness with which the lie rolled off his tongue, Reppa told both he could get a governor's subpoena if need be. Abstractly the woman said, "Oh, all right," and went to get Behrman, who agreed to see him that afternoon at four. Annabelle's secretary laughed and said, "A governor's whozit?" Nevertheless he took Reppa's office number, then called back in a while and informed Reppa that Annabelle would see him some evening in a week or so. It had to be sooner than that, Reppa said; he had only a few days to complete his investigation. With another laugh the secretary said, "Tonight, then. Nineish, between Annabelle's bath and her bewitching hour."

Most of the day Reppa browsed through the legacy of dictated reports McCreary had left in de Spirit's case folder and made notes to himself in a small blue notebook he had begun carrying. The three people he definitely had to see were Behrman, Annabelle, and Jill Wilkerson. Behrman had been in the phone book; Annabelle's unlisted number had been acquired from a special liaison officer at Ma Bell—but Wilkerson wasn't listed anywhere. No longer in New York? Married and going under her husband's name? An insoluble problem for the moment. He sat at his desk combing the reports for information about the people identified in *Andrea and Elizabeth* only by pseudonyms. "Jay," Andrea's former fiancé. The art gallery owner, "Claudio," who had been the first to exhibit Annabelle's work and later had a posthumous show of Andrea's paintings. But McCreary had been more interested in showing the police up as buffoons and scoundrels than in doing a plodding investigation of the case. Thus there were torrential recountings of phone calls to police detectives that had gone unreturned, visits to precincts where he had been kept cooling his heels for hours, contradictory statements, misplaced court records, broken appointments with lawyers, probation officers, and assistant district attorneys. It all added up to a scathing indictment of the judicial process that put Danny de Spirit away for life, but it left as many questions unanswered as it raised. Other than those with police officers and detectives, the only interviews of substance McCreary'd had were with de Spirit's mother, de Spirit himself, and Jill Wilkerson. He had also spoken briefly on the phone with Behrman and Annabelle, but both had refused to see him, claiming the police had advised them against talking to anyone acting on behalf of de Spirit. Stonewalled on every side, McCreary ended his last report: "The writer is herewith forced to close his professional interest in this case but will never allow anything to fetter his private interest."

For the past seventeen years Stanley Behrman had lived in a nine-room apartment on Park Avenue between Sixty-eighth and Sixty-ninth streets. McCreary's reports had described the building as "a palatial co-op" and added: "Unfortunately the writer, a mere esne, was unable to gain entrance to the palace to pay court to the royal personage there ensconced." After his presence was announced over the intercom, Reppa lingered in the lobby, held by a nervousness that had its roots in the knowledge of how removed this was from the apartment buildings he usually visited. Then, feeling the veiled curiosity in the door-man's eyes, he was compelled to show he wasn't just procrastinating.

"Worked here long?"

"It's an excellent building, sir."

"I'm sure it is. I was wondering if you remembered Mr. Behrman's stepdaughter."

The doorman was small, thin, cadaverous. Placing a bony hand on Reppa's elbow, he attempted to guide him toward a distant elevator where a spectral figure awaited in black wing-tip shoes and white gloves. "Mr. Behrman's on nine, sir," he said, the statement not only deliberately off the point but obviously final.

But Reppa didn't move. He allowed the doorman a glimpse of his shield.

"So I see, sir." Spoken easily, but Reppa saw the pinched cheeks quiver slightly.

It made round one feel like a draw. But round one of what?

He hesitated a moment outside the elevator, not yet ready, then stepped into the de Spirit investigation with both feet.

The royal personage answered the door of 9B himself and glanced indulgently at Reppa's shield and ID card.

"Ah, Officer Reppa. My pleasure."

Reppa took the smallish plump hand offered him, trying not to leap ahead to thoughts of whether it could have wielded a knife with deadly purpose twelve years ago. *Patience*, he swore at himself; *go slow and easy*. Using the moment of affability, he shook Behrman's hand at length while the impressions fell on his brain. Bald. Scarcely five feet tall. Round, almost cherubic face. Merry light-blue eyes. The genial visage that greeted Reppa seemed so innocuous that he nearly relaxed.

"Come in, come in. What's your beverage?"

"Nothing, thanks."

Swinging away from the door, Behrman became suddenly brusque and detached. Reppa, hoping for a glimpse of how Park Avenue lived, found himself being herded into a room where it was apparent no one had lived for a long time. A room of barren walls and long low-slung sofas, all of them covered by white sheets. There was a slight odor of must in the air.

"I'm still not here mentally," Behrman apologized. "Usually I don't get back to the city till June, but Marissa wanted to show off her tan before everyone else had one." He peeled the sheets off two of the sofas, baring—to

Reppa's dismay—plastic slipcovers. "Now, what's all this about the case being reopened?"

"Not exactly reopened. All we're trying to do is get a sense of the reaction in the event the governor decides to grant Danny de Spirit a pardon."

Between the slipcovers and the must Reppa had begun to feel that this might be no more than a home visit, like any other. He sat down on one sofa and watched Behrman arrange himself on the other in a decorative way, legs langorously crossed, arms stretched expansively along the back cushions. "Marissa?" Behrman called. "Here we are."

A tall blond girl, big-boned, with a deep tan, appeared in the doorway. She wore cutoff jeans and a white T-shirt with a bright-red heart between the words *I* and *Dirty Old Men*. Her face seemed young without really being youthful. Too sharp-featured. Too knowing. Her eyes caught and reflected the appraising glance Reppa gave her like mirrors in an empty refrigerator. Cold and without any expression of their own.

"Nice tan," he offered. "Where did you get it?"

"Outdoors."

"California?"

She looked toward Behrman like a defendant waiting for her lawyer to raise an objection. When none came, she said laconically, "Try Florida."

"Nice," Reppa repeated, feeling that with one arrow he'd disposed of two birds: where Behrman had spent the winter and who had answered his phone. Though the face was undeniably sixteen, the voice had all of the cool abstraction he saw in the eyes.

"Bring me a glass of orange juice, dear."

"And a wheelchair?" the girl snapped. "Since you're too feeble to get anything for yourself?"

Behrman decided to treat this as a joke and coughed. Reppa watched the girl shoot both of them a sideways glare as she left the room.

"Impossible to get decent help these days," Behrman said. Then, as if determined to maintain the pretense, he stared wistfully into his aging lap and sighed. "But that's true everywhere now, isn't it? My own business, for example. More and more I'm having to do it all myself."

"Furs?"

"A dying industry." Behrman made a sad face. "There's nobody around under fifty anymore who knows enough about it to make even the simplest deals. Now they're all going into suede and alpaca."

"I somehow thought you were retired."

"Because I spend half the year in Florida? You never retire. You're only forced to watch it slip through your hands." There was a difficult pause while Behrman again gazed deeply into the center of the lemon-colored slacks he wore. "A long day, officer. What is it specifically that you want from me?"

"As I started to say, the governor apparently thinks there's a strong possibility that Danny de Spirit was wrongfully convicted. Before he can grant him a pardon, however, he needs to know how the people who were most affected by the case would feel if de Spirit were released."

"Why doesn't he order a new trial instead? He'd get the same political benefit—public proof that he's concerned enough to intervene. And if the kid is found innocent, he won't have to suffer any of the static for the decision."

"Only a judge can order a new trial."

"But you and I both know governors have ways of ordering judges."

"Still . . ."

"Really, officer. Either the governor's being very naïve, or you are."

90

Reppa felt himself shift uncomfortably. "In what way?"

"Believing the information you obtain will be used to decide whether to give the kid a pardon."

There was much to resent in the direction Behrman had taken the conversation, but what disturbed Reppa most was how cavalier the fur dealer seemed about the notion of pardoning his stepdaughter's convicted killer. To test this, he said, "You asked me to be specific. What I'm here to find out is what your reaction would be if Danny de Spirit were to walk out of prison a free man."

"I don't believe I'd have one. I never did have much feeling about the kid, for or against."

"He's no longer a kid. He's over thirty now."

"All the more reason. He's probably matured in prison. I may even be able to find him a job. If he gets his pardon, tell him to come see me. Assuming he doesn't object to pushing around coatracks. I pushed a few myself in my day. For nearly a month before my father decided a nodding acquaintance with manual labor was as much as his heir apparent could tolerate."

It cleared up one puzzle—Behrman, who seemed too voluble for a fur dealer, wasn't one totally by choice. But it left the other, deeper puzzle.

"Aren't you being a little nonchalant for a man whose stepdaughter was brutally murdered?"

"You must remember she wasn't my own flesh and blood," the fur dealer said listlessly.

"But you raised her as if she were."

Behrman waved a hand as though to dismiss the effort to make this a matter of gravity. "Only in the sense that I gave her my name. My wife took all the responsibility for her actual rearing. After Adelaide died, Andrea and I were no more than friends. I think we were both immensely relieved. I know I was."

"Why?"

As Behrman sat forward, Reppa read on his face the subtle change that comes over all men when they embark on masking some deep emotion.

"I never felt even remotely like a father. Nor a husband either, for that matter. But I'm boring you, officer. You aren't here to listen to the memoirs of a late-blooming man. You want to know my attitude toward Danny de Spirit. Short and simple: My opinion from the first was that the kid was made a patsy. The killer wasn't a burglar. It was someone the girls knew."

"A number of people thought that. Including a detective who thought Andrea and one of her lovers might have been in the midst of some sort of sexual game when Elizabeth came home unexpectedly and interfered in such a way that the man wound up killing both girls."

"Sexual game." Behrman gave him a sideways elfish glance. "How delicately you've managed to phrase it."

"There was talk that you had that detective removed from the case. Is it true?"

A curt nod from Behrman. "But don't think that contradicts what I just said. Even though I believed the man was on the right track, I couldn't have him spouting his ideas to the Press. As a businessman, the last thing I needed was that kind of publicity. Andrea's being murdered was bad enough. Now, of course, it's all been so long ago, the truth can be of little harm."

"Why did you think he was on the right track?"

"Well, the girl *was* rather highly sexed." Behrman unleashed a self-deprecating sigh. "A reaction in part against her mother and myself, I'm sure. I have to confess it gave me pleasure when people mistakenly thought she was my offspring. Whoever her true father was, he must have been quite extraordinary. Perhaps some hot-blooded backwoods stud. It's certainly within the realm of possibility."

Reading *Andrea and Elizabeth*, Reppa had sped over the paragraphs on the childhoods of the victims. He seemed to remember that Andrea's family was originally from the South somewhere and that her father had been her mother's first husband. Had he remembered wrong? He asked. Behrman smiled and said, "Adelaide's great myth. She took it with her to her grave. Even poor Andrea died still believing her father was a soldier who'd married her mother just before going overseas. As a child she'd been given a cock and bull tale by Adelaide that he'd been killed in the Normandy invasion. I never told her the true story of her conception. How could I? I wasn't supposed to know the truth myself, and Adelaide never would have forgiven me if she'd found out I did. After working so hard to convince everyone she was a southern belle, to have it come out that she was really no more than the promiscuous daughter of a journeyman preacher?"

"Mmm." Reppa tried to sound thoroughly disinterested. Get him back to that detective who was taken off the case, he thought. But then he saw Behrman begin nodding gleefully in the manner of a man warming to his own subject, and he groaned inwardly. It was too late.

"The late Reverend Abilene Loomis," Behrman was saying. "It was all so transparent once I did a little checking into Adelaide's background after we were married. Oh, not myself personally. I hired a private detective. Adelaide billed herself as a debutante from Louisville. It took my man only a few days of nosing around Kentucky to learn she was really from Appalachia. Pity the dumb Jewish boy who thought he'd wooed and won a genuine Zelda Sayre. I should have known it was too good to be true. No woman had ever so much as acknowledged I existed until I met Adelaide. 'You have such an old-fashioned charm, Mr. Behrman'—I'll never forget her

93

exact words the first time she spoke to me—'so courteous and so refined. I don't suppose it's possible that you would be free to escort me home?' We were at one of my father's parties for buyers. Somehow she wangled her way in there alone, but I assumed she was some hotshot's date. I remember her eyes looking directly into mine. Who could have known it then, but it was to be our most passionate moment. We never did anything remotely as intimate again."

"You don't mean you . . . ?" Reppa halted abruptly upon realizing he did not really want an answer to his question.

But the fur dealer seemed to thrive on the pathetic implications of his tale. "We were married for twenty years. Legally—by Jewish law, anyway—it could have been annulled anytime. Impossible, you're thinking? Well, the fact is it's even worse than it sounds. I knew, you see, when we married that it would never be consummated. We even made a pact. Adelaide claimed her experiences with her first husband had been too awful for her to consider ever having sex again. I was just relieved to be in a situation which proclaimed to the world that I must be a normal man with normal sexual appetites without my actually having to try to climb the terrible wall that had always stood between me and women. It was a fair bargain, in all. Adelaide got someone who could provide for her and her daughter, and provide well. I got an attractive and charming woman who immediately improved my status in the business circles I traveled in."

Behrman sat back, giving Reppa an opportunity to talk if he were quick about it. Experience had taught Reppa that he often learned more about people by letting them do the talking, but the fur dealer gave him the feeling that he was revealing nothing about himself while seemingly revealing everything. Reppa's hand sought inside his jacket pocket for his notebook as he tried to recall what other areas he had meant to explore here. Then, sensing Behrman was about to speak again, he hastily asked the first semi-intelligent question that occurred to him.

"How old was Andrea when you and her mother married?"

Behrman's eyes met his momentarily, then looked away again as the fur dealer saw a way to expand the simple answer into another pontification. "Only two. But a very precocious two. Unusually big for her age, and already wise enough to realize I wasn't much of a substitute for the heroic father she'd supposedly lost. I remember when Adelaide first introduced us, she said, 'Who is this man, Mommy? He looks like Rumpelstiltskin.' It was difficult to forgive, even coming from a two-year-old. There were other impediments, too, to my marrying Adelaide, but they weren't enough to give me more than a moment's pause. What matter that she'd been married before and wasn't Jewish? Even after I learned the truth about her past, it didn't change anything. No one else knew, after all, and I certainly wasn't about to let the cat out of the bag. The private detective did his job. He got me the information I wanted, I paid him and dismissed him, and that was that."

"Who was he?"

There was a trace of hesitation in the eyes the fur dealer kept averted. "If you're thinking that perhaps you should confirm my story, I'll save you a bit of trouble. The police checked out the information he gave me twelve years ago, then were kind enough not to make any of it public since it had absolutely no bearing on the case."

Kind enough, Reppa wondered, or well enough paid? Casually he said, "Then you won't mind giving me his name."

Again that elfish sideways glance.

"There's no point. The man's dead now."

"How do you know?"

"I had occasion to use the services of his agency again later. For business reasons. When I asked for him in particular, since he'd done so well the first time, they told me he'd passed away."

Reppa took out his notebook. Behrman looked distastefully at it.

"Is it really necessary, officer, that you write all this down?"

"Not all of it. Just a word you used before."

"Which one?"

"When you were describing Andrea's first reaction to you."

"Precocious?"

"Rumpelstiltskin."

"It's not really a word." Behrman was responding to his interest with an anxious look. "It's a name from a fairy tale."

"I know," Reppa said. He kept his notebook open. "What originally prompted you to hire that private detective?"

Behrman seemed surprised by the question, as if the answer were self-evident. "Well—Adelaide's sister. Besides our mutual vow of celibacy, Adelaide imposed another condition on me before agreeing to our marriage. At first I didn't realize it was a condition. It seemed only a request—that I support Annabelle while she struggled to find herself. But when I tried to terminate my support, I learned otherwise. Adelaide threatened she wouldn't have anything more to do with a man who was too miserly to help a member of her family. Miserly indeed! Here I was, kicking in to the tune of several hundred dollars a month to support a woman who was flaming around like the last of the great bohemians.''

"Flaming around how?'' he asked, his curiosity genuinely piqued. For if interviewing Behrman had seemed from the first a chore, he was looking forward with an obscure eagerness to meeting Annabelle. She was someone; a celebrity. She was also, perhaps, not unattractive.

"Oh, *flaming*'s the wrong word. *Slinking* is more like it. After a few years of watching Annabelle in action I began to suspect the Loomis clan might be less than gentry. Although I gave her enough money to live anywhere in the city, she insisted on living in the worst hovels, making those absurd plaster dummies all day and then prowling the streets at night in long black dresses that looked as if they'd been torn off Dracula's daughter. And she used drugs. I didn't even know what drugs were then, but, my God, when I look back on those years, there wasn't much doubt. Her eyes were always crazed, her hair was unkempt, her hands and face were squalid. Every other week she had some new disease. Even VD, I wouldn't have been surprised, if it hadn't been so clear that she'd never let another human being come near her. Adelaide used to have to go down to her place for days at a time to stay with her and take care of her. I lived in dread that Adelaide would suggest the woman move in with us, but fortunately she never did. Though I wonder now if she wasn't just being careful not to expose me to Annabelle any more than was absolutely necessary. The woman was such a mess it didn't seem possible that she and Adelaide could be sisters. Yet they obviously were. They both had those huge blue eyes, much larger even than Andrea's. Adelaide wore mascara that downplayed hers, but Annabelle seemed determined to look as grotesque and unappealing as possible . . .'' Behrman paused and shook his head, as if disgusted by the memory.

Still unsatisfied, Reppa said, "So it was Annabelle's appearance and behavior that made you finally decide to check into your wife's background?"

"Not entirely. One night I mustered the courage to ask Adelaide why her parents didn't support her sister. Why should the burden fall on me? Adelaide had always been a little evasive about her family, implying that they were so violently opposed to her first marriage that they'd cut her off afterward. It seemed plausible, but when she told me they'd disowned Annabelle, too, because they couldn't stand her being an artist—well, I began to realize I might have been something of a fool. One daughter I could buy. Every family is entitled to one black sheep. But both daughters disowned? The Loomis family began to sound a little suspect, to say the least."

"And as your detective found out, they were. Besides your wife's father being a backwoods preacher, what else did he learn?"

"I'm getting there, officer. Don't be impatient."

Reppa shook off the admonition, too close now to the end of the thread he'd been following. "If Andrea's father wasn't a soldier who died in combat, who was he?"

"Oh, he was a soldier, all right. There's almost no doubt about that."

"Then the lie was that he'd been killed. Actually he was still alive."

Behrman flipped his hands noncommittally. "It's possible. Entirely possible."

"And also possible, therefore, that he was still in contact with Andrea and your wife?"

"What are you getting at, officer?"

"Jealousy. An ex-husband left behind in Kentucky by a woman who wanted more than he could give her. A woman who took his child away from him and came to

New York posing as a belle so she could meet a man of wealth and position.''

"Wealth and position." Behrman's tiny eyes turned merry. "Yes, that's certainly what Adelaide wanted, but again I could have saved you some trouble. You see, I was about to tell you she didn't have an ex-husband.''

Reppa took a breath and let it out slowly. "Andrea was illegitimate?''

"And conceived under the grimmest of circumstances—rape.''

As much baffled as astonished, Reppa felt his eyebrows soar.

"Reverend Loomis." Behrman stretched out a hand to silence him, to beg for silence while he sighed again before resuming. "My detective traced him to a shack outside of a place called Elizabethtown. It was Loomis's last stop after years of roaming the mountain towns in the southern part of the state. This was the summer of 1950, so long ago there's no more need for secrecy about Loomis and his miserable end. According to neighbors the detective spoke to, he'd lived better before the war. But then his son died, Adelaide was defiled, and he just seemed to give up. He died himself a year or so after my detective saw him. A broken man, a strict down-the-line fundamentalist whose life had been shattered, first by the death of his only son and then by the crime against his eldest daughter. Elizabethtown, you should be told, was a serviceman's haven—''

"Near Fort Knox," Reppa broke in to hurry things along. "Where I was stationed for two years. Among GI's it's called E-town.''

"Ah, then you're acquainted with the serviceman's mentality. Apparently a bunch of the boys who'd been whooping it up in a local bar ran into Adelaide one night

99

on their way back to the post. The rest I'll leave to your imagination. Loomis wouldn't speak of the incident at all.''

''Then how did your detective learn about it?''

''Neighbors. Needless to say, after hearing the story my attitude toward Adelaide changed. Where by rights I might have been angry upon learning the truth about her family background, I now could be nothing but sympathetic. Of course she wouldn't ever again want physical contact with a man. What woman would?''

''When Loomis discovered Adelaide had been assaulted, what did he do about it?''

''Sent her away somewhere to have the child, and apparently she decided never to return. You can't blame her. In a small town it would have been an impossible thing to live down. Whereas in New York creating a whole new identity for herself was rather easy. Besides, Annabelle was already here, having realized her personality wasn't much suited either for small-town living. How she supported herself in the early days I don't know. I imagine Adelaide must have sent her whatever money she could scrape together. Then Adelaide came to New York with Andrea and began the hunt for a meal ticket to take care of the whole Loomis brood. Too cynical a word? Marissa didn't think so when I told her the story. Of course some might argue that I'm rather a meal ticket for Marissa, too. It seems my fate, but at least I've learned that I can get more for my money than a bedmate in name only.''

Reppa interrupted to ask his question in a different way. ''I meant what happened to the soldiers who raped Adelaide?''

''Nothing, evidently. Loomis's neighbors said he refused to make an official report of the incident or let the police talk to Adelaide. When she told him what had

100

happened, he just whisked her out of town and tried to suppress the whole thing. But he couldn't suppress the effect it had on him. His life devoted to pacifism, then a war comes along and he loses his son, and his daughter is raped by servicemen. Quite a brutal irony.''

"How did his son die? In combat?"

"Actually, while home on leave. From some bug he'd picked up in training camp. Loomis was so embittered he refused to tell the army the boy was dead. He made them come looking for him in the belief they had a deserter on their hands, then dragged them out to the cemetery and threatened them with all of God's wrath. Adelaide told me this part herself, though of course she didn't mention the true source of her father's bitterness. He'd tried to have Alexander exempted from the service as the only son of a man of the cloth, but the army wouldn't accept his claim. They said he wasn't a practitioner of a recognized faith.''

"Alexander, Adelaide, and Annabelle. And Loomis's name, you said, was Abilene. Quite a fondness for assonance.'' Behrman looked startled that he knew the word. "What about Mother Loomis? What was her name?"

"Abigail," said Behrman with a grin. "You've picked up on the same family quirk that most intrigued me. I contemplated, if ever Adelaide and I had had a child of our own, what I would do if she insisted on continuing the Loomis name game.''

Fascinated now by Behrman's story, grudgingly fascinated, Reppa determined he might as well have it all. "You've been very quiet about Abigail. Any reason?"

The fur dealer looked strangely reverential.

"Granma Mooneyes. Her children's eyes were big, but hers reportedly were like saucers. After all the stories she heard about her grandmother from Adelaide, Andrea desperately wanted to meet the woman. Adelaide hoaxed her

101

along for years on the promise she one day would. But when Andrea got old enough to contemplate finding her grandmother on her own, the truth had to come out. Granma Mooneyes had died many years ago, Adelaide finally admitted, while giving birth to Annabelle. I say *the truth* reservedly, because with Adelaide I was never sure. It was definitely true, though, that Loomis lived out his last years alone, and there's evidence that he was a single parent for a good number of years before that.''

''What sort of evidence?''

Behrman appeared to debate something with himself, then climbed suddenly to his feet. ''Why not? Since you're going to talk to Annabelle, too, I presume.'' His face framed a reproachful look. ''Or perhaps you already have.''

''Not yet.''

''All the better, then. I haven't seen her in years myself. Not that I feel deprived, but it would still be interesting to see what middle age has done to that weird little face. You'll thank me later for having provided you with an instrument for comparative study.''

As Reppa watched the fur dealer rush from the room, the seat of the lemon-colored slacks snug as the skin of a new drum, he felt the last of his notion of a few minutes ago leaving him. In its place was nothing in particular. If there was no jealous husband in the distant past, who then? Someone closer to the present? Clearly. And it was also increasingly clear to him that the need to tell him the story of the Loomis family had been urgent within Stanley Behrman. He'd imagined the fur dealer would give him about five minutes of time; instead, glancing at his watch, he saw that forty minutes had passed, and Behrman was still going strong. With a parolee his instincts would long since have alerted him that he was being taken around the mulberry bush to keep him away from the real point. And of course, he realized now, it had been sloppy to let Behrman wriggle out of giving him the name of that private detective.

He glanced at his notebook but had time to jot down only a few words before Behrman came bouncing back into the room, bearing a wrinkled envelope, which he handed over with a flourish.

It contained an ancient sepia photograph of a man, two girls, and a boy. Reppa needed no confirmation from Behrman to know this was the Loomis clan. Reverend Loomis stood with his arms around his two daughters; his son knelt in front of the trio. Broad-shouldered, thick through the middle, Abilene Loomis bore little resemblance to his children, who were all thin and frail, yet hauntingly attractive in the way that Appalachian children often are: straight noses, finely chiseled features, plaintive expressions. Adelaide and Alexander looked dartingly at the camera, eyes round and wide and somewhat stricken, as if they'd been caught at a forbidden game. But it was the youngest child who captured and held Reppa's attention. She stood with her face turned to the side, long hair spilling down from her head and across the ruffled sleeves of the cotton dress she wore, reaching nearly to her waist. If the other children seemed wary of the camera, she seemed positively terrified of it. Reppa noticed her face was not just averted, it was hidden. The curtain of her dark hair covered everything but the tip of her nose, a patch of pale cheek, the flash of a cringing mouth.

"Don't make the mistake of thinking she was shy," Behrman said, retrieving the photograph. "She wasn't. It was part of her act, even back then. A delight in being weird."

Yes, *weird* was the right word. Weird, and somewhat otherworldly. Reppa asked how old Annabelle had been in the photograph. Seven or eight, Behrman thought. Difficult to judge since he didn't know exactly when the photograph had been taken. He ducked his head and took another look at it himself. "Loomis had this in his shack. In the back of a Bible. My detective spotted it and was enterprising enough to pilfer it. All by itself it was worth the price of his plane fare. For years I kept it in my safe at the office. My ace in the hole if ever Adelaide made any trouble." The fur dealer paused and sat down again, gingerly sliding the photograph back in its envelope. "But she didn't. She did me the great favor of dying instead."

"How did she die?"

Behrman fumbled at his shirt, undid two of the buttons, and plunged his hand inside, to demonstrate.

"Young for a heart attack."

"It wasn't quite that. More like a stroke."

"Was there an autopsy?"

"Of course. There had to be one, under the circumstances. It showed a combination of pills and booze."

"What sort of pills?"

"All sorts. Adelaide may have abstained from sex, but she made up for it in every other area."

"You're sure of that?"

"Absolutely. She drank like a fish and took pills like candy. Uppers . . . downers."

"I mean you're sure she abstained from sex?"

Behrman's eyes shrank. "What are you suggesting? That she was having an affair? I often prayed she would. It would have freed me from our covenant, knowing that she had broken faith with me. Unfortunately she would never even look at other men. I know. I watched her very closely."

"Where was she when she died?"

To Reppa's astonishment the fur dealer's face turned

color, not, it seemed, with anger, but with amusement. "Actually her lights went out at the opening of one of Annabelle's art shows. Right in the middle of several hundred people. The only time in her life she ever up-staged Annabelle."

"Were you there when it happened?"

"Happily."

"Why happily?"

"The gallery was next door to a bar. I was able to begin making up for lost time immediately."

For a moment Reppa thought Behrman was going to laugh at his own tasteless joke, but then he realized it wasn't a joke.

". . . picked up a lady of the evening," Behrman was murmuring "and brought her back here. I'd never dared to do anything like that in my whole life, never dreamed I even had it in me. But, sweet Jesus, it was like a miracle! No sooner was Adelaide's flower dead than mine bloomed!"

There was no help for it now that Behrman had started in on all the sordid details, smiling down into his lap. Visits to massage parlors. Lunch hours in the fur locker with an Argentinian girl who came in one day a week to help with the books.

Reppa said, "I get the picture—"

Behrman said, "I missed out on plenty, but I'm there now, all there," and went right on. When he arrived at his first encounter with Marissa, in a health food store, Reppa got out of hearing any more by rising and pleading the time.

"Mr. Behrman." He waited until he had the door open before turning back to the fur dealer. "I want to thank you for your help. You've put my finger on a lot of pulses that I'm going to have to feel before this investigation is finished."

"Pulses! Ha! More like pussies!"

"Anyway, thanks again—"

He got one foot out in the hall ahead of the reproving finger Behrman flung at him.

"You didn't ask me about Halliwell."

"Who?"

"The police treated him with kid gloves, too. What's the cape he has over your heads? It's a fur expression—cape."

"I caught it."

"Money? I've got more. Ivy League? Harvard means hands off? That girl who drowned in Chappaquiddick, they never did anything about that either."

"Halliwell?" Reppa repeated, to elicit more.

"Yes. Jeff Halliwell."

Jeff? Jay? He regretted now that he was halfway out the door. "Andrea's fiancé?"

"And perhaps her killer. Somebody should have at least explored the possibility."

"How do you know no one did?"

"Then explain how they failed to learn that he used to beat her. There were marks all over her body at times."

"What kind of marks?"

"In places that didn't show. He was careful, Halliwell. Never anything that couldn't be covered by clothing."

For several moments Reppa stood silent, mentally completing the syllogism. *Yet Behrman knew they were there. Which means he must have seen them somehow.*

CHAPTER FOUR

ANNABELLE

"This isn't a police investigation. All I'm supposed to be doing is finding out how people would react if de Spirit is given a pardon."

"So why did you ask him about his wife?"

"He gave me the opening. But there's no good way to ask a man if he was banging his stepdaughter. Besides, if you'd seen him, you wouldn't have believed it was possible. He looked like a troll studying to be an ogre."

"What about that blond girl who was there? She's your living proof it's possible."

"But he told me he didn't lose his cherry until his wife died—"

"And you of course believed him."

"You know me. I always give everyone the benefit of the doubt."

"So do I," Leilah said. "Which is why I don't go through your pockets looking for lipstick-stained handkerchiefs. Another reason is you insist on hanging your clothes where I can't reach them as long as I'm a prisoner in this damn bed."

It had been meant to be a cozy respite, spaghetti in front of the TV, between visits to Behrman and Annabelle. But the discussion had restored an uncomfortable tension between them, and he would not be able to leave now without a better explanation than the one he had planned. "At night?" Leilah would accuse. "What've you got going with her, Reppa?"

"Listen," he began, for it was already past eight o'clock.

"Aren't you lucky? There's no game on tonight. We can just lie here and let the hips fall where they may. Dr. Molnar said this morning that I can even begin lifting my legs now, one at a time."

"That's wonderful news, Sturm. Terrific. Now why don't you take your nap, and when I get back, we'll just test those legs."

"Where are you going?" she asked, beginning, predictably, to frown.

"Another visit. Someone who could see me only in the evening."

"Who?"

"Well, Annabelle Loomis."

"Annabelle!" She groaned, not duped for an instant by his use of the full name. "I suppose now you're going to fuck her, too."

"She's an old woman now, for Christ's sake. Middle fifties, at least."

He was reminded stonily: "You're thirty-eight."

"Still quite a difference."

Leilah tugged meditatively on a strand of her long raven hair. "She's also a lesbian, Reppa. But that won't stop you."

"Where did you hear that?"

"That was the book on her when she was in her heyday. A number of the beats were gay. The really famous ones. But you couldn't come out publicly then."

"So it's just a rumor she's a lesbian."

Leilah threw him a sardonic glance. "Now you've got it, don't you? A scientific reason to try with her. Anything in the name of research."

"If I'm successful, you won't have to look for lipstick stains. The evidence will be on my neck. Two little holes. Behrman even referred to her as Dracula's daughter."

"Come here. Let me look now."

"You can see from there."

"Will you ask her one question for me?"

"What is it?"

"If she's ever read *The King of Garbage*. Famous artist, precursor of the women's movement—my editor sent her bound galleys, hoping she'd say something they could use on the jacket. But she never responded."

"No promises. I'll have to get an opening where it doesn't sound too off the wall."

"And one more thing," Leilah said.

Reppa studied her face. It seemed oddly serene. The eyes regarded him with the equanimity of a doll's. Which probably meant she was in agony.

Finally he said, "All right. One more."

"If you fuck her, don't tell me about it. Our agreement was we'd tell each other everything, but now it's off. You're on your own." Leilah elevated her right foot about four inches, high enough so that the big toe came into view over the horizon of her brace. "Now I am, too, that means. So watch out, Reppa."

Annabelle lived in an eight-story loft building on West Eighteenth Street. On the wall beside the locked front door Reppa saw an intercom box and a vertical row of buttons. Imprinted on a strip of black plastic under the button for the top floor was an unadorned white *A*. He pushed the

109

button and stood in wait. After a while a male voice blared out of the intercom: "Yes?"

"Reppa." Then, realizing he had neglected to hold the button down so he could be heard: "Parole."

"Hercule Poirot?"

He began over, very slowly. "Frank Reppa. New York State Parole."

The door buzzed. He entered the lobby and pushed the button for the elevator. A bell clanged. Seconds later a girl's voice shouted down the shaft: "What floor?"

"First," he bellowed up.

The elevator descended haltingly, banging and jerking. When the door opened, a slat-thin girl stuck her head out. "Where're you going?"

"Eight."

"Do you know how to run one of these things?"

"I think so."

"Then drop me off and take it up yourself. Otherwise I'll still be stuck with it. Whichever floor uses it last has to keep it until somebody else rings for it."

Like drop the handkerchief, Reppa thought. The elevator was operated by pulling on a metal rod in the floor: up to go down, down to go up. The girl got out on the fifth floor, disappearing through a heavy steel door. A similar door greeted him when he reached the top floor. He knocked on it, heard a bolt turn, then a second.

The door opened onto a dimly lit foyer. Beyond it was a dark hallway that was bound on one side by the wall of the building and on the other by a white plasterboard wall that concealed the interior of the loft. As Reppa stepped into the foyer, the door slammed shut behind him. Turning, he saw a balding, bearded man blinking at him from behind thick rimless glasses, the same probably who had laughed over the phone and made the Hercule Poirot crack, though in person Annabelle's secretary looked ominously humorless. He could not have been much shorter than Reppa, a few inches at most, but he tilted his head as though looking up from the bottom of a well when Reppa displayed his shield and held out his hand.

"I'm Frank Reppa."

The hand was ignored.

"Kinder's my name. Come along and I'll tell the goddess you're here."

He followed the secretary down the hallway, passing three or four closed doors in the plasterboard wall, all of them bolted. He'd never been inside a famous artist's loft before, and he would not have known he was in one now if he hadn't seen the *A* on the wall outside the building.

The secretary threw open a door at the end of the hallway. On the door was a plastic nameplate: Lee S. Kinder. Inside was a spartanly furnished office. Desk. Metal swivel chair. Single plastic chair. Kinder picked up the phone on the desk, pushed a red button, and dialed a single digit number. Elsewhere in the loft a phone rang. Rang on and on.

Hanging up, Kinder announced that Annabelle must still be in the tub. Her nightly candlelight bath. In a hurry? If Reppa was, Kinder offered to ring her up on the bathroom extension to see if she'd speak to him while she soaked.

Reppa said he could wait. With a shrug Kinder sat in the swivel chair and coaxed him into the plastic chair by tilting his head again, querulously.

To Reppa's right was a partially open door. Through it he glimpsed a small, slovenly room, illuminated by a dingy floor lamp. Black plastic couch. Hot plate on a scarred wood table. Clothes and newspapers strewn about the floor. Unmade cot, sheets trailing . . .

Kinder shot an arm out and pulled the door shut.

111

"Your digs?"

"It comes with the job." Kinder gave him an enigmatic smile that sent him into a long silence, disturbed that the man lived on the premises. As if he were not only a secretary but a kept man of sorts. Or perhaps someone who fancied himself a keeper. The room reminded Reppa of a sheriff's that he had seen once while picking up a prisoner in a small upstate town. He'd been startled to find that the town's chief law officer inhabited a grungy cubicle behind the row of jail cells he watched over.

If Annabelle still lived in anything like the fashion she had in the days when Behrman supported her, here, plainly, was her ideal attendant.

Reppa glanced to his left, escaping the smiling, bearded countenance and at the same time observing another door, this in the plasterboard wall between the office and the main body of the loft. Across the face of it was a heavy steel bolt. On the secretary's side of the door?

He turned back to the room upon hearing Kinder say: "It rather appalled Annabelle when I told her why you insisted on seeing her. The mere thought that her niece's killer might be pardoned."

"Were you with her at the time of the murders?"

"*With her?* Is this your clever way of asking if we both had an alibi?"

"In her employ."

"Yes. Well, that's more clearly put. No, sir, I wasn't."

"When did you start working for her?"

"When did I start?" Kinder mimicked in a quiet, patient voice. "Oh, a while after the murders."

"How long?"

Kinder looked up from the desk in his oblique way. "Several months, if memory serves.

"So you've been with her nearly twelve years, then."

"That inimitable phrase again."

Annoyed, Reppa could no longer restrain himself from placing a row of knuckles on the wall beside the bolted door. He knocked sharply. Heard a cushioned thud instead of the hollow sound he expected. "There's a brick wall behind this plasterboard, isn't there?"

The secretary whipped off his thick, rimless glasses, as though the world were only altogether corporeal without them. "So many of these loft buildings are firetraps," he explained, his quizzical brown eyes squinting at the bolted door.

"What about the hallway? Is there brick behind that plasterboard, too?"

Another fleeting smile from Kinder. "Let's see if we can't get you in there to see for yourself. I'll page the goddess in her bath."

Putting his glasses back on, the secretary dialed another single-digit number on the phone while Reppa formed a picture of a dark tile sanctum, single candle flickering at the foot of a sunken tub . . . suddenly a ringing wall phone cleaves the silence, and a mottled arm rises slowly out of the water . . .

Kinder returned the phone to the cradle. "Sometimes she falls asleep—I suppose I'll have to check." He rose and began laboring over the bolt on the door. Finally he had to ask Reppa to give him a hand. Between them they managed to get the bolt to turn, very grudgingly.

"Needs oil," said Kinder, standing breathless before the open door, in Reppa's way, "now that it isn't used. Oops, I won't have to fish her out after all."

He quickly swung the door shut and bolted it again, but not before Reppa, craning over his shoulder, had seen at the far end of a long room, standing in front of a curtained window, a woman in a black floor-length dress. Head

113

partially turned toward the door, hand pressed to her throat, as if startled by the intrusion. Other, less certain impressions of what he had glimpsed continued to sift through after the door closed: long gray-black hair, streak of white face. He felt through his whole body the imminence of the moment, and because he had now seen her, it was strangely relaxing. Behrman's right, he thought, she's aged.

Kinder got back on the phone. Reppa heard two muted rings on the other side of the wall. In the middle of the second Kinder grabbed the phone off the desk and leaned back in the swivel chair. "Sorry, darling, but I got worried about you when . . . Yes, I knew you were in . . . Well, I *did* try to call you there, but . . . Anyway, Mr. Reppa is here now . . . *Reppa,* the parole . . . Now, I know you don't want to, but he's . . . I realize, darling. Of course I realize, and I fully agree. But we did tell him to come by this evening, didn't we? And that you'd . . . *Yes,* darling. Yes, yes. All right. I'll tell him . . . Yes, darling, *yes. Of* course."

With a final "*Yes-s-s*" Kinder slammed the phone into the cradle and stared fixedly at the bolted door. The receding forehead was deeply furrowed, the bearded face taut with the strain of having had to speak in the ingratiating tone of a parent talking to a spoiled child.

"Bitch is so obsessive about her little rituals. She thinks she's still a diva whose dressing room the whole fucking city is panting outside of the door of."

"When am I going to get to speak to her?"

"You heard. When she's ready."

"How long will that be?"

"Now, *how* do I know? I only work here." Kinder waited for his next question, brown eyes ablaze.

But Reppa had begun calculating with the input he already had. A stall had seemed, from the outset, inevitable.

Annabelle, being Annabelle, could do no less than keep him waiting as long as possible. The odd thing was Kinder. His fingers were tugging at his beard, but his eyes had turned vague, the cause of the nervousness that lay behind them well hidden. The sardonic semanticist of a few minutes ago had disappeared.

Suddenly the secretary faded to an inert gape behind his desk. "Hear it?" he said.

"Hear what?"

"The elevator bell."

"I didn't hear anything."

Kinder stood up, unpersuaded. "Somebody wants a ride. Shit, I'll have to run it downstairs."

He bounded into the hallway and shut the office door behind him. Reppa started to shake his head, convinced it had been the secretary's discomfort over his last question that had driven him from the room, but then, distinctly, he heard the elevator bell clang and Kinder's voice shout, "Coming! Christ's sake, I'm coming!"

While he waited, he opened his notebook and considered the questions he intended to ask Annabelle. Then he could no longer ignore the opportunity. After glancing around to make certain there were no peepholes in the walls, no glassy surfaces that could be one-way mirrors, he tried the door to Kinder's room. But the lock had been on when Kinder shut it. There was nothing of interest in the office wastebasket, and the desk drawer contained only a small black appointment book. He leafed through it to today's date. As expected, his name was there, but so were two others: Wilkes and Mald.

As he was returning the appointment book to the drawer, the phone rang on the desk, and it was his turn to jump.

Should he answer it himself or wait for Kinder to return?

By the third ring it was impossible not to pick up the

receiver. After all, he rationalized, it could be for him. Indirectly, anyway.

Which it was, though the voice at the other end caught him badly unawares at first. Mr. Kinder? Where was Mr. Kinder?

Not the tinge of anxiety. Not that at all. No, it was the husky, throaty quality. It sounded tremulous and a little eerie. And when it said, after he explained that Kinder had gone to pick up someone on the elevator, ''Well, then, you shall have to show yourself in to see me,'' he decided it was also more than a little sexy.

The bolt on the door was less stubborn this time, as though it only lacked use. Upon entering he looked for her first at the window at the far end of the room, and then, failing to see her there, he let his eyes sweep from an antique rocking chair to a black wicker settee, from the mirror and dressing table in one corner of the room to the oak table with four matching chairs around it in the other, from the wirehaired terrier asleep on a brass bed to the gaunt beagle which stood beside a mahogany dresser with one leg raised as if pointing out an invisible quarry to an invisible hunter. The room was perhaps fifty feet long by twenty feet wide. On the front wall, facing uptown Manhattan, there was a row of windows, a ring of white lights blinking atop the Empire State Building visible through their dark-red curtains; opposite them, as he'd anticipated, a forbidding brick wall. He had also anticipated he would see paintings, mobiles hanging from the ceiling, perhaps some posters advertising Annabelle's art shows. He saw none of these things. The room looked more as if it were inhabited by an austere baroness than an eccentric artist. The single decoration was a blowup of an old magazine cover, which was tacked to the wall above the bed at what was, now that he'd moved deeper into the room, below

116

eye level. Bending forward, peering intently—for the room's only light came from a recessed ceiling bulb above the oak table—he saw that the cover came from a journal called *Art Nouveau*. Featured on it was a picture of a shabbily dressed black woman carrying a shopping bag in each hand.

His eyes dropped to the dog on the bed. So motionless, so rigid and still that it looked dead. Dead, he realized suddenly, or stuffed. Feeling a chill, he turned back to the room. It felt awful damn dead in there now, the whole thing did. He tried to summon his memory of a while ago, closing his eyes and clutching for the image that would place her there again: a wedge of black dress, a window, face turning from it, and the pale hand at the end of the long-sleeved arm pressed to a high-collared throat.

And then it came, as some instinct in him had sensed all along it would. The grand entrance.

At the far end of the room, beyond the oak table, a door opened slowly.

She was still wearing the long black dress.

She stopped in the doorway to brush, strand by strand, several loose gray and black hairs from her face. Then five quick steps, the heels of the shoes she wore, hidden under the hem of the dress, clacking on the bare wood floor.

"Mr. Reppa?"

As he felt her fingertips briefly touch his, stiff and cool, a blurred object flitted across one corner of his eye like a mote of dust. Then his attention came back to the tall, spare figure in front of him. Even in the poor light he could see more gray hairs mingled with the black than he'd first perceived and that the skin around the mouth was deeply lined.

Aware that he was studying her, she turned her head

117

abruptly from the light, and now, where the eyes had been, there were only two deep, round hollows.

"Shall we sit down?"

She pointed toward the chairs around the oak table. But when he had seated himself in one of them, she slipped behind him and lay down on the wicker settee, staring up at the ceiling. He wondered whether the maneuver was intentional, sitting him under the only light in the room and then arranging it so neither of them could see the other.

"Would you mind . . . ?" He finished his request by turning his chair around to face her and pulling it off to one side of the light. When she didn't protest, but only lay rigidly still, her eyes half-closed, he said, "If you're too tired, I could come back another time."

"There must be no other times. I will speak with you this once and never again. Now please, begin whatever it is you must do."

She pressed her long hands together, and Reppa, observing the knots and gnarls on the knuckles, remembered that he was looking at the hands of an artist. He said, "First I'd like to thank you for talking to me. I know how rarely you see anyone anymore. Mr. Kinder explained to me—"

"Spare me any discussion of Mr. Kinder," she cut in sharply.

"Well, actually I can't. In making my report I have to say something about the living circumstances of each person I interview."

"Say mine are rid of everything irrelevant. My entire world now is in my loft. I see no one, I speak to no one."

"Mr. Kinder excepted?"

"Only when he has a message from the outside world to give me or I have a request to make of him. The messages from the outside world are few nowadays. My requests are

118

equally infrequent. Seldom more than a reminder now and then that it's time to walk Adelaide.''

''Adelaide?''

Annabelle reached out a hand and tapped a long finger on the floor to call his attention to the small form huddled in the shadows under the settee. A toy of a dog, it appeared to Reppa from his distance. So small that he did not wonder that he had failed to notice it until now. Still, he was not quite convinced it had been there all along. Had it followed her in when she entered, or was it just his imagination that he'd seen something dart past them when their hands met? He glanced toward the door at the end of the room and saw it was now closed. What was back there? A kitchen? Her bathroom?

And what about some sort of a studio where she did her work?

Leave the geography for later, he thought. As it was, there were already too many unknowns. The terrier and the beagle, for example.

''The other two—they're stuffed, aren't they?''

For an instant she glanced at him, and her whispery voice rose to a near laugh.

''Abigail and Alexander? *Stuffed?*''

''Well, they're obviously not real.''

''As real as I could make them. Abigail was my very first pet when I came to New York. My one and only friend. She slept with me every night. She still does. Alexander I found on a subway platform, all skin and bones. Somebody took him down there and abandoned him to starve. I had him for almost seven years, and then one day he disappeared. Went walking down by the river with me and ran off. Now he's back.''

It had been audible in her *Went walking down by the*

river. The faintest trace of a twang, a cadence from her past. Hearing it moved him to say, "Where's Abilene?"

Now she did laugh, a harsh sound that ended quickly. "You know, don't you? You know all my little secrets."

"Far from it. I still know nothing about Mr. Kinder and what his duties are."

"Precious few. For which he's paid very handsomely. The way I treat him, Mr. Kinder will soon be able to retire."

"From the looks of his room he's already semi-retired."

"Oh, he showed it to you?"

The husky voice faltered for a moment, and Reppa saw the long hands twitch when he explained that the door had been open while he and Kinder were talking.

"Careless. Careless of him, too, opening my door like that. What if I'd been . . . ?" She paused and completed the thought with a slow shake of her head. "Mr. Kinder, if you haven't already realized it on your own, is not a particularly well man."

"What's wrong with him?"

Annabelle, smiling, removed her face from his view by turning it toward the back of the settee. "You're very persistent, Mr. Reppa. What's your background? Surely you didn't grow up wanting to be a parole officer?"

"Football."

"You were a player of that gruesome sport?"

"Later a coach . . ." Reppa had started to explain when she turned to him, and they looked at each other directly for the first time, across the space and shadows between them. The blue irises of her large eyes were all but consumed in the dim light by the black pupils.

The thought that came to him, unwelcome and so unnerving, was: How bottomless those eyes look! How bottomless and how sad!

Then she turned away again, leaving him to contemplate the long, mostly barren room and the brick wall. Bringing his gaze back to the settee, he saw she had returned to her scrutiny of the ceiling.

"What do you think it costs to rent this place for a year—what's your guess?"

"I couldn't begin—"

"Nine thousand dollars. To say nothing of the utilities."

"Hmm."

But a moment later he understood the odd aside. She wasn't trying to distract him; she only wanted an excuse to talk about herself. "It wouldn't be so bad if my Annabelles were still selling, but no one wants them anymore."

"Why not?"

"I'm no longer *au courant,* some say. The more popular opinion is that I'm tainted. My sister had to drop dead at one of my openings, and then there were all those awful stories that were spread about Andrea after she was murdered. I'd always been a little strange in my own right, but that was acceptable. You had to be strange, the fact was. Once I realized that, I made myself a motto. Be freaky, it was, and it worked." Reppa saw her pause and press her hands together again, as if she held a secret between them that was trying to escape. "I never let myself be seen in anything other than a long black dress. Once I went for over three years without saying a single word in public. Not one single word. Meanwhile the more freaky I became, the more seriously I was taken as an artist. But when people began finding out about my family and seeing they were pretty freaky, too, well, then it was over. Because you have to understand, it's all right if an artist is bizarre—but only as long as the rest of her family is normal. People have to believe there's no explanation for what makes an artist. Artists are simply aberrations,

121

beyond all understanding. But give them a family as crazy and weird as they are, and their freakiness is no longer mystical.''

Annabelle's head was still lying on the settee, her eyes half-closed. Reppa observed that the lines about her mouth were no longer as deep as they had been earlier. Of course the light was bad, and he could not be completely sure of what he was seeing, but he felt that he was listening to a woman whose desire to explain herself was smoldering like an explosive inside her. His presence for the moment seemed incidental.

''After Andrea was murdered,'' she went on in a toneless whisper, her voice sinking even lower, ''I refused to have any new shows of my work. Then someone said I should do a memorial show, combining some of my Annabelles with Andrea's paintings. Not easy, since Andrea had very few paintings. Whatever talent I had, it didn't run in the family. Sadly for her, because while she idolized me, she was at the same time so jealous that it consumed her. The idea of a memorial show—I didn't like it, but it did seem as if it might be a way of making up a little for what I'd done to her. So I went ahead and had one, and you know what happened.''

Reppa nodded gravely, though he knew nothing. ''The show was a flop?'' he hazarded.

Dully she said, ''It was a disaster.''

''Nothing sold?''

''*Everything* sold. Everything of Andrea's. People fought over her paintings.''

''What was so terrible about that?''

''The critics.'' Annabelle's voice cracked as if the throat were dry and brittle inside. ''They said the whole thing was in unspeakably poor taste. They claimed I had the show because my popularity was slipping and I was trying to exploit my murdered niece's memory to give it a boost. Some of them even changed their opinion of my Annabelles and said that they were nothing but junk that belonged in a carnival sideshow.''

Reppa frowned. "I don't know much about how the art world operates, but from the little I do know, that kind of criticism should have made you even more popular."

"Perhaps," she said with an introspective smile, "it would have if Adelaide and Andrea hadn't died so sensationally. Being that they did . . . well, nobody'd known a single firm biographical fact about me before. Where I grew up, how old I was, what my family was like—any of it. But suddenly they knew everything."

It was his chance, and he knew it. "Not everything. Certainly not who your parents were."

"No, not that. Although some knew. I always thought Stanley Behrman did, for one. Adelaide told him a tall story or two when they married, but he was the type who'd go sneaking around behind her back. The truth about our parents wasn't that hard to discover if someone really wanted to do it. But that wasn't what I meant when I said people knew all about my family. Kentucky and my father may have interested Behrman, but the rest of the world cared only about Adelaide and Andrea. Now that I was seen as a member of this very strange family, my Annabelles began to seem very commonplace in comparison. But I still had my pride. I simply stopped making any more Annabelles. I ceased being an artist."

Her voice had grown so heavy that Reppa hardly dared register his disbelief. "Not entirely."

"Oh, yes. Entirely."

"How? This loft doesn't pay for itself."

"True. I still have to prostitute myself now and then."

Annabelle rose up on one elbow and gestured negligently toward the bed.

"The magazine cover on the wall?"

"No," she said faintly, "that's from my days as Annabelle. The one memento of my faded glory that I allowed myself. I was referring to Abigail."

"You make dogs?"

"Animals of all sorts. For people like myself who have lost loved ones. I draw the line at horses. There isn't enough space here for anything that large."

"Then you do keep a studio . . ." He waited for an offer to show it to him. When none came, he said, "I don't suppose you'd give me a tour?"

Her eyes opened wide in alarm. "I've willed everything here to an art institute to do with as they wish. But until I die, no one will ever see my studio. You're the first person, incidentally, to be allowed in this room in several years."

Reppa could only murmur that he appreciated the honor.

Annabelle sniffed away the compliment. "You gave me no choice. If the governor is thinking of letting that horrid young man out of prison, I'll do anything in my power to stop it."

"Why do you feel so strongly?"

"Why?" Annabelle looked up at the ceiling, her expression becoming hard and cold. "Because twelve years in prison isn't nearly enough punishment for two murders. If Danny de Spirit is pardoned, it will seem as if it is."

"That isn't the thinking at all behind pardons. They're not given to men the governor feels have been sufficiently punished but to those who probably shouldn't have been sent to prison in the first place."

"You're trying to confuse me."

"On the contrary. I'm trying to explain the principle involved here."

"The only principle I care about," Annabelle said firmly, "is punishment. And I say twelve years of punishment for two murders isn't enough. Andrea was a wonderful girl. The other girl was an equally great loss to the world. She was a social worker, you know."

"Draft counselor," he corrected.

"But she was saving money to go to social-work school. She told me so herself. She was a person of very deep qualities. Her tragedy was living with Andrea and that nonentity. They were too fast for her. She was a girl who needed a very different sort of atmosphere to emerge."

He recognized the affinity. In describing Elizabeth Moffett, Annabelle could have been describing herself. The girl from Appalachia who came to the big city over thirty years ago.

"Emerge in what sense?"

"We'll never know," Annabelle said with a small shrug. "Like me. Elizabeth was someone who experienced a great deal of difficulty in finding herself."

"Were she and Andrea close?"

"Why are you asking me all these questions? Learning about the girls certainly isn't part of your assignment."

"No. But you have very strong feelings against Danny de Spirit being given a pardon. I'm trying to find out why."

"I've told you why," Annabelle said. "In fact, I've told you everything I'm going to." She began to grope at the floor under the settee. "Adelaide?" she crooned. "Where's Adelaide?"

Reppa watched the dog crawl out and attach itself to its mistress's arm, clinging to the sleeve of her dress like a

125

monkey. It even looked, now that it was in the light, a little like a monkey.

"She seems very fond of you."

"*He*. A fact I learned very belatedly."

"Where did you get . . . him?"

"From Mr. Kinder. A gift."

"So your relationship with Mr. Kinder does have a personal side now and then."

"Now and—" She raised a hand to her forehead. "What *is* this? No more *questions*."

"One more. Who are Wilkes and Mald?"

"Wilkes and Mald," Annabelle repeated with a little laugh. "You say their names as if they were gangsters."

"Who are they?"

"Persistent." She laughed again. "Carlo Mald owns the gallery where I had all my shows. He was the one who had the bright idea to mix Andrea's paintings with my Annabelles. He had a lot of ideas, but the only one that was truly bright was giving me my first show. I made the Mald Gallery what it is today. Thirty years ago Carlo had a little storefront on the Bowery. Now he has one of the leading galleries in SoHo."

"I've heard of it," lied Reppa, realizing that he should have.

"But it pretends never to have heard of Annabelle. My name isn't even on its pub sheet of famous exhibitors anymore."

"Pub sheet?"

"Short for publicity. Which is the one thing Carlo is very long on. For himself, that is. Everything is Carlo Mald."

"What about Wilkes?"

"The nonentity," Annabelle said with a bitter sound.

"Wilkes is Jill Wilkerson?"

She changed her name to Wilkes after the girls were murdered to keep from being identified as their roommate. So she says. Everyone knows her true reason was something else.''

''What was it?''

''Wilkes has a harder, more masculine sound. It was also, you'll remember, the middle name of Lincoln's assassin. Both are important considerations when you do the kind of painting she does.''

''She's an artist? I hadn't realized.''

''Most artists prefer not to realize it either.

Reppa was sitting forward in his chair, intrigued. ''What's her work like?''

''See for yourself. She, too, was one of Carlo's discoveries. I'm sure he's still got a painting or two of hers around his gallery. Although not on display. I doubt that even he would be so stupid.''

''Are you still in contact with her?''

''*Never.*'' Annabelle's head shook vigorously.

''Can you think of any reason, then, why Mr. Kinder would want to get in touch with her and Mald, or they with him?''

''Mr. Kinder?'' She stared at him: her widest eyes. ''Well, Carlo perhaps. He still calls here occasionally, though I never speak to him.'' She paused. ''But Wilkes wouldn't dare call here. I can't stand her, and she knows it. She played up to Andrea in college when she learned I was Andrea's aunt. Eventually she even got Andrea to introduce her to me, hoping I'd do her some good, but she was rudely disappointed. I recognized right away that she was nothing but a little climber and told Andrea she'd be wise to get another roommate. Andrea, sadly, didn't listen to me, and you see what happened.''

"Are you saying that having Jill Wilkes for a roommate contributed in some way to Andrea's being murdered?"

Annabelle held her hands cupped and facing upward, as if holding a balance scale in them. "Jill insisted on having a bedroom to herself," she said. "And so Andrea was forced to share her room with Elizabeth. If Andrea had been the one with her own room, it all might have worked out very differently."

"Because Elizabeth wouldn't have walked in on her when she got home? She'd have gone to the room she was sharing with Jill and not gotten in the way of whatever was going on in Andrea's room?"

Annabelle's only response was another small shrug.

"Miss Loomis, I hesitate to ask this next question, but duty requires me to. What do you think was going on in your niece's room when Elizabeth Moffett walked in?"

"Duty?" For the first time the voice grew loud. "You're lying. You don't have a duty to ask such questions."

"All right, I don't," Reppa acknowledged. "But meanwhile—"

"Meanwhile," Annabelle cut in flatly, "we're through talking. Shall I get Mr. Kinder to show you out, or can you find your own way?"

He gave her a moment to calm herself, and then he said, "Will you answer one more question? Do you know where Jill Wilkes is living now?"

She rose from the settee. "Good-bye, Mr. Reppa. I trust you'll put what I said about Danny de Spirit in your report."

"Since you won't answer my question, will you grant me a request?"

Annabelle looked down at the tiny monkey-faced dog cradled in her arms and cooed huskily, "The strange man

128

is leaving. Don't be frightened, my little pet. He'll soon be gone."

"One last thing," he said stolidly. "Will you walk me to the elevator?"

"That won't be necessary."

"I'd still be grateful if you would."

A faint smile, then Annabelle turned and went quickly to the brick wall. With one hand she held the dog pressed to her while with the other she unbolted a door he hadn't noticed before because its face was covered by wallpaper that had a brick design. A thick metal door. When she stepped back to let him open it, he saw it led to the dark hallway.

"The elevator is all the way down at the end, Mr. Reppa."

He took two steps down the hallway, then realized she wasn't following him.

"Walk me there."

"Oh, I can't." She stood in the doorway, swinging one foot behind her coquettishly.

"Could you if you wanted to?"

Her forehead looked perplexed, as if she hadn't understood the question. Then the blue eyes widened. "*Go*, Mr. Reppa. Please."

She backed deeper into the doorway, leaving only a length of black dress, the shadow of a swinging foot.

"*Could you?*" he repeated.

She didn't answer.

He started to push the button for the elevator, but then he saw it was there, awaiting him. He looked back one last time.

More of Annabelle was in the doorway now, both feet, one still swinging, and a hand fluttering a little wave to him.

His eyes turned slowly, involuntarily, on down the hallway toward Kinder's office.

The door was open. The front of a balding head leaned around the corner of it. Even in the gloom the lenses of the rimless glasses glinted piercingly.

Reppa stepped backward into the elevator and pulled the door shut behind him. His fingers took hold of the metal floor rod. When he hauled it upward, he felt the floor bump under him. In a moment, beginning to descend, he heard the bolts being slammed on the door above him and he wondered if he only imagined that he also heard someone laugh.

CHAPTER FIVE

THE ROOMMATE

There was a lengthy pause after he explained how he'd gotten her unlisted number, and then he began hearing fragments of a hushed conversation at the other end of the line.

". . . parole . . . asking if . . . talk about . . ."

Finally he broke in. "Would you prefer I call back when you're alone?"

"A friend's here who also happens to be a lawyer," Jill Wilkes said tartly. "She says I don't have to talk to you."

"Your friend is right. Legally you don't. But I can give you a good reason why you should."

Her end of the phone went silent. In a while she said, "All right, parole officer. What's the pitch?"

"You testified against Danny de Spirit at his trial. He may remember."

"Are you threatening me?" After another hushed conversation at the other end of the line Wilkes said, "My lawyer says I can report you for this."

"It's not a threat, Miss Wilkes. There's a strong possibility de Spirit will be pardoned. Before the governor acts, however, he wants our agency to find out how people like yourself will feel if de Spirit is released. Nobody makes

131

any claims he was a nice kid. The likelihood is that twelve years in prison haven't improved his disposition. So I'm obliged to point out that there could be repercussions."

She snorted. "Meaning you're going around telling everybody they could be killed?"

"Hardly. I'm not telling you anything like that either. But since you were the only person who positively placed de Spirit near the scene of the murders, there may be something here for you to consider."

Wilkes clapped her hand over the phone. It was a minute before the hand was removed and she said, "I've been advised to tell you that all I'm going to say is in my opinion de Spirit should not, under any circumstances, be restored to the community. He was sentenced to life, and I feel the sentence was fair and should be made to stand as is."

"Will you agree to meet me someplace and tell me that in person?"

"No way."

"Then could I speak to your lawyer friend for a moment?"

There was a long hesitation. "Why?"

Reppa, who had spent the morning rereading *Andrea and Elizabeth*, answered straightforwardly. "You couldn't identify de Spirit in a police lineup after he was arrested. Yet at his trial you claimed you'd seen him outside your building a few days before your roommates were murdered. Something of a discrepancy there. Your lawyer may not be giving you the best advice in the event somebody decides that you perjured yourself."

Haughtily she said, "There's a statute of limitations on perjury. Nobody's going to come after me for something I said eleven years ago."

"You're right—from a legal point of view. But in de

Spirit's mind I doubt there are any statutes of limitations. You still haven't answered how you, personally, will feel if he's released."

"He won't be," she said coolly, "if enough people tell you the same thing I am. That he shouldn't be restored to the community under any circumstances."

"You keep repeating that phrase, Miss Wilkes. Where did you hear it? It's pretty legalistic, to say the least."

"Of course it is. My lawyer friend just whispered it to me."

Reppa grinned the grin that parolees saw when they claimed the needle marks on their arms were cat scratches. "Put her on for a minute."

Wilkes's hand smothered the phone again. Then: "She says she won't talk to you."

"It would've been a little difficult for her to say otherwise."

"It's her prerogative. She'd be stupid to talk to you."

"You're being stupid enough right now for both of you."

"I'm acting on advice."

"Your own. There's no one there with you. You're alone."

Jill Wilkes gasped but recovered quickly. "That's all. I told you my opinion of the idea of pardoning de Spirit. Stick it in your report, parole officer, and fuck off."

"Unfortunately, I won't be able to. Since you never gave me an opinion."

"But I did. You just heard me."

"No," Reppa said innocently. "No, when I called you, you refused to talk to me altogether. So I had no choice but to say something in my report to the effect that you were uncommunicative."

"Uncommun—you can't do that! I spoke to you. I gave you a very clear and very direct statement."

"Your word against mine. Now, if your lawyer friend really happens to be there as a witness that we spoke, my word might not be as good as yours. If she's not, who knows?"

"Prick," she said. "You're as bad as that other parole dude."

A left-handed score in his column.

"If you agree to see me in person," he promised, "I'll put your opinion about pardoning de Spirit in my report verbatim."

Wilkes was silent in what seemed a considering way. At last she said, "Oh, Christ, I don't know why . . . but okay, I'll see you."

Damn right, he thought. You're afraid not to. That much was obvious.

But afraid of what?

Two hundred and six Arion Place was a three-story concrete building in the Williamsburg section of Brooklyn that had been converted from the decrepit residence of three small factories that paid a modest rent to the decrepit residence of three artists who paid a small fortune. Economically 206 was a windfall for its owner now that rents in Manhattan had forced painters and sculptors to establish enclaves in other boroughs. Esthetically it was an eyesore.

Entering the lobby, however, Reppa had immediately noticed a wistful mural of a seascape on the wall opposite the freight elevator, and the smell of acrylic paint drifted pleasantly down the fire stairs. Certainly there were drearier places in which artists in this day and age chose to live; especially those who were not—and Jill Wilkes wasn't—

134

overly concerned with the physical appearance of their surroundings.

Right now, at a few minutes after four on Tuesday afternoon, Reppa was scanning the living space of Wilkes's second-floor loft for a chair that would not ruin his clothes. Dust lay everywhere. The ceiling had more cobwebs than the Carlsbad Caverns. At the rear was a bespattered plywood partition that reached from the floor to within a few inches of the ceiling. Underfoot was a gritty layer of kitty litter. Not surprisingly the four feline residents of the place skulked above it all on window ledges, and the one human resident was perched on a tall wood stool, wearing an army fatigue jacket and tattered jeans. Her hair—short, blond, and curly—sat atop her head like a spaniel's on a mastiff. She had a broad brow, eyes set well apart, flat cheekbones, and a thin, pale mouth that looked as if it would have regarded a smile as an expression of torture.

Upon arriving, Reppa had said to her, in the way he sometimes had of seeming laid-back when he was ill at ease, that it was some weather they were having and concocted a slim compliment to the effect that she really had a lot of living space. *Living space*, he had since decided, was too charitable a term. Wilkes had scads of chairs and three voluminous, overstuffed sofas but appeared to sleep and eat nowhere in particular. The closest thing to a bed was a bamboo mat on the floor, and dirty paper plates were scattered around randomly, under chairs as well as on window ledges and an enormous rolltop desk, like orphaned Frisbees.

He further observed that Wilkes was not in the least bashful about decorating her loft with samples of her work. The better part of two walls was taken up by unframed paintings of varying sizes, and a third wall had a single canvas, nearly six feet tall, squarely in the center of it. All the paintings were alarmingly realistic and instilled in Reppa no desire to see behind the plywood partition, which he presumed set off Wilkes's studio from the rest of her loft. Wilkes, like most figurative painters, no doubt worked with a human model in the formative stages of a painting. *Human* was again, in Wilkes's case, perhaps too charitable a term.

For each of her paintings was a hard, brutal study of a nude man. Reppa could not look at any of them for long, but the large one was the most disturbing. It depicted a pallid, boyish-looking man with the wrinkled, wasted limbs and genitalia of a modern Methuselah. Dorian Gray's face attached to the body that would have been seen in the fabled portrait if the clothes had been removed. Yet it was clear that a great deal of effort had gone into the painting, and that Wilkes had talent and even a sense of humor. Affixed to the wall beneath the canvas was a white card with the title of the work on it: *The Last American Prince*. Its effect on Reppa was as arresting as his first sight of a Goya nude had been. But the Goya had produced a pleasant sensation of arousal. *The Last American Prince* prompted only a spreading unease—and recognition that its creator was not someone whose work would be widely accepted.

Wilkes ignored him until he'd completed his appraisal of her place and settled on a deck chair that was adorned at the moment with a pair of frayed blue cotton underpants. As he was gingerly clearing off the chair, her left hand held up a teapot inquiringly. When he declined, she spilled some murky liquid into a plastic cup and handed it to him anyway. About to take a polite sip, he thought better of it.

"So." Then, with an involuntary glance at *The Last American Prince:* "Your latest?"

For an instant her eyes flashed.

136

Reading the signal, he said, "You'd rather not talk about your work."

"It speaks for itself."

To allay his nervousness, he took his notebook out and opened it on his lap. Looking up, he saw her slide forward on the stool.

"What's that?"

"Notes. The first of which concerns the day you saw Danny de Spirit outside your building."

"What about it?"

"You're the first person I've interviewed who claims to have set eyes on him outside the courtroom. I'd like to hear about it."

Wilkes studied him, as if trying to gauge whether his curiosity was sincere. Finally she shrugged and then told him virtually the same story he'd read in *Andrea and Elizabeth*. She was on her way home from the elementary school in Brooklyn where she taught art. She supposed it was around five o'clock. When she got to her building, de Spirit was sitting on the front steps and staring up at a window. She asked, keeping her distance, if she could help him. De Spirit's only response was to shake his head and slink away. She failed to recognize him in the police lineup because he'd then been much thinner than the kid she remembered; later she learned the reason for this— he'd been heavily into drugs since she'd last seen him. By the time the trial came, however, he'd put on weight and once again looked pretty much as he had that afternoon outside her building. Even so, she'd wrestled with herself a long time before making a positive identification in court. Not that she doubted de Spirit was the killer, but he terrified her. He looked so weaselly and psychopathic. What if he weren't convicted and came back to kill her, too? But then she'd realized her conscience would never let her alone if she didn't do everything in her power, however small it seemed, to help see that the man who'd murdered her two closest friends was put away someplace where he could never kill anyone else.

Reppa continued to stare at his notebook after she finished. He tried to remember when he'd first realized he didn't believe her, but it was one of those tiny, jarring sounds that weren't possible to isolate in his memory. Frowning, he said, "How much weight do you think your testimony carried?"

"Very little. De Spirit's lawyer didn't even bother to try to dispute my identification. Nobody seemed to think it meant very much."

"Not quite nobody. A book I read about the case said that one juror admitted later that as far as he was concerned your testimony was what sold him."

Wilkes gave a disinterested shrug. "Good. Now if de Spirit gets out of prison and bumps me off, I'll die knowing what I did wasn't in vain."

Still focused on his notebook, Reppa heard Wilkes take a swallow of tea and said quickly, "What will your feeling be if the real murderer comes after you?"

He raised his eyes, not certain what he expected but certainly expecting something. But his remark only drew what seemed an honestly disdainful look: *Do I really have to listen to this?*

She started to rise from her stool but dropped back again when he said, "Another point. You claim you testified out of strong friendship for your roommates. Everything I've heard suggests you didn't get along with them at all."

"Who said that? Halliwell?"

"Matter of fact, it was Annabelle."

"Annabelle? You spoke to *Annabelle?* How? Where?"

"Last night in her loft."

"Her . . . ?" She was looking at him now as if he were something more than a minor irritant. "She actually let *you* in to see her loft?"

Reppa consulted his notebook. "Claimed you were a little climber who tried to play up to Andrea in the hope that it would get you an in to her. But she sensed what you were up to and cut you dead. Evidently you and she didn't hit it off too well."

He looked up, certain that this time he would see something, but Jill Wilkes's eyes were once again bland, and her arms were calmly folded.

"On the contrary. I've never had anything but admiration for her."

"The feeling doesn't seem to be mutual. She even had some highly unflattering comments to make about your painting."

Wilkes nodded. "I get it. You're doing a number so I'll make a few choice remarks about her in turn."

"Such as?"

"Sorry, but I have a different philosophy than Annabelle does. I don't vocalize my feelings about people. I demonstrate them."

She gave a careless wave toward the plywood partition. "Your studio?"

"Want to check it out?"

"Will I have to stay and pose?"

"That depends." For a moment Wilkes smiled an assured porcelain smile. "Would you make an interesting subject?"

"Not by your standards. My wares are pretty run-of-the-mill."

Her eyes thawing for an instant, as if acknowledging he'd held up his side of the repartee, she said, "Anyway, the offer's there. Unlike Annabelle, I open my door to everyone. Art is ten percent genius, forty percent luck, and fifty percent public relations. To make dough, you have to show.''

''Which brings me to another point. Are you able to support yourself on the money you get selling your paintings?''

Wilkes glumly followed his gaze around the walls. ''Not very well, obviously, since you see so many of them here. Fucking Mald. He had me tone down my image, and they're the result.''

''You consider these paintings toned down?''

''Way down.'' Her left hand swept the room. ''They're good, but they lack the brilliance my earlier work had. And now I can't get it back. Mald insisted the world wasn't ready for Wilkes the social commentator, and I stupidly listened to him. Now I'm paying for it. My work falls too much in the middle.''

The middle of what? Reppa wondered. ''When you were in your social commentator phase, what was your work like?''

''Dynamite,'' she said more staunchly. ''It really spoke to the point. Nobody wanted to listen, but not many listened to Van Gogh in his lifetime either.''

''Van Gogh was the one who cut his ear off, wasn't he?''

''Because he couldn't act out his *angst* on canvas. I didn't have that problem.''

He watched Wilkes take a drawing pencil out of her jacket pocket and pantomime a chopping motion with her left hand. The gesture was so decisive and so abrupt that the topic suddenly seemed exhausted.

''These social commentary paintings, were you doing them while you were living with Andrea and Elizabeth?''

Her head shook. ''I couldn't. After I finished art school,

I had to go out and earn a buck. I didn't have rich relatives beating down my door with offers to pick up my tab while I sat home and played with my paintbrushes."

"Is that a dig at Andrea?"

"Believe it. She was born with a silver spoon in her mouth and another one up her ass."

A bright vein of envy decorated the rage in Wilkes's eyes. Reppa wondered how best to tap it. Tentatively he said, "The one in her mouth being her stepfather's money?"

"Right. And the other one was Annabelle. Having her for an aunt should have been a sweet break, but you had to know how to handle it. Andrea didn't. Annabelle lived wrapped up inside herself. Andrea let it all hang out. They were so different they could barely communicate with each other. Eventually Andrea stopped trying altogether. I tried to tell her that was foolish. Annabelle was too valuable. Being her niece was worth a lot more than Behrman's dough."

"Valuable in what sense?"

Wilkes stared speculatively at him. "All Andrea had to do to make it as a painter was let a piece of Annabelle rub off on her, but she couldn't. There were too many other things she enjoyed. Partying. Men. In college she used to do all her paintings for her studio courses on the last night before they were due. That was her pattern in everything. No discipline. What tore her apart was the realization that she'd been handed every chance in the world to be R and F and she couldn't take advantage."

"R and F?"

"Rich and famous. Andrea was the first by birth, but she knew she had to become famous on her own, and she also knew she didn't have it in her to do it. The last few months before she was killed, she got incredibly angry

141

every time people mentioned Annabelle and told her how much they envied her.''

"One of those people being you?''

"I'll admit it,'' Wilkes said defiantly. "I was damned envious. Who wouldn't be of someone who had Annabelle for an aunt, and a mother who had known every art dealer and gallery owner in town? I had nobody, not one single fucking connection. A two-bit scholarship to Cooper Union from the women's club in Garden City, where I went to high school. Everything else I got, I had to hustle for. Hustle my ass off.''

She threw him a searching look, as if to see how literally he'd taken that.

"The old story,'' he said neutrally.

"Mine, at least. All Andrea had to do was turn out a few half-decent paintings, and the whole art world would have come crawling to her. Young, beautiful, the niece of a famous artist—she didn't have to shake it to make it. It was all right there in her lap, and she blew it.''

"In your envy of her you seem to give her stepfather pretty short shrift. Wouldn't it have been nice to have someone with his money behind you?''

"Behind me?'' she said jeeringly. "More likely he'd have had me on my behind.''

"Meaning what?''

"Why don't you just ask me, parole officer? You want to know it Behrman and Andrea fucked.''

Annoyed at her crudeness, more annoyed at his inability to hide his reaction to it, Reppa could feel the color rising in his face. "Did they?''

She gave him another of her cool porcelain smiles. "Begging your pardon, but aren't we going a little beyond the limits of your investigation?''

"Not really. I've been given a pretty wide latitude.''

142

"By whom? Certainly not by the governor."

"It was a very complex case. Therefore the feelings and opinions of the people I interview are going to be complex. I'm expected not only to report their feelings and opinions but also to try and find out what they're based on."

"Bullshit," said Wilkes. "Pure bullshit. But smooth. You're almost as smooth as the other parole dude who came to see me."

"McCreary?"

"John Jacob McCreary. I've still got his card around somewhere. 'Call me J.J.,' he said. Smiling, teeth showing like little penises. What happened to him? Why didn't they send him back over the same trail? He fall off his high horse on his head?"

"They thought they'd try someone with shorter teeth. So Little Red Riding Hood wouldn't realize she was talking to the wolf."

"Hohoho. McCreary was not only smoother, he was a lot more amusing."

Resistance to the needle was no longer possible. Reppa said harshly, "But you're going to tell me things you didn't tell him. Do you know why?"

Jill Wilkes regarded him silently, curiously.

"Because I think you're afraid. I think you've known something for twelve years that no one else knows, and that knowledge has become dangerous again."

"Again?" she inquired calmly. "Why again?"

"Because if de Spirit gets a pardon, it means some influential people think he's innocent, and the whole case could be reopened. If that happens, the real killer may suddenly remember you're still around."

Unexpectedly Wilkes laughed again. "Who's been coaching you? McCreary? He tried that same shit to browbeat me into talking about Andrea's boyfriends. It got him zip."

"I'm my own coach, and I've got something McCreary didn't have."

"Your color? You think because you're white—?"

"Twelve years," Reppa cut in sharply. "I can look back over twelve years and see what's happened to each and every person connected with the case. You, Behrman, Annabelle. Halliwell and Mald after I've finished talking to them. Cupach, if I can—"

"Mald?" A signal flashed in her eyes. "You can't go bothering Carlo. He had nothing to do with the case."

"Then you shouldn't have a worry in the world if I talk to him."

"What's your game?" she asked stonily. "What's your real buzz in this?"

"Buzz? I'll tell you what my *buzz* is. Making it hot for liars."

"You can exclude me. I haven't lied about anything."

"Then your conscience should be as cold as your tea is by now. I'd say clear, but your tea looks like mud."

Glaring at him, Jill Wilkes rose from her stool. "That's all, parole officer. I don't have to listen to this shit."

Reppa rose with her. Standing, he realized his heart was hammering.

"Just one more question. Tell me how your art career happened to pick up so quickly after your two roommates were murdered."

There was a moment of silence, brief, heavy, and then Jill Wilkes snarled, "Yeah, I'll tell you. I paid my dues, fucker. I worked—worked my buns off—and I was rewarded for it."

"Mighty small dues. One day you were teaching school and saving your pennies, and a few days later you were

144

suddenly supporting yourself on your painting. A pretty rapid ascension. Meteoric, I would say.''

''It was more than a few days! It took months of *hard, hard* work!''

''Months is still a few days in my world. I coached football for nearly ten years before I was even close to moving off square one.''

''Maybe you just weren't any good, parole officer.''

''Or maybe,'' Reppa countered, ''I didn't have a sugar daddy to pay my bills so I could stay home and paint. Or maybe I didn't *need* a sugar daddy because a certain gallery owner decided to have a show of my work. For a reason, let's say, that had very little to do with art.''

Wilkes batted her eyes mockingly. ''Are you suggesting I gave my body to Carlo Mald in return for being given a show in his gallery?''

''You know damn well that's not what I'm suggesting.''

''What then?'' she taunted. ''That I know who killed Andrea and Elizabeth and the show was a bribe for my keeping my mouth shut? Your investigation has no limits, and neither does your imagination.''

''Oh, but it does. There's one place it keeps getting stopped. Why in all this time hasn't the person who killed Andrea and Elizabeth killed you, too?''

''Because he's been locked up.'' Wilkes fashioned one of her unreadable smiles. ''Face it, parole officer, you're trying to pry open a clamshell with a limp prick.''

She wheeled and started for the door. Reppa followed slowly, brooding under the weight of the questions he had not gotten to ask and the sense that he'd been wrong about her. If she had agreed to talk to him because she was frightened, it was not a fear he could understand.

''I may be back again with something harder,'' he said tightly.

Her smile again. Bright. Meaningless.

"No, you won't. I really did talk to a lawyer after you called, you know. Agencies like yours only allow you one interview per person on an investigation like this, and you just had it."

CHAPTER SIX

MALD

Since Leilah couldn't move off her back or tolerate any weight being put on her, the only activities that were medically permissible were manual and oral. And even then, as Dr. Molnar had cautioned, the main objective shouldn't be sexual gratification but revving up her circulation so that she would avoid pneumonia, kidney failure, and any of the sundry other disorders that threatened the bed-bound. Her orgasms thus were incidental. In fact, if they didn't occur after five minutes or so, the prescription was to cease activity so as not to get her back muscles too tense.

It was such restrictions as these, together with Molnar's prognosis that Leilah wouldn't be back on all cylinders for a good six months yet, that were the bane of Reppa. Why, since they weren't married and had never even discussed marriage, didn't he feel free to get a little something going on the side while she was recovering? Hadn't she told him just the other night that he was on his own now? A green light, on the face of it, but he'd been around too many women not to have learned to listen to what was going on below the surface.

A bind. But a more painful bind was that other women

didn't turn him on much anymore. One possible explanation was that Leilah while intact had fulfilled all his desires so completely that he had no curiosity left for anyone else. A second (and far more likely) possibility was that he was feeling too guilty about his part in what had happened to her. Still another reason may have been that between his job and his domestic life he was seldom thrown into contact with interesting women. True, there were a couple of moderately attractive female parole officers roaming around the Fortieth Street office, but he'd never even gotten on a first-name basis with them.

And yet there were inklings that a fourth possible explanation for his current celibacy might be the most nearly correct. What if the de Spirit investigation was devouring not just his time and his intellect but his passions as well? Its original appeal had been to the strain in him that had tangled with the 26th Precinct over Jimmy Wallace. Some people would get away with murder over there unless he blew the whistle on them for pressuring Wallace to lie. Somebody in the Behrman-Moffett case, namely Cupach, had gotten away with murder, if you believed, and he was finding it increasingly difficult not to, that de Spirit was innocent.

Up till yesterday afternoon that was as far as Reppa had taken it. But now, after talking to Jill Wilkes, there was some additional distance to travel, a final corner to be turned. He had stated it to Wilkes himself in so many words. What would her feeling be if the real murderer came after her?

The real murderer. Not anybody at the 26th. This wasn't a matter of figurative murder. No, there was someone out there who—if Reppa hadn't just been talking to shake up Wilkes's infuriating appearance of calm, though that was certainly part of it—had literally gotten away with murder.

Leilah still didn't share his indignation, but at least she was no longer listening just to be polite. She was beginning to lament, in fact, that she was getting everything secondhand and that he was no Archie Goodwin at reporting.

"Stop being such a romantic. I ask for one good reason why you think de Spirit was railroaded, and you tell me you saw in this Wilkes woman's eyes that she was hiding something. Stare deep into my eyes, Reppa, right now—right this minute—and tell me what I'm thinking."

They were lying together in bed for the last few minutes before the alarm rang, his hand wedged around the metal rail between them and under the covers, lightly massaging her shoulders. A radio was playing in the apartment above them—the Hungarian couple Leilah had been trying to evict ever since she'd bought the building, because they only paid $97.52 a month after forty years there under Rent Control. Street traffic outside. Watery sunlight crawling in between the bars on the window gate.

"Why not invite the whole crew over here?" she said, meaning all the suspects. "The obligatory final gathering in the great Nero Sturm's boudoir."

"I haven't spoken to everyone yet myself."

"So? You're not going to find out anything anyway. You're too busy peering into people's eyes to listen to what they're saying. If you'd brought Wilkes to me and let us talk, woman to woman, instead of getting her all riled up with your Bogart routine, the issue would be settled now. Either she's hiding something or she isn't."

"What would you have done that I didn't do?"

"For one thing, asked her how she and Andrea got Elizabeth Moffett for a roommate."

"What else?"

"It would have depended on her answer to that."

"I'll tell you what her answer would have been. It was

149

in the book I read about the case. She and Andrea originally had another roommate, a third girl from Cooper Union who left to get married. They needed a replacement to help out with the rent, so they ran an ad in the paper. Elizabeth answered it. She was living in a women's hotel, having just come to New York fresh out of college. Since her share of the rent was less than what she was paying in the hotel and the apartment was within walking distance of her job, she moved in.''

"Was she the only one who responded to the ad?"

"I see. You're wondering why they chose her, this drab little mouse, ahead of everyone else. What makes you think Wilkes would have told you?"

"The answer could have been something as simple as the fact that she *was* a drab little mouse, and neither of them wanted any more competition in that apartment."

"For men? That may have been true for Andrea, but it wasn't for Wilkes. To put it right on, she doesn't seem overly interested in the opposite sex."

"But she might have been interested in Andrea. Another attractive woman around the place would have only been in the way."

"According to Annabelle—"

"Reppa, that's exactly my point. You can't just buy everything Annabelle and the others tell you. You've got to go over each and every detail with each and every person and then compare their answers. That story Behrman told you about the Loomis family, for—"

"You don't understand. I'm on thin ice as it is. I can't ask all the questions I want to, because it's not my job."

"Tell the others that. Don't try to tell it to me, Reppa. I see how much time you're putting in."

"Because I have to. There's a deadline. I've only got another six days to finish this and do my report."

"But what are you doing during all that time you're out there if you're not asking questions? Oh, why do I always have to say the obvious. . . ." She pushed his hand away. "Do you know what I think is going to happen? I'm afraid you're going to meet somebody and leave me."

"Where?" Reppa said. "Sure as hell not on this investigation. I've got a hotshot art gallery owner left to interview, some Wall Street prick, maybe a couple of cops, and that's it."

"Okay. But I notice you didn't say it wasn't possible."

She rolled away, and he was left looking at the back of her long black hair. The alarm clock began to ring. There was a car for him to move, and Mrs. Gore would be down in a few minutes.

The Mald Gallery was open weekdays from eleven to six. Mald himself seldom came in before one o'clock, the woman who answered the phone at the gallery informed Reppa, and never saw anyone during business hours except artists and collectors. Asked for Mald's home phone number, the woman said frostily that a parole investigation on behalf of a convicted murderer didn't really sound like any of Mr. Mald's concern. Could she be persuaded to let Mald be the judge of that? When the woman said the best she could do was give Mald a message that Reppa had called, Reppa said, "Put in your message that one of the women who was murdered was a former artist of Mr. Mald's. As was her aunt. And add that I'll call back around five."

Cupach was a different matter. His only present connection with the NYPD was as a special consultant on films and TV shows that depicted New York's finest at work. It was unclear whether he was on the NYPD payroll or received his daily bread from the producers of the projects

151

that utilized his expertise. No one with the NYPD knew his present whereabouts, who his theatrical agent was, or even how a message could be gotten to him. No one, anyhow, who was about to tell Reppa.

Meanwhile his most pressing problem was the one that faces any investigator trying to do authorized work without the authorization to do it: how to interview a man who refused to be interviewed, namely Andrea's ex-fiancé.

Reppa had a few ideas. One of them was more or less the same as McCreary's: "Tell him if he doesn't see you, you'll put in your report that he was uncooperative. If enough people are uncooperative, tell him, the governor won't be able to risk granting de Spirit a pardon. What'll happen then, chances are, is there'll have to be a new trial. Ask him if he wants to be called on to testify about his relations with the Behrman broad. And *use* words like *broad*. Tell him de Spirit's lawyer is an ace who'd like nothing better than to get some Wall Street asshole on the stand and make mincemeat out of his personal life."

"Is that true?" Reppa, standing, watched McCreary tilt his chair back and swing his feet up on his desk. "Can he be called on to testify this time around if he wasn't called in the first trial?"

"Hell, yes. Halliwell will know it, too. He's got a law degree. Just tell him what I said. Guaranteed, he'll take a different attitude."

"I was thinking more or less along the same lines but—"

"The most he can do," McCreary interrupted, "is call them upstairs and say he's got a guy bugging him for an interview he's within his legal rights not to grant."

"And they'll gong me off the investigation."

"Not anymore they won't. You're in too tight now."

"Tight with whom?"

152

"Just make sure, baby, the mileage you turn in on your expense account isn't padded too much. I'll take care of the rest."

"Tight with whom, McCreary?" Even that *care* had sounded ominous.

McCreary's sunglasses regarded him implacably. "Your ass is covered. Take my word. There's a rabbi in parole-officer heaven looking out for you."

But on one point Reppa was firm. He got McCreary to promise not to pester him for any progress reports until the interview phase of the investigation was completed. Then, if McCreary wanted to help him write some of the more sensitive passages in the report he had to send up to Albany, it would be accepted. Neither of them was ready to acknowledge openly that matters had reached a state where they would both be monumentally disappointed if Reppa's only concern at the end of the investigation was his grammar.

There was a message stuck in the dial of the phone when Reppa got back to his desk.

CALL: *Zippy Dwersky*
Legal Aid
577-3328

It was in Spielman's handwriting. Spielman was his current partner, and he had a lifetime allegiance to the minds that gave the world *Mad* magazine. Once Reppa had opened the folder of a new case he'd been assigned to and found a picture of Alfred E. Neuman where the prison photo should have been. Another time there had been a message awaiting him when he returned from lunch that a Melvin Coznowski had called him collect from Neptune,

153

New Jersey, while he was out. Spielman, who had been out on personal leave that day, lived in Neptune. Most of his disguises were a little thin.

Zippy Dwersky. Reppa tossed the message out and then left one for Spielman to find: One of Spielman's longtime absconders had called to report he was ready to turn himself in; the man was sitting by the phone awaiting Spielman's return call. Reppa added the number of Dial-A-Prayer and went off to spend his lunch hour at the Y.

He returned to the office around two: exercised, saunaed, invigorated. And suddenly somewhat melancholy. Spielman had done one of his vanishing acts; after being at his desk all morning, he was now nowhere to be found, so there was no one to ask if any absconders had turned themselves in lately. The office was an invidious place to be even under the most convivial circumstances. Alone in it, Reppa could feel himself aging with each passing moment. His joints stiffened. His eyelids drooped. His back seemed to be melting into the padded contours of his swivel chair. He was a field parole officer if he was anything, and most of the time even that seemed a dim substitute for the dream of Frank Reppa stalking the sideline in Cleveland Stadium, hired to lead the Browns out of their recent doldrums to the Super Bowl. He had a sudden vision of a headline: PAROLE OFFICER'S INVESTIGATION FORCES POLICE TO RE-OPEN BEHRMAN-MOFFETT CASE. He shook his head, stood up, stretched, sat down again, and laboriously began writing an account of the stances Stanley Behrman, Annabelle Loomis, and Jill Wilkes had taken on the governor's notion of pardoning Danny de Spirit.

When five o'clock came, he called the Mald Gallery, and the gallery owner himself answered the phone. Rich, vibrant baritone. Pronounced foreign accent. French? Castilian? Polite in any event. By all means, Mr. Reppa.

Any help I can give. Anytime. Today? Yes, if you can get here before six.

Reppa walked to his car, which was parked on a block between Eleventh and Twelfth avenues that had been a freebie for over a month now while the city procrastinated over replacing a no-parking sign that had been sheared off by a truck that took the corner too sharply. He headed downtown on Twelfth Avenue. By the time he arrived in SoHo, it was twenty to six. The signs on all the side streets said parking was illegal between 8 A.M. and 6 P.M., but most of the blocks were already packed solid with cars. He found a spot near the corner of Spring and Wooster streets, stuck his Division of Parole parking placard on the window visor just in case some traffic cop got a last minute sadistic urge, and strolled back to West Broadway.

The Mald Gallery occupied the entire third floor of a shabby concrete building on the block between Spring and Prince streets. Reppa had allowed himself to be dragged around SoHo by Leilah several afternoons last fall, and he supposed this must have been one of their stops. But it looked neither familiar nor unfamiliar. It looked pretty much like all the galleries Leilah had taken him to, which was to say it registered as a lot of indirect recessed lights and waxed wood floors. In one room he saw a stack of perfectly square wooden boxes that he immediately labeled *Study in Bowling Ball Crates,* and in a second, somewhat larger room, were some half dozen paintings of what looked like grease spots on pages of lined notebook paper.

A young woman who sat behind the reception desk with the listless manner of a security guard in a broom factory directed him through a rear exit. Outside it was a hallway with a door at either end. The door to Reppa's left was closed, but the other was open wide. Through it boomed

155

the baritone he had heard on the phone. "Oh, my dear, have you thought of becoming an illustrator? . . . Yes, yes, I know. But I can only repeat . . . My dear, now, please. This is not at all the reaction one would expect of one who wishes to be called a mature artist."

Judging from the syncopated pauses that Mald was in the midst of a phone conversation, Reppa stuck his head in the door to make his arrival known. But the hand he held up in signal, instead of finding Mald's eyes, found a gangly rawboned woman's, which at the moment were blurred with tears. She was on her feet, too anguished to speak as she gesticulated despairingly toward a row of soft-toned cityscapes that were propped against the back wall of the office. Between her and the door a man sat slumped behind a Formica desk, long fingers kneading black eyebrows.

Reppa retreated to a chair outside the door, where he became a reluctant audience.

"Please, no more tears," Mald's voice said. "Otherwise I will begin to think your life is like your paintings. All emotion and no substance."

"But if you'd come to my studio . . . I mean, in here . . . can't even see in this light."

"Unfortunately I can see all too well. You told me modern realism. This is French impressionism. Go home and take out all those shimmering greens and yellows and put in lines. Straight black lines."

"There's a market . . . I know there's a market. That you don't know makes you and your gallery—"

"But of course there is a market. For circus clowns and flowers in vases people go to the Village Art Show. For order they come to Carlo Mald."

". . . saying I should peddle my work on the street? These are good paintings, Mr. Mald, not something you—"

"Technically they are splendid. Commercially they are a disaster. Good day, now. I will get someone to help you carry your canvases outside to a cab."

". . . my fare . . . to say nothing of—"

"The inconvenience I apologize for. The money for your cab fare has been reimbursed on my advice. No more French impressionism. Order. People today buy what they know they *must* feel, not what they wish they *could* feel."

The woman's voice murmured something then that was inaudible to Reppa. Whatever it was, it caused Mald's voice to grow venomous.

"*Vete!*"

A hand slammed on a desk top. A chair creaked. Suddenly the office door was no longer empty. The tall man who filled it was gaunt, almost skeletal. Straight black hair and a sallow complexion. Dark, mica-hard eyes. The gray suit he wore had creases like razors, and a yellow marquise stone gleamed like a tooth in the center of his orange tie. Unexpectedly there were camel-colored Hush Puppies on his feet.

Reppa bolted to his feet. "Mr. Mald? Frank Reppa."

"Oh, yes." Mald clutched for his composure as for a hat a stiff wind had tried to lift from his head. "Forgive me this distasteful spectacle. It will be a very few minutes and I will be with you."

The office door was shut. In a while it opened again, the gangly woman staggering out under an armload of paintings, Mald behind her carrying a single painting with the forebearing expression of a professional pallbearer.

"An ape's ego in a giraffe's body," he murmured to Reppa in an aside as he ushered the woman through the entrance to the gallery.

When she wheeled around with a final word to deliver, rocking from one leg to the other, coddling her humiliation,

157

Mald preempted her by cocking his arm as if to heave away the painting he held. Instead he laid it almost tenderly against the wall, handed Reppa into his office, and shut the door—but not before the woman got out a strangled *"Cucaracha!"*

"So sorry for this spectacle," Mald repeated when the two of them were seated, Reppa aware that his chair—a kind of cloth basket that held his rump like a sling—was going to make it difficult to sound brisk and forceful. "These artists never appreciate that I am one of a very few gallery owners who is willing to see everyone who claims to have talent. As a result they make me the receiver of all their frustration when I reject their work, as I often must."

Reppa nodded somberly, sinking deeper into his chair and his observations that he was in an essentially one-person room: one comfortable chair, one ashtray, one man's taste represented by the one-color, one-theme paintings on the walls. He watched Mald open an ivory cigarette case and offer him a selection of what appeared to be neatly rolled joints. When he shook his head, Mald chose one and lit up. Half of it disintegrated with his first puff, and Reppa noticed the room was filled immediately with an unfamiliar but not unpleasant aroma. He asked what it was.

"The tree of life," Mald said mechanically. He took another voracious drag from the joint, stubbed it out in the ashtray, and wreathed his dark eyes with wrinkles from a smile that reached no part of the eyes themselves. "So good of you to think of me while you were doing your investigation. I would have been most unhappy if we had not spoken."

"Oh?"

The smile lingered like a lone wave on a cold, empty sea. "After all, every man should be given the chance to correct false impressions that have been whispered about him by others."

"What sort of false impressions?"

"Come, come, Mr. Reppa. You are seeking answers to certain questions, and now here I am. Perfectly willing to give them to you."

"All of which leads me to believe someone called you to say I'd be in touch with you. Who was it?"

"Perhaps you misunderstood. I did not say I would answer *all* your questions."

Mald's tone of voice was still cordial, but his eyes contradicted it. As Reppa watched the gallery owner, he could clearly discern that this man's face would never reveal anything to him. On the other hand, his very presence here revealed much. Mald, no less than the others, had some inscrutable reason for speaking to him—some reason that went beyond simple curiosity.

"Was it Lee Kinder? Jill Wilkes?"

"Mr. Reppa, all of this is taking time, and I do not have much more to give you. Surely you have more important matters to discuss."

"Foremost of which," he said coldly, tiring of Mald's elaborate evasiveness, "is that I have to turn in a report with a recommendation of whether or not a convicted murderer should be pardoned. The recommendation might carry some weight, it might not. I tend to think it will, because everyone I've spoken to has given me the same feeling. There may be a difference of opinion over whether Danny de Spirit should be released from prison. But I've gone away from each person increasingly convinced that there are enough questions still unanswered to warrant reopening the whole case."

"Then, by all means," Mald said easily, "you must say this in your report."

159

"I intend to. But first I'd like to find answers to as many of these questions as I can. Coincidentally a number of them center around you. So many of them, in fact, that I felt I had to talk to you even though you're not officially part of my investigation."

"This between us, then, is off the record, as you say?"

The slick black hair lay absolutely flat against Mald's skull. It looked like a helmet, as dark and gleaming as polished metal. It also looked as false as Mald's studied unfamiliarity with the English idiom was beginning to sound.

"Not necessarily. What you tell me won't go in my report, but I still might make use of it."

"Mr. Reppa, you must explain to me, a man who knows nothing about your profession. What is your position with respect to other law enforcement agencies?"

"As a parole officer I'm required to cooperate with them and assist them whenever I'm able. Not legally required in every instance. Sometimes only ethically required. Even you, a man not completely at home with the English language, will appreciate the distinction."

Mald regarded him with a considering smile.

"It does sound as if you have chosen to pursue a most interesting career."

"Yourself also. I've heard gallery owners can make or break an artist with a snap of their fingers. That woman who was just in here, for example. If you'd decided to give her a show, it could have changed her whole life."

"A popular misconception of my influence," Mald said modestly.

Reppa stared at the narrow, triangular face before him. Cheekbones sharply jutting, tight skin, the long curved eyebrows acting almost as frames for the eyes. "Yet the fact is you *have* changed the course of people's lives. Jill

160

Wilkes for one. Twelve years ago you launched her like a rocket. Now you seem to have dropped her like a hot potato."

He observed, with some perverse satisfaction, that Mald's smile did not flicker. The gallery owner was clearly prepared on this front.

"A rocket and a hot potato. Rather clichéd metaphors, Mr. Reppa."

"I often speak in clichés when I'm afraid of being misunderstood."

"You cannot imagine," Mald said tonelessly, "how little danger you are in of that happening here. Jill Wilkes, you seem of the belief, has some sinister power over me. It will suffice to say it is untrue."

"Then why did you show her work? Looking around your gallery, I wouldn't think her style of painting was in keeping with your philosophy of straight lines and order."

"Philosophies change with the times. Ten years ago there was a vogue for her kind of work. The country was in Vietnam, women were starting to organize, people in general were more political. Jill Wilkes seemed as if she one day might become important, so I put her under contract. I often do that with young artists. Pay them a stipend while they are in the embryonic stages of their development. Many gallery owners now do the same. In some cases it bears rich dividends. Artists being subsidized suddenly become very popular and more than pay back the money we have invested in them. For when they accept our stipends, they also give us exclusive rights to represent their work."

"For life?"

Mald clasped his hands behind his head. "If they are so stupid as to agree to that. Most artists now are growing wiser. I, too, am somewhat wiser. No more will I subsidize someone for longer than a year."

161

"How long was Wilkes under contract to you?"

"And I equally bound to her," Mald hastened to interject. "A two-way street. Ten years we traveled it together. But her work showed no development. It only grew increasingly hysterical. When her contract with me expired, we parted ways."

"On good terms?"

"I like to think I am always a friend to the artists I have represented. Unhappily some of them cannot reciprocate in kind. But no matter what Miss Wilkes thinks of me, I shall continue to have nothing but the highest professional esteem for her."

Reppa frowned. "I suppose if it ever came down to it, you could produce a copy of this contract with her."

"Uncle Sam's income tax people would make short work of me if I could not."

Glib as Mald's explanation was, it also sounded disappointingly like the truth.

"When I spoke to Miss Wilkes, she didn't say anything about this business arrangement the two of you had. Any reason why she'd want to keep it a secret?"

"Obviously so I'd be cast in an unfavorable light in your eyes. A very bitter woman. She was given every opportunity to change with the times, but she refused."

"What brought the two of you together originally?"

Mald eyed him absently for several moments, as if considering deeply. "Andrea Behrman told me about her, I believe. It has been so long ago now. It may even have been that she came in here one day on her own and said she was Andrea's roommate. I really cannot recall the exact circumstances."

"Was your first meeting with her before or after Andrea was murdered?"

"Oh, before, I'm sure. I remember she had very little

work to show me. Later, when she had more, she contacted me again, and we made another appointment to meet.''

''In her studio?''

''I would assume so. That was my custom then. Out of curiosity I always used to visit an artist in his own domain.'' Mald grinned in his peculiarly disengaging way. ''I am no longer so foolish. I might make an appointment to go to an artist's studio out of the old curiosity, but then wisdom will intervene. This woman today—from what you saw of her, you can well imagine the slanderous accusations I would undoubtedly have had to defend myself against if I'd made the mistake of going to her studio.''

An ape's ego in a giraffe's body. The memory goaded Reppa to ask one of the questions his own simian ego had short-circuited him from asking Wilkes: ''How long after her roommates were murdered did Wilkes wait before getting in touch with you the second time?''

''A while.''

''A month? Two months? Six months?''

Mald smiled unctuously. ''I really don't remember.''

''Had she changed her name as yet from Wilkerson to Wilkes?''

''These questions grow tedious. Mr. Reppa, what is your point?''

''That Wilkes had no time to paint while her roommates were alive because she was too busy working to support herself. Consequently, as you said yourself, she had very little work to show you. After the murders she continued to teach and have no time to paint. Yet she suddenly had enough work to convince you to subsidize her for ten years. As for the name change, if she did it before she got in touch with you, it would be a pretty fair indication that she was confident her art career was about to take a decisive turn.''

163

"Go on. Get to the point."

The smile continued to regard him fixedly, but he seemed to detect the faintest trace of anxiety in the gallery owner's voice. "Just that I don't believe Wilkes had any more work to show you the second time than she had originally. What you saw on the first occasion didn't interest you in the least. But what she *told* you the second time she contacted you interested you very much. So much, in fact, that you didn't care if she had any work to show you or not. You had no choice but to make an arrangement with her."

"Have you given anyone else the honor of hearing this theory of yours?"

"Wilkes."

Mald gazed at him, disconcertingly speculative. "And what was her response?"

"To make a joke out of it. To pretend I was suggesting that she'd slept with you in return for your giving her a show."

"Why are you so sure it was a joke? If you believe my reputation, I sleep with all the female artists I represent."

"Including lesbians?"

"I seldom inquire into a woman's political affiliations," Mald said, unconcerned.

Reppa sat back, stopped for a moment. Then he came forward again in his chair and said, "Did you ever sleep with Annabelle?"

For the first time he saw the weary, joyless smile waver.

"Don't be absurd. No man has ever slept with Annabelle."

It had the sound, he thought, of self-apotheosis. If the great Carlo hadn't succeeded, who else could have? "What was the nature of your relationship with her in her heyday?"

"That of a dealer to his client. There is nothing else to be said."

"Annabelle has told me you were the first to give her a show. What made you do it?"

"Talent. She was brilliant when she was young. Some would say a genius."

"How did you discover her?"

Mald's face showed that this was the right way to ask the question. "Thirty years ago I had a tiny gallery on the Bowery. Making the youthful mistake of exhibiting only artists who appealed to my taste, I filled my walls with abstract expressionism. Now and then I sold a painting, but most of the time I sold nothing. Then one day Annabelle walked in, and my life and hers changed."

"Was it really that simple?"

"Simple? If you believe the ability to recognize genius is simple, then, yes—it was extraordinarily simple. But if you are not so naïve, you know that kind of ability is in itself genius. Before meeting Annabelle I had heard about her, of course. Other gallery owners were frightened away by what they heard. The mark of my genius is that I was not."

"What sort of things had you heard about her?"

Mald's eyes drifted away, retreating into an interior mood that brought an almost youthful look to his face. For a time that began to seem endless to Reppa he sat without speaking. Then, quietly and with an unmistakable and disturbing tinge of nostalgia, he said, "Oh . . . that she was bizarre. That she was even perhaps demented. It was an image that she was presenting to some extent, but until she met me, it hadn't been successful. Women artists traditionally were not allowed to have such an image. Even if they were starving, they had to maintain an appearance of refinement and elegance. Annabelle was one of the first to try and change this, and *I* was the first to realize the world was ready for the change. In November of 1950 I

165

gave her a one-woman show. Almost no one came to the opening. There was a single review, and it was unfavorable. Annabelle's people looked too much like Tobacco Road moved to Times Square, it said. But some who read the review understood what Annabelle and I understood: that parts of New York were becoming more like Tobacco Road every day. Curious, they came to look. Then they returned, bringing friends. A year later I gave Annabelle another show, and now there were many reviews. One critic called her an anthropologist with a mortar-board. Another described her as a bard who used a chisel instead of a pen. Her fame and fortune came quickly after that, and by association with her mine did, too.''

Reppa sat silent, scratching his way slowly toward the itch Stanley Behrman had left in him: those long intervals when Adelaide was supposedly away caring for her ailing sister. Backing up a moment, he said, ''Did you know Adelaide Behrman?''

''Who?''

''Annabelle's sister.''

This returned the gallery owner abruptly to the present. For a moment his eyes seemed reluctant to lose their soft cast, but then they once again grew indifferent.

''A well-meaning but superficial woman. She wanted so much to be thought an aesthete. I am afraid many thought her only a fool. Yes, I knew her. Who did not? She rushed to every gallery opening as if afraid Leonardo would be there if perchance she missed it.''

''A celebrity seeker, in other words.''

''Precisely.''

''Why did she do it?''

''How should I know? I am not a psychiatrist.''

Reppa could no longer avoid seizing it directly, the area that itched. ''Mr. Mald, Annabelle didn't walk into your gallery in the Bowery thirty years ago. Her sister walked in, acting for her. Walked in and offered you something in return for something. Isn't that the way it really happened?"

Reppa's throat constricted; he felt suddenly too warm as he watched the gallery owner's eyes rise again to meet his. But there was still no worry in them. Mald only gave him another one of his tired smiles and stood up, offering down a hand as if to help him climb out of a hole.

"Come. Rather than haggle over these tedious theories of yours, let me show you what we really should be talking about."

Reppa got out of the basket chair unassisted, but the hand stayed around anyway to give his shoulder a squeeze.

"Have you ever seen an early Annabelle, Mr. Reppa?"

"No. I don't think so."

"You must. Unavoidably, like all artists, she started to repeat herself, but once she was one of the most outstanding talents of the era. . . ."

The rich baritone voice faded to a mordant hum (it was, to Reppa's amazement, the theme music to *Alfred Hitchcock Presents*) as Mald led the way out of his office and commenced trying a set of keys in the door at the other end of the hallway.

Sensing Mald's enthusiasm but without any reason to share it, Reppa said uneasily, "What's in here?"

The answer was a very long, very narrow storeroom. Mald threw on a fluorescent light. He seemed to grow taller under it and greener. "Well, now, hello." There was a dead mouse just inside the door. Beyond it, as far as Reppa's eyes could see before becoming lost in labyrinthine shadows, were three tiers of paintings efficiently stacked against the wall. In the aisle, seemingly at random, metal, stone, and wood sculptures stood around like old clocks whose time had long ago run out. Mald pointed vaguely into the maze. "Down there."

Reppa took a step in that direction and nearly a second, but then leaped back.

The man was crouching behind a large stone horseshoe that might have been someone's attempt to stand a toilet seat on end. His face was suffused with murderous intentions, and there was a straight razor in his hand. He wore a cloth cap, ragged jeans, and black basketball sneakers.

"Mme. Tussaud's would pay thousands for him," said Mald, standing in the doorway, discreetly ignoring the fact that Reppa had reached instinctively under his jacket for the holster he had given up wearing during the investigation. "If he were not just a common hoodlum. Annabelle named him *Uptown Local* because she saw him mugging somebody on a subway platform in Washington Heights."

The man, on second look, was only plaster, and he was far from perfect. There were signs that his clothes were starting to rot, and a chunk had been gouged out of his jaw, leaving a crater that made havoc out of his larcenous profile. Even so, he wasn't anything you would look forward to meeting, and in any case the straight razor was real.

As Mald was reaching for the light switch, Reppa remembered another thing he ought to see here.

"Do you have any of Andrea Behrman's paintings?"

"Sorry. At the one show I had of her work it all sold out."

"Well, how about some of Jill Wilkes's early things, then?"

"Her early *things*?" repeated Mald with malicious emphasis, as if seeing the inquiry about Andrea had only been a smokescreen. "Yes, there are probably still a few around."

He pondered a moment, then glided down the long line

of paintings. Stopping short, he stooped, grabbed a canvas at the end of the lowermost tier that was turned face inward, and twirled it around.

There, not five feet in front of Reppa, was social commentary in its purest form. Sprawled on a bed, great gouts of blood spurting from between his legs, eyes closed, arms flung out, long hair haloing his ascetic face, was a man. Standing beside the bed, a long kitchen knife held lovingly in her hands like a scepter, was one of the most exotic girls Reppa had ever seen, with a beatific oval face and large blue eyes. The girl, judging from the high school photographs of the two ill-fated roommates that had been reproduced in *Andrea and Elizabeth*, was meant to be Andrea Behrman. There was no model in Reppa's mind for the man, but some face, a blurred image, did fade in and out at the perimeter of his consciousness, as when sometimes, while he was watching TV late at night, his drowsy mind would for the hell of it superimpose a football star of yore on the bland countenance on the screen. So Johnny Carson became for an instant Dick Butkus. Now he saw . . .

No, that was too far out. Even Jill Wilkes, for whom the myth of the male God was like a perpetual chicken bone caught in her throat, would never dare anything so sacrilegious. Or, now, just a minute: Beneath the face in the painting was there not another face flickering at the threshold of the intelligible?

CHAPTER SEVEN

THE FIANCÉ

Leilah looked up from her notebook. "Are you trying to read what I'm writing?"

Reppa froze, for he had been leaning gradually closer to her with just that aim. Apart from jotting down scraps of thought like all great writers, she poured her soul into her notebook twice a day, immediately upon awakening, so as not to lose any interesting dreams she'd had, and again just before going to sleep at night. Mist for the grill, she called it.

Studying the empty and silent TV screen at the foot of the bed, he reflected that this was the first weekday morning in months he'd been home past eight o'clock, and wondered how long did he have to go on watching her scribble in the damn notebook? Inside him a grain of anger rubbed against this woman who was beside him but was not there in any real way. *(Where does she go when her eyes glaze over like that?)* He would never, of course, try to sneak a look at anything she'd written when she wasn't around, though he had to acknowledge this resolve had yet to be seriously tested—when was the last time she had not been around? *New Year's Eve. For about five minutes after I got in from the field, I had the place to myself, and*

170

then she came home. He remembered vividly the picture of her standing in the door, keys still in her hand, himself rising to greet her, but the rest of that night was still, mercifully, a blur.

"What are you doing, Reppa? Don't you have to move your car?"

"It's in a legal spot."

"Aren't you going to work?"

"Not till ten. When I have to meet Halliwell in a restaurant downtown."

"Halliwell?"

"Andrea's ex-fiancé." He waited for her to turn to him with interest. But it didn't happen. "Anyway, I don't have anything to do until then, and I thought . . . "

"You thought what?"

"We could work on a project together." *Christ, when had he started this sort of hedging?* "Two hands are always better than one."

"Mine's already got a project. Move. You're in my light."

He sank back into a wounded silence. Ten minutes later he was still there when the phone rang and a harassed, slightly hoarse female voice at the other end demanded to speak to Parole Officer Reppa.

"You've got him. Who's this?"

"Zippy Dwersky. I just called your office, and they said I could probably catch you at home."

"Hi, Spielman. Nab any absconders lately?"

"What?"

Spielman's female impersonations had usually collapsed by now into a series of lewd grunts, but this one was pretty good.

"Where'd you get that name Zippy? It sounds like an old single-wing scatback."

171

After a long pause Reppa heard himself being told icily: "There's not a whole lot else you can do with Zipporah."

Spielman didn't have the imagination for anything this elaborate. Unless he'd gotten one of the secretaries in the office to call. "Patsy?" he tried. "Veronica?"

"Did I wake you up, Mr. Reppa? Or are you just naturally this churlish?"

"No, no, I've been up."

"You're a difficult man to reach. You're never in your office, and you don't return calls."

"One. I only got one call." *One message. Now, what had it been?*

"Anyway, I have to talk to you. You're doing de Spirit's pardon investigation, and I'm representing him on his new appeal. We're at cross-purposes. We have to have a strategy discussion."

"Cross-purposes?" Legal Aid. She was with Legal Aid. Zipporah Dwersky. Zippy.

"I'll explain when we get together. Lunch today?"

"Oh, now, today . . . "

"You know where our offices are? Fifteen Park Row. I'm on the eighteenth floor. Meet me here around one, and we'll negotiate on a restaurant. Unless you just want to agree right now on Chinese."

He loved Chinese, but he was determined to hold out for anything but until his dying breath. He'd been overrun by women before, but this one stampeded. "Downtown? Hang on here. My office is way up on Fortieth Street—"

"You're on a field investigation, Mr. Reppa. I know the state. You guys can go wherever you want to and just put in for the mileage. Myself, I can only allow an hour today for lunch. If I come uptown, that's twenty-five minutes each way. Which leaves me all of ten minutes to shake

172

hands, wolf down a Big Mac, and plead with you not to blow de Spirit's chances for a new trial."

It made a fair amount of sense, though he had the feeling there was still an underlying premise that had eluded him. "It just so happens that I'm going to be downtown this morning anyway, but I still don't—"

"Terrific. We're on, then, for one o'clock. Sorry for disturbing you at home. But."

Once he realized the dead line he was left listening to wasn't going to tell him but what, he hung up. Who was it? Leilah wanted to know.

"A lawyer named Zippy Dwersky. We're meeting for lunch."

"Hahaha," she said without looking up from her notebook. "No, seriously. Who?"

The Green Turtle was not a place where anyone could form attachments other than to quick service. Of all the restaurants Halliwell could have chosen, and Reppa had passed several in the three blocks he had walked from the subway station, there were none more dismal. In another part of town its plastic green decor and raffish waitresses would have attracted motorcycle gangs. Around the corner from Wall Street it appealed to a different breed of easy rider: a Dobbs Ferry commuter keeping an appointment with a man he couldn't have cared less about impressing.

Reppa had already felt it in the pit of his stomach: an untrammeled impulse to loathe Halliwell, as though all the man had to do to trigger it was glance at him wrong when he entered the restaurant. Over the phone last week Halliwell's "I have nothing to say to a parole officer" had been like a reveille call. Yesterday afternoon his "Don't smooth talk me—you're not talking to one of your cretins from Attica" had fallen on Reppa's ears like a battle cry.

173

As it turned out, Halliwell was wearing tweeds, but there the pretense ended. Halliwell was the kind of man who hid a room of crumbling furniture behind a door of solid gold. He was the palest shade of white, with stoop shoulders and watery blue eyes and a rather moist handshake. Tall, though. Well over six feet, hoisting Reppa's eyes upward with wonder, when Halliwell's bolted away, that a man so full of himself had apparently not yet heard of the miracles of est.

"Let's sit down."

A voice that barked it like a command, accompanied by a timorous glance. Reppa noticed the contradiction immediately.

The waitress lugged over two cups of coffee and left behind the scent of some syrupy perfume.

"Who's paying for this, by the way?" Halliwell inquired.

"The state'll spring if you keep it under a dollar."

"Just asking, just asking," Halliwell said with a condescending smile. "Doesn't come under the heading of an event I'd care to use my company MasterCard for, and I didn't bring any cash with me."

Reppa hiked one leg up, crossed it over the other, and said, "A couple of times when I tried to reach you at the office, your secretary said you were on the floor. The Stock Exchange? What exactly do you do?"

"Make money. More than that I don't really care to discuss, and you don't really need to know."

"Fine." Rankled, Reppa fought not to show it. "Anyway." A smile which felt half-sincere. "This started out to be a fairly straightforward investigation. On one level it still is, but I'll tell you in advance that I'm going to ask you some fairly direct questions about your involvement in the Behrman-Moffett case. Why am I telling you this? Because you, having a law degree, will know I'm going

174

out on a limb. Also that you don't have to answer anything you don't want to. Hopefully you won't exercise that right too often, because, as I said yesterday on the phone, it looks as if de Spirit will push for a new trial if his pardon falls through and—"

"And," Halliwell broke in with a snort, "as you so subtly implied yesterday, if I don't answer your questions, you'll see to it that his lawyer calls on me to testify."

Reppa made a sound of his own, neither assent nor objection. "I can't speak for her. That would be entirely her decision. All I know is that I'm scheduled to speak to her later on—"

"You know, don't you, that if you reveal anything to her of our discussion here this morning, it'll be a violation of the law."

"Really?" Reppa smiled. "Which one?"

"As a law officer, you're not permitted to—"

Reppa waved a hand. "There's something here you're apparently not aware of. A parole officer doesn't function as a *law* officer. He's a kind of hybrid. Part peace officer, part social worker, part about a dozen other things. Not the least of which, in my case anyway, is an ex-football coach."

"Fascinating. Are you going to quote Rockne?"

"Not Rockne." His smile broadened. "Reppa. You see, being hybrids, parole officers don't really have anyone looking too closely over their shoulders. Or anybody special looking out for them. The advantage is nobody cares how I go about doing this investigation so long as there isn't too much flak from the people I interview—"

"In summary," Halliwell cut in with a sour smile, "you see yourself as a vigilante."

"Maverick," Reppa said quietly. "I'd leave it at maverick."

175

For a moment Halliwell's eyes brushed his. "What are you hoping to turn up?"

"The real Behrman-Moffett killer. Because the deeper I get into this, the more convinced I become that Danny de Spirit is innocent."

He had been watching the damp eyes closely when he spoke, but to his disappointment they did not so much as blink.

"Good for you," Halliwell said, looking down. "That makes two of us."

"How long have you felt that way?"

Halliwell dallied with the handle of his coffee cup. "If I could, believe me, I would have done something long ago on my own. Never felt the same way about a woman again. Not even my wife. Any of my wives . . ."

"How many have there been?"

There was the briefest of pauses before the broker said, "Should have been just one. No question. Each of us has only one great love. Andrea was mine."

"Yet you broke your engagement to her. Why?"

"Couldn't bear it anymore." Halliwell shook his head. "Wanted just to put it down to youthful promiscuity, but it wasn't that. Something very complex. Never really understood. Tried to stick it out with her, but it finally got to be too much."

How easily sympathy could be provoked, Reppa realized, once the favorite pronoun was abandoned. He was certain Halliwell realized this, too. Dubious, he said, "There must have been some part of her that wanted to settle down. Otherwise, why did she agree to marry you?"

"Marriage? No, the engagement was only a sop to her mother. Girl living in her own apartment, Mama could accept it if there was a male protector close to the scene. Later our engagement became a blind. A way of account-

176

ing to her roommates for all her nights away from home. Supposedly, they were to think, she was with me. Many nights she was, but then . . ." Halliwell lowered his head and squeezed his little finger into the handle of the coffee cup before continuing. "Finally had no choice. Had to call her on it. Just what she was waiting for. Her mother was dead now, so there was no more need to keep up the show. It was the end between us."

The beginning, back in Halliwell's senior year in college, proved nearly as easy for Reppa to extract. The broker's story was that Andrea had been invited up to Cambridge for a winter weekend by his roommate, who had met her in New York over Christmas vacation. On Friday the roommate came down with the flu, leaving her without an escort. Would Halliwell . . . as a favor? At first he expected from her beauty that she'd be snobbish and aloof, but instead she was lively, full of laughs and puns, and . . . well, quite frankly, amenable. Amazed at his success with her, Halliwell presumed she must be infatuated with him. But when he wrote to her after she returned to New York, she didn't respond. He wrote again. Then called her home. Got her mother, who summoned her to the phone. But when he identified himself, she hung up immediately. Confused, feeling enormously shot down, he worked at putting her out of his mind.

But he never did, entirely. Three years later he finished law school and decided, after weighing various offers, to leave Boston and take a position in a New York firm. Moved into an apartment on East Sixty-ninth Street and, not knowing anyone, began haunting the singles bars in the neighborhood. And one night, in one of them, there she was. Get her out of this zoo, she said, grabbing his arm almost the moment she saw him, as if they were old cronies. Later he grew to understand that she'd occasionally used singles bars to pick up men, but that night he was too caught up with seeing her again to wonder why she'd been in one. They went to his apartment, where she told him, in the intervals between atoning for their three lost years, that she'd just finished school and taken an apartment with two other women and a job on a magazine. But what she really wanted to do was get a loft and paint all day. Live like her aunt, the famous sculptor. Annabelle. What? He'd never *heard* of her?

Halliwell, aware he'd lost vital points, saw he had to do something extraordinary to redeem himself. There was only one thing he wanted to do right then anyway. So he did it.

To his joy and amazement she accepted his proposal, and for a long while he didn't object when she stalled over setting an actual date and avoided introducing him to her aunt or her stepfather or even her roommates. Of course he understood what was going on. Andrea was using him—he was her nice Harvard boy she could bring home to Mother. It disturbed him, sure, but not for long—because the tables turned a bit when he took a job with one of the brokerage houses his law firm represented. It not only meant more money, but it also put him in with a new crowd of people, many of them young and attractive. When Andrea saw his social circle had expanded, she began to introduce him to more of her own friends, starting with her roommates. Jill, a real man-eater, and Elizabeth. Sad case, was his initial reaction, but she kind of grew on him after a while. And one night, around the same time, he even got to meet Annabelle at one of her openings. A really weird woman. And those spooky statues of hers—if they were art and she was a typical artist, he didn't want Andrea to have any part of it.

But she wasn't overly fond of his family either. His

father in particular. *A man on a riderless horse* was her phrase for him, just dismissing the fact that he was one of the top lawyers in the city. Oh, hadn't he mentioned that? The old man was a partner in the firm that had originally hired him.

Andrea's father? Well, she never talked much about him, not her real one. Down South somewhere; oh, right, Reppa, right—Kentucky. Louisville. She was born there after her father'd died. Soldier killed during the Second World War, she'd said. And as for her stepfather, she'd maintained he and her mother had this asexual thing, like two neuters. Being around Adelaide, he had to think Andrea was putting him on. The woman was just too attractive for any man to let her pot sit cold on a back burner. But when, finally, he got to meet Stanley Behrman, he understood at once why Andrea had tried to keep her stepfather in the closet. Shame and embarrassment. Why, the man looked like . . . Rumpelstiltskin? Right, Reppa. Good. Exactly. In any event, the bargain Adelaide Behrman had made couldn't have been anything but one of those old-fashioned marriages of convenience. When he thought of her now, she began to seem to him, as she must have seemed all along to Andrea, something of a sellout. A woman who'd sacrificed her own life so her daughter would have opportunities she hadn't had. It made sense now, all of it did. By becoming engaged to him Andrea had fulfilled her mother's expectations for her. At the same time she couldn't help but see everyone who did things for money in the same light as she saw her mother's marriage.

As he and Andrea got to know each other more deeply, he tried to find ways to share his insights with her. With some of them she agreed. When he got on the subject of Behrman, though, he met with a shock. Stanley hadn't been kept in the closet out of shame and embarrassment. On the contrary, he, Jeff Halliwell, had been the one kept in the closet—until she'd felt safe that Stanley would approve of *him*! Stanley was shrewd, not only in business but about people, too. Incredibly shrewd. And she ought to make it very clear that when she'd called him a neuter, it was only with respect to her mother.

Since they were making things very clear, what exactly did *that* mean, he'd demanded to know. Just that Stanley was a deceptively sexy man, that was what. Deceptively sexy with whom? Well, she hoped he didn't think with *her*, Andrea had said, but with a look that would not quite meet his.

It was not a conversation that Halliwell could bear to pursue at that moment, and there'd never come another. Less than a week later Andrea's roommates had had a surprise birthday party for her—family and close friends—and afterward she'd snuck off with somebody and spent the night with him. Next day she tried to deny it, claiming she'd just wanted to be by herself awhile, and since Halliwell had been gone when she got back, she went off to bed. Yes, her *own* bed. Impossible, he said. She ought to have checked with her roommates before concocting that story. Elizabeth Moffett had called him early the next morning, almost hysterical, needing to talk to her, obviously thinking she was at his place. Now, was it possible that Elizabeth, sleeping in the same room, wouldn't have noticed Andrea if she had been in her *own* bed?

It was an issue that had arisen more than once before, and each time Andrea had devised a wild story that was impossible to check, involving gypsy cab drivers who didn't speak English and whisked her off mistakenly to New Jersey or friends on bad acid trips she couldn't just go off and leave. The story she told him now was that Jill had dragged her to a party in SoHo to meet Frank Stella, and she had wound up on the Staten Island ferry, riding it back and forth until dawn in order to think.

"Who was Stella?" Reppa would always wonder whether he had just chosen a convenient moment to interrupt or there had already been an inner voice telling him not to let Halliwell slip past that surprise party. None of this was in *Andrea and Elizabeth*, he remarked to himself, watching Halliwell gaze down into his as yet untouched cup of coffee. But then he remembered that the police must have been over all this with Halliwell twelve years ago. So how important could it be?

"A painter Andrea admired. I think it was Stella. Some woman's name anyway. Hard to remember now, except that her story was plausible. Which told me at once that it probably wasn't true."

"Why?"

"Andrea was one of those women who are constitutionally incapable of telling a straight story. She'd save her most outrageous lies to embellish the most trivial incidents. Say she was late somewhere because her alarm didn't go off—she'd claim she was nearly mugged on the way. But if she told you she was late because her alarm didn't go off, watch out. Her night in SoHo and the ferry ride was that kind of excuse. Too tame."

"Where do you think she really went?"

Halliwell looked around as if he sought his way out of a corner into which he had painted himself. "It depends," he relented at last, "on whether she left the party alone or with the Spanish Flycaster."

"The what?"

"The guy who owned the art gallery where her aunt used to exhibit."

"Carlo Mald?" Reppa squinted one eye. "It was a

surprise party, you said. Family and close friends. What was he doing there?''

"My question, too. He stood out like Hugh Hefner at a Wellesley reunion. But so, in her own way, did Annabelle. My idea was he'd been invited just to balance her off. As it was, a lot of people were made uncomfortable by them. Especially Elizabeth Moffett. She'd never met Mald before. Or Annabelle either, for that matter. She was so nervous around them at first that she couldn't stay in the same room. Eventually she got over it a little, with Annabelle at least. The two of them even talked awhile, off in a corner. But not for long, because Mald walked past where they were sitting and apparently said something to Elizabeth. Or it might just been being in his presence. Whatever, she dropped her drink. It shattered on the floor, and she got so flustered she ran out of the room.'' Halliwell grimaced sardonically. "A real Don Juan. But Andrea couldn't get enough of him. Neither could Jill Wilkerson. They both fawned over him all evening.''

"Fawned?'' Reppa could not imagine Jill Wilkes ever having *fawned* over anyone.

"Oh, you know. 'Carlo, what do you think of so-and-so's work? Do you really think Warhol will last?' Jill I could understand. She was hung up on making it at all costs. The party had been largely her idea, probably an excuse, when you get right down to it, for luring Annabelle and Mald there. But it backfired. Annabelle ignored her completely. And every time she cornered Mald, Andrea hauled him off to meet somebody or start another of her deep philosophical discourses about art. It was sickening to watch. Not until later did I realize it might have been an act.''

"For what purpose?''

"Well . . .'' Halliwell donned his painted-into-a-corner

182

look again. "So that when she snuck off, I'd be led to think it was to be with Mald."

"Didn't anyone see her leave?"

"Not actually. Around midnight I was in the kitchen talking to Stanley Behrman. He didn't like the sudden schmooziness between Mald and Andrea either. When we returned to the party, Andrea was gone, and so was Mald. I hung around awhile in the hope she'd come back, then took a cab across town with Behrman"—Halliwell paused to shoot him a sideways look—"who by that point seemed in an even greater hurry to leave than I was. Went home and tried to sleep, but all I could think of, lying there, was how closely she'd clung to Mald at the party. What if the two of them—? Immediately all sorts of hideous pictures began rushing at me there in the dark. Never did fall asleep. By the time Elizabeth called, I was so knotted up I couldn't talk to her. Having it positively confirmed that Andrea hadn't been home all night was like the final blow. Because if she'd been with Mald . . ."

The broker stopped and pulled a tormented face.

"But you implied you later decided she wasn't."

"Later, yes. But at the time it still hadn't occurred to me that . . ." Halliwell paused again, this time with another darting glance across the table.

Reppa's first impulse was to stand mute: the bait was being dangled in front of him; why should he plunge after it? "That what?"

"Nothing," Halliwell said stiffly. "Anyway . . . the next evening Andrea and I had it out over where she'd gone. 'Mald?' She laughed. 'I may be pretty liberated, but I do draw the line at being second to my mother with any man.' I hadn't known Adelaide had been having an affair before she died—much less with someone like Mald. I began to feel I'd been something of a fool in my view of

183

her. Andrea's laughter gave me the same feeling. I was meant to believe she'd gone off with Mald, and now I wasn't meant to believe her denials. One of her tricks when she lied was to laugh mockingly. I'd called her on it so often that she'd know I'd think she was lying if she tried it again. Instead I said, 'Okay, I believe you, you weren't with Mald. Now for the last time, really, where were you last night?' And she said . . .'' Here Halliwell hesitated for a long moment but without an accompanying glance at Reppa. ''Well, actually, she stopped talking altogether after that,'' he concluded softly.

''So you never really found out where she went after she left the party.''

''No . . . not for sure.''

''When you said Behrman suddenly seemed in a hurry to leave the party, does that mean you think he had somewhere special to go?''

Halliwell nodded with poorly feigned reluctance, hanging the bait out again.

''Where do you think he went?''

''Oh, probably to take care of a few loose pelts.''

The sarcasm fell so heavily that Reppa could no longer ignore the obvious.

''Tell me, did you ever think . . . ?''

''Yes?''

''That Andrea could be involved somehow with her stepfather?''

Halliwell's hands were twisting together.

''Impossible . . . that fat little . . . totally impossible.''

''Did you ever ask her?''

''Couldn't,'' Halliwell interrupted tensely. He closed his eyes and shook his head violently, as if to rid it of all memories. ''I just know that after that party for the first time in my life I started having . . . trouble. Andrea made her stupid jokes about how Jack is all work. Which made it even worse. Would almost have believed there was something physically wrong with me if it hadn't been so clear the trouble was . . . well, not in the lower deck but upstairs.''

Halliwell laughed nervously and hung his head, a mop of blond hair falling forward to hide his eyes. Watching him, Reppa was convinced he had never met a man who took such delight in portraying himself as a victim, unless it was Behrman. He'd also, except for Behrman, never met a man whose candor was less refreshing.

"How long did this trouble, as you call it, last?''

"Weeks. And the strange thing was it didn't seem to bother Andrea in the least. But then I realized—there was only one possible explanation for her being so blasé. She was getting all she wanted somewhere else. Now that I really *did* confront her about." Halliwell threw his head back suddenly, the hair flinging back into place and the eyes bolting open to stare vacantly. "And this time when she laughed at me . . .''

Reppa waited. Hands clenched. Intently watching the blank blue eyes begin to water. Face turning wretchedly pale. Mouth quivering to get it out.

"I didn't *lie* there and *take* it. I dragged her out of my bed and pitched her right straight out in the hall. Naked. Locked the door and shouted that I wasn't going to let her back in until she told the truth. The whole truth. And do you know what she did?''

Reppa glanced at the waitress, who was no less interested than he and pretending to freshen their coffee cups.

"Got on the elevator, went downstairs, hopped in a cab like Lady Godiva, and rode off!''

The waitress crept away, nodding. Reppa tried to remember there was another thread he'd been following, but

185

for the moment this one had him by the proverbial fruit of the loom. "Where did she go?"

"No idea. Kept calling her place all night until her roommates got angry and took the phone off the hook. At one point I even considered calling the police."

"Why didn't you?"

Something in Halliwell's eyes became wary. "They wouldn't have done anything anyway. Finally I just waited until morning and then called her place again. The phone was back on the hook. This time she answered. But when she heard my voice, she hung up. It was just like college all over again. Later that day I got a telegram from her, saying she wanted her freedom. By freedom I took her to mean—"

Reppa cut in sharply, returning to his original thread, "When did this Lady Godiva incident happen?"

"A couple of weeks before she was murdered. Why?"

"I'm just trying to put all this into some kind of order. When was the party for Andrea?"

"March seventh. I remember because it fell right on her actual birthday. My job was to take her out to dinner and then get her over to her place around nine. Never forget the look on her face when that door opened . . ." Halliwell sat back as if overwhelmed by the memory and then came quickly to a frown. "The fact still remains that she ruined the whole evening by sneaking off to spend the night with someone else."

"How do you know she didn't leave to get *away* from someone?"

"Who?"

"I don't know. I'm just wondering if something didn't happen at the party. Something that upset her so much she had to get out of there."

"Like what? I was there. I didn't see anything."

"How do you know *she* didn't?"

"Because *I* didn't."

"Maybe you weren't looking at things in the same—"

Reppa stopped suddenly, seeing Halliwell's pupils dilate, the veins spring out in his forehead.

"I *was* looking! I *saw*! I saw *everything*! And I knew Andrea! I *knew* when she was lying, and she *lied* about that night! It was an awful goddamn *night*!"

"Easy," Reppa said, holding up both hands, palms out. "I agree with you. But I think something important happened that night. All I'm asking you—"

"I've told you everything I know," Halliwell muttered sullenly, lapsing back in his chair. "Now, if you'll excuse me, I've got to be getting back to my office."

He started to rise. There was a brief hesitation, and then his eyes ranged Reppa's way glancingly. Both men poised themselves there, watching each other for a moment. Finally, Halliwell sat down again. "Sorry. But you have to understand. I loved that woman." He spoke quite softly.

The transition from rage to a kind of burned-out calm, all in the space of a few seconds, stunned Reppa. What goes here? he thought, and then: Why is he staying?

"When Elizabeth Moffett called you the morning after the party, what did she want to talk to Andrea about?"

"She didn't say."

"But didn't you ask? You said she sounded almost hysterical."

The broker looked around the restaurant, apparently ignoring Reppa's question. "All I remember is my first instinct when she told me Andrea hadn't come home that night. Should've followed it." Halliwell breathed deeply. "It might all never have happened if I had," he almost whispered.

"What was your instinct?"

187

"To hire somebody. A private detective or something. Then, when she told me she wanted her freedom, I nearly did. . . ."

"What stopped you?"

"The fact that she didn't return my ring. It meant . . :" Halliwell looked down and discovered he had begun stirring his coffee with his finger. Wiping it on a napkin, he sighed heavily and murmured, "We were still, technically anyway, engaged. So I decided just to let her have her freedom, knowing deep down that it was really all over . . . but still having that one faint . . . hope."

Reppa waited. He saw Halliwell stare straight ahead at nothing for several moments and then pale visibly and resume stirring his coffee, very agitatedly, with two fingers.

"When the police found my ring in her jewelry box, the first thing they did was suspect me. Jilted lover, all that."

Not unnatural, Reppa thought. But he continued to sit silently.

"They hounded me," Halliwell went on, looking at him in challenging incredulity, "because I wasn't in my office the morning it happened. No alibi, they said. Hell, I had the best alibi in the world. I was where every American with an ounce of God in him was that morning—in church praying for Bobby Kennedy. Bastards ridiculed me because I didn't have any witnesses. Man, at a moment like that who notices who's kneeling beside him?"

Since Reppa could recall having passed that same morning in a shocked daze, he wasn't able to disagree. Nor probably, when all was said and done, had the cops on the case been able to. But before the moment could sink into a wake for shattered dreams, he came out of his silence to get in a word for hard, cold reality.

"Did you ever take a lie detector test?"

For a moment Halliwell's fingers ceased their stirring,

and a vein jumped in his eyelid. "Wasn't necessary. Told the police everything. Completely open with them. Must've gone over my whole history with Andrea, from college to the day of the murders, twenty different times from twenty different angles."

Reppa held his gaze for a moment with some effort.

"But surely somebody at some point must have asked you to take one."

"As a matter of form," Halliwell acknowledged petulantly. "And I refused, of course. Worthless instrument. Totally unreliable. Every law school now advises you not to let your client be subjected to it. You, a parole officer, should know that."

He turned in his chair, presenting one angular tweed shoulder to Reppa.

"One final question."

"Oh, no!"

Reppa had seen it coming, but he was still startled when Halliwell's hand jerked suddenly and knocked his coffee cup into his own lap. The waitress materialized instantly with a handful of napkins. "Can I help?"

She stood there limp-fingered as Halliwell reeled into the rest room.

"Looking for a back window?" Reppa said, following him in.

"Which is better? Cold water or hot?"

"Try cold."

"Coffee's a bitch to get out. What do you mean, a back window? I don't have anything to hide. If I did, would I have come here today of my own free will?"

Reppa decided it was wise to let this pass as a rhetorical question.

"My lawyer said I was making a mistake talking to you.

Goes to show, I should have known better than to try to do the Christian thing."

"Can I ask my question now?"

Halliwell glanced quickly at him. "I know your question. Did I kill Andrea? And it infuriates me that a parole officer thinks he has the license to ask me that. Where do you come off, Reppa? The cops did all this twelve years ago. And did it a thousand times better."

"And wound up putting a kid in the can we both believe is innocent."

"Let him out then." Halliwell began mopping himself with paper towels, rapidly, flushed with impatience. "Put it in your report that I'm all for his being released."

"I will." Reppa's tone remained mild, but his heart pounded. "First, though, my question. Nothing so final as whether you killed Andrea. I'll settle for knowing if you ever beat her."

The flush had faded in an instant, and the soft white face was before him again. Halliwell's quivering lips could not speak the "Who said . . . ?" which Reppa saw rather than heard.

"Someone who saw marks on her in places even her best friends wouldn't customarily have occasion to look."

"Obviously someone you've spoken to on your investigation." Halliwell recovered himself by the supreme effort of closing his eyes. Then, opening them and waving an index finger: "I have a right to know who it was."

"Unfortunately not the police. If they'd been told what I was told, those twenty different angles they came at you from would have been two hundred and twenty."

"But they weren't told, and that means that whoever laid that story on you must feel safe from the hornet's nest he would have stirred up with himself in the center if he'd spoken up twelve years ago."

Reppa nodded, conceding the point. "Shall we continue our discussion in a more congenial atmosphere?"

"There's nothing to continue," Halliwell said frostily. "I was morally bound to talk to you. I'm not bound to make you my father confessor."

The statement was unarguable. It took Reppa a moment to realize that it was also somewhat revealing.

"You're sticking with the story that you told me today and the police twelve years ago? It may be a problem for you if de Spirit gets a new trial and his lawyer decides to call on you to testify."

"About what?" Halliwell's voice assumed more confidence. "An allegation? Who's going to make it? You? Hearsay. No judge will even allow you to open your mouth in his courtroom."

"You're forgetting that the allegation has a source other than me."

"Who'll repeat it in court? I doubt anybody would. Which reminds me, Reppa. You said that if I cooperated with you, there'd be no reason to say anything about me to de Spirit's lawyer."

"Did I? When?"

"Well, you at least implied it."

"True."

Halliwell straightened up and moved toward the urinal. His voice was suddenly brusque and forceful. "We're square, then. I've told you everything I know that's pertinent to your investigation. I want your solemn oath now that you'll live up to your part."

It was out now. The reason the broker had not dared leave prematurely.

"You have it. At least as far as de Spirit's lawyer is concerned."

"What do you mean?" Halliwell said, a wary note returning to his voice.

"You gave me what I need for my investigation. But I've been given some information about you that I can't ignore."

Halliwell stepped back, zipper gaping.

"You're playing loose, Reppa. Fast and loose. I warn you . . ."

The broker's mouth hung open, lips stiff and nearly white, and his eyes began blinking rapidly.

Startled by his vehemence, Reppa watched him stalk abruptly from the rest room.

CHAPTER EIGHT

ZIPPY

For an instant when he first saw her, for the blinking of an eye, Reppa felt all the loose fragments of himself come together like pieces of glass in a kaleidoscope.

It may have been the dress, he later told himself. The pale blue dress with ruffled sleeves, when he had been prepared for a severely tailored suit. Or it may have been the dark-blue eyes, which seemed to penetrate all the way through his own at some moments, and at others seemed so far away and abstracted. Or the face, whose features were so delicate and finely etched and whose skin had the kind of transparency that colors at the slightest provocation. Or the black hair, thick and lustrous, parted in the middle. Or the body, its precise curves and definitions undefined because the dress fit so loosely, but undeniably strong and firm judging by the assured angle at which the shoulders were set, the head was cocked—and especially by the slim but dizzyingly warm hand that gripped his and shook it just a fraction longer than necessary.

"Hong Wah, okay?" He could not associate the voice with the woman in front of him. There was simply no way someone who transported him to Victorian England could have spoken those syllables from twentieth-century New York.

"Fine. Sure. Wherever."

On the elevator ride down he observed she had a mole on her right earlobe. Walking to Chinatown, she commented on how high the sky was today but looked blank when he said it was a perfect punter's sky. In front of the restaurant she said, "The reason I suggested this is it's Mandarin. All that hot Szechuan gives me gas." When they were seated, she announced that she didn't subscribe to the traditional practice in Chinese restaurants of ordering two dishes they both agreed on and then sharing them. Her dish would be hers, and his would be his—though she had no objection to splitting the check straight down the middle even if his cost a little more.

It was good that he had discovered these enormous imperfections, because now he could revert to his pledge to himself that his Ohio tenderfoot would not be trampled by her roughshod Manhattan herd. Already she was no longer anything spectacular. She was still a light year away, though, from his preconceived picture of Zippy Dwersky.

The talk meandered for a long while. Nothing of an innocent man rotting away in an upstate prison. Just the Arab-Israeli conflict juxtaposed to the muddle in Ireland, the latest near disaster at a nuclear plant, her dissatisfaction with Koch, the eternal war between New York City and the rest of the state over virtually every present-day survival issue.

"Just supposing Norman Mailer had been elected mayor back in 1969 and delivered on his campaign promise to make the city the fifty-first state. No comment on what Mailer would have been like as a mayor in other respects, but say he'd managed to do that one thing. Would it have changed the whole course of the last decade? Or is it just that we in New York have a superinflated opinion of the size of the niche we occupy in relation to the rest of the world?''

Reppa stared at her, aware by now that she wasn't meandering but had taken him down the old garden path so she could examine the color and trim of his political foliage.

''Well, what's your view?''

''Of the struggle between the city and Albany? We have much the same thing in Ohio between Cleveland and Columbus.''

''Is that where you're from?''

''Cleveland, Ohio State, ten years of coaching high school football, two with a couple of off-brand pro teams.'' He looked directly at her: *and you?*

''How long have you been a parole officer?''

''Three years. How long have you been with Legal Aid?''

''About the same. Married?''

''I was. Divorced now.''

''I am, too,'' she said, as if excusing him.

''Kids?''

One shoulder under the blue dress was raised slightly, perhaps in a negative shrug, perhaps in a signal that this had gone far enough.

''Like it? Being a parole officer, I mean.''

''Sometimes. When I'm not just checking pay stubs and arms.''

''Lots of junkies on your case load?''

''My share.''

''Drugs are our biggest problem, too,'' Zippy said solemnly. ''Everything's always so murky. The undercover narc who makes the buy tells one story. My client tells another, claiming he was just there as an observer. The money used to make the buy is marked, but somehow

195

all but a dollar of it has disappeared. Or else it's this song. My client is picked up for loitering, and when his pockets are emptied, several glassine envelopes tumble out. His story: They were planted on him. Their story: He's been under surveillance for a long time as a major drug dealer. Whom do you believe?''

Here we go, Reppa thought. With the nod of an actor picking up his cue, he said, ''I had an instance like that just the other day. Kid named Jimmy Wallace.''

He looked at her pointedly. She returned his gaze blankly. ''And? What did you do?''

''Nothing yet. It's still in limbo. Under investigation.''

''There, you see—our jobs are very similar. A shadowy world out there on the street, and if you're like me, it starts to wear you down.''

''Very shadowy,'' he agreed and waited for the inevitable: ''Jimmy Wallace, did you say? Isn't he . . . ?''

But she'd resumed eating, her attention seemingly bent only on getting this grain of rice and that strip of broccoli between her chopsticks. Could it be that he had not been given a cue? That his senses were merely frayed and hyperactive after the long week of listening to and observing people whose every word and gesture had to be examined for a hidden signal? *Relax*, he told himself. But he heard his voice say a little too stiffly: ''What did you mean on the phone when you said we were at cross-purposes?''

''Oh''—she looked up, startled—''I'd thought we wouldn't talk until we finished eating.''

''Didn't you say you only had an hour for lunch?''

''Ordinarily. But I—after I spoke to you this morning, I rearranged things a little.''

Her voice seemed artificially casual, somewhat tense, but her laugh sounded genuine enough.

''Then I have an idea.'' He waited until she touched

196

eyes with him briefly. "Let's walk up to Little Italy and get a *cremolato*."

"Your turf?"

Her laugh again. It stirred him to make an odd statement. "Not really. I live on the Lower East Side."

"Where?" she said teasingly. "Avenue B?"

"Not quite that far east. Off Second Avenue. Ninth Street."

"The Ukranian section. Reppa—what sort of name is it?"

"A mixture of several Eastern European tribes. What about Dwersky?"

"Oh—you could say it's a *mixture*, too."

Perhaps not so odd a statement after all. For her smile, now that he'd been given his first glimpse of it, completed the revival of interest her laugh had begun. Reppa found sudden solace in having kept his apartment. Even if he'd never take a goat there in its present condition, it was a relief not to have to come right out with it that he was living with someone. Of course, he'd acknowledge Leilah's place in his life if the question arose, but for now he could just return once more to the days of being Reppa, resident of the Lower East Side, and didn't that promote a sense of ease and freedom all by itself? Didn't it, though?

All she'd meant by cross-purposes, Zippy explained, as they were moving, *cremolatos* in hand, unbeknownst to her toward another of Reppa's ideas, an elementary school playground where there were sometimes terrific paddleball games in the afternoon, was that de Spirit was 100-percent sure of getting a new trial if the governor didn't come through with a pardon first. Thus, from her standpoint, Reppa's investigation represented a danger. If he came out strongly in favor of a pardon and the governor went along

197

with his recommendation, the corrupt mechanism that had sent an innocent man to prison would escape unscathed. Also it was vital, she felt, that de Spirit be totally vindicated. A pardon wouldn't accomplish that because there'd still be a lingering public suspicion that he was really guilty and that the governor had succumbed to some clandestine political pressure to release him. De Spirit basically agreed with her. She hadn't had a chance to talk personally with him yet, but his letters to her confirmed he wanted a new trial above everything else.

How had she heard about the pardon investigation?

A memo from Albany. But while they were on the subject of channels of communication, she was surprised he hadn't known that de Spirit had an appeal for a new trial pending.

They'd heard rumors, Reppa said.

Well, didn't it behoove him to explore the rumors?

How? he defended. Working for parole, you were given your corner of the puzzle to do. Other agencies had theirs. Most of the time you never got to see the total picture even after it was all assembled.

She sympathized. The whole criminal justice system was the same way.

Legal Aid included?

Not quite as bad, she hoped.

It was at that juncture that Reppa, still bristling from the criticism implied in her *behoove,* said, Oh, no? How was it, then, that she'd never heard of Jimmy Wallace? When she said, "The client you were talking about before?" he said with a sense of triumph, "A client it might *behoove* us both to talk about."

She stopped short, turned to him, awaiting an explanation. With a sense, now that his pride was assuaged, of what a sucker he still might be, he gave it.

"I was wondering if you had a personal reason for taking on this investigation."

"What about you? How did you come to be assigned the appeal?"

"By asking for it." She smiled fleetingly. "Others wanted it, too, of course. It's an interesting case. Mildly put. I got it because I had something they didn't."

"Seniority?"

"Sex. De Spirit specifically requested a woman be assigned to represent him."

"Why?"

She read his frown and shrugged. "If you believe his letters, because he's read about Caryl Chessman and seen the obvious parallels to his own case. Continued protestations of innocence, years of appealing on his own behalf unsuccessfully—and finally, when all else failed, Chessman grudgingly allowed a young woman to represent him, and she did a fantastic job."

"But also ultimately failed. Unless de Spirit has a death wish, he can't be too pleased by the obvious parallels. Since Chessman was executed."

"It can't happen to de Spirit. The worst he could get if he's retried is the same sentence."

"Life," Reppa said flatly.

"But there's no way he can lose this time. The state may not even want to go through with the time and expense of an actual trial. Just the formalities, plea of innocence entered and accepted."

"Is that why the cops are going to all the trouble of getting Wallace to perjure himself?"

"You said it yourself. Everyone in the system only gets to see their piece of the puzzle. Often the police will do that, work months on a case. And then the DA will pull the rug out from under them when it gets to trial stage."

"You seem very confident. Why?"

She shrugged, smiled, and started walking again, rapidly, without waiting for him.

"Sit in the sun?" he asked after they'd gone some additional distance, putting them near the benches outside the school playground. To his disappointment there was no one he knew playing paddleball. No one to say, "Hey, Reppa, how's your game? Still whipping everybody's ass?" All the same his chagrin was only momentary, a small twinge, for he had decided, once more and finally, that there was nothing all that extraordinary about this woman.

He saw her look at her watch, heard her remark that the school would be letting its horde out at three o'clock. Shouldn't they go someplace more peaceful? A glance at his own wrist told him it was only two twenty, so by her measurements they must still have a fair amount of talking to do. His own impulse, on reminding himself that his original aim with her was to be whenever possible contrary, was to hurry things along. Still, he could spare a few moments to watch a cloud slide across the sky from down below Canal Street, over the block where they stood, and past the sun. A gust of wind assailed the back of her hair. It became his excuse, which soon disappeared, for offering his shoulder when her head went in search of a shield.

Later, and this also was over too quickly, her hand sought his arm when she stumbled over a curb. And then they were somewhere on Mercer Street, a corner with a bar they could both agree looked quiet enough. No jukebox, a lone man eating a cheese sandwich in an otherwise empty back room. Deeply scarred table. Rickety chairs. Pools of sunlight on the bare wood floor.

"Where's your case load?"

He glanced at her. He'd hoped for a few minutes of silence, of communication between himself and the place,

200

while he thought through what had brought them here when he had intended to walk her back down to her office. "Central Harlem."

"By choice?"

"Seniority. The lack of it."

"So you'd like to string this investigation out as long as possible."

"There's a deadline." He felt insulted; resentful. "Four more days. Unless I ask for an extension."

"Will you?"

"There's no real reason to. I know what I'm going to recommend."

Zippy drew back. "A pardon?"

"The whole case smells. Half the people I've spoken to openly admitted they thought de Spirit was innocent."

"Is that what you want?" Zippy leaned forward until her face was close, and he saw twin spots of color appear above each of her high, delicate cheekbones. "Is that *all* you want?"

Reppa could give no answer but the wisp of a shrug.

"Say the pardon does come through. Jimmy Wallace never has to take the stand and perjure himself. Will that be enough for you?"

He felt her eyes trying to pull in his.

"Will it, Frank?"

His half-empty glass of beer awaited him when he looked down.

The "I don't know" he heard himself murmur had been framed, he was aware, in response to more than one question.

"I'm not asking what you've learned while making your investigation. It's privileged information, and some of the information I have I'm not free to share either. But there is one thing we have in common, unless I'm very wrong about you. And I don't think I am, any more than you're wrong about me. We've both gotten a very strong sense of each other.''

Reppa continued to look down at his glass. ''In what way?''

''But don't you know, Frank? Don't you know yet what we both feel? Two girls were brutally murdered, and the real killer got away with it.''

Suddenly Zippy seemed very distant, and the walls of the bar receded. Reppa felt himself suspended in the wide air, and he heard something like fear in his voice. ''But it's just a feeling.''

''For me,'' Zippy said softly, ''it's more than that.''

''But how do you know? How can you be so sure de Spirit is innocent?''

''You are, too,'' she said very slowly. ''You know it's not enough just seeing that he's pardoned.''

''True.'' He swallowed. ''It wouldn't be.''

''You see why, don't you, Frank? The police would say the pardon was only a political ploy, and most of the public would feel the same way. Because it's been too long since the crime occurred. All anyone will remember now is that two grisly murders were committed, and a man with a long criminal record was convicted of them and sent to prison. At best pardoning de Spirit will be taken as a statement that he was convicted improperly. It won't be a declaration of his innocence. Only a new trial can accomplish that.''

''Even if de Spirit were exonerated, what guarantee is there that the case . . . ?''

''Would be reopened?''

Reppa nodded silently.

''None, finally. No guarantee. Unless.''

"Unless what?" he asked, though he saw what her answer would be. Absolutely.

"De Spirit's new trial draws so much attention to the case again that the police won't be able to let it die."

"How can it?"

"I'm not sure. All I have at the moment are ideas. Please don't ask what they are, because I'm not at liberty now to tell you," she finished in an earnest tone. But her look said: *Soon, let's hope. Soon* . . .

It was difficult not to surrender then and there to her plea that they become conspirators. Difficult but still not impossible. Reppa wet his lips and shifted the beer glass in front of him. "You're not thinking, are you, of asking me to slant the report I'll be doing when I finish the investigation? Slant it in such a way that the governor will refuse to grant de Spirit a pardon?"

Her head shook emphatically. "No, Frank. Even if your report carried that much weight—which, of course, it won't—I'd never ask you to change a word of it."

"Good. Because I wouldn't. But what do you mean, my report won't carry that much weight?"

"Don't you realize there's no way in the world the governor would ever grant a pardon in a case like this unless the real murderer made a deathbed confession? Even then there'd have to be corroborative evidence. No, all the governor is doing is pressuring the State Supreme Court to act quickly and favorably on de Spirit's latest appeal. The pardon possibility is like an ax being held over their heads. In this instance, literally an ax."

"Literally—what do you mean?"

"Does the name Robert Gooden mean anything to you?"

"No. Should it?"

"What about Ax? Ax Gooden?"

"Gooden? Was that his last name? I wasn't aware."

203

"Right." Zippy nodded somberly. "The pimp who gave de Spirit to Cupach."

"Whatever happened to the murder charge against him?"

"It was reduced to manslaughter, and he went to prison. Came out after a couple of years and went right back in on another charge. The pattern continued until he got a federal drug rap last fall. They offered him an even better deal than the one Cupach did. A quashed indictment if he became an informer for them. He agreed to do it, and a couple of months ago he was found stabbed in a hallway on Manhattan Avenue by two undercover feds. He couldn't tell them who stabbed him, but he did tell them something else before he died. On the ambulance ride to the hospital he said he'd lied about having been told by one of his hookers that de Spirit killed two girls. He'd only given Cupach de Spirit's name to get the murder rap off him. So you see what that meant. Once de Spirit learned what Ax had said, he immediately filed a 440 motion sending his whole appeal back to trial court on the basis of newly discovered evidence. Namely that the entrapment setup to get a taped confession out of him was the result of a perjured statement. It's enough alone to get him a new trial. And once he does, all the state has left in the way of a case against him is the oral confession he made while undergoing heroin withdrawal. The judge at his first trial wouldn't even allow particulars of his confession to be introduced in court, and there have been several precedents in the years since for throwing out that kind of confession altogether." Zippy paused to lean back in her chair and tap her fingertips together. "Now do you see why I'm feeling so confident?"

"Frankly, no. Why should the Supreme Court accept Ax's statement to the feds? Who's to say he wasn't lying again?"

Zippy was looking curiously at him. "But they have to accept it. It's a dying declaration."

"Merely because he died after he made it? You mean to tell me anything someone says as he's dying has to be taken as the gospel truth?"

"Even if he doesn't die. Just so long as the deponent genuinely *believes* he's dying when he makes the statement." Zippy shook her head admonishingly. "I'm surprised you don't know that. I thought most parole officers had some legal training. At least a nodding acquaintance with Blackstone."

"Not me. I got all my legal training at the school of Hayes."

Puzzled, Zippy said, "What's the school of Hayes?"

"Named after the pride of Ohio."

"Oh—you mean Rutherford B. Hayes."

"No," said Reppa. "Wayne Woodrow. The only dying declarations he was interested in hearing were from referees who blew penalty calls in the Michigan game."

Zippy frowned. "Are you talking about Woody Hayes the football coach?"

"Do you know the principle, Avoid getting in a bind?"

"I can't say that I do."

"It's Woody's first principle. Essentially it means keep the wind at your back and the ball away from your own goal line. Sitting here, I'm beginning to feel a pretty stiff breeze in my face and that shadow over my shoulder looks suspiciously like goalposts."

Zippy's frown had disappeared, and a blank look had slipped into her eyes.

"You want something from me," he continued. "You still haven't told me what it is. Instead you keep backing me farther and farther downfield with a lot of political and legal mumbo jumbo. Easy to do. I'm not one of your great

205

scholars in either area. But I'm pretty good inside my own ten-yard line."

She looked directly at him for several moments. "You know—if I've been spouting too much shop talk, it's because I'm nervous. Real nervous. This is my first big case."

Her voice was so soft, so strained that he felt a hasty wash of guilt. "I'm pretty damn nervous myself."

"Because of your investigation?"

"Because of this afternoon." Reppa hesitated as the need for simple honesty rose within him, overwhelming the complexity of feeling he had had all afternoon. "I'm very attracted to you, and I think you know it. I just don't want you to feel you can get some play businesswise on that attraction."

She turned sharply away from him.

"Wait," he called after her. "That didn't come out right. You've got me all rattled."

In a few moments she turned back. For the first time her eyes could not meet his gaze. "I feel your attraction. I think I have more than a little of my own. No, not think—I know. But it disturbs me that you're so fragile that you have to protect yourself against it."

"Fragile?"

He started laughing but stopped immediately. His laughter had sounded stupid in his ears.

"Do you have a similar reaction to all the women you meet?" she said. "That if they're straightforward with you, they're trying to exploit you?"

"Only those who have blue eyes and wear blue dresses."

She threw her head back in mock disdain. "I suppose you think I put this dress on expressly for your benefit."

"It crossed my mind," he admitted. "Until I remem-

206

bered you were already at your office when we made the date."

"How do you know I didn't run home and change after I called you?"

"I don't," said Reppa, who realized that he also didn't positively know she'd made the call from her office and not her apartment.

"You almost have me believing you're serious, you know."

"Almost is like saying half. Which is about what I am. Half serious."

For some moments Zippy did not reply. And then she said, "Oh, Frank," and reached out her hand to touch him, to be touched.

And seeing his hand reach out, too, Reppa felt lifted from him a burden of tension and anxiety. The relief was quite physical, and he felt instantly lighter.

For a long while they both stared silently and gravely down at their clasped hands. Then her eyes shifted to her glass. "What should we drink to?"

He shrugged. Smiling unsteadily, still holding on tightly to her hand, he picked up his glass and spilled some on the table in raising it. Then, getting her message: "To us."

"Yes . . ." She nodded vigorously. "You and I—two rebels with a cause!"

They toasted each other, then the seeds of their rebellion, then the seeds of those seeds, meanwhile changing from beer to red wine. She told him she had married at eighteen, worked in a law office to put her husband through medical school. No, it wasn't the usual story—he hadn't abandoned her once he got his degree. She had left him because she found him too narrow, too dependent, and because she wanted a career of her own, not just a rooting interest in his. At first, upon finishing law school, she had worked

207

for a corporate firm, but she found it deadly. Legal Aid was where she belonged, at least until she got enough trial experience to hang up her own shingle. He told her about Ohio State, coaching, Irene and his three daughters. Joan, Hillary, and Catherine. "No Zipporahs?" she said, and he remembered, amid her laughter, that someone had once said, What's in a name, anyway? After that they spoke less frequently, but their eyes continued to meet in long and eloquent dialogues.

Eventually, though in dialogue that was more often elliptical than eloquent, he told her about Leilah.

They had met during a criminal justice conference at John Jay College. In the morning their eyes met across the auditorium at the beginning of a panel discussion on prison reform, and then again after each of the panelists had made an opening remark or two. *I have the feeling this is all going to be something I've heard before,* his said. Hers said she wasn't going to listen to it even once. He watched her take out a notebook and lower her head to it. Throughout the rest of the morning, glancing at her every second or third minute, he only once caught her looking up, but it was not at him. Her eyes were turned inward, deeply inward, and even then he had an inkling that his most serious competition might be whatever was going on in that notebook.

It was no easy matter at lunch, in the upstairs dining room, to finagle a seat at her table. The John Jay group she was part of claimed all but one chair, and three men got to it ahead of him. All four stood around awkwardly, making polite head motions, acquiescent gestures with their cocktail glasses. Stiffly smiling, "You go ahead." "No, you were here first . . ." Smiling, smiling. A situation, definitely, that called for a deck of cards: high man gets his chance with her. Or a round of Russian roulette.

Reppa resolved everything by spilling his drink on the floor and plummeting into the vacant chair while the others leaped aside to avoid getting splashed.

"One too many?" he heard her inquire.

"Many too few," he said, looking around the table with a fiercely affable smile.

From then on it was all downhill. Leilah refused to look his way again until coffee was served, and then, when her eyes found him there ahead of her, waiting with his smile, she said, "And who is the strong, silent type at the end of the table? Anybody know him?"

"I'm Frank Reppa. Double *p*, as in *apple*."

"Also as in *hippopotamus*," Leilah said. The whole table laughed. Someone asked him whether he taught. When he said no, he was the Division of Parole's emissary to the conference, Leilah said, "Oh, it's explained. He's on parole." This time there was only a nervous titter, as the others at the table sensed from her attack, which was so out of proportion to its provocation, the real source of her distress.

At the end of the day she remained behind in the auditorium. When she saw he was determined not to let her be the last to leave, she said, "I teach a course here on women and the law. I've published a novel that reviewers say makes Marilyn French read like Mary Worth. Men who look at me like you're doing always wind up hating me. The bottom line is I'm thirty-five years old, never been married, never even lived with anybody. Still in there? Hello? Anybody home?"

"Right here," Reppa said.

"Want more? I can't cook, don't intend to learn. My shrink says if I'm lucky I may finish therapy before I begin collecting social security. I have a chronic bladder infection. One of my knees is worse than Joe Namath's. When I'm writing, I often don't see or talk to anybody for days."

"What are your bad points?"

"I know what's going on in your head, Reppa. I'm giving you the Germaine Greer equivalent, you think, of the old Bogart routine: 'I'm warning you, sweetheart, stay away or I'll break your heart.' "

"There's still an hour or so of light. If you walk me to my car, I'll show you a place not far from here to watch the sunset."

"You're either a masochist or you live on adolescent fantasies. Which is it?"

"Both. Sixteen was a painful year, but I'd be very happy to repeat it."

Her ferocious deprecations had excited him all the more. He couldn't believe himself. He was speaking to her in the same lethally bantering way she spoke to him, and it was easy.

In climbing into his car she gave him a glimpse, as she gathered her skirt around her, of firm, full buttocks, and he wanted to make love to her on the spot. His fantasies up till a moment ago had all been wisecracks, but the creature who sat beside him as he headed for the pier at the foot of Fifty-seventh Street suddenly looked and smelled soberingly three-dimensional. He tried to smile at her, but her manner no longer allowed it. She wasn't talking anymore. Silent, she was awesome.

"What are you thinking?" he asked.

"How scared I am."

"Of what? I'm a terrific driver."

"Yeah, Reppa, but you're not too hot at pretending you don't know what I'm scared of."

"Will you go to a movie with me this weekend?"

"No, but I'll take you up to this lake I know about if you promise not to laugh at my body."

He nearly ran the car into an oncoming road divider.

"She certainly sounds interesting," said Zippy.

Reppa nodded and pretended to examine the knotholes in the table, hoping he could get away with telling her only the bare essentials. Writer: feminist: teacher. It was not an unwillingness to answer anything Zippy might ask him. Rather, he feared the questions he had not yet seen how he could ask himself.

"How long have you been living together?"

"Since December, more or less. The less being that I've never officially given up my apartment."

Still, she was perhaps thinking, a step short of TC. Two steps, if she counted marriage. Leilah at this point would have been thinking, *Smart to keep his apartment with places so impossible to come by now.* To her the only thing that constituted total commitment was if everybody ganged up on you and signed you into Bellevue.

"How does she feel about the parole investigation?"

He scrambled in his mind for an alternative to the first word that had occurred to him: *jealous.* "All right. She's been a lot of help, actually."

"You've discussed it with her?"

"Don't you think I should have? No one's told me not to."

"Then probably it's okay. You're lucky in that respect." She paused. "Even more lucky in that you have someone to talk to about what you're doing."

"How about yourself?"

"My turn now?" Zippy smiled carefully. "Well, I'm not living with anybody."

211

He took her hesitancy for disappointment. "But you're seeing someone you'd like to be more serious about."

"Why do you say that?"

Having seen her smile freeze for an instant, he shrugged, advisedly. "You're too attractive and too interesting not to be with someone. And my sense of you is that you'd want a lot from whomever you were with."

"Why do men always think every attractive, interesting woman automatically has someone? So many don't. Leilah, for example, before she met you."

"But I'm right, aren't I?" He fought, unsuccessfully, against his curiosity and her obvious reticence. "What's he like?"

"You, unfortunately," she said with a quick glance at her watch. "Very stubborn, very self-willed, very driven and"—she consulted her watch again—"very unavailable."

"Married?"

He watched her finger trace the circle left on the table by his beer glass.

"Yes," she said finally and then looked at him sidelong. "But not in the way you mean."

"Then why is he unavailable?"

"Let's put it this way. If I said I didn't want to have dinner alone tonight, what would you say?"

"It would depend." Then, after the question had settled in him more deeply: "Is this hypothetical?"

Zippy replied with a smile, but Reppa seemed to read in her eyes a trace of evasion. "He wouldn't respond at all to my not wanting to be alone. He'd only agree to have dinner with me if *he* wanted to. So everything we do together revolves around him. His needs . . . ambitions for himself . . ."

"Sounds difficult."

"Unstoppable."

212

Her eyes were dull, removed, hopeless. Reppa didn't trust himself to speak for several moments. "Well."

"Well," Zippy echoed, continuing to smile without much force. "That's only one side of it, of course. The good side is he's the most inner-directed man I've ever met. And the most self-reliant. Obsolete phrases now, but that's because the qualities they describe are so rare. Meanwhile"—she took another glance at her watch— "there's still the question of dinner."

"You mean you were serious?"

"Yes, I guess that's what I was. Dutch again. And it would have to be something besides Italian."

The assertive tone annoyed him for an instant, but a glance at the delicate pale face and dark-blue eyes made him swallow, nod, swallow again. "I'll have to make a call."

"To Leilah? Before you do, let's think a moment. . . ."

He found himself incapable of dealing head-on with what he knew she was saying. "About what?"

"Something impossible, probably."

The *probably* had an edge of impatience, as if she'd begun to resent his hesitation. He raised her hand from the table and stroked it in all the places where his own hand yearned.

"Are you feeling what I am or not?"

He nodded.

"Then, for God's sake."

Her eyes came up from the table. Their pupils were suddenly spinning so close to his that they drew him in like whirlwinds.

"Where can we go?" she said when her lips were hers to speak with again.

"Well." He raised his eyebrows. "I don't think you'd care much for Ninth Street and Second Avenue."

"Thank you, but you're wrong. I was born only four blocks from there."

"Fifth Street?"

"The other way. Avenue C." She smiled quickly. "So it won't come as a shock. I've taken more than my share of baths in the kitchen."

After all these years, the first time with a woman he wanted badly could still feel like the first time ever. Her dress, when it was removed, had very little under it. Just a pair of white cotton pants and a thin bra that came apart with a single tug, like a shoelace. Then her breasts were in front of him, small, pale, lemon-shaped. The natural smell of her, under the faint scent of rose water, was enough to tell him that he would never quite get enough of her. His hands, sliding the pants down, cupped her buttocks, which were surprisingly full considering her overall smallness. Hers explored the buttons on his shirt. One breast, then the other brushed against his forehead; he swung his head to kiss one nipple, then the other.

"Mmm," she said. "You're incredible."

That quickly it all changed, and the only thing that mattered now was that nothing either of them said or did here could possibly be new.

A minute later, in bed, he felt as if something dreadful were about to occur. Something truly dreadful. A heart attack, at the very least, if he was to get what he really had coming to him. As he knelt on the sheet, which was clean in the sense that it hadn't been used since it was last changed six months ago, he saw Zippy's legs part, rise, bend, to form a basket for him, and it came home, the wellspring of the confusion in which he was wallowing.

The feeling of utter familiarity, then the sense of awful foreboding: boredom and dread, the frantic search for

214

reasons that would explain away both. Reppa didn't know all of what his nerves were trying to tell him, but it was clear, watching Zippy make her basket, that he had better admit to himself that there was someone else in the room with them. He could not keep her out. He could now see himself dimly, too, as he must have looked that night. *Not here,* he pleaded helplessly. *Not now!*

Of course, his plea to himself that night last winter had been that they would have to stop this—now, right now— but he had also pleaded with himself not to give her the satisfaction of jeering at him for being the first to stop. Below them, five stories down, beyond the maze of fire-escape ladders and platforms, was Bank Street. Two minutes till the New Year, the first they had celebrated together.

To make it special they'd pledged to spend it alone, just the two of them, drinking hot buttered rum and reading passages to each other from their favorite novels. Long passages. His from *Studs Lonigan*, hers from *The Golden Notebook*. By eleven thirty they had both developed really epic tension headaches and gone up on the roof for air. It was the end of a decade. It was the beginning of a decade. There was almost a full moon. The night was incredibly still and soft for almost January. All they had on were sneakers and trench coats. At eleven forty-five Leilah opened hers to the sky north of the city and got up on the ledge so that those who were earthbound would not be deprived of the view. Not wanting to be outdone, he scrambled up beside her, though he could not get his hands out of his pockets to unbutton his trenchcoat. Many of the lighted windows in the buildings across the street had potential spectators inside them, he told himself, and besides, while it was amazingly warm, it wasn't all *that* warm. (He might, God help him, just also have been less drunk.) They both sat down after a minute or two. When he glanced over at her, she was lying back on her elbows.

"Do you know what I've always wanted to do?" Just playing around, but already it verged on a dare. And yet, Reppa knew, he was not beyond confusing her dares and his desires. People could watch them, the whole world could watch—when you had a wicked headache and only two minutes to come up with something extraordinary to usher out the decade, your rum-ridden brain wasn't entirely itself. "Just like this," she said, straddling the ledge with her anklebones to show him how the tomboys in Bensonhurst had done it.

He was still convinced this was going to stop just as soon as they both felt they would one day have a story to tell about their first New Year's Eve together.

Then she held her arm up and gestured frantically at her watch. "Hurry! Hurry up! There's only a minute left!"

But she was laughing with the same daredevil zest he'd heard way back in October, when she'd plunged into the lake on their first day together. It persuaded him that they were only clowning around.

"Here I am," he said. "The original sixty-second man."

Straddling the ledge, he couldn't get up much momentum and was therefore not surprised when he felt his hard-on (barely token to begin with) quickly fade. Too late he heard her moan "No-o-o" and realized, feeling her legs rise and flail to keep him from slipping out of her, that he had indeed confused something tonight, but it had not been dare and desire.

As they lurched out over the ledge, he grabbed the ladder on the fire escape with one hand and held on, trying to throw his other arm around her at the same time. But she was too far gone. The most he could do was yank her out of the wide open air and fling her into the ladder. She went clattering down it and landed on the fire escape platform one flight down.

"Happy New Year, Studs," she groaned, holding out a hand as he clambered after her. "Help me up."

But he couldn't.

Zippy's hand now, reaching for him, searching out the reason for his hesitation. And then, her fingers moving with warm confidence, there no longer was one.

His legs glided downward, sank between hers, and she turned her head away and cried, "Oh, Frank! Jesus!"

And he cried, "Zipporah!"

Identities affirmed, they closed their eyes, kissed, merged. Reppa felt through his loins the imminence of betrayal, and because he could now feel it as that, it was no longer terrifying. For the first time in his life he confessed to himself that he was committing adultery (though the fact was that, in a strict sense, he had committed it many times over after separating from Irene and waiting for his divorce to come through). It wasn't so awful. Still, as he came, he whispered aloud, once: "Leilah." For whatever it was worth in the cosmic scheme, however much or little.

After a drowsy while Zippy slid out from under him and went in search of the bathroom. "The seat's loose," he warned her. "There's a bolt missing."

"It happens in the best of homes," she said, and when she returned too quickly and found him sweeping an array of dust balls under the bed: "I have a suggestion."

"Your place next time?"

"My place has its own problems. I was going to say I know a law student who takes on cleaning jobs to pay her rent. We can split whatever it costs to get her in here every other week or so."

217

He overrode all the poetic lines that were being said, by implication, to focus on the one clinker. "What's wrong with your place?"

"Nothing. It's lovely. But it's way uptown, and yours is much more convenient."

"For?"

She began gathering her clothes. "Well, I want to be as straight as possible. I'd like to see you again, but it can only be for a few hours here and there. On afternoons when we're both able to get away."

"What if I prefer evenings?"

"Prime time." She was speaking so coolly now that he could imagine her addressing a jury. "Fine, but we both face the same logistical problems. If you don't want to spell them out, I will. A job we're both interested in doing well and another relationship we don't want to jeopardize."

"It sounds as if you already have everything carefully analyzed."

"My nature whenever I've been overwhelmed. You blew me away. I never expected anything like this to happen."

What *had* she expected? He looked at her with faint surprise as it occurred to him that he still didn't know. "But you arranged it in advance so we could spend several hours together if need be."

"This wasn't the if I had in . . ." She turned away with a frown, and it seemed to Reppa that her distress was genuine. But then, still frowning, she slipped her dress over her head and came out with a smile. "God, you have hands. When you touched me in the bar, it was like something electric."

Nothing explained that really had to be explained. It was like his whispered "Leilah." Some personal hole being filled, not the chasm between them. Which suddenly felt

218

vast. Already, even though she was standing beside his bed, separating her underwear from his, it seemed only a dream that she had been in it just minutes ago.

"Want a cup of tea or something? Wine?"

"No. No, thanks. God, what time is it? It's late, isn't it?"

Her watch said, give or take a minute, the same thing as his: a little before six.

"Do you like Indian food? There's a great place on Sixth Street."

"Dinner? I know what we said before, but—whose stocking is this behind the door? Mine?"

"You didn't wear any."

"Shit." She was having trouble fastening her bra.

"Want help?"

"No. What are you doing now?"

"Getting a pencil so I can write down your phone number."

"It's five-seven-seven something. I can never remember it. Just call the number for Legal Aid in the book and ask for me."

"And your home number?"

"Well, that's not in the book. Actually we still have to negotiate whether I should give it to you. Let's put it on the list for next time."

"Is there really going to be one?"

"As soon as possible." Her eyes glanced incessantly from him to the door. "Call me, or I'll call you. No, I'll call you. At your office. Who is that man who answers your phone as if he had a handkerchief over his mouth?"

"Spielman. My partner."

"Spielman. And what's Leilah's last name again?"

"Why? Are you making up a dossier on me?"

She laughed—hurriedly, he thought. "People tend to

surround themselves with people who have similar names. Have you ever noticed?"

"I've noticed you didn't tell me the name of the man you're seeing."

"Put that on the list, too. It keeps getting longer."

She spoke unconcernedly, but he saw a flush pass quickly over her face.

"Maybe we'd better knock off one or two items on it now, before you go."

"Can't." She stopped at the door, frowning. "I really was blown away, you know."

"Sure. We both were."

She surprised him then. "Do you want to make a definite date right now to get together again? Noon Monday? Or I could do it tomorrow after four."

"Tomorrow. Where?"

"Here. Say four thirty."

She turned from the door. Kissed him quickly. Fled. Reppa went to the front window and opened it. Sticking his head out, he watched her emerge from his building and walk west on Ninth Street until her blue dress disappeared behind a row of parked cars on the other side of Second Avenue. She did not look back once.

And the hell of it was she came to his place the following afternoon at four thirty on the dot. And she seemed to crave him every bit as much as he craved her.

CHAPTER NINE

THE SEVEN BLOCKS
OF GRANITE

The Moffetts, George and Lucy, were no longer living in Charleston. Reppa wanted to call the Charleston postmaster and find out if they'd left a forwarding address, but when he tried to get authorization to make the call, he was told first by Lidsky, who was still his first link on the chain of command, and then by the assistant area director, to whom he appealed in protest, that the cost of tracking down the Moffetts was prohibitive, considering how little significance they had.

"What can they tell you?" Lidsky said. "Twelve years ago they came to New York for probably the only time in their lives to claim their daughter's body. Then they went back to Zipville and tried to put the whole thing behind them. If you dig them up now, they'll only resent it."

Reppa argued that they had a right to know that their daughter's convicted killer might be pardoned but had no counter when the assistant area director said, "Okay, so you tell them a pardon's in the works. And then, say, it comes through. Now they know de Spirit's out, and they feel rotten. Whereas chances are, way the hell down in South Carolina, they'll never find out if you don't contact them."

A reasonable position, but it didn't prevent Reppa from grumbling inwardly about the agency's being too uptight to approve the expenditure of a single dollar that did not absolutely have to be spent. For the want of a couple of long distance phone calls, his report would not include a single word from the two people who had given life to and then been deprived of their beloved daughter. He recognized, too well, that his sense of injustice here was something of a cloak to hide from himself a deeper sense of unease. Of purposelessness. Now that the Moffetts had been crossed off his list, there were suddenly no more names on it. The investigation was over, finished, completed. The fun part, that was. Still left to do was the report, put off till the bitter end like a term paper. But unlike his term papers in college, which he had procrastinated over because he loathed the seemingly endless job of research that awaited him, the report made him want to cry out in frustration that his research had been too finite, too circumscribed.

Sitting at his desk the morning before the report was due, yellow pad in front of him, notebook open atop the blotter, intensified his restiveness. The investigation had answered the governor's question. Some people were opposed to pardoning Danny de Spirit; others thought he should be pardoned; a few couldn't have cared less. But the questions the investigation itself had posed were still unanswered. The nagging void they left in him was not imagined, it was real.

Under it all, damn it, he still did not have a single concrete reason to tell himself that it was more than an intuition that he had spoken to the real murderer of Andrea Behrman and Elizabeth Moffett. In the beginning the notion of uncovering the murderer in the course of his investigation had stirred the romantic in him. Now it seemed arrogant and remote. One report, a few hours of writing

222

and then a few minutes to dictate what he'd written, and he would become a parole officer again, once more confined to the routine of office reports and home visits, of trips to Rikers Island to lodge warrants and attend parole violation hearings, of transporting prisoners and chasing absconders across rooftops.

Over the distance of the last week he watched movements, facial expressions, mannerisms; listened to voices, changes in tone, dissembled accents; and he tried to pull his thoughts together. Slowly, as he probed his memory, old habits of concentration took command. Slowly a doodle began to form on the yellow pad. There were only six X's at first, one short of the number he needed. So he threw in de Spirit. That gave him his forward wall, all seven of them. Like the Seven Blocks of Granite, he thought, Fordham's legendary impregnable frontline. And now that they were all in a row in front of him, they looked every bit as formidable as Lombardi, Wojciehowicz, and company.

But he couldn't go up against them himself. That was the bind.

A week ago, under Leilah's goading, he'd begun making notes to himself that Behrman's true relationship with Andrea should be probed, his story about hiring a private detective to investigate his wife's background checked out, his current girl friend questioned about her impressions of him. It seemed just a bit much that a man could reach middle age still a virgin and then smoothly become a lothario. Likewise, Annabelle's hermitage seemed incredible unless she was being kept prisoner for some reason by Kinder. And who was Kinder, anyhow? What was his history? His personal life? Did he ever leave Annabelle's loft other than to run errands and the like?

And Mald. What about that toupee and phony accent? His reputation with women? His glib accounts of how he'd

223

astutely recognized that Annabelle and Jill Wilkes were talented and taken them on as clients? His evasiveness when questioned about what he had going with Adelaide Behrman? Halliwell's speculation that he might have had something going with Andrea, too?

This last depended, of course, on how much of what Halliwell told you could be believed. Really, now, was Halliwell anything like the loyal, selfless, worshipful swain he made himself out to be? He'd alluded to a period of impotence with Andrea—had there been lapses since with other women? Good chance. And a damn good chance, from what he'd seen, that Halliwell didn't just tuck his tail meekly between his legs when they occurred.

But the real block of granite, who even looked the part, perched defiantly on a stool, was Jill Wilkes. He'd gotten to know her well enough in the hour he was in her loft to realize his first assessment of her was wrong. She hadn't agreed to talk to him because she was afraid not to. She had done it out of curiosity. *She wanted to know if he knew something that she, too, ought to know.* The rub was that he still didn't know whether or not he did.

Which left Danny de Spirit. The whole impetus for this investigation and the only one of the seven X's he hadn't interviewed. For the simple reason that he couldn't. De Spirit's opinion on whether or not he should be pardoned was immaterial, and the agency wasn't about to authorize a trip up to Auburn just so Reppa could see that the subject of his investigation really existed. Any more than the agency would authorize him to talk to Behrman's girl friend, put Annabelle's loft under surveillance, follow Kinder around, pry into Mald's background or Halliwell's sex life. He couldn't even take another crack at Wilkes. If he did any of those things, it would be a step over a finely drawn but very clear line, the line between which activities

224

by a parole officer doing a pardon investigation were permissible and which were not.

But so what? Even if he were brought up on charges, which he surely would be, so what? There were other jobs around. Plenty of other jobs. But how many of them, realistically, could someone with his record get? An ex-football coach who'd left the profession under a cloud. An ex-parole officer, fired after being brought up on charges. With an ex-wife and three kids back in Ohio. A disabled ex-tomboy for a roommate. And now an extracurricular affair with the Legal Aid lawyer of the very same client on whose behalf he was supposed to be conducting an impartial investigation.

But still (stay with this now, Reppa), so what? Sure, he'd backed himself into a corner. He could continue poking around in the Behrman-Moffett case on his own time, get fired, and wind up pushing a broom somewhere. Or he could drop his interest in the case and retreat to where he'd started, square one, Parole Officer Reppa. Pretty dreary choice, when put like that. But suppose in his poking around he discovered the real killer. It was always a possibility. Then what was stopping him?

He looked down abruptly. Ignoring the yellow pad (the seven blocks of granite were not his only barrier), he seized the notebook and leafed rapidly through it. *You see yourself as a vigilante.* Who had . . . ? But who wasn't important. *Maverick . . . I'd leave it at maverick.* Why had he said *that*? What did *leave it* mean?

Soon, soon now, he would have to look deep into himself: no more evasions whenever he sat down like this to puzzle out what had really pulled him into the investigation, no more wisecracks to Leilah in response to her digs about his vacillation. One day left. One more and he would have to come down off the fence to . . . go on

225

playing detective as long as he could before they took his shield and gun away? Or write his report and dump the whole mess back in the laps of the Powers That Be, where it would probably lie dormant for another twelve or twenty or two hundred years? Not that there wasn't still a third alternative, of course, though it too had its own dreary consequences. For it was just barely possible that tucked away in his notes he already had in his possession the key to the Behrman-Moffett case. And maybe, he thought morosely, it was also possible that even though he couldn't find the key, others could.

The Lone Ranger had Tonto. Nero Wolfe had Archie. Holmes had Watson. Sidekicks all, and not overly swift. His own two sidekicks in this were more on the order of Robespierre and Lady Macbeth.

He flung his jacket over a chair as he entered the room, but Leilah didn't look up until he got close enough to the bed for his shadow to fall across her notebook.

"Home already?"

"It's almost six, Sturm."

She tossed her head, flip-flop of raven hair. "Six is early for you these days."

"Time for Roger Grimsby." He started to switch on the TV.

"Don't," Leilah said. "Take it in the living room if you're going to watch it."

"All work and no play is bad, Sturm. It's making you impossible to be around."

"It's also making a five-hundred-page novel."

"When are you going to tell me what it's about?"

Silence.

"Does it have a title?"

Leilah lowered her head, as though confiding a secret to

a microphone in her armpit. *"Sugar and Spice and Everything Nice."*

"Well, at least it isn't autobiographical."

Another long silence.

"You can't keep ignoring me, Sturm. You've been buried in that damn thing all week."

"That's three Sturm's in less than three minutes. Who is she?"

"Who's who?"

"You never call me Sturm unless I call you Reppa first. My shrink would say it's a clear example of aggressive behavior to hide a guilty conscience."

"My shrink, if I had one, would say your shrink was redundant. There's no other kind of conscience."

"Keep it up, Reppa. You won't get off the hook, but it's fun listening to you try."

"Hook?" He shook his head in a pantomime of amazement. "What hook?"

"Gore told me she's not going to do our laundry anymore. It pulls too hard at her heartstrings, since she knows I never wear lipstick."

"Neither do any of the other women I'm sleeping with."

The lean face creased with disappointment. The accusations had been sprinkled in his path like landmines, but he'd kept slipping past. She *knew* there was someone else, but now *he* knew she couldn't prove it.

"Here's the deal, Reppa. Let me work for another hour without any interruptions, and then I'll let you make dinner."

"Only if you'll go over my notes on the investigation with me afterward. Agreed?"

But her brown eyes wouldn't stir from the page she was filling with her slow but steady hand. It was astonishing how much strength her fingers had regained since he'd started this investigation.

227

The dark brown eyes were straying from him again.

"You're not listening, Sturm."

"Yes, I am. You said the scene in the painting was the reverse of the murder scene."

"Whose painting?"

Leilah snuck a look in her notebook, as if it contained a crib sheet. "Wilkes's."

Reppa nodded. "A woman mutilating a man with a knife. The woman looked like Andrea, the man a little like Christ."

"And from *that* you think Wilkes intended the painting to be a clue to the murderer?"

"There's more. Somehow I just can't put my finger on it."

"Well, pardon me then. While I put *all* my fingers on what I mean."

She blatantly opened her notebook, found her place, and was off and writing before Reppa could invent another group enterprise.

"I'm not done, kid. Lots more. For instance, Adelaide Behrman."

"What about her?"

"What would make a woman marry a man like Behrman so her daughter could have all the economic and social advantages she hadn't had? And then sleep with a man like Mald so her sister would have a gallery to show her work?"

"Uh-uh. If I let you sit here any longer and pick my brain, there'll be that much less in it for me."

"How about putting that notebook down? Haven't you written enough for one day?"

Her head didn't stir. She turned the page, yanked on a

pulley to bring fresh blood into her arm, and went right on.

"You've never written at night before. What's going on?"

"Nothing." And then, as if aware she had betrayed herself by speaking, she said, "I've never had to lie here all day crying over spilled beer before."

"Spilled beer? What're you trying to tell me—this investigation is making me an alcoholic?"

"The aroma was all over your sleeve when you came home the other evening. As if you'd been sitting somewhere with your arm in a puddle of beer. You're not a drunk, Reppa, and you're not much of a sitter. So I had to think something was holding your arm down. You said that morning you were going to talk to Andrea's ex-fiancé, and then you were meeting de Spirit's lawyer for lunch. Nero Sturm deduced that you either got into an arm-wrestling contest with him or held hands across the table with her."

He heard the controlled vibrato of her larynx, saw the mouth strain not to quiver, the eyes endeavor to regard him coolly sidelong.

"Brilliant. You missed your calling. You'd have made a great cop with that kind of ability to manufacture evidence."

"Men have been sent to the chair on less."

"Maybe I was just in a conversation that was so absorbing I lost track of where my sleeve was."

"About what?"

Reppa searched his inner linen drawer, pulled out the first article that looked clean. "Woody Hayes."

"And this person was so interested in Woody Hayes that this person went back to your apartment for a look at your old football scrapbooks?"

"Who said I went to my apartment?"

229

I have eyes, Reppa.''

"That see what?''

"The knees of your pants.''

"Oh? What was on them? Lipstick?''

"Dust. What happened, her glass eye fall out and roll under the bed?''

Reppa knew better than to keep trying to laugh her off. He might get free of the knot again, but like a spider she would just throw out another silken thread.

"Where are you going with this, Sturm? I've already been boxed into a corner on the investigation. One bind at the moment is enough.''

Lying there at anchor under her steel brace, Leilah gave him a long, level look. Who was he to talk to *her* about binds?

"If your object is to lay a little guilt on my side of the bed, you can't miss. If it's something else . . .'' He paused. Then, with quiet emphasis: "Do you want me to move out?''

"Where? To live with her?''

"Let's stick to you and me—what you want and I want.''

"Who is she, Reppa? That Legal Aid twit? She going to help you sue me for alimony? Half the royalties on my new book? I knew when you moved in here we ought to draw up a contract. If I give you my old baseball cards and the TV, will you call it even?''

"Look, talk seriously. For one moment.''

"I only talk seriously to myself. If you want to listen, learn telepathy.''

"I would listen, you know, if you gave me the chance. There isn't anything I wouldn't listen to.''

Leilah spread her notebook over her face, covering all but her chin, which began to tremble. She wept silently for well over ten minutes. Then the alarm clock went off: the Mets were in Cincinnati tonight, and Seaver was pitching for the Reds. Tom Terrific. She didn't know whether to root for the Mets or for Seaver, and that kind of ambivalence made everything else in her life seem momentarily black or white. She stopped weeping and watched the game. All Reppa had to do to become a good guy again was restrict himself to talking to her only between innings.

"Your trouble," Leilah said before the bottom of the fourth, "is you don't know how to listen to women. It's not entirely your fault. Being in the army, playing football, you're used to having things given to you like commands. You've never learned how to draw inferences."

"I'm not going to start now. If you're going to tell me I misunderstood something you said, you're going to have to spell it out."

"The other day is a good example," she said while they awaited the top of the fifth.

"Which other day?"

"When I asked you why Elizabeth Moffett was living with Andrea and Jill, and you explained that she answered an ad for a roommate to share their place. Then we got off into a discussion of why they accepted her ahead of other women who'd answered the ad."

"And I thought we both had more or less the same idea. Are you going to tell me now I was wrong?"

"Sssh. Mazzilli's up."

The camera did a pan of Seaver's wife behind the Reds' dugout, and then the focus was on Tom Terrific versus the Wop Fop. A fastball came in, and Ralph Kiner reported it was a slider. Some ten minutes later Leilah said, "Not wrong. But you didn't go far enough. I wasn't just asking why they accepted her. What made *her* accept *them*?"

231

"We went over that, too. The price was right, and it was near her job."

"Not the apartment, Reppa. *Them*. I thought about it afterward. Can the same be said for you?"

He wasn't going to tell her it couldn't.

"They weren't a pair most Catholic girls from Charleston would choose for roommates."

"She was interested in becoming a social worker," he pointed out. "Maybe she thought they'd be good subjects to study."

"Now who isn't talking seriously. See me before the top of the seventh. While you're standing up and stretching for both of us, I'll tell you another inference you've missed."

"What is it?"

"At the end of the inning."

She was true to her word and as direct as she was true: He'd fantasized too much about finding the real Behrman-Moffett slayer and not enough about what he'd do if his fantasy became reality. Anyone who had killed two girls and gotten away with it for over twelve years wasn't going to go along peacefully just because a parole officer said the jig was up. He seemed to hold the opinion that Jill Wilkes knew who the killer was. All right, suppose she really did. The fact that she apparently wasn't afraid did not mean there was nothing to be feared. It only meant that she felt she personally did not have anything to fear.

"And meanwhile," Leilah added diplomatically, "here I lie. Flat on my back. After you get done flushing the killer out of hiding, one day when you're not here, he'll come looking for you and zap me."

"Not if I move back to my place until this is over."

Scornfully she threw her head back, hard enough to jolt

even a healthy spinal column. Twinge of pain, thin firing-squad smile to cover it. "And give that twit a clear field?"

"Then, if I'm staying, we'll have to do something so that you feel safe."

"How about a bulletproof vest? Only it seems I already have one."

Tears started glistening again. Reppa, at his best with women who flew their emotions only on special occasions, like flags, nevertheless wrapped an arm around her flannel-covered shoulders.

Then he saw it wasn't anything to do with him.

"Bastard McNamara." She struggled in his arms, stuck out her chin, glared at the TV.

The Reds were taking Tom Terrific out for a pinch hitter.

He put a rough draft of his report in front of McCreary's nose the following morning. McCreary wafted cigar smoke under his while he read it.

"No dice saying the case should be reopened. Cross out that whole paragraph and just write that some of the people you interviewed were being, in your opinion, less than candid. Then say a further investigation of certain issues that are still unresolved would seem warranted."

"That's not nearly strong enough."

"I'm just going by what's on the page," McCreary said with a glance at the palm of his hand, which had two mints in it. He offered one to Reppa, who regarded it as he would have a piece of silver. "Why're you looking at me like that? You sure didn't expect me to send this report up to the governor as it stands. Before I put my head on the chopping block, I've got to smell raw meat. All you have here are the same chicken bones everybody's been chewing on for years. Wilkes couldn't identify de Spirit in a police lineup, but she identified him at his trial. So what else is new? Behrman and Halliwell think de Spirit is innocent. Big deal. Annabelle's a recluse. Who gives a shit? They all raised questions about each other that demand answers. What does that mean?''

"I didn't want to spell it out on paper, but Behrman claims Halliwell used to beat Andrea. A number of people think Behrman was sleeping with her. There's speculation that she was also sleeping with a gallery owner named Carlo Mald who probably had an affair with her mother at one time."

"Where's Mald? I didn't see any mention of him."

"I left him out because his opinion doesn't have any real bearing on whether de Spirit should be pardoned."

"But you talked to him?"

Reppa nodded.

"Speak to anybody else whose name isn't in the report?"

"A couple of cops on the phone who wouldn't give me their names when I asked about Cupach."

"Couldn't find him, eh, Rep?" McCreary grinned in the manner of a teacher listening to a lazy pupil trying to explain an incomplete homework assignment. "Too bad. Any others you spoke to who aren't down in writing?"

"Well . . ." Reppa sat back in his chair. "De Spirit's Legal Aid lawyer. I met with her one afternoon to discuss whether my investigation would harm his chances for a new trial."

"Why should it?"

"She's afraid if de Spirit is offered a pardon, he'll take it and not go ahead with his appeal."

"Be crazy not to."

"That's what I think, too," said Reppa, who also thought McCreary seemed far too pragmatic all of a sudden. He had expected, if anything, to be told to juice up his report

234

with the material he'd excluded, not to tone down what was there.

"His lawyer any good, you think?"

"She's got a lot of energy."

"That's pretty fucking cryptic," McCreary said. "What's it mean?"

"For one thing, she seems to want as badly as you do to shake people up so the case will be reopened. Or anyway, as badly as I thought you did."

"You poking her?"

The accuracy of it stopped his heart. Seated beside McCreary's desk, he clenched his hands out of sight below it until he felt the blood begin to flow again. "Get serious. What's happened to your attitude toward this investigation? It's changed."

"I was just about to ask you the same, Rep. Two weeks ago you sat in that same chair and came on like getting this assignment was the biggest thing in your life. You ain't, from what I see in this report, done diddlyshit since."

"Look—I've done a hell of a lot more than you did twelve years ago."

McCreary fixed his gaze on the remaining knuckles on his maimed hand. He blew lightly on them. "Did you smoke Cupach out and talk to him?"

"I tried."

"Trying's for judges. What about all those questions the people you interviewed raised about each other? Where are the answers?"

"To get them I'd have had to do a whole different kind of investigation."

"Yeah?" McCreary brought his gaze up from his hand; his sunglasses were shining, as if a light had gone on behind them. "Well, what stopped you?"

Reppa shook his head; he was unable to return McCreary's

look. "Are you going to back me if I start putting people under surveillance—checking into their backgrounds?"

"You caught any static from anybody so far?"

"No, but I've stayed pretty much within the boundaries of what I'm allowed to do." He paused, thinking of Zippy. "I somehow don't see you being able to cover my ass if somebody upstairs finds out I've switched from doing a pardon investigation to digging around in a closed murder case."

McCreary raised his brows and smiled. "What do you need, a written guarantee that you won't be brought up on charges?"

"I'll settle for a two-week extension on the investigation."

McCreary pulled a long face. "No can do."

"How about one week?"

"The governor's waiting on your report, Rep, before he makes his decision. What reason are you going to give him for holding his water?"

"We'll send him a preliminary report with a recommendation that a pardon seems feasible on the basis of the information I've gotten so far. That way he's got something to work with. Then we'll say that an addendum will follow when I've spoken to the people I haven't been able to interview yet."

"Which people?"

"Cupach for one. If I'm given another week, I'll have time to make an all-out effort to find him."

McCreary's smile went thoughtful and cool.

"And meanwhile what will you *really* be doing?"

"Discreetly looking for the answers to those questions."

"Discreetly like how?"

"I'd rather not say. You'll have to leave it up to me."

"That's what I've been doing, Rep—leaving it up to you. The results have been less than exhilarating. You

236

ain't come up with one thing I didn't know or at least suspect twelve years ago."

Reppa sat straighter in his chair, while his hand languished on the notebook in his pocket. So much in it that had not gone into the report . . . yet his mind was made up.

"Another question arose during my investigation. This one centering around Jill Wilkerson, known now as Wilkes. Were you aware she was a painter?"

"I seem to remember she mentioned it. But when I asked her if I could see some of her paintings as a way of thawing her out, she said she didn't have any to show me."

"The truth is she probably didn't. But a few months after her roommates were murdered, she was suddenly able to stop teaching school and paint full time. Because Mald took her on as a client and gave her a stipend. He admits that he picked up her tab for ten years and claims the reason was he thought she had commercial possibilities."

"And you're of course convinced he had another reason."

"No question."

"Which you're going to make me guess. So," McCreary said, elbows on his desk, eyes gazing boredly at the ceiling, "what can it be? Having met Wilkes, née Wilkerson, myself, I can discard the natural conclusion that her fair white body was offered to Mald. That leads me to—" McCreary burst all at once into a braying laugh. "Shit, Rep. You don't really believe she knew Mald bumped off her roommates and blackmailed him into promoting her career?"

"Mald or more likely—someone else. Someone who was either owed a favor by Mald or could make it worth his while to subsidize Wilkes. Paying him a nice piece of change over and above what he was paying her."

237

"Got any proof of this?"

"No, but I've seen one of her early paintings. The scene in it is almost a carbon copy of the murders. Only in reverse. Instead of Andrea Behrman being stabbed, a woman who looks very much like her has just finished castrating a man. Now maybe, just maybe, Wilkes meant that painting to be a hint as to who the real murderer is."

"Far out."

"But you'll have to admit, having met Wilkes yourself, it fits her personality."

"Sure, babe. And it fits the murderer's personality that he's going to let Wilkes run around doing paintings that reveal his identity to the whole world."

"Maybe he doesn't know those paintings exist. Maybe he's someone who doesn't have much knowledge of the art world and isn't aware what Wilkes's work is like."

"This hypothetical cat meanwhile is the same person who's hip enough about the art world to make a deal with Mald that was acceptable to both him and Wilkes."

"It could have been arranged by an intermediary who enabled him to stay out of it entirely. Say a father who's a lawyer."

"Come right out and say Halliwell, why don't you?"

"Not yet." Reppa shook his head. "This is all still just speculation. The only thing solid is that Wilkes knows who the killer is, I think."

"Glad you added that *I think*, Rep. Because the only thing solid I see is the block you've got between yourself and reality. Face it. I am. I took a chance—that you'd be the one guy in this outfit who could do what I could have done if I'd ever gotten the opportunity. But you came up short."

Reppa plunged before he thought. "Wait. I've got something else." His hand came out of his pocket. "I made complete notes after each interview—'' He stopped sharply, awaiting a glance that was too quick, a gesture that was too eager, but McCreary still didn't rise above scorn.

"What do you want, a medal? I'd hope to Christ you didn't try to write a report this sensitive based all on your memory."

A look passed between them, and then another look passed between Reppa and his notebook. He couldn't exactly trust McCreary. And yet. If he wanted to keep going, he had to have a teammate. The worst that could happen if he put all his cards on the table was he'd be told to fold the hand. He was only hours away, as things stood, from having to fold it anyway.

"That the notebook you used, Rep?"

"I thought I'd read portions of it to you."

McCreary withdrew the hand he had let drift languidly out over the desk.

"In the hope I'll see something you missed? I've already seen too much that you missed. But go ahead and lay it on me. Maybe one of the people you talked to said something only a dumb nigger will understand."

How could he, McCreary interrupted as Reppa was reviewing Behrman's story of his marriage and the Loomis family, have sat there all that time and not gotten Behrman to tell him the name of the private detective he'd sent to Kentucky? When Reppa argued that he hadn't pressed it because he figured the police had the name in their files on the Behrman-Moffett case, McCreary said, "Swell. And how do you propose we get it from them when you couldn't even get them to tell you where Cupach is?"

Next McCreary ridiculed his making a note that Andrea had called Behrman Rumpelstiltskin upon first meeting him.

"Are you familiar with the fairy tale? If you'd seen

239

Behrman, you'd realize the name describes him perfectly. Coming from a kid, right in front of the kid's mother, whom he wants to marry, it must have nailed him right between the eyes.''

"You really think he's going to let it frost his nuts for twenty years? And then stick her and her roommate one day when it gets to be too much for him? All because of something she said when she was five years old?''

"Two," Reppa said. "Right here I have it written down: 'A very precocious two.' ''

"All the more—" McCreary stopped and reconnoitered his forehead with his fingertips. "You got any kids, Rep, kids of your own? Kids are always—" He stopped again and snapped to a frown. "You sure he said Rumpelstiltskin?''

"Positive.''

"What year did Behrman and Andrea's mother get hitched?''

"Nineteen forty-seven, it must have been. I remember him saying they'd been married twenty years when she died. Which was late in 1967.''

It took a moment for McCreary to answer. "So Andrea must have been born sometime in 1945. You got her exact birth date anywhere, Rep?''

Reppa leafed ahead to his notes on the Halliwell interview. "March 7. There was a surprise party for her the year she was murdered that I want to say something about now that we're on the subject.''

"Later.'' McCreary beat a quick tattoo on the desk with his fingers. "Say she was two and a half the first time she met Behrman—listen, Rep, did you ask Annabelle anything about her sister's rape?''

"Not really. The topic never came up naturally, and it

seemed a little too sensitive just to pop on her out of nowhere."

"Did she know Behrman told you all this stuff about her family?"

Reppa stared intently at McCreary.

"What are you getting at? Do you see something I missed?"

"My trouble," McCreary said with a large sigh, "is you seem to have believed everything you were told. Consequently I don't have much choice now but to believe it all, too."

"In the beginning I might have let a few get by me," Reppa admitted. "But I got sharper as I went along."

"Great, but this ain't on-the-job training. I thought from the way you handled Leddy you had a few smarts. The more I hear, the more convinced I am I made a bad mistake. Tell me about this guy Kinder, now. What's his full name?"

"Lee, I think." Reppa checked his notebook. "Here it is—Lee S. Kinder."

"I don't suppose you got any bio info on him."

"Such as?"

"You say in your report that his role in Annabelle's life seems to be a little broader than that of a personal secretary. Broader like how?"

Reppa told of his interview with Annabelle and his suspicion that she might somehow be being kept a prisoner in her own loft. McCreary nodded for a while, then said condescendingly, "And thinking that, you just waltzed out of her pad without doing anything to verify it."

"Short of putting the place under surveillance, what could I have done?"

"Beats me, Rep. But if I'd been there, I wouldn't have left until I had something with Kinder's prints on it. If he's

241

anything like you describe him, chances are he's got a rap sheet somewhere.''

They moved on to his interview with Jill Wilkes. McCreary yawned mechanically, removed the wraparound sunglasses to reveal closed eyes when Reppa began describing his efforts to interrogate her about her impressions of Stanley Behrman.

"Am I boring you?"

"Yeah, actually. She wasn't about to tell you anything about Behrman, but there was somebody she *was* ripe to tell you about."

"Who?"

"Halliwell. Only you missed the signal."

"When?"

"Correct me, Rep, if I'm mistaken. What did she say when you told her you'd heard she didn't get along with her roommates?"

"She couldn't believe Annabelle had said that about her."

"But you slipped in another bit of info. Her first instinct was Halliwell had given you that scoop. If you'd been on the ball, it would have hit you that there must be some bad vibes between them. Again, correct me if I'm wrong. Ten-to-one odds, you split without asking her a single question about Halliwell."

Reppa said hotly, "I was just getting to it when she made me leave."

"How? She threaten to cut your dick off?"

"Look, McCreary—I read your reports. I don't recall that you got much of anywhere with her either."

"But she remembered me, babe, even after twelve years. I'd say that meant I had a pretty fair-sized effect. Think you can claim the same?"

Reminding himself to massage McCreary's ego, Reppa

managed a sheepish smile. "Well, I should have asked her about Halliwell. You're right. But I did a little better when I spoke to Halliwell about her."

Turning back to his notebook, he relayed what Halliwell had told him about Wilkes's fawning behavior toward Mald at Andrea's surprise party, added Halliwell's description of the impact Mald had had on the company there, Elizabeth Moffett in particular, and then started to discuss the aftermath of the party. But when he glanced up, McCreary once again was sitting with his sunglasses in his hand and his eyes squeezed shut. "What's the matter *now*?"

"Back up. You said Moffett was sitting off in a corner with Annabelle, the two of them talking, and Mald did something that made her drop her drink. What was it?"

"Halliwell couldn't really tell. He just said when Mald came near her she got all flustered."

"This was the first time she met Annabelle and Mald?"

"According to Halliwell."

"And she dropped her drink—*literally* dropped her drink?"

Apparently."

"Man, people don't just *drop* drinks. What the hell did Mald do to her?"

"You're making too much out of this. Mald's a pretty heavy guy. He wouldn't have to say or do very much to freak out a girl like Moffett."

"Maybe not." McCreary grinned and nodded. "But in her own way Annabelle's just as heavy. And Moffett winds up in a corner with her, pouring out her life story."

"Halliwell didn't say that. He just said they spent a little time together."

"Right, but *you* said Annabelle had quite a bit to say on the subject of Moffett and her ambitions. Me, my kind of mind wouldn't have let her get off the subject without exploring her interest in Moffett a little more deeply.''

"By interest you mean something sexual?''

"The scouting report is she's a dyke, right?''

"If she's anything. But Moffett wasn't.''

"Anybody know for sure? You do any checking into her background? Talk to any friends or relatives whose mouths might be aching to say something they couldn't twelve years ago?''

Reppa told of his thwarted efforts to call Elizabeth Moffett's parents. McCreary was silent awhile. He restored his sunglasses to a perch on the end of his nose and then gazed at Reppa over the top of them. "You were saying a minute ago that Moffett called up Halliwell all excited the morning after Andrea's birthday party. What did she want?''

"To talk to Andrea. She thought she was with Halliwell, but—''

"Talk to her about what?''

"Halliwell didn't know. He was too upset to stay on the phone with her after she told him Andrea hadn't spent the night at home.''

Reppa went over Halliwell's report of the charges, countercharges, lies, evasions, and so on that had been raised by Andrea's vanishing act the night of her party. Then he moved ahead to Halliwell's tale of how he and Andrea had broken up.

"Did you talk to any of the doormen in the building where Halliwell used to live?''

"No. Why?''

"To get their version of the night he supposedly tossed Andrea out bare-assed.''

"This was twelve years ago—''

"So? You think a doorman would forget something like

that? How often do you think he sees a naked broad come running out of his building? Sad. Behrman tells you Halliwell's into S&M with Andrea. You're given a perfect opportunity to find out if it's true, *and you blow it!*''

''Where was my opportunity?''

''The doorman, dummy. Did he see any bruises on her—scratches—whiplashes? Halliwell was careful, Behrman said, not to mark her in any place that showed. Well, that night was one time it would've *all* hung out!''

Reppa felt two scarlet patches burning on his cheekbones. His lips trembled. He started to say, ''I didn't have time—''

''You had over a week,'' McCreary said. ''Most of this stuff you didn't do wouldn't have taken ten minutes.''

''But it wasn't part of the investigation. I couldn't go around taking fingerprints and tracking down private detectives and witnesses to incidents that happened twelve years ago.''

McCreary lit a fresh cigar and grinned at him. ''Yet you're asking me to give you an extension. To do what, Rep? Pick up on all the broads you missed scoring with the first time around?''

''That's the second reference you've made . . .'' Reppa paused, feeling the dark glasses trained on him, and said placatingly, ''Look, I did a decent job. You can see for yourself that I turned up a lot of new information. Give me an extension so I'll have a shot at doing something with that information.''

''Can't be done, Rep.'' McCreary shrugged and then added casually, ''Which ain't to say you couldn't go ahead on your own.''

Reppa sensed that his face was still aflame. ''As a *parole officer*? I'd be up on charges the minute I tried—''

''Sure. As a parole officer.'' McCreary nodded gravely. ''Absolutely.''

"But with authorization there's a lot I could do. Mald, for example. If Wilkes knows who the real killer is, chances are he does, too. And I think with the right approach he can be reached."

"Not on *my* authorization. I can just see you putting one of your deft approaches on him, and about a week from now we'll get a call that you were found floating in the East River." McCreary smacked his desk with his open palm. "Go do your report, Rep. Do it up the way I told you and dictate it. Tell them in steno it's got to be on my desk by COB this afternoon."

With that McCreary rose and gestured toward the door, to signal COB for their venture, too. Reppa couldn't allow it.

"A week, McCreary. Just one more week."

McCreary stared morosely at him and shook his head.

"Why not? What have you got to lose? You want the same thing I do, and you want it just as bad. Meanwhile, regardless of how much you put down what I've done, I'm still the only hope you've got."

McCreary continued to shake his head.

"So you'd have some explaining to do if you gave me an extension. Wouldn't it be worth it if I turned up something? If I found the answers to just a couple of those questions?"

McCreary removed the cigar from his mouth and contemplated it sadly. "No, Rep. Trying to keep this investigation going would be suicide for both of us." For the first time that morning all trace of scorn had vanished from his voice; he sounded almost melancholy. "It's okay. I ain't going to hold it against you. If I came down on you a little heavy, it's only because I'm so damn disappointed."

"But all this stuff in my notebook . . ." Reppa paused in the numbing realization that they really had reached the

246

close of business between them. "The cops never had a lot of this information. Nobody did."

"The cops had something, though, that we don't. The license to dig, Rep. And there ain't no amount of dirty socks that can get us that."

"Even without it. If I were just given the authorization—"

Suddenly, unexpectedly, McCreary stumbled.

"Jesus," he said. "I really had my hopes up." He shook his head slowly, heavily, and reached for Reppa's hand. "Well, we gave it a good try anyway, good buddy. Maybe if de Spirit doesn't get out and we're both still around, we can take a shot at it again in another dozen years or so.

Spielman was absorbed in a crossword puzzle but looked up when Reppa entered the office.

"Back on the old case load?"

Reppa nodded.

"Good news for me," Spielman said laconically. "Bad for you."

He passed Reppa a note from Lidsky. Jimmy Wallace's aunt had called while Reppa was talking to McCreary. Wallace had been arrested again.

CHAPTER TEN

BETRAYAL

While Spielman's eyes roved the street in search of a parking place that wasn't too deep in broken glass, Reppa transferred his set of handcuffs from the leather case on his belt to his jacket pocket. Except when they went on bread runs together, he and Spielman traveled very separate routes, Spielman's bringing him around the parole office so infrequently he was known as the Phantom. Their relationship was not in any sense a friendship; occasionally, just to be sociable, they had spoken about football and their kids, but Reppa couldn't remember whether Spielman had three or four, and he couldn't seem to get Spielman to grasp that his name was not pronounced "Ruppa."

What brought them together at seven o'clock this morning was the sad, inescapable fact that Jimmy Wallace had to be taken into custody. Apart from writing a memo to the commissioners to justify his allowing a parolee with two arrests in less than a month to remain on the street, Lidsky had given Reppa no alternative but to request a warrant. It seemed absurd that the day after he'd completed the de Spirit investigation he was going to have to lock up the man whose threatened freedom had first gotten him embroiled in it. Reppa hadn't heard Wallace's version of this latest arrest yet, and he was not looking forward to it. Neither Graham nor Sweet had been around when he called the 26th Precinct yesterday evening, but the desk officer, after checking the arrest book, informed him that Wallace had been picked up on a charge of loitering, then released on his own recognizance after being given a summons. It didn't sound nearly as bad as the first bust. But Reppa had a grim premonition that the loitering charge, which was only a violation, had started out as something far more serious.

"Roof?" Spielman asked as they were entering Wallace's building.

"No. He's not going to run." Spielman huffing along behind him, he mounted the stairs.

"How the hell can anybody live in a place like this?"

"Nobody does."

"The kid's just using it as a shooting gallery?"

Reppa had meant that the two people here were prisoners, not tenants, but a display of social consciousness suddenly seemed hypocritical. He was climbing these stairs, after all, not as a caseworker but with a warrant in his pocket.

Outside Wallace's door Spielman muttered, "The meterman bit?"

"No need. If anything, he'll be happy to see us."

Whatever happened, Reppa decided, he wasn't going to let it bring him down too far. He had plugged himself into the idea that Wallace was better off out of circulation for a while. Until the governor made a decision on de Spirit's pardon and the fog had cleared a little over the battleground. If de Spirit was released from prison, the 26th Precinct would stop lassoing Wallace every time he went out on the street. Though if the pardon was denied, matters would remain murky.

"You don't need no riot squad," Wallace's aunt said

when she opened the door and saw Spielman. "He just been lying in the bed like dead since you was here."

"He must get up once in a while." To go out and get arrested if nothing else, Reppa added to himself.

"Only for the drugs."

"He's using again?"

The aunt stepped back, her mouth opening involuntarily.

"Since when?"

"I don't know. Couple weeks."

Her look wasn't accusing, but it still wanted to know if Reppa didn't think he had slipped up last time. He felt miserable. *Damn his eyes for talking him out of checking Wallace's arms.*

"Spielman?"

"That's my name."

"End of the hall. And you can put your piece away."

"You sure? This lady could be conning us."

"I'm sure." Wallace's aunt was wadded up over the kitchen table, one hand inside her housecoat, holding her chest as she struggled to clear her throat.

They found Wallace lying on the cot in skivvies and a turtleneck shirt.

"Don't tell my aunt," he murmured as Reppa rolled up the sleeves. "It'll kill her if she finds out."

Reppa nodded obligingly, but Spielman had to say: "It won't be anything she doesn't already know."

Wallace shrank away from the handcuffs. "You're lying. She don't know I'm dipping.

Reppa glared at Spielman as he said, "It's okay, Jimmy. They'll put you on methadone, and when you come back out, you'll be starting off clean again."

"Don't wanna come back out. Ever. Man, before you take me in, you gotta promise they can't come after me next time they got another paper for me to sign."

Their eyes met. Wallace's skittered away, but they'd stayed long enough to tell Reppa he'd dropped another nickel on top of that dime.

He went up alongside Wallace and took hold of a spindly arm. Together they left the apartment, Wallace refusing to look at his aunt, Reppa nodding good-bye to her as she closed the door behind them.

When they got to the car, they had to wait for Spielman to clear some toys off the back seat. Stuffed bunny. Plastic fire truck. Spielman held up a rubber mask that looked like Howdy Doody. Actually it was Alfred E. Neuman. For a moment Reppa was terrified Spielman was going to put it on and try to give Wallace a laugh. But then the mask went on the front seat, and Reppa climbed in the back with Wallace.

"What did they make you sign this time?"

Wallace gave one of his one-shoulder shrugs.

"An addition to your first statement—saying that you cut school on the morning you supposedly saw Danny?"

Wallace half-nodded.

"It's all a lie, isn't it, Jimmy?"

Wallace's eyes stared out the window as the car started up the ramp to the Triborough Bridge. In another few minutes they would be crossing the long, low bridge to Rikers Island, and for Wallace it could not be soon enough.

"We have to talk. One of four things is going to happen. Danny could get a pardon. Or he could win a new trial and be released because the state doesn't have a case against him anymore. Or he could get nothing and be kept in prison. In all of those events any statements you signed won't be used. The fourth possibility is the one we have to worry about—if Danny gets a new trial, and you have to testify."

251

Wallace could not tolerate the plural pronoun. "Man, there ain't none of this your problem that I can see."

"I'm trying to help you."

"How?" Wallace blurted. "You gonna go to court for me? Be the one to sit up there and lie?"

"Maybe I can see to it that you won't have to go to court. But you've got to level with me about these arrests. What did they pick you up for this time?"

"Another twenty years."

"Drugs again?"

Wallace could not look up. His face was frozen. "Only not like they tried to make it go down. I didn't sell nothing. I was only holding, like."

"What did they charge you with at first? Or what did they *say* they were going to charge you with?"

"Another big A."

"And then after you gave them the statement they wanted, they reduced it to loitering as a violation?"

Wallace sat silent, flexing his handcuffed arms behind his back.

"Too tight?"

"It ain't the time," Wallace said suddenly. "Twenty years, a hundred years—it's what they're gonna do to me in there."

"The guards?"

"The dudes, man. All them dudes. They're waiting on me—waiting up in Attica to fuck me in the ass."

Reppa turned and looked steadily at Wallace.

"You're not going to Attica, Jimmy. In a few days you'll get a preliminary parole violation hearing if you want it. I'm not supposed to tell you what to do, but I'm telling you. On the paper I'm going to send out to Rikers, check the box where it says you want a hearing. It's just to show we have grounds to hold you. Later, when you get

252

your final hearing, is the important time. There you'll tell your side of the story, and I'll say we held you chiefly to protect you from being harassed by the cops who were trying to get you to perjure yourself against your step-brother.''

A slip. *Half brother*, Wallace's eyes pleaded mutely.

"In any case, we're only getting you off the street now for your own protection. If I have any say in it—and at most hearings what the parole officer says counts for a lot—you'll be out again in a few weeks."

Wallace's eyes continued to look trapped. "You can't take me someplace else? You gotta take me out to the Rock?"

"As long as you're under twenty-one."

"Man, it's the same there. There's all them dudes out there, too."

"You'll be all right. Look at me. Jimmy, look at me." He heard his voice grow strident as what had been a plea to Wallace became a plea to himself as well. "It's only temporary, and you said yourself that you wanted to get off the street."

"Yeah," Wallace said lifelessly. "But this ain't gonna be far enough."

The dull, dark eyes glanced briefly at Reppa and then dropped to the car seat, where Reppa's fist lay clenched between them, the skin pulled taut and white across the knuckles.

Later that same morning, returning to the office so he could file the warrant receipt and tell Lidsky the bread run had accomplished its mission, Reppa found himself being pulled down the stairs to the first floor and through the hall to the Assignment Control Center, like an arsonist return-

253

ing to an explosives warehouse, in disbelief that his fuse has failed to ignite.

The door of McCreary's office was closed, and when he knocked on it, a secretary jabbed her head around a partition across the hall. If he was looking for McCreary, she said, McCreary was on annual leave.

Already seeing a glimpse of it all the way through, Reppa demanded to know since when and learned that McCreary had put in a memo late yesterday afternoon requesting two weeks off so he could attend to a suddenly emergent personal crisis.

Then the secretary said, "You're Mr. Reppa, aren't you? Mr. McCreary left this for you."

She handed him a sealed envelope. Inside it was one of McCreary's business cards. On the back of it McCreary had written: *Thanks, Rep*.

And though that was all, Reppa understood instantly how completely he had been had.

By midnight most of the windows along Riverside Drive were dark. Reppa sat behind the wheel of his car on the west side of the Drive, the focus of his attention a row of windows that were among the scattering still lit. These were the three windows that belonged to the D apartment on the eighth floor of the building on the corner of 116th Street and the Drive. Two people had gone up to the apartment over three hours ago, and he was relying on his intuition that one of them would leave before the night was out.

Dark clouds rolled across the sky. A low wind whipped along the Drive, rattling tree limbs, snatching pedestrians off their course. Earlier there had been a violent rainstorm. He'd gotten to the building shortly before it started and informed the doorman that he was a parole officer trying to

254

track down an absconder who was reportedly living in the neighborhood. After being shown the building directory, he confided that one of the residents had a name that matched the alias his absconder sometimes used. An extreme long shot that this was his man, but he had to make sure. He was allowed to take the elevator unannounced to the eighth floor, where he learned the D apartment faced Riverside Drive. Up that high its windows couldn't be seen inside from the street, but the alternation of light and dark in their panes would tell him when someone came home or went out.

Usually Reppa hated this kind of surveillance. It was boring and most often fruitless. But McCreary's message this morning had flailed him until he could no longer turn away from either his misguided faith in McCreary or his nagging distrust of Zippy. Even though he had been outside her building going on four hours now, a scalding anger still boiled in him.

Only when he recalled going through her purse that afternoon while she was in the bathroom did he have a twinge of regret. She trusted him, after all, enough, anyway, to believe his intentions toward her were benign, and it seemed sheer paranoia on his part that he could not make himself place an equivalent trust in her. Seriously, now, was it even remotely possible that the man in her life (the man she'd described as being very much like him) was J. J. McCreary? And furthermore, wasn't it going off the deep end to believe the two of them had conspired to swipe the material he'd uncovered during his investigation and use it to win de Spirit an acquittal, to force the NYPD to reopen the case, and perhaps even to take a stab at solving it themselves?

Paranoia. Sheer paranoia. And yet, having experienced both of them in close and intimate circumstances, he had to acknowledge that it was maddeningly possible. McCreary was a skillful actor, quite capable of seeming to scorn Reppa's information and ideas while actually finding them illuminating; Zippy was no less deft at dodging personal questions, scooting away from serious discussions. And what was more—what was perhaps the most damning proof—McCreary seemed to know there was something going on between him and Zippy. Just a shot in the dark? A shrewd guess based on some change in his face or voice when he spoke about her?

Her address had been on her driver's license. Told five days ago by the liaison officer at Ma Bell that there were no telephone subscribers in all of New York named Zipporah Dwersky, he had two choices, now that he had definite proof that she lived in the city: either she didn't have a phone (highly unlikely) or it was listed under another name. Reppa knew (although he could not stop himself from calling information to make sure) that she would never be so stupid as to list it under McCreary's name. He also knew, without having the will power to keep himself from putting her building under surveillance, that he did not want to find out any more. The thought that she was linked with McCreary was hurtful and enraging, but it remained only a thought. Should he learn it was true, he would have to do something, and while he did not know what it would be, he wished he had not begun wearing his gun again after the investigation. With it holstered now on his belt, sitting in a car for four hours was uncomfortable and thinking for four hours dangerous.

Even conceding that the thing between him and Zippy— the affair or whatever it was they were having—had not meant to her what it meant to him, he'd gotten to know her too well over the last few days, and his objectivity was eroded by passion. Night before last, parrying with Leilah, he had convinced himself that he would stop seeing Zippy in a week or two, certainly no longer than that. Now he could easily have told himself, if he had not been so vigorously denying it, that he was in love with her.

Around ten o'clock, as he'd been watching her building, she had entered it with a man. It happened so quickly, the two of them lurching around the corner of the building under an umbrella, and it was raining so hard at the time that he caught only a whirl of long, dark hair and the backs of two trench coats, one blue and the other tan, before they vanished through the entrance. He hadn't been sure at first that it was she, but two minutes and ten seconds later, by his watch, the lights went on in her apartment. Just about right for an eight-floor elevator trip.

A short while later the lights had gone out and then come on again about half an hour ago. During that interval, steadfastly refusing to abandon his mind to images of what was occurring in 8D, he sat hatching the strategy that would carry him through the rest of the night. By one o'clock, if the man was still up there, he'd face the fact that the two of them were in for the night and go home. If the man left, however, he would follow him. McCreary (and the longer he sat there, the more positive he grew that it could be no one else) lived in Demarest, a small New Jersey town just a few miles north of the George Washington Bridge. What he ought to do, logically, was get close enough to the building for a good look at the man when he left; or, failing that, tail his car until he made certain whether it was or was not headed for Demarest.

As Reppa stared at the row of windows, a light went out in one of them and a shadow flitted across the blind in another, swelling for an instant from an amorphic blob to a tall and unmistakably masculine profile. The shadow as suddenly disappeared. A second window darkened. Then the third. Then, several beats after Reppa had decided they'd bedded down again, this time for the night, his heart caught.

A man in a tan trench coat—McCreary's height and moving with McCreary's customary swiftness—was leaving the building under a dark, wide-brimmed hat that hid his face.

Reppa's hands began trembling so hard that it was several moments before he could turn his key in the ignition. By then McCreary was walking up 116th Street toward Broadway.

Reppa made a U-turn and cruised slowly past the foot of the street. He saw McCreary disappear from view over the rise in the center of the block. He pulled up to the curb and waited. His thought was that McCreary had parked somewhere up the hill. In a few moments McCreary's car would come down 116th Street and then go speeding off up Riverside Drive toward the bridge, and he would follow. But suppose McCreary was parked on Claremont Avenue, or on Broadway, and took another route to the bridge? He got out of his car and stood on tiptoe, craning to see over the rise.

McCreary was standing on the corner of Broadway with one hand clamped to his hat, holding it on his head against the wind, and the other hand waving in the air. A cab? Where would McCreary be going in a cab? Unless . . .

He vaulted back into his car and raced around the corner, even as it came to him that McCreary had taken a hotel room in town. It all suddenly made perfect sense. That emergent personal crisis—the last-minute memo requesting annual leave. For the next two weeks McCreary was going underground right here in the city, so he could follow at close range the scent his stooge had naïvely dangled under his nose! It was a serious game. One that, if

McCreary was discovered, would cost him his career and pension. Its success depended almost entirely on McCreary: how good he was at it. It also, Reppa realized, depended partly on him. The issue all at once became clear: *Could he allow McCreary to get away with the very thing that he had not been able to find a way to allow himself to get away with?*

His face was tingling, and his fingertips were numb; he drove as if he were asleep, yet he was intensely aware of his surroundings. He saw McCreary get into a cab when he was still more than a hundred yards from Broadway. When he turned the corner, he saw the cab waiting for the light at 115th Street. His foot hit the brake, and he slowed to a crawl, not sure how closely he should follow. McCreary might know his car, having looked up the make and license plate number in his personnel folder against just this kind of situation, and McCreary would also know how to spot a tail.

Reppa saw the light had changed. He waited until a car had slipped between his own and the cab. Then he put his foot on the gas pedal and went forward, watching as the blocks and traffic lights passed before him like a great unevenly illuminated diorama.

He was unsurprised when the cab turned east at 110th Street. His recognition of McCreary's game had included a hunch that McCreary was using as his temporary home base some fleabag on the edge of Harlem, where he could come and go unnoticed.

But at Central Park West the cab went south rather than north toward Harlem, and at Eighty-sixth Street it turned east and entered the park.

Reppa frowned. The East Side? Not only were there few hotels on the Upper East Side, but it was the section of town where McCreary—black, shaven skull—would be the most conspicuous.

His surroundings very different now, his eyes wandered among the trees and did not notice at first that the cab had disappeared around a bend. Speeding up, he splashed through a deep puddle left by the rainstorm. He turned on his windshield wipers. When the glaze of water cleared from in front of him, he saw the cab at the end of a line of traffic waiting for the light at Fifth Avenue. He fell back again, in panicky confusion over what he would do when the trip ended. Grab McCreary on the street and have it out with him then and there? Find out where he was holed up and leave it at that for the time being?

The light changed. Up ahead, the light at Madison Avenue was still green. The cab raced to make it. Reppa, trying to keep pace, saw the cab clobber a pothole as it skittered through the intersection. Its taillights flickered and went out. A few yards farther on it sputtered to a stop. Reppa braked and allowed himself to be caught at the light while he sat watching the hackie vainly try to revive his engine. In a few moments the man got out and opened his hood. Then McCreary got out, too, handed the man some bills, and started to walk rapidly toward Park Avenue.

Following again when the light changed, Reppa saw McCreary clutch at his hat as the wind threatened to lift it. Finally, turning the corner of Park Avenue and heading south, McCreary surrendered to the elements and removed the hat. That was when Reppa gaped at the full head of gray hair and broad, fair-skinned face that were now bared to him and realized he had not been following McCreary.

The man strolled down Park Avenue to Eighty-first Street and turned east. Since Eighty-first Street was one-way westbound, Reppa could no longer follow by car. Looking wildly around for a legal parking place, he saw

260

none and pulled up to a hydrant. Throwing his Division of Parole placard in the windshield, he set off at a trot.

The man was now more than a block ahead of him. The excitement draining from his legs, Reppa pursued mostly out of curiosity and a perverse satisfaction that the man, married, was hurrying simply to get home under the wire. He still could hardly believe that he had been so wrong about Zippy. Her reason for concealing her boyfriend's identity from him had been merely the universal instinct of her sex for secrecy. It was relieving to know that he could trust her now, tell her about McCreary and his duplicity (though never, of course, of his suspicions concerning her and McCreary). Perhaps she could even advise him. Should he track McCreary down and demand . . . demand what? Should he report McCreary to the agency for . . . for what? For doing without authorization what he hadn't been able to do without authorization himself? Envy, not outrage but simple envy—wasn't that really the largest part of what he was feeling now?

Stung by the realization, Reppa almost ran blindly into a woman walking a great Dane. With a muttered apology he careened past her and saw the man enter a high rise on the corner of Third Avenue.

Now what? Flash his shield and ask the doorman for the name of the man who'd just come in? The doorman, if he wasn't too swift, would give it to him questioningly. If he happened to get a doorman who was on the ball, though, it could be awkward. Why'd he want to know? What kind of a badge was that, exactly? And in any case the doorman would probably call the man on the intercom after he left and let him know a parole officer had just been inquiring about him. And if that were to get back to Zippy, who, perhaps to provoke a little jealousy, had told the night man in her life about the day man in her life—

261

He couldn't believe himself. A few minutes ago he'd been tracking the man as if he were a wounded lion. So the doorman gave him a hard time. So Zippy learned he'd done a little checking up on her. So?

For a final moment he stood outside the building, the wind cutting through his clothing. Then he stepped toward the door and entered. The doorman listened to his request, glanced at his shield, and broke into a grin. Hey, what was his problem? Couldn't he tell the players on his own team without a scorecard?

Reppa was afraid he was going to be told the man was a fellow parole officer. But it was worse than that.

Within half an hour he was home and shaking Leilah awake because he sure as hell had to have help with this one.

CHAPTER ELEVEN

THE BARGAIN

As soon as he had confessed all, he felt uncomfortably unguilty. Having publicly named the culprit, he resented the freedom with which he could now curse her. Lying beside the victim, he was disturbed by the equanimity with which she accepted his confession.

Even more galling was the idea that Leilah, who hadn't left her bed during the whole investigation, could have seen all along a design forming from his descriptions of the people and places he'd visited, while he saw only disparate fragments, and he kept trying to shrug it away. In the last tremor of each shrug he felt that if there were just a way she could give him a few pointers without making it feel as if she were in competition with him, he could bear it.

And yet the need to be in competition with her was tonight a physical craving, as though his affair with Zippy could not, finally, be condoned unless she refused to condone it. If she would blame him, he could trot out all the reasons he was blameless. But when she told him she could see where he might have an excuse or two for what he'd done, he no longer saw where he had any.

After a while, happily, her baser nature began to rumble.

"Just because I understand why you got it on with her doesn't mean I don't hate your guts. The question is, would you have told me about it if you hadn't found out who her boyfriend is?"

"In a way I wanted to tell you about it a hundred different times, and in a way I never wanted to tell you. Even now there's more I want to say, and at the same time I feel I've already said too much. What puzzles me is I still don't see why she did it. She never tried to pump me for information . . . or asked me to slant my report . . . or hinted that maybe I should stop trying to dig so hard. Still, she must have wanted something. If it had been McCreary she was hooked up with, I could think she'd been put up to it just to keep tabs on me."

"But you're still convinced he knew the two of you were getting it on?"

"My guess is he has one of the girls on the office switchboard helping him out. All she had to do was plug into my line while I was talking to Zippy and report what she'd overheard to him. It couldn't have been much, because we never said anything, really. But McCreary wouldn't need much. He's slick, that bastard."

"Maybe," Leilah said carefully, "she's equally slick. You claim she never tried to pump you for information. How do you know she didn't get what she wanted without your being aware of it?" He looked up sharply. "But I'm more inclined to think she got something from you she didn't want. You overpowered the poor woman, Reppa. She wasn't supposed to wind up in the sack with you, but she couldn't help herself."

"Overpowered! It was about as mutual—"

"Oh, quit being so dense. I don't say she didn't have a lot of ambivalence at first about what she was doing. And no doubt it was part of her plan to flirt a little. But at some point she got carried away. What did you do—your drag-them-off-to-look-at-the-sunset number?"

"I didn't really do much of anything. It just happened."

"Believe that and you also have to believe that God made the atom bomb. But anyway, you're both stuck now with the consequences. You haven't looked at this thing from her side. She had a mission with you, and she blew it. Her boyfriend, I'm sure, isn't any happier at the moment with her performance than I am with yours. Now he's got McCreary hot on the case, and I have a cheat in my bed."

"Oho," said Reppa, "so that's your *real* opinion."

Faced away from him, Leilah said, "Not someone who cheated on me. Someone who's cheated himself. You did all the work on that investigation. And then you went to McCreary and threw it away."

"But I had to go to him. I needed more authorization, and he was the only one who could give it to me."

Leilah shook her head. But she was kind enough not to say: "And why did you feel you needed more authorization?" Reppa knew that despite all his thinking about this question, he still had hovered on the perimeter of it, but for tonight, at least, he finally seemed exiled to the depths of himself, examining his actions and trying to come to grips with them realistically. The flaw, he decided, was in his own character. He was stupid. He had handed the bird to McCreary on a platter and then heaped on the trimmings when McCreary told him all he had were the same old bones. Even Leilah saw further than he did. It was wisdom on her part. A firmer grasp of human nature. He not only was stupid—he felt stupid. With McCreary he had gone along on the assumption that he might be robbed of the credit for a job well done but not of the opportunity to do the job, and Zippy, toasting him across the table in

265

the bar with shining eyes, had beguiled him into thinking that her rebel had the same cause as his own.

The window behind the TV set lightened from mauve to a dark russet, and then it was nearly daylight. Leilah had slept restlessly, and he hadn't slept at all. "Poor Reppa," she said. "What are you going to do?"

"What would you do?"

"Now? There's only *one* thing I can see for you to do."

"I know." He sighed heavily. "But it's really going to be rough."

"Not necessarily."

He looked over at her and saw she didn't mean now. She meant *right now*. He got up and walked quickly around the bed. She reached for the pulley above her and then for him beside her. She showed him that Dr. Molnar's caution to treat her as a woman who was in her ninth month of pregnancy didn't mean it had to be the same as making love to a woman who was nine months pregnant. Gently, kneeling, he was surprised to discover that she'd put her diaphragm in at some point during the night. As if she knew he needed reassurance that he wasn't stupid about people—he was just a little underdeveloped.

He was pacing the sidewalk in front of his building when she arrived. He was ready for her to ask him why he hadn't waited for her inside, but first she wrapped her arms around him and held up her chin, her mouth expectant. He heard himself clear his throat, too loudly.

"Let's go somewhere and have a drink."

Her eyes opened. "What's wrong?"

"There's a bar around the corner on Second Avenue."

"Bad day?"

"Better than yesterday." He paused. "I didn't tell you—

266

the guy who assigned me the investigation apparently has decided now to follow up on it on his own.''

"McCreary?''

"Oh, you know about him. Did I mention him to you?''

"No—I don't know—you may have. But we knew he was the parole officer in charge of making the assignment.''

"We?''

"The memo we got from Albany—Legal Aid.''

She looked fleetingly at him as they walked and then off in another direction. *You've still got a chance to tell me on your own,* his glance had said. Now his words followed. "You know about McCreary. Anything I should know about?''

"De Spirit is getting a new trial. It's not official yet, but it's definite. Now I've got to see about getting the court to release him without bail, since he's indigent.''

"*Release* him?''

"They have to. At least they have to set a reasonable bail. He's like any other defendant now.''

"What about the pardon?''

Zippy shook her head. "Evidently it was turned down.''

"Already? My report just went up to the governor two days ago.''

He gazed at her and did not miss what he thought was a superior look passing over her face. *Told you it wouldn't mean anything.*

Stopping and waiting until she had no alternative but to stop, too, and look at him, he said coldly, "Anything else I should know about?''

"It's McCreary, isn't it? You feel he's stealing your thunder.'' Then, as if realizing she had spoken too lightly, she took his hand and squeezed it. "But, Frank, what can he do that you didn't? He's only a parole officer, and besides, he looks so militant now, who's going to—?''

"How do you know what he looks like?"

"By reputation. Everyone in our field who's been around any length of time becomes known. You will, too, if you stick it out long enough. You've already cut a fair-sized swath in certain sectors."

She kissed him quickly on the cheek, just in time for the rabbit in her eyes to elude the hound in his, which was baying that she didn't know McCreary—not even by reputation. But someone else knew him. Someone she'd just better hope to hell *she* knew.

In the bar Reppa, feeling nothing but his transparency, watched her pick up his hand and hold it.

When they had sat there in silence for several suffocating moments, she asked offhandedly, as though it had just occurred to her: "What did you mean when you called— that you absolutely had to see me today?"

"We had to lock up Jimmy Wallace the other morning. He's sitting out on Rikers Island now until we see which way the current's flowing."

"De Spirit's cousin?"

"Stepbrother."

"You're hurting my hand."

"I guess I'm angry that you haven't even given Wallace enough thought to get the bloodlines straight." She flushed. "Because if he does something like hang himself in his cell, I'm going to feel it's on my head. And I'm not going to let myself carry that kind of weight around alone."

"You're saying I'll have to bear my share of the guilt, too, because I pushed for a new trial?"

"A little more than that."

She looked at him, and her pupils darkened as he leaned forward and nodded.

"I know, Zippy," he said quietly. "I know who he is."

268

The admission, though made with a sense of release, was not without pain. He still could not accept that he'd been so wrong about her.

Sitting there, he watched the flush bloom more hectically on her cheeks, their hands unclasp, her lips form a silent "When?"

"Last night. I saw him come out of your building and followed him to his. The doorman told me who he was."

Her head lowered, and her eyes became invisible to him. "How did you find out where I live?"

"Your driver's license. I went through your purse yesterday." Her eyes remained lowered. "I'm not proud of it, but you were so secretive about your personal life that I finally had to make sure you weren't concealing anything that could be harmful to me."

The truth, but not all of it.

"One might wonder," she said listlessly, "why I didn't take better care of my purse. Who knows?"

"Only you," he said, suspecting he might, too.

"Anyway." She gave a bitter, ironic laugh. Then, still gazing downward, she said, "So you had to ask his doorman who he was."

Reppa nodded. "Until last night the only time I'd ever seen him was in that movie, and that was a long while ago."

"And he's so sure everyone still knows him by sight. I told him you weren't . . ."

"I wasn't what?"

She reached for his hand. "What are you going to do, Frank, now that you know?"

He folded his arms and sat back.

"Get in touch with de Spirit. Let him know he's being represented by a lawyer who's sleeping with the cop who sent him up. Then I suppose the people at Legal Aid should be told there may be a slight conflict of interest in your handling of the appeal. After that I think I'd like to hear from Big Steve himself what the plan is.''

"You're feeling very self-righteous about this, aren't you?''

"Actually . . .'' Reppa pulled his chair forward and frowned down at the table. "Why did you do it, Zippy? What were you after?''

"I really didn't—''

"Information about the investigation? Whether I'd found out anything?''

"Steve just wanted to make sure—''

"Whether people had forgotten about the case?''

"No. I was only supposed to—''

"Keep tabs on me? What about Cupach? Was he keeping tabs on us in the meantime?''

Angrily she shouted, "At least he didn't stoop to spying on you and following you around!''

"He didn't have to. He had you to do all his spying for him.'' Reppa paused. "Though what he learned about me from you I still can't figure out.''

"That you were honest,'' she murmured.

"That's *all*?''

"And that you had a personal motive for undertaking the investigation, but that it had nothing to do with any of the people associated with either Andrea or Elizabeth.''

"What else? There's got to be more.''

Her head shook slowly. She held the sleeve of her dress between her fingers, pinching the thin material, twisting it. "I keep telling you. I really was overwhelmed—we were just supposed to—''

"Just supposed to what?''

"Stop attacking me. You're no big, wide-eyed innocent in this either. From the first you didn't trust me.''

"The only instinct I had about you that was right, it turns out."

Zippy seemed to shrink, and her shoulders sagged. "Do you really believe that?"

"No." His eyes dropped. "But I still don't understand— what are you and Cupach up to, anyway?" He looked at her. "Or better, what's he up to?"

"What do you think? That I'm just doing his bidding in this?"

"You have to admit it seems like it might be more than just a coincidence that Cupach is sleeping with the lawyer for the last man in the world he wants to see win an appeal and get out of prison."

"We were already seeing each other," Zippy said with pursed lips, "long before I asked to be assigned the case."

"Oh, *that* makes it much better. That *really* eliminates the possibility that Cupach had an ulterior motive for starting an affair with you. To say nothing about *your* motive for requesting the assignment!"

"I'll tell you my motive. He's willful, he's stubborn, but above all, Frank, he's extremely direct. He knows what he wants and what he believes in, and he's inspired me to feel that I, too, can become all those things."

"So direct that he can't stay overnight with you and has to come and go from your building in a hat that hides his face?"

"Being direct doesn't mean being stupid. Obviously we have to cool it while I'm handling the appeal. And besides, he's separated from his wife. She isn't contesting the divorce, but he's afraid she will if she finds out he's seeing someone."

Reppa half-nodded, half-frowned. "How long have you been seeing each other?"

"About four months."

"What's he doing now? Other than acting as a consultant on cop movies?"

"That's not really any of your business."

"For real, Zippy. Unless I get some good answers, I'm going to walk out of here and go straight to your supervisor at Legal Aid."

"Go ahead," she blurted. "It'll ruin my career—but go ahead."

"I don't see where it's going to do much for Cupach's career, either."

Reluctantly she said, "It won't. You're right. You could ruin his chances to be appointed a deputy commissioner. It's what he wants now more than anything." She shrugged dispiritedly. "Oh, it's not what he really wants. He'd really like to become chief of detectives or something equivalent. But that's out, because they won't let him back in the department."

"Why not?"

"Because—he resigned when he took that movie role. It's every cop's dream to come into a case like Behrman-Moffett. The credit for breaking it is the only kind of recognition he can ever really get. But so few ever get it that the ones who do wind up being hated."

"Not if they don't exploit it to become instant celebrities."

"Instant *what*? If anything, Steve was exploited. They put him in one stupid movie, and then, when he didn't *instantly* become Sylvester Stallone, they dropped him. Leaving him nowhere. He can't get back on the force. The case was so long ago they don't even call him for cameo roles on TV cop shows anymore. The most he can get now is an occasional consulting job. Sure, they pay well—better than being a cop ever would have. But he wants more. He got a taste of the kind of power a man of his ability deserves, and he wants it again. So when he heard about this new deputy commissioner's position they're creating, he put in for it."

"Put in for it with whom?"

Zippy hesitated. "Well, he's still got a few friends."

"Who owe him one?"

"Who know the city will be a lot better off if he gets the job rather than someone who doesn't know the first thing about what it's like to be a cop but is owed a political favor. The only thing that can stop his appointment is if de Spirit's pardoned or found innocent at a new trial. The pardon was never a real worry. Now that any possibility of its happening has been eliminated—"

"What about the trial? Or is that all rigged? A perjured statement from Wallace that will guarantee de Spirit is convicted again?"

Her eyes took on their faraway look—the same look he'd seen whenever she felt him looming too close.

"There isn't going to be a new trial. So you don't have to worry. You can promise Wallace that he won't have to testify against his *step*brother."

"But you just finished telling me the Supreme Court had granted the appeal."

She shrugged again, and Reppa cocked his head to one side. With a sigh she said, "It's been arranged."

"*What's* been arranged?"

"Between me and the ADA who's going to be handling the case. Once the appeal went through, and we were both positive it would. I did a good job on that appeal, drafting it, getting it through channels. I learned a lot on this case."

So have I, love, Reppa thought. He said, "Congratulations, but that still doesn't answer my question."

A voice so low that he could barely hear it. "Don't ask

273

me . . . please . . . Just take my word that no one's going to be hurt by it.''

He shook his head. "You're going to have to tell me. This arrangement, what is it?"

"It's only verbal at this point. A gentlemen's agreement. If you have any ideas of taking this to somebody, it'll be denied."

"As are most gentlemen's agreements now," Reppa said stonily.

She lifted her head then and stared at him: Was he so perfect?

"Do you want me to say that I won't go to anybody with what you tell me? Again, I can't. It depends."

"On what?"

"How bad it sounds. Outside of Wallace I don't have any commitment to anyone in this."

"What about Parole?"

"I work for them. They get their money's worth in sweat. My blood belongs only to me."

Zippy continued to stare at him. "You really are like him, you know." She gave another long sigh and then murmured, "All right. What more do I have to lose?"

She told him that the ADA was prepared to reduce the charge against de Spirit to manslaughter if she, in turn, would persuade de Spirit to plead guilty. The ADA would then tell the judge that the state recommended that de Spirit be sentenced to time served in the view of his good record while in prison and his relative youth at the time of the offense. The judge, prepped in advance for what was going down, would agree. De Spirit would thus be released immediately, and at the same time the manslaughter conviction against him would stand. Everyone would emerge a winner. Not so terrible, now, was it?

Perhaps she would be kind enough, Reppa said, to

274

explain to him just how she was going to convince de Spirit to plead guilty when he'd spent the last twelve years claiming he wasn't.

She looked at him perplexed. "But why shouldn't he? He'll get out of prison in any event."

Reppa said dryly, "Not everyone wants to go through life with a conviction for a double homicide on his record."

Zippy shook her head. "You're not going to believe this, I know, but it's true."

"What's true?"

"He really is guilty."

Reppa sat stunned for several moments. "Oh, come on . . ."

"Really. Steve said that in his oral confession de Spirit admitted it happened just about the way Steve thought it did. But when it came time to make a written statement he refused. Later he denied having made a confession—even orally. As a result a lot of things he told Steve didn't come out at the trial, because the judge ruled that the particulars of his confession couldn't be admitted—"

"Things like what?"

"How he got into the apartment. The big problem all along was that there was only one logical way for a burglar to get in—through the kitchen window. But it would have taken an acrobat to reach it from the fire escape."

"Or someone extremely tall," interjected Reppa, remembering *Andrea and Elizabeth*.

"Neither of which de Spirit is. He's average height and has no special athletic ability. Steve was convinced he didn't get into the apartment through the window. He got in a much easier way."

"How?"

"Through the door."

"One of the girls let him in?"

Zippy nodded.

"Andrea?"

"Not Andrea. Andrea wasn't even home when he came."

"Elizabeth?"

Zippy smiled at his surprise. "Steve's idea all along was that Elizabeth was the first one to come home that morning. And that as far as she knew, she was going to have the place to herself."

"And knowing that she was there alone, she opened the door without checking to see who it was, and de Spirit forced his way in? I can't believe she would have been that careless."

"She wasn't. At least not in that way. She let him in willingly."

"Why? What story could he have possibly given her?"

"None. She knew him."

"You're not serious."

Zippy nodded mutely. "They met, Steve thinks, at the center where she did draft counseling. De Spirit didn't have to worry about the draft, being a convicted felon, but he pretended he did. She looked like an easy mark to him. White, young, not terribly attractive, a high degree of social consciousness, and very little street wisdom to go with it. All de Spirit had to do was charm her a little in the hope that it would pay off someday. Then, the morning the center was closed early because of the Kennedy assassination, he walked her home and convinced her somehow to invite him up. It looked like a sure score to him with very little risk. She'd be too embarrassed by her own stupidity to admit to the police that she knew the burglar and had invited him in voluntarily. And even if she did file charges against him, it would be her word against his that she hadn't given him the clock radios and whatever else he took as gifts. But when he tied her up, he got aroused.

276

Deciding to rape her on top of it, he removed her clothes. Then Andrea came home unexpectedly, and the whole thing exploded."

"You started out by saying 'Steve thinks.' This is all just his idea of what happened, in other words."

She shook her head. "De Spirit admitted when he confessed orally that he knew Elizabeth. He just wouldn't put it in writing."

"So it really is only Cupach's word that he said any of this."

"There's more than his word, Frank. There's proof that Elizabeth and not Andrea was the one alone with the killer in the apartment."

"What sort of proof?"

"Before I tell you any more"—Zippy swallowed visibly—"you've got to promise not to go to anybody with this. I'm giving you information that no one but Steve and a few others know about, and in return I want your pledge that you won't do anything with it to hurt me."

The bargains you're making, he thought. "All right," he said but then reconsidered. "Unless it turns out that someone besides de Spirit is the killer. Then the whole thing's off."

He sat back to await her protest, still half-convinced it was a trick. But she said firmly, "Fair enough. If de Spirit is innocent, you're free to do whatever you want. Including turn me in to my supervisor for what I'm doing."

For a long moment she stared at him, silently communicating the message.

"Oh, yes," she said then. "That's part of it. You're not to say a word to anyone about my relationship with Steve or my real reason for wanting to handle de Spirit's appeal."

The twin spots of color high on each cheekbone . . . another blue dress, this one with a low collar that revealed

277

all of her long, smooth throat. Reppa remembered, seeing her swallow again, that it, too, colored when she was excited.

"Once more," he said slowly, aware of his own difficulty in swallowing, "only if de Spirit is guilty."

She turned away and looked off across the bar, as if to make certain they were unobserved. Then turned back and parted her lips. In a near whisper she said, "Andrea was murdered with her clothes on, though she was found naked. Elizabeth was found with her clothes on, but the evidence indicated she was naked when she was murdered."

"What evidence?"

"Cloth fibers in the stab wounds. Andrea had them, Elizabeth didn't. Which doesn't positively mean she was naked when she was stabbed, but it strongly suggests it. Steve thinks de Spirit was afraid people at the draft center had seen him hanging around Elizabeth. To hide the fact that she was the one in the bedroom with him, he dressed her and stripped Andrea after he killed them. There was even a hint that he might have had some feeling for Elizabeth in the way he laid her out on the bed."

With her arms folded so peacefully over her wounds . . . Reppa let out a groan when still another memory struck him. Was it possible that Jill Wilkes hadn't been lying after all when she claimed she'd seen de Spirit outside her building?

"Why didn't any of this come out at de Spirit's trial?"

"Do you remember the Sam Sheppard case?" Zippy countered. "Well, why didn't it come out at his first trial that the murderer was almost definitely lefthanded whereas Sheppard was righthanded?"

"But there the prosecution naturally wanted to conceal that information from Sheppard's lawyer. If they'd leveled about the physical evidence at the scene of the crime, it

278

would have wrecked their whole case. De Spirit's trial was different. What was the point of holding back the fact that the killer had reversed the actual circumstances under which Andrea and Elizabeth were stabbed?"

"It was a strategy decision. The prosecution felt that as long as they couldn't bring into court any of de Spirit's statements to Steve as to how he got into the apartment, they'd have a better shot with the jury by going along with the theory that Andrea was the prime target. Since she was by far the more attractive, it was much simpler to convince twelve people that a burglar had been sidetracked by her. So, really, de Spirit's trick of reversing the victims backfired on him. It allowed the prosecution to make the case against him that much stronger, especially knowing that de Spirit or his lawyer couldn't mention the switch in clothing either. If they had, the ballgame was over. Because, theoretically, they couldn't possibly know a switch had occurred.

Reppa said grimly, "So the prosecution knowingly suppressed an important piece of evidence."

"Don't you? Every time you do a violation report? So the case against your client looks either better or worse?"

"To an extent maybe. But that's not—"

"The same? Isn't it? Really, isn't it? I'm not trying to score a point, Frank. That's just the way it is. We all have to resort to it or something like it if we're going to do our jobs."

Hearing her argument, Reppa could not believe his own slowness to understand. She was not pleading for forgiveness—she was pleading for him to wise up. "Did the prosecution have any witnesses who ever actually saw de Spirit and Elizabeth together?"

"Jill Wilkerson, for one."

"She saw de Spirit—de Spirit alone—outside her building. She says.''

"You seem doubtful.''

"Doubtful is putting it kindly.''

Zippy had been giving him the full force of her angry eyes, but now she looked past him, concentrating on the wall of the bar. "Steve believed her.''

"Because he wanted to. Just like he wanted to believe Ax Gooden. It makes it a lot easier to believe someone when you're staking your whole career on his story being true.''

Her eyes still refused to look at him. "You're not just talking about Steve, are you?'' When he shook his head slowly, hers began shaking rapidly. "You think I'm a fool for believing him, but you don't understand. You're only a parole officer, and you're out of touch. You talk to them in your office, and you visit them in their homes. You see only the surface—only what they want you to see. You never see what they're really like. You didn't see Andrea Behrman and Elizabeth Moffett after they were murdered. Steve did. He was one of the first to see their bodies, and he knew right away that whoever did it had to be removed. One way or another. Whatever it took to do it. As a cop you don't have the luxury of waiting until you've built an airtight case. By the time you do, you've got a Son of Sam on your hands, and a dozen people are dead. You have to act quickly. Act on your instincts. And Steve's were that Danny de Spirit was a very evil kid. He'd killed two women, and if he wasn't removed, he'd kill more.''

Reppa shifted in his chair, made uncomfortable by the very obvious sincerity of her passion. "When did his instincts about de Spirit change?''

"*Change?* They've never changed. He's still just as firmly convinced as ever that de Spirit's guilty.''

"Then why is he willing to be party to a deal that would give de Spirit time served and let him back out on the street?"

"Not *willing* to be," Zippy said, cuttingly. "*Forced* to be. He wants that deputy commissioner's job, and he won't get it if de Spirit is cleared now, after all the controversy that's been stirred up. He's compromising, Frank. Compromising his ethics, if you want to call it that. He doesn't. There are no hard and fast ethics anymore. Not in the criminal justice system. There are only personal codes at best. At very best there are still some who have personal codes. Steve is one, and his is that if you've given society twelve years of freedom from a Danny de Spirit, you've done a hell of a lot more, for instance, than a parole officer who's operating on some kind of phony idealism."

"Is that his for instance or yours?"

"Neither of ours," Zippy said more gently. "He knows you got into this mostly because of your concern for Jimmy Wallace, and he respects you for it."

"What else does he know about me?"

"Don't you mean about us?"

He nodded silently, unable to look her in the eyes.

"Nothing directly," she said. "Only what he's sensed."

Which, Reppa thought, was probably everything.

"And Leilah?" she asked.

"A lot that she's sensed. A fair amount that I've told her." He glanced toward Zippy, she away from him. Her eyes returned when he said, "This deal you and the ADA have cooked up. If everything's all set, why have the cops gone to so much trouble to get perjured statements from Wallace?"

"Leverage."

"In the event de Spirit won't agree to plead guilty? Then you'll—?"

"Tell him his own stepbrother is prepared to testify against him," she finished reluctantly.

"You've really got it all figured out, don't you?"

"No. Not all of it."

Her eyes dropped away again.

"Do you want to?" she said then. Very quietly. "One last time?"

He discovered that he could not say he didn't.

CHAPTER TWELVE

THE INVITATION

It was Friday morning and all the offices on Reppa's aisle were empty, their occupants either in the field or taking a long weekend. Reppa was owed one for the extra time he'd logged during the de Spirit investigation, but he had to be in the office today. He was the duty officer in his unit, which meant keeping himself available in the event someone's absconder decided to turn himself in, a warrant had to be lodged, or one of the female parole officers needed a male body to accompany her on a bread run or a home visit to a dangerous building.

He put away his dictating machine and for perhaps the fiftieth time that morning looked at his watch. Ten minutes to eleven. There was no longer any escape from it: the moment had come to shit or get off the pot. He still didn't know what he ought to do, but he definitely had to do something. McCreary was out there somewhere; he was in here. It hadn't just worked out that way.

He stood up, massaged his cramped leg muscles, walked out of his office, and gazed down the aisle. The row of closed doors stretched on and on. There was no one between him and the secretary's desk at the end of the aisle. Nevertheless he rode the elevator down and went outside to find a pay phone. It was just possible that if McCreary had an ally on the switchboard, she was still monitoring his calls.

Behind him, on Thirty-ninth Street, a factory whistle blew once over the din of traffic to announce the hour.

Reppa cleared his throat in preparation. At the same time he held his finger on the coin return until his dime came back. It was useless. She would refuse to talk to him. Keeping within her rights. And threaten to report him. Knowing that he was exceeding his.

But calling her . . . the act alone of calling her.

With the feeling that a door had closed and locked behind him, or that another kind of whistle had blown and he had turned and found himself on the field alone, he shoved the dime in again.

The phone rang six times before she answered it.

"Miss Wilkes? Frank Reppa."

"Oh." A sullen pause and then: "What's this now, the old Mutt-and-Jeff bit? Don't tell me your next line. I already know it. 'Listen, Miss Wilkes, I'm really sorry for the way my partner behaved yesterday.'"

He understood at once. "McCreary? You mean McCreary talked to you?"

Her reply was to fart into the receiver with her lips and tongue.

Afraid she was going to hang up, he said quickly, "Wait, now. McCreary and I aren't working together on this any—"

"That's not what he said. He told me you were his legman. Like errand boy."

Not far wrong, unfortunately. "No, that's no longer—"

She broke in once more. "Who gets to play Mutt when you guys go back for Mald? Better hope it's not you,

284

because frankly, Frankie, I don't think you've got the balls."

Reppa took a deep breath and tried to remind himself that the only way to communicate with this woman was to stay on the same coldly sardonic wave length.

"Now, listen. I'm no longer working with McCreary." He raised his voice, overriding her "Yeah, sure." "He finessed me out of the information I picked up while doing my investigation. But there's something I've learned since that I'm fairly sure he doesn't know yet. The killer was playing house with Elizabeth—not Andrea—the morning of the murders. Now, if Danny de Spirit is the killer, no problem. If it's someone else . . . well, who knows what my having learned this information could lead to?"

There were several moments of tense silence. Then Wilkes said, "Does anybody else at your place know what McCreary's doing?"

"I doubt it."

"If he finessed you out of the investigation, like you say, why haven't you reported him?"

"Because, as pissed off as I am at what he did, I'm more pissed off at myself for letting it happen."

He could almost feel her weighing his explanation. To her it was just about the perfect balance. Angry, but not so angry that you cut your own nose off. At last she said tonelessly, "What are you hoping to accomplish by this call?"

Reppa didn't have an answer for her. He wasn't quite sure himself.

There was another long silence. He heard her breathing, evenly and rhythmically. Then a new sound came into her voice. "What you were saying before about Elizabeth, where did you hear it?"

"Why?"

"Because it's bullshit—pure bullshit!"

She spoke with such vehemence that Reppa might have been convinced if she'd followed by hanging up immediately. Instead she remained on the line for several more moments, breathing no less evenly, no less rhythmically. Then, as if it were an afterthought, she banged the phone into the cradle.

He stood holding the dead receiver as it occurred to him that all he'd intended this morning was to stick his foot in the water. Though what that meant, beyond calling Wilkes, was vague. She was at one and the same time the easiest person to talk to and the most difficult. She might never reveal a thing to him, but she would be the last to run to anyone and complain that he was harassing her.

There was no use trying to explain it to himself in any other terms. He was still sure she was lying. It angered him, because, like a headpin, if she toppled, others would go down with her.

He could no longer escape it. The investigation had been a test for him. Of his ingenuity and imagination, clearly, and of some other qualities that were far less clear. His overall game plan, the code he lived by. More accurately, his lack of a code since he'd left football behind him. That was the source, at bottom, of the conflict he felt about Zippy. Loyalty to something was the key. Hers went out (misguidedly, he felt sure) to Cupach. But disheartening as this was, it exhilarated him that she could be so strongly loyal. If he could just find something that inspired a similar loyalty in him. As things stood, he still could not decide whether he hoped, for Zippy's sake, that de Spirit was the Behrman-Moffett killer or whether he hoped for his own sake that it was someone else.

All of it was hazy in his mind, but he knew he was on the right track. He returned to his office and worked on reports till noon, and then went to the Y, played four games of paddleball, swam twenty laps, and stumbled into the steam room. The mist surrounding him was now a real mist rather than a mental one. Faces were just blurs. An eye or a hand would rise into focus for an instant, but that was all. Even so, he felt a moment of clarity. He was free, his own agent, and that was as much of a system to live by as he would ever need. But he began floating again as soon as he got back to the office, like a dead log sinking into the water, rising up briefly, sinking again, as if it had all only been the effects of a good workout. Around three o'clock the phone on his desk wakened him with a start.

"Parole—Reppa."

"Reppa, this is Jill Wilkes. Can you come to my place tonight?"

He came instantly wide awake.

"I might have something for you."

"Might?"

"Nine o'clock. If I'm here, we talk. If I'm not, you wasted the trip. But the invitation's only good for one person. No McCreary, understand?"

He started to say he did, but she'd already hung up.

The temperature seemed to drop ten degrees when he left Delancey Street behind him and started across the Williamsburg Bridge. Wreaths of mist that were close to rain drifted around his car and changed on the windshield into cold spangles of moisture. An eerie pallor had crept into the darkness out over the river, and the vague shapes of ramps and bridge supports hovered above him. Far down toward the Manhattan Bridge a tug hooted. The air smelled dank and unhealthful.

He felt at once numb and oversensitized. His stomach seemed huge and bottomless and in control of his entire

287

body. It was a familiar sensation but one he had not had for many years. There was a time when he had looked forward to it. In high school the worse he'd felt before a game, the more separated from his body he'd felt, the better he usually played. At Ohio State, where he rarely played, he sometimes had to carry the sensation for the whole game. He'd had it today ever since Jill Wilkes had called him more than five hours ago.

As he headed into the dark and winding streets of Williamsburg, he listened again to his two telephone conversations with her. He closed his ears to everything but her voice. And he decided he would be very surprised if he found her home.

His first thought this afternoon had been that she wanted to see him because she was frightened at long last and in need of a confidant. Then he considered that she might have contacted the killer after his call to her and been told that it was time to get rid of him because he was becoming too much of a nuisance. That made him think about not keeping the appointment, until he reflected how improbable it was that anyone who had been clever enough to get away with a double murder for twelve years would be so stupid as to kill a parole officer responding to an invitation from a woman who was already strongly suspected of knowing more than she'd admitted. Of course it could be that Wilkes intended to kill him herself—or at least put a good scare into him. That was conceivable. Just conceivable enough that he'd brought his gun along and told Leilah where he was going.

And it was Leilah who, once she'd learned of his two conversations with Wilkes, had steered him toward the realization he was coming to now.

Wilkes had no intention of telling him anything. No, it was simply a power play. A demonstration to her former

288

benefactor of what she was capable of doing if she wasn't put back on the payroll. Reppa had given her the inspiration for it when he said he'd learned Elizabeth had been the killer's playmate. After his call she had contacted her benefactor with a new proposition: They were hounding her, these two parole officers, and they were getting closer to the right scent. Some renegotiations were in order, starting with the money for, say, an extended vacation so she could get away until things cooled down again. Sure, take a little time to think about it. Take till, oh, say, eight o'clock tonight. Sorry the deadline is so short, but it just so happens that at *nine* o'clock . . .

Why was she so cocksure her benefactor would keep on allowing her to bleed him? Since this benefactor had likely killed her two roommates, wouldn't the wisest move be to kill her, too? But she was still alive and seemed in no fear that this condition would change. Again, why? Perhaps because her benefactor knew she could be trusted never to reveal anything. And the basis for that trust? All at once Reppa saw it. If the truth about how her roommates had died came out, *so would the truth about how her painting career had been launched.* And Wilkes, if he knew nothing else about her, was determined to be regarded by posterity as a serious (albeit badly misunderstood) artist.

But while she and her benefactor knew she would never spill any secrets, there had been that flicker in her eyes for an instant when he'd told her he was going to talk to Mald. What had it meant? That she was afraid Mald might say too much? That Mald might think, since Reppa's curiosity had been roused about him, that *she* had said too much?

Reppa's feeling had been that Mald could be dismissed. But now that he'd learned that Elizabeth had been the killer's playmate, it threw a new light on the whole matter of motive. His thinking all along had been that Andrea was playing house with the killer when Elizabeth came home unexpectedly. Finding Mald with Andrea might have shocked Elizabeth, but it was difficult to imagine anything she could have done or said that would have triggered Mald to kill both girls. Put Mald in with Elizabeth, though, the saintly and supposedly virginal Elizabeth, and then picture Andrea—

Reppa braked for a stoplight and sat considering. An ex-fiancé who had been scorned and humiliated. A stepfather who seemingly was just getting around to sowing his wild oats at the time of the murders. A lesbian aunt and her secretary of sorts, who himself gave off sexual vibrations that were a little odd. Even de Spirit, after what Zippy had told him, had to be put back in the viewfinder.

All kinds of half-baked motives could be attributed to each of them, but none held up for long. The same questions that had puzzled him when it had seemed Andrea was home alone with the killer were now more puzzling than ever. The sexless roommate surprised in the act by the sexy roommate—if it had really happened like that, what could the act have been that someone had felt compelled to murder two people upon being discovered at it? *Or was it the person and not the act that could not bear discovery?*

It was still five minutes short of nine o'clock when he pulled up in front of 206 Arion Place. Lights blazed in the two windows at the westernmost end of the second floor. Her studio, Reppa thought, recalling the layout of the loft. It was a hopeful sign. He parked behind a Ford van, switched off the engine and the lights, and sat motionless until nine o'clock. In that interval no one passed him. No cars. No pedestrians.

Finally he slid cautiously out of his car. He was amazed at how empty the street looked. A block down two men sat talking on a stoop, but they were too far away for their voices to reach him. Still he stood listening for several moments. That was when he realized how quiet everything was. And how much he yearned for a sound.

The front door of 206 was locked. He scanned the vertical row of buttons beside the door and jabbed the one under *Wilkes*.

An answering buzz resounded almost immediately.

Reppa stepped into the dim lobby and saw that someone— an irate landlord?—had painted over the seascape. The wall opposite the elevator was now a solid institutional white. It removed what little feeling of warmth the building had had.

The elevator was there, waiting. When he emerged from it, he saw the door to Wilkes's loft had also been painted recently. He knocked. When nothing happened, he knocked again. Waited twenty seconds. Then tried the knob.

The door was not locked. Opening it a few inches, he called, "Miss Wilkes?" No response. He swung the door farther open and peered around it. At the far end of the loft a thin ray of light shone over the top of the plywood partition. The musty-smelling living space between the door and the partition was dark and silent.

"Miss Wilkes?"

Still nothing. Not a sound anywhere in the place. It came to Reppa what he was going to have to decide. Whether to walk out of here and leave it to McCreary and Cupach and the others to whom it had become a cause, or stay and admit it had become that to him, too. The dread returned. What are you really afraid of? he asked himself; and the dread grew. For the answer was himself. It wasn't a fear that he would do the wrong thing but that he had allowed himself to get into a situation where he felt absolutely *on his own*.

291

He saw a light switch beside him on the wall. When he flipped it, a bare bulb went on over his head. It cast a dirty brownish light over Wilkes's cluttered living space and brought two of her cats out from under a sofa to investigate. Her rolltop desk was open, typewriter sitting on it. Draped over the wood stool where she'd sat during his last visit was a soiled cotton smock. All around him her paintings loomed bleak and immense. But there was no sign of Wilkes herself.

Sodden paper plates, trails of popcorn and kitty litter, a vine from a hanging plant that brushed his arm . . . As he moved toward the partition, from the space where Wilkes lived to the space where she worked, his hand hesitated and then came down firmly on the butt of his gun.

He only realized how tense he had really been when he stepped around the partition and the tension lifted from him. Wilkes sat on the floor, doubled over in what looked like a poorly executed lotus position. She was alone—meditating?

Then he saw the easel in front of her. Mounted on it was a large canvas. And her posture became to him that of a painter considering her next stroke. Then, moving closer so he could see what was on the canvas, he felt a cold pain in his groin.

A nude woman stood at a window, turned halfway around to the room behind her. As yet her features had not been defined; she held a knife in her hand, and she was gazing toward a bed where lay the figure of a nude man. The man and the bed had been sketched lightly in black pencil. The woman, Reppa now saw, was also drawn only in pencil, but in much darker and much fuller detail than the man. Quick bold strokes delineated her legs, her arms, her breasts. The framework was there for another of Wilkes's stark social commentaries.

But it was ruined.

For thrusting toward the woman, suspended in space a few inches from the knife in her hand, was a clumsily drawn penis. Attached to nothing, just hanging in the air, it looked like a bit of graffiti.

Wilkes must know he was there, but she still refused to move or speak. She sat with a black drawing pencil in her right hand, leaning slightly to her left, supporting herself on one elbow, head tilted, as if trying to get a ground-level perspective on the canvas.

"Miss Wilkes?"

Reppa walked over to her, with each step more unsure of himself. She was sitting so still and in such an odd position, it looked bad.

He didn't want to touch her. He called her name one last time. Then he had no other choice. He put a hand on her shoulder. At his touch a spasm seemed to take her across the back of the neck, and her head jerked. Slowly she started to fall.

It was clear to Reppa, even before she reached the floor and sprawled on her side, that she was dead. But how? Bending over her, feeling her cool flesh, her pulseless wrist, he saw no marks anywhere. No blood. No wounds.

Yet she was very definitively dead.

He wheeled around.

Because someone—*someone who was very definitively alive*—had buzzed to let him in.

For an instant he thought he heard a sound behind him. He spun back around; there was no one, but his arm struck the easel. He seized it before it fell.

"Christ's sake, Rep, careful—don't touch anything."

That voice . . . where had it come from? But then all thought in him dulled as he saw McCreary stride jauntily into the studio. He had on pigskin gloves, a denim jacket,

293

the ubiquitous sunglasses. As if to counter the image, a black leather briefcase was jammed under his arm.

Reppa stood staring stupidly. "What the hell are—*you* doing here?"

Same thing you are. Whatever she had to say, she was going to say it to both of us."

"How did you . . . ?"

"Know you were coming?" McCreary stood frozen in position, his face a curious mixture of scorn and sympathy. When he spoke again, his voice was flat. "Immaterial, Rep. Wilkes told you nine. I got here early. Unfortunately it wasn't early enough."

The switchboard. Someone must have plugged into his line when Wilkes called him. He met McCreary's gaze. "How did she die?"

"There's a note stuck in her typewriter."

"A suicide note?"

"It says she lost faith in her ability as an artist."

Reppa glanced down at the floor. Took in the closed eyelids, clutched pencil, outflung arms. And then brought his gaze skeptically back to McCreary. "Poison?"

"In effect. A big hit of smack or speed. Look at her left arm. There's a fresh needle mark in the glory hole."

Reppa looked. It was there. "Where's the needle?"

"On the desk beside her typewriter." McCreary paused, his eyes turned away from Reppa. But the rest of his face could no longer hide an inner glee. "No, Rep, it all fits. It's a clear case of suicide. At least it would have been if the killer hadn't made one little mistake."

"What was it?"

"Obvious. He dragged her in here while she was still alive."

"How do you know?"

"This painting she was working on. From what you

294

described, it's the same style she had when she first started out. People finding the suicide note and her dead in front of this painting were meant to think she'd tried to go back to her roots in a last-ditch attempt to salvage her career. Seeing the hopelessness of it, she loaded up a hypo and smacked herself off the map."

"And the cock?"

"Like I said, Rep. The killer's mistake was bringing her in here while she was still alive. Look at the pencil in her hand. She drew that cock as a way of saying who killed her."

"So you're telling me she was left in here for dead. Only she wasn't. Not quite. And while the killer was in the other room typing up the suicide note, she crawled—"

"Exactly," McCreary broke in impatiently, like a teacher hurrying along a slow pupil. "And the killer was too rattled to notice what she did. Or maybe he noticed but didn't see its significance. Or maybe he thought he had plenty of time to deal with it because you weren't due here till nine o'clock. But I came a few minutes ahead of you, and he had to split quicker than he'd planned when he heard me."

"How did you get in the building?" Reppa said suddenly.

"The door was open."

"Downstairs?"

"No, but her door was. Downstairs ain't important. Downstairs was easy. But are you listening, Rep? I keep repeating the same pronoun in talking about the killer. Because Wilkes gave it to us when she drew that cock. Now we know for sure it ain't no broad we're chasing. And I don't know about you, but it eliminates—"

"The downstairs door, McCreary. How did you get in the building?"

Did he only imagine he saw McCreary's eyes dart away behind the dark glasses?

"Hey, when you've been dealing with the criminal population as long as I have, you can't help but learn a few tricks of the trade."

"You picked the lock?"

"In a minute. But yet and still, I wasn't quick enough. Because when I got on the elevator, the killer must've heard it and bolted down the stairs."

It was too pat. Too much explanation. Given in quick clipped words as if McCreary were trying to rush him off somewhere.

"And when you got here, you found her body?"

"Just like you did. And just like you, I thought at first she was still alive. But once I saw the suicide note and the hypo—"

"The thing is," Reppa interrupted harshly, "you knew when I buzzed downstairs who it was. Yet you let me in. *Why?*"

The reaction was surprising: McCreary grinned.

"Because I know you, Rep. I knew you'd do just what you're doing—staying cool and giving me a chance to explain."

"Explain what? That you're sorry for making a stooge out of me? Save the apologies, McCreary. I don't need them."

"Good. Because there ain't gonna be any. The way I look at it, you had your shot, and it ain't my fault you weren't big enough to take it. You could even say I knew when I gave you the assignment that you weren't big enough. But I also knew you were smart. And if you were smart enough to do the investigation as good as you did, you weren't going to stay dumb forever. So it's no surprise that you grew up on me, Rep. The surprise is that you

296

grew up so *fast*. Because how else did you get Wilkes to invite you over here unless you caught something? Something big—something that maybe even I don't have. What is it?''

Reppa silently shook his head.

"This ain't no time to get heroic, Rep. Because you need me too much. Whatever you and Wilkes had going tonight, it got her killed. And you're standing here now with her body on your hands. You given any thought yet to calling the cops? They generally like to know about things like this.''

"And then what do we do? Wait for them and explain how we happened to be here?''

"Not we, Rep. *You*. Because unless you show me your cards, you're playing this hand alone.''

Reppa gazed at McCreary's immobile face and then stepped around the partition and went to examine Wilkes's rolltop desk. Amid the papers scattered about it, he saw a hypodermic syringe. As he finished reading the note in the carriage of the typewriter, he heard McCreary come up behind him.

"Satisfied?''

"How do I know you didn't type it?''

"You don't, Rep. You don't know anything here for sure—except that it's your ass entirely that needs a cover. Because mine is already dead. The agency's going to find out what I'm doing, if they haven't already. It's only a matter of time. But a little more time is all I need. I'm playing for time, babe. Hours at this point.''

"You're that close?''

You *know* I'm that close. You scored big on that investigation. Bigger than I ever expected you would. Now, if we pool what the two of us have got since—along with what Wilkes was trying to say when she drew that cock—my guess is we're home."

Reppa looked at him, at the will to succeed veiled by scorn. "What do you think her drawing meant?"

"For openers, a man iced her. The same cat that iced her two roommates."

"That somehow doesn't tell me anything new."

"Then maybe you ain't as smart as I think you are."

McCreary smiled, patted the briefcase under his arm. The gesture, in its smug superiority, made Reppa's stomach sink. "What's in there?"

"A few loose ends. Like notes from a talk I had with a certain detective."

"Graham?"

"*Private* detective."

"The one Behrman sent to Kentucky?" McCreary continued to smile. "He's still alive?"

"As is a doorman who remembers the night Halliwell threw Andrea out bare-assed."

"What else is in there?"

McCreary gave the briefcase another pat. "We partners again?"

"Until when—when you get all the credit, and I get my ass in a sling?"

"*Credit?*" McCreary spat the word at him. "Man, you think I give a shit about credit? Truth. The truth about a man who's sat for the last twelve years—sat with his pecker tied in a knot because he couldn't get anybody to listen to him."

"De Spirit?"

"Fuck de Spirit. *Me*—John Jacob McCreary. I know the streets. I know prisons. I know lawyers. I know courts. I know judges. Man, I know the whole goddam criminal justice system. Where it's fucked. Why it's fucked. Who's fucked it up. Call me an egomaniac? Goddam right, I'm an egomaniac. But if you'd put in nearly thirty years on a job and learned as much as I have—and there was never a chance for you to show what you could do, not one single chance—baby, you'd grab your brass ring when it finally came along just like I'm grabbing this one.''

"It really means that much to you to find out who killed those two girls?''

McCreary sneered. "You got three years in. *Three years* as compared to thirty, and you're standing here shitting your pants over what to do. Man, you're wasting my time. You're keeping me from finding out who I'm after and then going out and *getting* him.''

"And then?''

"Still thinking about glory? Worried that you'll be cut out of your share?''

Reppa focused intently on McCreary. "I want to know what you're *really* in this for.''

"Man, I *told* you—the satisfaction of showing all them assholes just one time how good this nigger really is.''

"There's more in it. There has to be.''

McCreary turned away and stood motionless for a moment, his body rigid. Slowly he turned back to Reppa with a faint smile.

"Yeah, babe, you're right. There is a little something more. But not so little there ain't enough for both of us. First let me ask you, ain't you ever wondered what I did that was so bad they pulled me off a case load and slammed me behind a desk?''

"I've heard stories. Nothing that sounded big enough.''

"Because there wasn't anything big. You know what they finally nailed me on? Putting fake information in reports that I sent to the commissioners recommending cats for three-year discharges. You know, really seditious stuff, like they'd been working for a year at the same job when they'd really only been working a couple of months. Or that they had stable home lives when the truth was their old lady had run off with some other cat. This was so guys who had maybe twenty years to do on parole could get their self-respect back after only three or four years. Black guys. Street cats who weren't bad anymore but weren't ever gonna get it together enough that you could put in the papers for a discharge without having to fictionalize a little.

"Did you ever take any money from them?"

"I told you nothing big, Rep. No bribes. Never a penny. And I had opportunities. I had Lower Manhattan for a while. Little Italy. Mafia cats who were always looking to put something in my pocket. I ain't gonna claim on a civil-service salary with five kids I wasn't ever tempted, but I stayed cool."

"What about now? Is anyone trying to put something in your pocket?"

"Sure." McCreary's face was lit with scorn. "They're lining up."

"Then if it's not money that's driving you to find the real killer, what is it?"

For just a second McCreary hesitated, and then he said sharply, "It's a long story, and you're standing here with a keg of dynamite that's got a short fuse. You've got a stiff on your hands, Rep. Decided yet what you're going to do with her?"

Reppa had begun to feel a change within himself. The confusion—the sense of isolation—were replaced by an inner calm. The more McCreary tried to hurry him, the more he felt he had all the time in the world.

"Somehow I'm not too worried. I've got a reason for being here. I was invited."

"For nine o'clock. Time's flying. You don't think the cops are gonna wonder where it all went between when you got here and when you finally got around to announcing your discovery that your hostess was no longer in a condition to entertain?"

Reppa shrugged. His indifferent response caused McCreary to shuck the pigskin gloves and then take a quick turn up and down the room.

"Gonna show you something," he said, rubbing the top of his head as if smoothing a decision that still had an edge of doubt.

He flipped the latch on his briefcase and sifted through its contents. Pulled out two sheets of paper. Smiled. Then wordlessly handed one of them to Reppa.

It was a photostat of an arrest sheet belonging to a man named Carlos Maldonado. On September 4, 1938, Maldonado had been arrested in Bayonne, New Jersey, for murder. Charge reduced to manslaughter at sentencing on February 11, 1939. Paroled October 14, 1946, from Rahway state prison. "Mald," said McCreary when Reppa looked up.

"Where did you get this?"

"Caught a sample of his prints the other day and had a friend with the NYPD send them through."

Reppa glanced at the other paper McCreary was holding. "Who else's prints did you get a positive on?"

McCreary casually ignored this. "Not only did Mald change his name, but he grew up in Bayonne, not Barcelona. See, Rep, you were right. His socks have class, but his feet are *cuchifritos*. After he was paroled, Jersey let him open up an art gallery in the city. They continued to surpervise him because he was living in Hoboken. Which is why we don't have anything on him in our office. But I

301

drove over to Jersey City the other day and got a look at one of their old case folders. Highly informative."

"What did he do?"

Again McCreary hesitated; smiled. "We trade. You tell me why Wilkes invited you over here tonight, and I'll give you the rest on Mald."

"Meanwhile holding back everything that's really important."

"You don't see what this rap sheet means?" McCreary stared opaquely at him. "Man, it's the ball game."

"If it were, you wouldn't have shown it to me."

McCreary took another quick turn up and down the room and came back with a sneer. "Know what Mald did? This is the guy you were convinced was a marshmallow. He snuffed a girl he met in Palisades Amusement Park by holding his finger on her carotid artery. The two of them were playing a game, he said, that was popular in those days. Back before kids discovered dope. A way of making each other light-headed and high. The cops thought he was trying to put her out cold so he could rape her, only he went too far. But they couldn't prove it."

"All this must have turned up twelve years ago, and nobody thought it was important then. Why is it now?"

"Sure, the cops found out Mald had a record, but so what? He'd changed his name and had a class operation. He'd been clean for over twenty years. There was nothing to link him to the Behrman-Moffett murders."

"As far as I can see, there still isn't."

McCreary looked coldly at him. "Better think that one through again, Rep."

"That other rap sheet you have—whose is it?"

"Gonna tell me why Wilkes invited you here tonight?"

McCreary wafted the second paper teasingly. Annoyed, Reppa snatched it out of the air and started to examine it.

302

He stopped when McCreary said tautly, "Hold it, babe. Drop both them sheets, and you get down on the floor with them."

Looking up, Reppa felt his mouth go dry. Pointed at his head was a small black revolver. His hands opened, and the papers fluttered to the floor.

"You next. On your belly. Hands behind your back."

Reppa heard a sharp metallic click as he complied. But when he glanced up in alarm, he saw McCreary had only opened his briefcase again and was bending to retrieve Mald's arrest sheet. The other paper lay inches from his hand. One of the cats was stalking it, back arched. He just had time to glimpse Stanley Behrman's name before the cat pounced on it.

He couldn't bring himself to feel calm anymore, not even when McCreary chased the cat away and began smiling again after he'd sealed the papers in the briefcase. The gun was still in McCreary's hand, and one of McCreary's stubbed fingers was curled around the trigger in complete earnest.

"Bastard." He saw two sharp lines appear at the corners of McCreary's mouth. "I've got it all now except one thing—and you won't give it to me."

"What's that?"

"*Why*. I know who killed Behrman and Moffett—and now Wilkes. But the only one I know for sure why he killed is Wilkes."

"Then you really are way ahead of me. I would have bet my bottom dollar Wilkes wouldn't get it."

"Yeah?" McCreary's voice hung for an instant, as if uncertain. "Well, you would've died broke."

"True, but maybe not for the reason you think. You're still a step short."

McCreary laughed scornfully and gathered himself

303

together, his pigskin gloves, his briefcase, holding the gun steady all the while. Reppa had a final glimpse of him standing lean, dark, and truculent against the background of garish paintings and black windows. Then he was gone.

Reppa got slowly to his feet, wondering what McCreary had seen in Wilkes's drawing that he hadn't. Going past that for the moment, wasn't the whole point of killing Wilkes to keep her from talking? What kind of killer would so painstakingly arrange her death to look like suicide and then carelessly allow her to drop a clue to his identity? And hadn't it required a moment or so of carelessness on Wilkes's part to get that needle into her arm? But perhaps she'd been forced to inject herself. At gunpoint, say. Seen in that light, the theory that her drawing contained a clue suddenly became more plausible to him, and he went to take another look at it. Someone had given Wilkes a lethal dose of something and left her for dead, but out of sheer stubbornness she'd hung on long enough to take one last swipe at the canvas with her drawing pencil. Her intention was to say her killer was a man, but there was more. McCreary had seen it. Now, surely, if he took his time, he could, too.

Reppa felt obliged to have something intelligent to tell himself before he gave up staring at the canvas on the easel, but at the same time he felt stupid. Would the shape dangling in thin air form, if you tilted your head this way or that, something other than a cock? The start of a name that she hadn't been able to finish? Well, it was straining the imagination, but he supposed you could see a sloppy, sideways *J*. And before he could think *J for Jeff*, his brain had superimposed over the shape the upper arc of an *S*—for Stanley. He shook his head. McCreary had experienced no such confusion over what he had seen. Clearly, then, it was not meant to be an initial. It was beyond him, though (goddam fucking beyond him), whatever it was; and he started to turn away with the reminder to himself, as his eyes skimmed over Wilkes's rigid outstretched body, that it was time to get out of there: time to wipe off the easel and the doorknob (the only two things here he'd touched) and call 911 from a pay phone. Handkerchief over the receiver, because they recorded—

Her right hand! With so much that was odd about the way she was sitting, he had missed seeing how wrong the pencil had looked in her right hand when all his memories of her—pouring tea, gesturing—were of a southpaw.

Of course it might mean nothing. Someone dying would grab desperately, wildly. The cock, the hook, the initial, whatever, was misshapen enough to have been drawn by Wilkes using the wrong hand. Then again—there was no saying it had not been drawn by someone who had then crammed the pencil between her stiffening fingers.

Someone who hadn't realized she was left-handed. And the needle mark, belying the theory that it had been self-administered, was in her left arm.

Before leaving the loft he took a handkerchief to the easel and the doorknob and then went down the stairs. As he drove along looking for a pay phone, he tried to decide whether he should go back and wait for the cops after he called. What purpose would it serve? They would want to know what he was doing there, and what could he tell them? "We became friendly while I was doing the de Spirit pardon investigation and she asked me over tonight to look at her latest painting."

Reppa took his inner turmoil for another sign of conflict. Damned for confusing the wheels of justice if he did. Guilty of obstructing them if he didn't. He thought of McCreary, and in him there arose very suddenly that feeling of alienation that comes to a traveler left to grope alone in the deep jungle by a merciless tour guide.

It had occurred to him that part of the reason the drawing had been a little clumsy might be because the hand that had done it was missing a couple of fingertips.

But if true, then McCreary had been deliberately trying to mislead him. Where? Or away from what?

And, even more disturbing, how possible was it that the drawing pencil had been employed by the same hand that had inserted the hypodermic needle?

CHAPTER THIRTEEN

McCREARY

On the Tuesday morning after Jill Wilkes was killed, Jimmy Wallace's preliminary hearing was held at Rikers Island. It was all but automatic. Wallace's two arrests were cited by Reppa, as were his failure to find a job and his reversion to drugs, and the hearing officer swiftly found probable cause to hold Wallace in violation of his parole, pending a final hearing at a later date. Afterward Reppa was able to spend a few minutes alone with Wallace and reassure him that well before the final hearing matters should have straightened themselves out to the point where he could recommend that Wallace be restored to supervision. Wallace remained unconvinced when Reppa told him again that he would never have to testify against his half brother. The story going around Rikers was that de Spirit was scheduled for a new trial in a few weeks. He had some snappy young bloom for a lawyer who'd gotten him out on dime-store bail and hustled him up a room at a YMCA in midtown that was paid by the state to set aside the top floor of its residence hall for indigent parolees and ex-offenders. Most of this was news to Reppa, but he didn't doubt Wallace. Word traditionally traveled much faster and more reliably among those restrained by the criminal justice system than among those sworn to uphold it. He left Wallace with a promise that there would be no new trial, though he carefully skirted any discussion of how he intended to keep it.

The one thing he had not been expecting, the weirdest thing, was that Jill Wilkes's death would have so little impact. The body had been found too late for the story to make the morning papers, but Saturday afternoon's *Post* had given two columns to it on the fourth page:

POLICE TO PROBE DEATH OF BROOKLYN ARTIST

A complete autopsy was ordered today on Jill Wilkes, the 35-year-old painter whose body was found last night in her Williamsburg loft.

"At first glance it looked like a suicide," said one detective investigating the death, which occurred at 206 Arion Place. "But after looking further, now we're just not entirely sure."

A preliminary examination indicated Wilkes died of a drug overdose but in a manner that is not typical of suicide victims. Detectives were vague on the exact circumstances in which her body was found.

Another source claimed that her body was found as the result of an anonymous phone tip to the Police Department, but detectives were close-mouthed about this angle. "Pending test results and review of a few odds and ends that don't add up as yet, we're proceeding on the assumption that this woman killed herself because she was despondent about her lack of progress as an artist," one investigator said.

He added that the "odds and ends" being checked had to do with her artistic career.

*　　*　　*

All three papers on Monday had had brief articles, the one in the *News* being the most to the point.

NEW ANGLE IN PAINTER'S DEATH

Brooklyn detectives have discovered that the true name of Jill Wilkes, the painter whose death last Friday is still under investigation, was Jill Wilkerson and that she was a former roommate of Andrea Behrman and Elizabeth Moffett, two women murdered in a notorious case in 1968.

In an odd note Danny de Spirit, the convicted Behrman-Moffett slayer, has appealed successfully for a new trial and is scheduled to be released on bail today after being incarcerated since 1969.

No connection has been established as yet between the two events, but detectives have not ruled out the possibility that Wilkes-Wilkerson, who testified against de Spirit at his original trial, may have been a homicide victim and not a suicide.

"In which case we're going to have to take a hard look at whether this is entirely a coincidence of events," one investigator said.

De Spirit was definitely still at Auburn state prison last Friday night, detectives have confirmed, and there has been no known contact between him and Wilkes-Wilkerson since his trial in 1969.

And since Monday all had been silent.

Reppa knew that the police seldom had much to say to the Press while an investigation was still in progress. As a result even the most sensational stories faded from the public eye after a day or two, once reporters ran out of pots to boil. Of course interest in Wilkes would revive immediately if developments showed there was a connection between her death and the Behrman-Moffett case. But for the moment she was just an obscure artist who had died under circumstances that as yet were not satisfactorily explained.

So, on second thought, it was no surprise that her picture was not splashed on all the front pages. Nor did it surprise Reppa that no one from the NYPD came to visit him and inquire where he had been on the night of. Or whether it was true that he had received a phone call last Friday afternoon from. Or whether he was the owner of a car that had been seen parked in front of. The odds that anything he'd done on Friday would come to the attention of the police were extremely long. Eventually, if and when the probe into Wilkes's death went deep enough, someone would discover he had spoken to her during his pardon investigation, but until that happened, he was reasonably secure. Maybe next week he'd be asked a few questions. The end of this week, at the very outside. And long before then it should all be over.

Each day since Wilkes's death he'd expected some grand-stand play by McCreary, some startling revelation. His most acute fantasy was of turning on the TV and watching McCreary, flashbulbs popping all around him, announce that after a quest that had been begun twelve years ago by a lone parole officer with an unstoppable lust for truth, the real Behrman-Moffett killer was in custody. Reppa, loath as he was to admit to unstoppable envy, could not come out of the bathroom in the morning until Leilah pledged that McCreary's face hadn't appeared on *Good Morning America*. By the fourth day, when there was still no explosion from McCreary, his dread changed to puzzlement, and by Wednesday morning he could almost dare to believe his own parting shot that McCreary was walking out on him a step short of the solution to the puzzle.

Nevertheless, when Leilah's assessment of the situation

310

echoed his hope, he had to say that he was still a long way from being convinced that McCreary had been bluffing.

"Then where is he? What's he waiting for?"

"Proof maybe. Enough so it'll stick if he makes an arrest. Or maybe he's playing some sort of cat-and-mouse game."

"With?" Leilah baited.

Reppa shook his head. "I have no more idea now than when I first started."

"Not true. You may not know who the killer is yet, but you know the most important thing. Andrea's coming home unexpectedly was the real catalyst for the murders. If McCreary hasn't realized that yet, it's the reason he's still floundering."

"So it really would have been the ball game if I'd told him Elizabeth was the killer's playmate."

"Not quite. He'd also have to understand *why* she was the killer's playmate."

The person or the act?

"Do you?"

She could see he meant to push it a rung higher, so she anticipated him. "No, Reppa—I don't know who the killer is. Don't you think I would have told you if I did?"

Reppa had to say he sometimes wondered.

"But something I am fairly sure of. You're right in thinking there's something very strange about Wilkes's murder. Especially that little extra tidbit that was added to the painting she was working on."

Nodding slowly, Reppa said, "I still think McCreary put it there especially for me to see. Otherwise I have to believe Wilkes did it herself, and it's a legitimate clue." Seeing Leilah frown, he went on more quickly. "It makes no sense for someone to kill her and make it look like a

311

suicide. Then spoil the effect by doctoring her painting so that it looks like she was trying to signal she was murdered.''

"Cogent, Reppa.''

"I'm not finished. If the killer doctored her painting, why would he botch it by sticking the drawing pencil in her wrong hand? That way everyone who knew her has to wonder if she did it.''

"He may not have realized she was left-handed.''

"After knowing her for twelve years?''

Leilah said coolly, "I haven't heard any proof that she was killed by someone who's known her for twelve years. At least not by someone who's been around her enough to know which hand she favored.''

"That's saying her benefactor was either incredibly unobservant or else he had an intermediary take care of all his business with her.''

"No, it's not. It's saying she might have been killed by someone who didn't have any business to take care of with her until the other night. For one thing, she apparently didn't feel she was in any danger. There was no sign of a struggle. No sign any force was used on her. As if she'd been taken totally by surprise. How could that be if she'd invited this mysterious benefactor you keep talking about over to bleed him for more money? She'd have been very much on her guard.''

"I'm sure she was. But she never thought he'd kill her. Something must have changed his mind about her. I was thinking—''

He left off abruptly when Leilah threw him a look. "About her last painting?''

"Right. It looked as if it was going to be a variation on the one I saw in Mald's gallery. The killer could have flipped when he saw it. He might have thought she was making a statement of some kind about him and panicked.''

"Don't you think he would have destroyed the painting if he saw its implication?"

"If he had time."

"For something that important he'd have made time. So we know that either he didn't see its implication—unlikely—or else it didn't have one. Or else . . ."

"Or else what?"

"He didn't see its implication because it didn't apply to *him*."

"How can that be?"

"I don't know," said Leilah. "But when was the last time a man panicked into killing someone just happened to have a hypodermic in his pocket to do the job?"

"Why did he bring it with him, then? What changed his mind about her?"

It was never one of Leilah's favorite moments when she had to admit she didn't know something. "Before we can answer that," came reluctantly from her side of the bed, "I'm afraid we're going to have to know who killed her."

When had she started saying "we"? It was cheering to Reppa but only moderately. Two heads were still not getting them any further, it seemed, than one.

He said moodily, "At least the cops can't tag de Spirit for this one. He didn't get out of the can till Monday morning."

Leilah gave a stifled exclamation.

"What is it?"

"Well, of course you're right. The killer didn't doctor Wilkes's painting. Her death was meant to pass for a suicide."

"Because if it looked like murder, it couldn't be blamed on de Spirit?"

Leilah was half-sitting up now in her excitement. "Even more—he couldn't wait till de Spirit got out so that it *could* be blamed on him. He was desperate, Reppa. He was too afraid she was going to talk to somebody.''

''But she wouldn't have. I'm sure of it.''

''Not to you, maybe. But McCreary'd already been to see her once, and the murderer must have known that. It may not have been anything she did as a consequence of your phone call to her that got her killed. Much as I hate to say it,'' said Leilah with uncharacteristic shyness, perhaps because now that the metal rail had been removed, the bed was all one unit again, ''in the murderer's eyes the threat probably wasn't anything we knew but something McCreary *didn't*.''

Two mornings earlier, at a few minutes past eight, J. J. McCreary had been sitting in his car on a side street in West Harlem and coming to much the same conclusion. His eyes riveted impatiently on the row of parked cars on the opposite side of the street in the hope that one of them would leave and free a legal parking spot, he cursed the city that had dragged him out of the sack after only three hours of sleep to keep his car from being hauled away. Already one Traffic Control tow truck had pulled up beside him, the cop at the wheel all set to drop anchor, until he rose up in his seat and gave the vulture the full force of his sunglasses and shaven head in warning that this car wasn't carrion because it very much had an occupant.

And now he had a foot patrolman training an eye on him from across the street. He stared back: *Waiting for something, fella?* But the clown seemed unaware that every black man wearing sunglasses and sitting alone in a parked car had to be treated as a potential drug dealer. Just as well, for McCreary realized, edging a hand into his pocket in preparation for the anticipated encounter, that he had come out of Mattie's pad so hastily he had left his

314

shield in the pants he'd been wearing last night. On the other hand, he was not unprotected. His gun was in its clip holster inside his belt, and his brain had been pumping forth its usual barrage of ideas and insights ever since the alarm went off. Which was not to say it had been idle during the three hours he'd been asleep. The truth was, he had not really slept at all last night. Tossing relentlessly, he had lost track after a while of being consciously awake, but he had never quite been able to lose the question that had hammered in his head for nearly sixty hours now:

What had made her ready to spill? He knew now where he had made his mistake the other night: He had allowed Reppa to wriggle off the hook without telling him the reason behind Wilkes's invitation. But he'd been afraid that if he stayed there any longer, Reppa's slowness to grasp the significance of that arrest sheet would lure him into a false confidence. As it was, he had very nearly anted up another bit of information in the hope that Reppa would come across. Not that *he* would have in Reppa's place—but, Christ, when had that prick become so sly? The other day, pissing away his notes on the investigation, Reppa had left him totally convinced that he'd been stripped of every last scrap of information he had. But apparently not. It was either believe that or believe that Reppa had continued the investigation on his own without his *precious* authorization and stumbled over something new. (No, not stumbled—careful now, this was exactly the sort of over-confidence he had to be on guard against: Reppa was no more an idiot than Jill Wilkes had been a simple little mercenary.)

But if Reppa had gone out on his lonesome, why hadn't they crossed paths last week long before Friday night? Nearly all the people he'd spoken to and the places he'd gone had been in direct response to the gaps he'd so witheringly chided Reppa for leaving, and not once had he gotten there less than first.

Since it was too hard to believe Reppa'd been slick enough to deliberately hold back something he'd learned during his investigation, and there were no outward signs that he was still actively pursuing it, what did that leave? Someone must have told him something after he'd turned in his report—something so juicy that when Wilkes found out he had possession of it, she called him. Moreover, either Reppa or someone else must have contacted her in some way before her call and told her what he had. But who had the source been?

Dwersky. The only person Reppa had spoken to during the investigation who was *simpatico*. Had to be her.

He wondered why he hadn't seen this so clearly before.

It had begun to get stuffy inside the car. As McCreary rolled down the window, he glanced in the side-view mirror and noticed that the patrolman had moved farther down the block. For a moment his gaze lingered over his own reflection. He smiled, then smiled at himself smiling at himself.

This might finally be it, he thought. The only thing stopping him from turning his key in the ignition right now and picking up the Behrman-Moffett killer was the laughing-stock he would make of himself when he went to explain his grounds for the collar. Rumpelstiltskin . . . plaster dogs . . . that dropped drink . . . Moffett's hysterical phone call . . . the killer's confession . . . and, of course, deciphering the *real* meaning of that painting. (Getting one of Mald's assistants to show it to him had been smooth work; his misreading of Wilkes not so smooth.) But what, when you added all those pieces together, was the sum total? Sure, he knew who had really wasted Andrea Behrman and Elizabeth Moffett. Damn right, he could explain where the NYPD had gone off course and when and why the killer had in effect confessed to Reppa while being interviewed by him. But a confession in effect was far from a confession, and he was still as far away as ever from the thing that would shut the NYPD's laughter off like a switch when he handed the killer over.

Motive, motive—the little matter of m-o-t-i-v-e.

The sad-assed fact was he still didn't have one single shred of solid psychological (forget physical—physical after twelve years, in this case at least, was impossible) evidence that the killer was not Danny de Spirit. Those documents Behrman's dick had held back thirty years ago: Even they, if they were what he thought they were, wouldn't do it. But that wasn't why he had refused to buy them up. He'd been sure at the time that the Fund money could be better used on Wilkes. Though he personally would never have given that bitch a dime, he could see his way to doing it as long as it wasn't coming out of his own pocket. But who, seeing how meagerly she was forced to live, would've believed she'd turn down *ten grand?*

Shit, after hearing her so coolly tell him to fuck off, he would have guaranteed she couldn't be reached. And yet someone had obviously not agreed with his appraisal.

Her killer.

He had been so busy trying to steer Reppa away from her killer (even if that goddam doodad had been, in his haste to throw something in Reppa's way before he arrived, more a Freudian slip than a red herring) that he hadn't fully absorbed until a long while after he'd split how *off* that hypo had looked. It had been enough to shoot him down out of the clouds for a whole day and it still had him battling to soar up anywhere near as high as he'd been the second he'd finally gotten Reppa out of his office last week and been able to throw up his fists in triumph that

317

he'd just spent his last day behind that desk. Because if he was right about who the killer was, then he had to be wrong about something equally critical. Otherwise how had hard-nosed Wilkes, knowing the hypo must contain something lethal, allowed herself to be stuck (or been forced to stick herself) without putting up a violent and at least semisuccessful struggle? It could only be that she'd been taken thoroughly by surprise, or else been thoroughly terrified, and the candidate he had in mind didn't seem capable of accomplishing either. Wilkes, in fact, on anything close to even terms, would have been more than a match, withal.

What the fuck, then, had gone down in that loft the other night?

McCreary hated to admit that he might have added the pieces together wrong, but he was even more reluctant to dismiss Reppa's send-off too casually. Was it possible he still—?

Or how about if it wasn't a step he hadn't taken but a turn he had missed? Backing up a moment to Reppa's description—such a nice eye for detail it had almost put him right there in the room with the two of them—could he have misinterpreted the signals that a mask had been worn? And then, gazing again into the side-view mirror and trying to find his own eyes behind the sunglasses, he saw all at once that he had misinterpreted nothing but misunderstood everything.

As in the mirror, he had been looking at the whole picture in *reverse!*

The word clicked like the last turn of the tumbler on the combination lock his brain had been feverishly spinning for the past twelve years.

He knew now that Wilkes had been less than a physical equal for her killer. But it still left the hypo.

A moment later, his impatience no longer stemming from his having to wait inert for a parking spot, he looked away from the mirror and stared hard into the middle distance. *Who the hell trying to fake a suicide would use a hypo?*

Then he saw out of the corner of his eye that he was going to have to deal with an interruption.

For a moment he experienced a faint, peripheral annoyance with the intruder on his thoughts, but when he swung his gaze reluctantly back to the side-view mirror, he recognized too late that they had at some point gone off in a very wrong direction.

At a quarter to ten on Thursday morning Reppa found himself sitting outside the office of Senior Parole Officer Donald Smail. Smail was in charge of the unit in the Bureau of Special Services that handled internal investigations. The bureau (known within the agency as BSS) had been devised to cope with situations that were beyond the scope of the average parole officer. Long-term surveillances of organized crime figures. Hunts for escaped convicts. Probes of fellow parole officers suspected of being on the take. BSS officers considered themselves the elite of the Division of Parole, and a case could be made that they were. Most were crack marksmen and skilled in hand-to-hand combat. One or two had karate black belts. There was an ex-heavyweight boxer, two finishers in the last New York City marathon, and several men who would have been career FBI agents or police officers but for their inability to pass the stringent vision requirements of those agencies.

Smail supervised six of these men but was himself the possessor of no special abilities. He had gotten the job sheerly by dint of his passing score on the last senior parole officer's exam and the fact that his name had been next on the appointments list when a senior's slot fell open in BSS. He was short, pallid, and white-haired, with a round face, round shoulders, and a round belly. The antithesis in every respect of J. J. McCreary. A comparison that Reppa would have had no reason to make if the moment had not been one that begged for comparisons. The last and only time he had requested an assignment since becoming a parole officer had been less than a month ago. And now he was about to request a second assignment from Smail because the man who had given him his first assignment was dead.

It was nearly ten before Smail opened the door of his office and beckoned to him. When he was seated beside Smail's desk, he saw a yellow pad on the blotter with his name printed on the top sheet, followed by several lines of shorthand notes.

"Poop," Smail said, almost dreamily watching his efforts to read upside down. "I made a few calls around the farmhouse while you were outside. You got McCreary to assign you the de Spirit pardon investigation out of rotation. How? You did the job, and the day you finished, McCreary fired off a memo asking for emergency leave. To do what? You're no particular friend of McCreary's, yet the morning after we learn he's been blown away, you turn up on my doorstep. Why?"

"Your unit is investigating his death. I want to be temporarily assigned to BSS so I can take part in the investigation."

Smail looked at Reppa. "I figured that much out on my own. As for the rest of it . . ." His voice trailed away.

Reppa felt a tension rise within him, and an anger at that tension. He waited several moments before he replied, and he made his voice as flat and expressionless as possible.

"The pardon investigation I volunteered for because I supervise de Spirit's stepbrother, and he was being coerced by the cops into making false statements that could be used against de Spirit in the event there's a new trial. I didn't like it, and I wanted to put a stop to it."

"Am I missing something? How did you expect a pardon investigation to accomplish that?"

"I wasn't sure when I started, but I found a way." Reppa paused, carefully considering his next words. "The statements still stand. But now I can stop them from ever being used."

Smail retained traces of his dreamy expression. "Oh? How?"

"I can't say. There are things I've been told that I've been sworn to keep in confidence for the moment."

"You can't . . ." Smail lifted his right hand to his lips as if to blot out a wrong approach. "Well, would you at least tell me how you got McCreary to assign you the investigation?"

"De Spirit's stepbrother is a young black who's had a rough row to hoe. I imagine McCreary decided as long as somebody had to do the investigation, it might as well be a parole officer who had an interest he could identify with."

Smail looked at him sideways, frowning slightly. "That's it? *All* of it?"

"At first it was. By the time I finished the investigation, I had a pretty strong feeling de Spirit was innocent. So strong, in fact, that I felt the whole case should be reopened. I tried to say this in my report. McCreary made me tone it down. My impression, though, was that he felt as I did and was just trying to keep the report strictly to the point. The feasibility of a pardon was all we were asked to investigate, so that was all—"

Smail cut him off sharply. "You knew that McCreary was de Spirit's parole officer at the time of the Behrman-Moffett murders and that he got in hot water over becoming too involved in the case?"

Nodding, Reppa said, "McCreary even told me he found it highly ironic that he was in charge of assigning the very sort of investigation he would have given his eyeteeth to do himself."

Smail turned to stare at him in silence for several moments.

"So highly ironic that he decided to take up where you left off after you finished?"

Reppa said gravely, "It does certainly look that way."

"Don't you think you had an obligation to inform someone here of your suspicions?"

"Quite frankly," Reppa said, "no."

"Why not?"

"Did anyone bother to tell me three years ago that my first partner was a drunk and a racist and that it could cost me my neck if I went on delinquency work with him?"

Smail tried to put some vehemence into his voice. "So you felt one bad turn deserved another?"

"There's more. McCreary was doing something that had to be done. De Spirit is innocent. The murder of the third Behrman-Moffett roommate the other night proved it. A new trial for de Spirit isn't going to be enough. The case has to be reopened."

"Murder?" Smail retrieved his dreamy look. "The Wilkes woman? First I've heard she was murdered."

"You may hear a lot here for the first time before I'm through. It depends, number one, on whether I'm assigned to your unit. And number two, on how much freedom you give me . . ." Reppa had other stipulations, too, that he wanted to make. But he caught on Smail's face an expression of such anxiety, dismay, and something like fear that he was surprised into silence.

"Freedom to do what?" Smail said warily.

"Whatever I have to to find McCreary's murderer."

Smail seemed to freeze. "The police are handling it. We're limited to giving them whatever help we can. Any information you have, of course, has to be turned over to them."

Of course? Phrases like that had in the past often sold Reppa when they were uttered with casual authority, but he heard the forlorn prayer behind this one. "The police don't have the same interest I do. At any rate, enough of them don't so that it's impossible for me to distinguish those I can trust from those I can't."

"McCreary quite evidently had a similar feeling. Not only about the police but about us. His own outfit. I hope you don't think there can be any justification for the way he operated. Suffice it to say that if we'd known what he was doing a few days ago, he'd still be alive."

It was not the emptiest of proclamations. "If you're thinking," Reppa said in an angry tone, for he did not want to hear anyone voice, even insincerely, the thing that he could not yet entirely dismiss, "I'm responsible for his being murdered because I didn't report my suspicions, you don't know McCreary. Even knowing what he was doing, there's no one here who could have stopped him. He'd committed himself too far, and he was too close to getting what he was after."

"The real Behrman-Moffett murderer?" When he wasn't contradicted, Smail murmured, "How do you know he was?"

"He left behind a briefcase. In it are some papers and notes telling what he did during the last few days before he was murdered."

323

Smail's eyes skittishly examined Reppa's face. "Where is it?"

Reppa produced a key and deposited it on the corner of Smail's desk. Smail glanced away as he picked it up and turned it over between his fingers.

"How did you get this?"

I paid a quarter for it at the lockers in Port Authority."

Smail nodded, conceding him his little joke. "What I assumed you were saying was this key fell into your hands somehow."

"Not the key—the briefcase. And it didn't *fall* into my hands. It was given to me last night by a friend of McCreary's."

"Who?"

"A woman. I don't know her name. Her only contact with me was to hand over the briefcase."

Smail let the key drop from his fingers to his palm, and his eyes took on a guarded expression. "And its contents—you've examined them?"

"Thoroughly."

"And now . . . on the basis of what you know and the fact that the briefcase is in your possession, you feel you should be assigned to BSS."

Reppa nodded.

"Is it your belief that McCreary's murderer and the Behrman-Moffett murderer are one and the same?"

"You can add Jill Wilkes to that list, too."

Smail closed one eye, lifted the other brow. "That's a lot of loose change for one hand to pick up. Most of it in coins that aren't in our currency."

"But McCreary is. If you want my pledge to concentrate on getting his killer and leaving the rest to the NYPD, you've got it."

"I already have my entire unit working on McCreary. Why do I need you?"

"The information I have that your men don't."

"Without the expertise to use it. You don't have any of the skills my men do.

But he had the information. Reppa thought that went without repeating. There was one thing, however, that had not yet been said, and now was the moment.

"I'll work this alone if I have to."

"Yet you came to me first." Smail looked at him in silent speculation. "Why?"

"I have a score to settle, but I'd still prefer not to do it on my own."

"A score to settle with whom?"

"McCreary's the closest I've come in this outfit to a partner I can respect. Since he left me the briefcase, I have to think he had a little respect for me, too. And when a man's partner is killed, he does something about it."

Smail's other eye closed partway, and the dreamy look was back. "Where have I heard that before? *The Godfather?*"

"The weed of crime bears bitter fruit."

"Oh, now, that's—"

"A stitch in time saves nine."

Smail stared glassily.

"What I'm saying," Reppa told him roughly, "is the score I have to settle is personal. There's no neat code behind it. No super sayings. I want to win—to feel like a winner—and it's been a long time since I have. I can now, and in a big way. They don't come along this big very often, and I intend to ride it to the end. Because if I get off this now, someone else is just going to get on in my place."

"Now look at it this way—" Smail began.

"No. I've already looked at it every which way, and here's the only view that makes sense. I'm a team player. I've played team sports all my life, but I'm starting to think they don't work when it comes to teaching you how the rest of the game is played. Don't push me over the brink. Transfer me to your unit and give me the authorization to go after McCreary's murderer. Because if you don't, I'll be forced to go out on my own, and nobody in this outfit is ever going to learn what's in that briefcase."

Smail glanced at his palm and then closed it into a fist. Reppa watched him reach his other hand toward the phone on his desk. "Not only am I not going to transfer you to my unit"—Smail waited for more spit to form in his mouth—"but I'm going to call the area director and recommend you be brought up on charges."

"Fine. But before you do, I'd like my key back."

Reppa's voice was nothing but mild, but Smail glanced toward the door, as if regretting he'd closed it. His hand let go of the phone, and his eyes assumed the guarded look again. Rising suddenly, he thrust his closed fist under his armpit. "This is going up to the area director. Don't try to stop me."

"From making an ass of yourself?" Reppa remained seated. Impassively he said, "That key will get you a pair of old sweat socks. You don't believe me? Send one of your men across the street to look."

"Where's the briefcase? You lied to me, Reppa. Where is it?"

"I didn't lie. I showed you a key to a locker. I didn't say what was in it."

"You're lying. How do I know there even *is* a briefcase?"

Curiously, almost detachedly Reppa watched his hands, which had been shaking a little, become perfectly steady. "I knew before I came in here that you'd try to crap all

326

over me. It won't work, Smail. When I had McCreary do it to me, I had the best. I said I'm ready to work this alone if I have to. If I get up from this chair and walk out of here, I start.''

Smail said despairingly, ''I can't request that you be assigned to my unit. I don't have the authority.''

''I know better. Right now McCreary takes precedence over everything else.''

''It's not the same as when a cop—''

''You can get anyone you want into your unit. All you have to do is ask.''

Smail tried to resurrect some dignity, but he was close to a whine. ''People will demand to know why—''

''Tell them.''

''What can I—?'' Smail halted, as if stricken by the ineffectual tone of his voice. ''Give me something—anything—as proof.''

Reppa gave him the only thing in the briefcase that had not been paper.

McCreary's shield.

The phone call had come the previous night, even before he'd learned McCreary's body had been found. The woman's words were Jill Wilkes all over again, cryptic and oblique. If he came to the Empire Bar on 125th Street at eleven o'clock, she would give him something. But the voice had none of Wilkes's astringency. It sounded drained and diffident, and when it mentioned the place of assignation, Reppa began to listen for clues that its owner was black. But if there were any, they were too subtle; and besides, he had the Mets' game blaring in his other ear.

The alarm clock on the night table said it was twenty past nine. Plenty of time to get uptown if he was going, but why should he? To meet with a woman who'd given him no real information and allowed him no time for questions?

And yet she'd asked for him by his full name. Not Mr. Reppa. Frank Reppa. And apart from the office and one or two paddleball cronies, he'd given out Leilah's phone number to no one.

The ball game was still yammering away when the phone rang again.

This time, once he learned it was Spielman calling long distance from New Jersey (collect, naturally), he got Leilah to turn the TV down. Spielman said, "Wahoo." Reppa knew that this, rather than being a greeting, was only a parenthesis from the tumultuous monologue Spielman had begun even before he'd finished dialing Leilah's number. Reppa sat down on the bed, and within three minutes he'd been told, amid Spielman's idiosyncratic blasts of punctuation when excited, that McCreary wahoo had been found earlier that evening in the trunk of his own car, which had been towed by the cops to the auto zoo on the pier, where it had sat around for a couple of days before wahoo somebody'd noticed an aroma coming from it, and wahoo the early line was McCreary'd been blown away with his own gun, which was stuffed in his mouth, which in turn was going to make everybody think wahoo, especially since the cops had snatched his car off Mulberry Street right in the heart of Little wahoo.

No sooner did he put the phone down than Leilah turned up the TV again, but when she saw his face, she switched it off completely. After he told her about McCreary, they were both still for a long time.

"You can't go meet that woman," she said halfheartedly. "You don't even know who she is."

"I can make a pretty good guess: the girl on the switchboard who's been helping McCreary out."

"But a Hundred and Twenty-fifth Street—what do you think she has for you? It could be a bullet in the head. You still don't know what McCreary's real reason was for going AWOL from his job."

"What's going on? You didn't do this when I went to see Wilkes."

"I'm pissed off, Reppa."

He looked at her in quiet amazement. "About what?"

"It's frustrating being Nero. Would you take me with you tonight? Would you if you could?"

"You wouldn't be too afraid?"

Leilah slipped her hand under his wrist to take his pulse. "Unbelievable," she said. "Feel mine."

"What's mine like?"

"You don't know, do you? That's what's so unbelievable."

Reppa pulled his hand away. "I'm not in the mood right now for a physical exam."

"Well, maybe others are."

Leilah began writing furiously in her notebook.

Fifteen minutes later he was listening to his car radio as he went up Tenth Avenue. One detail Spielman had either omitted or not known: The car had been towed on Monday morning, so McCreary had been dead for at least two days. Nobody had any theories to offer, at least not over the air. A career parole officer. Wife and five children. Dedicated, according to parole officials, to his job; devoted to his family. What, Reppa had to wonder, would they have found to say about him? He put that thought and others like it away. To focus on the immediate. *Slow down . . . you're doing almost fifty. Columbus Circle and now where? Broadway to Seventy-second Street . . . Amsterdam Avenue.*

It was roughly the same journey he made each time he

went to the field, but at night he could never get oriented. Harlem, approaching it up Amsterdam Avenue, was indistinguishable from the rest of the city. Until you got to 125th Street, turned right, and there it was.

The Empire Bar was between Lenox and Fifth avenues. He parked near the corner of Lenox, acutely conscious as he got out that his was the only white face for miles. But people passing him seemed scarcely to notice. An active corner. He turned all the way around. Nobody he could see whose interest was in him. The neon sign in front of the bar had two letters out: M IRE. There was a full moon, but the clouds were so thick that only a pallid disc shone through. He entered the bar, wishing he'd done what Cupach and probably every smart cop would have done in this situation: worn a hat. And sure enough, there they were. All along the bar. Eyes watching him with the same half-amused, half-hostile curiosity shown little boys who'd ventured into the wrong rest room.

He took a seat in an empty booth, which became in a matter of seconds one of a string of three empty booths as the people behind and in front of him defected to the bar. Faces receded. Voices swelled. Other noises. A jukebox. What remaining composure he had wavered and then held firm. He looked around a little. A barmaid seemed to be debating whether to come over to him, which, if she didn't do soon, would force him to get up and order a beer at the bar. His throat felt too dry and stiff to conduct any oral business, while his hands wouldn't stay still, nervously garrulous, like a mute's talking to relieve an uncomfortable silence.

Another barmaid was listening to a woman in smoked glasses at the end of the bar. The woman handed her a shopping bag to hold while she got into her coat, but then left without it. When the barmaid turned and looked at him, he realized he should have paid more attention to the woman. Other than the smoked glasses, what had registered? Young; late twenties; decent legs; nothing fantastic. But not familiar. Not one of the girls on the switchboard. McCreary'd had more than one on the string, then.

He got up when the barmaid, not so young, started toward him. Heads swiveled his way again.

"For me?"

The barmaid made as if to return to the bar after depositing the shopping bag in front of him, so he had to be fast.

"Who was the woman who gave this to you?"

"She gone."

"I know, but who was she?"

"She say give this to the white man. You telling me I got the wrong white man?"

He waited until he was out of Harlem, somewhere on Columbus Avenue, before he pulled his car over and opened the shopping bag. The briefcase was wrapped in a newspaper, that day's, which told him the woman had probably prepared the package for him herself, probably not till after she knew that McCreary was dead, probably being careful that none of her fingerprints got on it. The folder stuffed with papers that was inside the briefcase had a note scribbled in pencil across the front of it: *Get this right away to Frank Reppa, anything happens.* Also on the folder was Leilah's phone number.

He drove back downtown quickly, but he and Leilah made no haste going through the folder. Only after they finished did they look at each other and visibly acknowledge their disappointment. There was plenty that was new, but there wasn't enough. If McCreary had figured out which way the final step had to be taken, he hadn't put it in writing. They read every note, every scrap of paper, so surely one of them would have found it if it was there.

And Reppa's disappointment became frustration when he understood how thoroughly McCreary had hooked him while once more, and this time finally and forever, escaping without revealing who or what he had been hooked by himself.

CHAPTER FOURTEEN

THE LEGACY

McCreary had been a pain in the ass to them for so long the NYPD would not have been unhappy to chalk off his murder to some cross-up between him and the Mob and let it go at that. So the major burden of proving otherwise fell on the Division of Parole. Bill Timberlake, the BSS parole officer who was assigned to work with him, seemed about as sharp as they came. After his initial incredulity and resentment when he realized Reppa not only had his own ideas as to how the investigation should proceed but also had been given free rein by Smail to act on them, Timberlake semipeaceably accepted his role as the junior member of their team. Timberlake knew McCreary well, having been with the agency over twenty years himself, and recognized that the briefcase had been willed to Reppa for good reason. It was in a sense a legacy, handed down from a man whose ego had demanded he be king to his chosen prince.

"What I'm seeing," said Reppa, once Timberlake had sifted through the contents of the briefcase, "is McCreary must have been killed because he was right on the edge of exposing the real Behrman-Moffett killer. But like Jill Wilkes, he was caught by surprise somehow. Badly by surprise. Else how could he have allowed anyone to take his gun away from him? Also it's weird that he wasn't carrying his shield at the time."

"Not necessarily. Maybe he got nailed when he stepped out of the place where he was crashing just to pick up a pack of cigarettes or something."

"Meaning the murderer both knew where he was staying and wasn't afraid to hang around Harlem until a chance came to take him? Neither seems very likely."

Timberlake shook his squarish head. Pushing fifty, he still had the torso of an Olympic weight lifter. Not terribly large, only about five nine, but he was the unofficial arm-wrestling champion of the entire agency.

"What we ought to do is go up there and lean on that barmaid a little. Chances are if she doesn't know the woman herself, she can put us on to somebody who does."

"That's on the list," Reppa said, beginning his captaincy, "of things for you to do. What I've done is divided it up according to the areas in which each of us functions best. You'd be stronger, I think, at finding out who the woman was that delivered the briefcase. Also at learning whether or not McCreary had somebody here on the switchboard helping him out. Then I thought you could handle getting the information from other agencies that we need. Such as the full story on the offenses on the arrest sheets McCreary turned up. Mald's manslaughter and the three busts Behrman had for soliciting hookers. I'm also wondering whether Annabelle's secretary has a record. McCreary's notes say he couldn't get either Kinder or Mald to talk to him, but he managed to get Mald's prints by tricking him into handling his ID card at the gallery before Mald realized who he was. Kinder, on the other hand, refused to answer the door when he tried to get in to see Annabelle."

"It shouldn't be hard to get Kinder's prints. Maybe from the Division of Criminal Justice Services."

"Try. Last but not least, we've got to learn what McCreary was really up to. There was more to it, I'm certain, than just finding out who the real Behrman-Moffett murderer is."

"Why so certain?"

Reppa hesitated, having told no one in the agency of his last encounter with McCreary—no one anywhere except Leilah. Should he now? After swearing Timberlake to secrecy? He decided not. Timberlake, a career man, would not allow himself to be bound by the oath if told Reppa'd gone up the creek without a paddle by going to Wilkes's loft the other night. "McCreary kept insisting he only wanted the personal satisfaction of showing everybody for once just how good he really was. That may have been all of what made him take the risks he did, but you knew him even better than I. Do you buy it?"

Timberlake didn't respond. Instead his eyes flicked curiously over Reppa's face. "You haven't said what you're going to be doing while I'm running down all this other stuff."

"First of all, making another visit to each of the people I interviewed during the pardon investigation." Reading Timberlake's look, Reppa said, "Alone. Having spoken to me once, they'll know me. You, if I take you with me as a strange face, may be an inhibiting factor."

"It's standard, you know, for two men to do what you're going to do."

Reppa nodded. He'd considered this a long time before deciding that he absolutely did not want another partner. It belonged now solely to him—and to Leilah, though this was not, as yet, so clearly established. "I have to go with my instinct that it's best if I work this part solo."

"It might be nice," Timberlake pointed out dryly, "to have a backup along in the event one of them tries to waste you."

"That's occurred to me. But I've got a way of covering myself. I'm going to contact each person in advance and let him know I'm coming. When I get to his place, I'll call the woman I live with from a pay phone outside and let her know I'm there. She'll wait five minutes or so for me to get inside, then call him and ask to speak to me. I'll then tell her in his presence that I'll call her back as soon as I leave."

"Fine. But what makes you so sure the killer won't bump you off even if he's known to be the last person you were with?"

"Because he's kept his identity a secret for twelve years. He's not going to blow it now. At least not in such an obvious way."

Hearing this, Timberlake seemed appeased. They argued awhile, though, over which of them should talk to the private detective Behrman had hired thirty years ago to investigate his wife's background. In the end Reppa won out, because he knew best the material McCreary had most likely gone over in talking to the detective. Also, McCreary's notes said the detective lived on the Lower East Side. Reppa and he would at least have that in common.

His name was Lowell Muntz. In 1962, after fifteen years of service with the Wakefield Detective Bureau, he had been fired after trying to extort money from a client. By checking police records McCreary had discovered that, although no formal charges had ever been pressed against Muntz, his license had been permanently revoked. Neither the police nor the Wakefield Bureau would tell McCreary the details of Muntz's crime, but someone at Wakefield had verified that Behrman utilized their services in 1950, and again in 1964. McCreary's notes implied that he'd gotten Behrman to give him the detective's name effortlessly— "Subject hedged a moment, then a hopeless shrug slithered across his shoulders . . ."

Muntz lived on the ground floor of a walk-up on the corner of Second Avenue and East Third Street. Though only six blocks from Reppa's own digs, it was not a building he'd ever noticed before. McCreary's description of Muntz: ". . . cripple, wheelchair; arthritis (so sub. says); living w/ old woman claims is wife but two last names on mailbox."

The second name was Cerny, and the woman mumbled it when she answered the door. If she gave a first name, Reppa didn't catch it. She had a coat on even though the thermometer was pushing eighty. A frayed wool coat. Was there anything under it? And her hair, the color of iron, the texture of rope—could anything so unkempt be real? There were women like this sitting on park benches all day, but it was the first time Reppa had ever been in the home of one.

She seemed to lead him nowhere in particular, just started wandering down a hallway that smelled of garlic and other equally strong but less definable odors. At the end of the hallway was a tiny room with a rocker, a throw rug, and a small TV set, which was turned to a soap opera. She paused with her hand on the knob of the door as if waiting to be told that whatever duties she had here were finished. Had he missed something? There was another partially closed door back the way he'd come, and there inside it, with a chessboard on his aged lap, was a man in a wheelchair. It had to be Muntz. But was there ever a man who looked less like a detective? Hair, bone, and skin, and of the three hair predominated. Full gray beard, ragged bushy eyebrows, long ponytail that was tied with a piece of dirty string.

"Mr. Muntz? Frank Reppa. New York State Parole."

The mass of hair didn't stir.

"I called you this morning . . . J. J. McCreary, the parole officer you spoke to last week?"

The head remained slumped over, but the eyes widened, and Reppa saw their keenness. He held out his shield and ID, but Muntz was uninterested.

"Make a move," the old man said. "Any move. Either side of the board. White or black."

"I didn't come here to play games."

"You're supposed to take white," Muntz said querulously. "McCreary took black, and I mated him in four moves." But he folded up the board obediently and shoveled the pieces into a cigar box at his side.

Reppa sat down, uninvited, and opened his notebook, unnoticed. Muntz was gazing at a spot on the carpet that looked like dried blood.

"Dogs," he announced glumly. "Guy brought his bitch with him while she was in heat. Blind, so I had to let him do it."

"A client?"

"Last one. Muntz's last case . . ."

The old man's voice receded when Reppa cleared his throat, gazing meanwhile at the ceiling, which retained its own mementoes of past adventures. In one corner an egg stain, hunk of dried shell adhering. Overhead two round dots that looked like empty eye sockets. Bullet holes? The sensation creeping over him that he was in a room out of a dim and distant past, he cleared his throat again. "As I explained over the phone, we're checking back over McCreary's activities the last few days before he was shot. We know he talked to you about an investigation you once

338

did for a man named Stanley Behrman. Our hope is that something the two of you discussed can give us a lead as to who killed him.

Muntz grunted. "Talked about only one thing."

"What was it?"

Muntz grunted again but then remained silent, considering.

"McCreary left some notes," Reppa pursued. "They show he had several questions he intended to ask you about the family background of Behrman's wife. But there's no mention in his notes of your answers."

"Because I gave him none."

"You didn't remember the investigation?"

"Never forgotten it."

"Then . . . ?"

"The price is still the same."

"Price?" Muntz looked, but only looked, as though he were at the mercy of his wheelchair. Sit down across from him, and those eyes became incandescent.

"Ten big ones."

Like candles behind frosted windows, that kind of incandescent: Muntz had cataracts. "Ten hundred?"

"Grand. Same as I told McCreary. Foolishly he didn't pay. Thought he could get the same info or better from another source."

"Did he say where?"

Muntz's shoulders went up half an inch. "Just said he had other avenues to explore. So I told him go ahead. Which is what he must have done. Tragic."

"This information you have . . ." Reppa paused for several moments, in the hope Muntz would fill the silence, but the old man sat like a lump of stone. "Does it pertain in some way to the Behrman-Moffett case?"

"Might."

"And just *might* it tell me who killed Behrman and Moffett?"

Muntz snickered. "You think I'd let gold go for the price of tin?"

"Tin? Ten grand is a lot of money."

"Cheap at twice the price. If McCreary'd wanted to, he could've scraped up the dough, easy."

It was said expressionlessly, as if to end this phase of the conversation, but Reppa stared intently at the old man. "How do you know he could have?"

"My business." Muntz returned his stare with another faint shrug. "When it's an issue of whether there's dough to pay for information, I know."

"There's another more important issue. A parole officer has been murdered, along with three women. If you have information that would help reveal who—"

Muntz didn't let him finish. "Spare the horses. And forget any ideas you have about bringing the cops here with a search warrant. They won't find what you want. Ten big ones. You work for a big outfit. One of your men was killed. If you guys want what I've got, you'll figure out a way to come up with the dough.

"Sight unseen?"

"Ah." Muntz smiled for the first time, and it was surprisingly warm. "Smart. McCreary didn't think to ask that."

Before Reppa could feel the satisfaction this might understandably have brought him, Muntz suddenly banged both hands on the arms of the wheelchair and cried, "Who are you? How much do you know about Behrman-Moffett?"

"I did the de Spirit pardon investigation. McCreary may have told you about it."

"McCreary didn't tell me *bupkis*, but I read. I still read everything. And I keep up my scrapbooks. Behrman-Moffett.

'welve years ago the cops came around and asked if I had
nything to add to the report I wrote after I finished
nvestigating Adelaide Behrman's family background. I
old them to take a hike. Bastards never got a thing from
ne after they pulled my license.''

"Who spoke to you?"

"The movie star. The big guy and his partner. But it
vasn't only my grudge against the NYPD that made me
hut the door on them. I had a dollar to make, and they
on't like to pay. Not for the kind of stuff I have, anyway.

"Then why should our outfit?"

"Because you're not just looking for some guy who
tuck a couple of girls. You lost one of your own men. It's
vorth ten grand. Even the bare chance that what I have
an lead you to who killed him. That's why the price is so
igh."

See my logic, Muntz's look said, but Reppa had also
een given another glimpse of the loose piece. "Yet it's
he same price you quoted McCreary, and all he was
ooking for at the time was the person who killed Behrman
nd Moffett. Since the stakes have gone up, why hasn't
he price?"

Muntz flicked his eyes to the box of chessmen, as if
fraid one of them might talk.

"To put it right on, why did you think your information
vas worth as much to McCreary as it is to us?"

A glance at the wheelchair was all the answer he would
et. Muntz had seized one of his hands with the other, to
top a violent tremor.

"Take a charitable view," he said at last. "Nothing
oming in anymore but disability. It ends when I go. Don't
ou think Lois is entitled to a little nest egg?"

Muntz coughed listlessly, as if to intimate, in the event
Reppa was unimpressed by wheelchairs, that there were

341

other factors to consider. But then a genuine coughing fi
seemed to overtake him. Bright red flecks appeared in the
gray beard.

"Water?"

Muntz hacked on, gaspingly, all the while shaking his
head. Suddenly he sagged to one side, but when Reppa
jumped up to assist him, he saw the old man was reaching
for the chessmen.

Upright again, Muntz held out two closed fists. *Which
hand?*

"If you're trying again to get me into a game—"

"No games. Just pick."

Puzzled now, Reppa pointed. The left hand burst open
like a hairy gray flower, revealing a white pawn.

"Behind you. On the desk under the blotter."

Turning, Reppa lifted the blotter and found a small
white envelope.

"Open it. A present. Compliments of Lowell Muntz."

A copy, he saw when he unfolded it, of Andrea
Behrman's birth certificate. Mother: Adellaide Loomis
Father: Unknown. Born: March 7, 1945, in Murfreesboro
Tennessee.

"Well?" Muntz grunted. "Interesting, no?"

"Not very."

"Look again."

He still didn't notice, until Muntz asked him how to
spell *Adelaide,* that the name on the document had a
double *l.* Okay. So it had been misspelled. In backwood
hospitals those things happened.

"Murfreesboro isn't the backwoods," Muntz said testily
"And in the forties it had several homes for unwed
mothers."

"So what? Adelaide went there to have her kid. All this
does is corroborate the report you gave Behrman when you

342

got back from Kentucky." Reppa paused. "Unless Andrea's father isn't really unknown. That's it, isn't it? You know who he is."

Muntz gave a tidy shrug, and his eyes went blank, hiding whatever was behind them. "Does happen I know who her real mother is."

Once more the old man held out closed fists but then opened them before Reppa could choose. Each palm had a white pawn. Muntz's little joke. No losers here, though the prize could still be a bummer.

Reppa was sent this time to the top right-hand drawer of the desk, where another small sealed envelope awaited him. And another folded photostat of Andrea Behrman's birth certificate. He started to read it to himself but then halted, stunned, and read aloud: "Annabelle Loomis!"

"The date," Muntz prodded. "Look at the date."

March 7, 1944. A year earlier . . .

"Moth-eaten trick," the old man went on. "Like kids used to do with draft cards. Clumsy, but it works. Paste one number over another and make a photostat. A five over a four, no problem. Single digit. But Adelaide over Annabelle? One letter short."

Then it had been Annabelle who went to Murfreesboro. But in 1944, not 1945. Reppa's eyes flew back and forth between the two birth certificates. "Where did you get these?"

"One was in Loomis's Bible. The McCoy I had to go to Murfreesboro for."

"What made you think the one in the Bible wasn't authentic?"

"The story about the rape. Made me suspicious. Especially when I found out from Loomis's neighbors that *both* Annabelle and Adelaide left town right after it supposedly happened. The whole thing had a sour smell. So I went to

Murfreesboro. Paid my own way. Didn't even put in for expenses."

Reppa looked at the old man steadily for several moments. "Why not?"

"To avoid questions. Once I got my hands on a copy of the real birth certificate, I saw immediately that it might one day be profitable if nobody knew I'd been to Murfreesboro." Muntz coughed and then spoke more firmly. "Especially when I put that birth certificate up beside a couple of other little items I located."

"Like what?"

Muntz smiled. "Ten big ones. Take along the birth certificates. Prove to your boys at Parole that Muntz knew his job."

"Why didn't you ever show these to Stanley Behrman?"

"Oh," the old man said distantly, summoning pleasure to his voice. "There was a rule we followed. The smart ones among us. Never give a client more than he's paid for. Behrman wanted to know about his wife's pedigree. It would've cost him extra to find out he was raising a girl who wasn't really his stepdaughter, and my hunch was he wouldn't pay it. I went by my hunches. One of the few times I didn't, I got burned. My own fault. My hunch was that someday when she was old enough, Andrea Behrman would be willing to buy these birth certificates. She or whoever the guy was she married. So I saved them.

"Did you ever consider trying to sell them to Annabelle Loomis?"

Muntz laughed, stopped short, and began coughing rackingly, the worst siege yet. Reppa felt his eyes being pulled away from the wheelchair. He was aware suddenly of the Cerny woman in the doorway. She stood in her old wool coat, peering in at them. He was struck by the worry on her face and the concern in her voice.

"Lowell, that's enough, now. You know you mustn't get yourself overwrought."

"Goddam lungs . . ."

"Go," she said to Reppa. "Please."

As he rose, Muntz managed to rasp, "Ten big ones . . . a bargain," before falling back in a fresh seizure.

Mother: Annabelle Loomis. Date of birth: March 7, 1944.

Later, when he showed the birth certificates to Leilah, he remembered Rumpelstiltskin. McCreary's barely suppressed excitement when he heard the name, as if he'd realized that a child of two, even a very precocious two, would hardly know such a word, much less be able to pronounce it.

The error glared in retrospect, but Leilah wouldn't let him feel witless for long. It wasn't so critical, after all, that Andrea had been older than two when she first met Behrman. What was liable to be critical was why it couldn't be acknowledged that she was older. Where had she been during that lost first year of her life? And why had she been taken away from Annabelle?

"It's weird," Reppa said, "but the whole time I was with her she didn't let on for an instant that she was Andrea's mother."

"It would be even weirder if she had," Leilah replied dryly. "No, Reppa, what's really weird is that neither she nor any of the other people you spoke to during your investigation refused to see you. If one of them really is the murderer, logically he should have. But he didn't. Why?"

"It would have made me suspicious if he had."

"What did he care if you were suspicious? No, he saw you because he wanted to. Because after twelve years of

345

keeping it locked inside him, he was fairly crying out for someone to talk to about it."

Sometimes she reminded him that he was getting his training on the job and hers came out of books. "The old theory? Every murderer secretly wants to be caught?"

"Not caught." Leilah, after a moment of emphatic silence, said very softly, "Understood. Something was said to you or shown to you. Something seemingly unnecessary.

"They all said or did things they didn't have to. Behrman laid that story about the Loomis family on me—"

"And in telling you about them he tucked in some very revealing things about himself, including his reaction to Andrea's first words to him."

"And Annabelle said more than she had to about Elizabeth and less than she should have about Andrea. And Halliwell didn't have to tell me about the Lady Godiva incident—"

"Mald did something equally unnecessary. Why did he drag you off to see samples of Annabelle's and Wilkes's work?"

"And why did Kinder leave me alone in his office so I could find an appointment book with two names in it that I wouldn't have otherwise known in time to ask Annabelle about them? He also took Annabelle by surprise when he opened the door to her room. It may have been deliberate. It almost seemed he wanted to jar her."

"Halliwell's spilling coffee on himself definitely was deliberate. He must have known what question you were about to ask him and hoped to avoid it.

"I'm sure he did."

Leilah's hands gripped each other, forming a rock of thoughtfulness, which she planted under her chin. She faced him then across the rock with a deepening gleam in her eyes. It was time to discuss the strategy he would take when he interviewed the blocks of granite again.

The following morning Reppa told Timberlake about his talk with Muntz. When Timberlake saw the two birth certificates, he agreed they were interesting but couldn't see where they were enough to make anyone spring for ten grand to learn what else Muntz had. How important could something a private detective had turned up thirty years ago be, anyway? For one thing, Reppa suggested, the identity of Andrea Behrman's real father. Terrific, and just how was that going to get them any closer to McCreary's killer? That was their objective here—their one and only objective—in case Reppa'd forgotten.

They argued. Finally Timberlake agreed to talk to the president of the Parole Officers Association. A few years earlier the POA had tapped each parole officer for fifty dollars so a lawyer from Louis Nizer's office could be hired to represent them in their fight with the state for a grade hike. It could be, since McCreary's murder had cast the agency in such a bad light, that the POA might consider trying something similar to raise Muntz's ante. Especially if this thing dragged on much longer. Already many parole officers were mutinous over the lackadaisical way the police were responding to the incident as well as over the agency's failure to treat it with the same seriousness as the NYPD would the murder of a police officer. The crowning demonstration that PO's were the lackeys of the law enforcement system. Meanwhile the agency was also catching it from another direction. McCreary's widow was filing a suit against the state, claiming her husband had been killed in the line of duty—prove otherwise.

The issue of Muntz tabled for the moment, Timberlake told Reppa that he'd been unable to unearth any information on Stanley Behrman's three arrests other than that they had occurred under the new "john" law. Whether the cases had been dropped because they were too flimsy, because Behrman had paid off someone, or because, as was most probable, the DA's office couldn't muster the enthusiasm to prosecute a prominent local businessman for violating an unpopular statute, Timberlake could not determine. Too bad. Reppa wanted as much ammunition as possible when he tackled Behrman again.

A young woman, but too polite to be Marissa, answered when he dialed Behrman's number. Informed he had reached a message service, he tried again in an hour. Same young woman. This time, when he identified himself, he was given over to her supervisor, who told him that Behrman's directions were that all important callers be told he was in New York Hospital.

Reppa looked up the number of the hospital and learned, when he reached In-Patient Information, that Behrman had been there since Monday. What was wrong with the fur dealer couldn't be divulged, but it wasn't so serious that Behrman couldn't have visitors.

He found his man in a private room. A fan circulated air freely in the room, but a strong medicinal smell assailed his nostrils nevertheless. It emanated from the bed where the cherubic face was regarding him with a limp smile. Pudgy fingers fluttered a greeting. Words were croaked.

"Officer . . . Teppa, isn't it?"

"Reppa."

The phone rang. Behrman picked it up, listened, and then handed it to him. It seemed ridiculous, standing beside a man in a hospital bed, to be checking in with Leilah, but it was wise, in any event, to establish the habit.

"So you see," Behrman said when he'd hung up. "I was right. A new trial. No pardon."

"You were right." The concession cost Reppa nothing but earned a sturdier smile from Behrman. In a moment, though, the fur dealer's face crumpled in a wince.

"Hernia operation," he murmured after suffering awhile in stoic silence. "Damn stitches."

Reppa offered the appropriate condolences as he seated himself and then said, "This isn't the ideal time to talk to you, but I can't wait. You've heard, I suppose, that the parole officer who talked to you last week was murdered."

Behrman acknowledged that he'd seen the papers. Terrible thing.

"I'm here because our agency is helping the police investigate his murder. Some notes he left show the two of you talked a week ago Wednesday in your apartment." Receiving a faint affirmative nod from Behrman, he said sharply, "What was the main topic of discussion?"

"Hmmm"—the pale round forehead wrinkled, the creases running almost vertically down the center—"I don't know quite how to put this."

"Briefly," Reppa said. "As briefly as possible."

"Well, it seems we talked mostly about your investigation. Officer McCreary said as your supervisor he was obliged to check up on the report you turned in to him. There was fear on his part that you may have distorted some of the facts. After I assured him that wasn't the case, we spoke in general terms about other matters for a few minutes. And then he left."

"But not until you'd given him the name of the private detective you hired to check into your wife's background." Seeing the shrug that elicited, he thought, McCreary was right—it is a sort of slither. His voice still sharp, he said, "Those other matters you talked about, what were they?"

Behrman frowned deeply. "I must say, officer, I didn't find you nearly this officious last time."

"Last time we were talking about someone who hadn't killed anybody in twelve years. Now we're talking about someone who's killed two people in less than a week."

"Two?"

"The police are coming to the conclusion that Jill Wilkes's death wasn't a suicide. Their next conclusion ought to be that the same person who killed her killed McCreary because he was getting too close to discovering who really killed your niece."

"Andrea?" Behrman gave him a chiding smile. "You mean my stepdaughter."

"No," Reppa said. "No. I mean your niece."

Behrman stared at him, his smile diminishing.

"It appears, you see, that your wife wasn't Andrea's mother. Her sister was."

"Annabelle?" Behrman let loose a hoarse gasp. "Impossible."

Reppa presented him with the two birth certificates. After examining them Behrman waved the original angrily and cried it was a fake. His reaction looked and sounded depressingly legitimate. It all did. Behrman hadn't known that Andrea was Annabelle's daughter.

"According to Muntz, the other one is the phony. Look at the way your wife's name is spelled—"

"Muntz? Where did you get these? Muntz? He's dead."

"So you claimed. McCreary found out differently."

"But that's what I was told. When I went back to his agency, they said he'd passed away."

"You're either lying, or you—"

"No. Now, listen—when I asked about him, the secretary lowered her eyes and said, 'Mr. Muntz is no longer with us.' What would you take that to mean?"

"You misunderstood her. But it's no longer important. What still is, though, is why you refused to tell me his name when we spoke last time. Was it because you didn't want me to trace him to the agency where he worked? When you went back to the Wakefield Bureau in 1964, Mr. Behrman, what did you ask them to do?"

To this there was no reply.

"Was it, by any chance, to put a tail on your wife because you suspected she was having an affair?"

"I've already made it clear," Behrman said frigidly, "I trusted Adelaide completely."

"Even in the company of Carlo Mald?"

Behrman momentarily shut his eyes. "Sweet Jesus," he murmured, and then: "Look here—you can't attack me like this. Not only am I a sick man, but I'm sure if I consulted my attorneys, they'd say I don't have to talk to you."

"No doubt. And there's none about what will happen if you take their advice. Danny de Spirit is up for a new trial. The DA's office might decide to scratch it and go after somebody else instead if I tell them a certain uncle didn't tell the police his niece was beaten up by her fiancé because it would have meant some embarrassing questions about how he came to see the marks on her."

"Uncle . . ." Behrman fidgeted under the stiff white hospital sheet. "These birth certificates . . . how did you get them?"

"Muntz gave them to me as a sample. He has something else. Something bigger."

"What is it?"

"I don't know. I was hoping you would."

Behrman shook his head—in relief? In any event his forehead unwrinkled.

Over the next minutes Reppa threw out the rest of the

351

lines he'd intended to cast here—when had Behrman seen
the marks on Andrea that indicated Halliwell had beaten
her, what were his three arrests about, and once more what
exactly had he and McCreary discussed?

Since this last topic was by far the safest, Behrman
waxed prolifically now on McCreary's visit. Rumpelstiltskin?
Yes, the name had been mentioned, but after that McCreary
had asked him next to nothing about Andrea. Or about
Adelaide. But there were some moments of interest in
Annabelle. McCreary had heard about the old Loomis
family photograph. Point of curiosity: He'd always wondered what the famous Annabelle had looked like as a
child. And after he was shown, he left.

"Before he did, was there anything else that you and he
discussed?"

If there was, Behrman couldn't think of it.

"What about your arrests?"

"Oh, now," Behrman said with garish affability, "there
was nothing to those things. Minor indiscretions."

"If it had been one, I might agree. But most men would
take the hint after they were picked up the first time. You
didn't. Or couldn't. Three busts for soliciting hookers
begins to look a little compulsive."

The fur dealer made no reply. Reppa let a silence exist
for several moments and then said, "Shall we move on to
Halliwell?"

Behrman shook his head, but to no real purpose; his
eyes looked hopeless.

"The occasion when you saw belt marks on Andrea that
indicated she'd been beaten—how long before her murder
was it?"

"They weren't really belt marks." Behrman made a
most unhappy gesture. "Not that the distinction matters, I
don't suppose."

352

"It could. We might not be talking about the same incident. McCreary talked to someone who described them as belt marks."

"He did? Who?"

"A doorman in the building where Halliwell used to live. He was on duty the night Halliwell and Andrea fought and Halliwell threw her out naked."

The fur dealer started another weary gesture and then halted himself abruptly.

"She came to your place that night, didn't she? What happened? Why were you too afraid to tell the police about the incident?"

"I wasn't afraid—" Behrman said and saw his mistake. "It's difficult to explain," he mumbled.

"Give it your best shot." When Behrman continued to eye him with an unbridled lack of enthusiasm, Reppa said, "Either you talk to me, or I talk to the DA."

"It wasn't what everyone thought. People wondered about us. But if they'd understood about me, they wouldn't have wondered."

"Wondered what?"

Behrman hesitated for a long moment; then, seeing Reppa was not going to let him do less than put a name to it, he said heavily, "Whether we slept together. But we never did."

"Never?"

"Until"—Behrman sought refuge in a sigh—"that night."

"What made it so special? That she came to your place naked?"

"She wasn't naked. She'd grabbed a curtain out of one of the windows in the lobby of Halliwell's building and wrapped herself in it. But it was thin. The marks showed through. Not from a belt. A TV cord, she said. When I

353

saw them, my heart went out to her. And then, when she asked me for money to pay the cabby who'd driven her over . . .

Behrman looked at him with such an effaced air, compounded half of profound embarrassment and half of a debased sort of comradeship, that Reppa found himself unable to speak.

"It was putting the money in her hand—physically giving her the money," the fur dealer went on dully. "That's what did it—that's what *always* does it—that's *all* that can do it. You'll say I should have told the police about the rest of the incident and left that part out. But I knew I'd give away everything if they challenged me. As you've done."

"If it wasn't fear, then, that stopped you from talking—"

"Shame," Behrman finished morosely. "It was still too new to me then. It had only been a few months since Adelaide's death. Now I'm more accustomed to myself. My *thing*, as it were."

Hearing the word, thinking of its many current meanings, evoked Reppa's next question. "Have you ever seen any of Jill Wilkes's paintings?"

Behrman seemed to feel the ground firm beneath him again. "Why, no," he said with an obliging chuckle. "But I've heard they're rather bizarre."

"Bizarre?"

"Yes. The papers. After her death I believe they used that word to describe her paintings."

"Not her paintings. Her loft. Her paintings weren't described at all."

Behrman shrugged as if the distinction Reppa had made eluded him.

"Two final questions. Have you had any contact since your niece's murder with Carlo Mald?"

"Niece," Behrman repeated, savoring the word.

"In a business sense, particularly. Have you and Mald ever had any business dealings?"

"Do I look insane? The man is an asp."

"What about Elizabeth Moffett? Did you ever have any business dealings with her?"

"Elizabeth?"

"Yes. Did you, to be precise, ever put any money in her hand?"

Behrman said, "Don't be absurd," with the same obliging chuckle. But he seemed at pains to find a comfortable place for his eyes.

CHAPTER FIFTEEN

WHEN YOU STOP
AT NOTHING

Mald had not been in to the gallery all week, and nothing Reppa said could get the woman on the other end of the phone to divulge his home address. Kinder refused to speak to Reppa or call Annabelle to the phone so that she could be asked about some new information he'd uncovered. Over the phone Halliwell accused him of breaking confidence by telling McCreary everything the two of them had spoken about. McCreary had appeared on Halliwell's doorstep in Dobbs Ferry one night. He'd turned McCreary away flatly, of course—even after McCreary threatened to talk to his wife if he wouldn't cooperate. From now on any meetings between him and the Division of Parole would occur in the office of his attorney, and then only if he'd been served with a subpoena.

Reppa asked Timberlake the morning after Memorial Day if they could get one. Not until the cops had finished with Halliwell, Timberlake didn't think, and probably not even then. The same applied unfortunately to Kinder, Annabelle, and Mald. To make sure, Timberlake promised to check with someone on the agency legal staff. But meantime he could tell Reppa with grim certainty that the NYPD was playing it close to the vest. What strides they'd made in finding out who killed McCreary were not about to be shared with their brethren at Parole.

Even though he'd worked all his life under bureaucratic restraint of one form or another, Reppa now felt in himself a latent seed of independence. He cultivated it. He allowed himself to become neither defiant nor dispirited by Timberlake's report. His nonreaction didn't exactly inspire Timberlake, who controlled his voice and went on to say, fairly mildly, that he had completed most of his end of the tasks they had divvied up the other day. Mald had been discharged from parole by New Jersey in 1953; his adjustment while under their supervision had been deemed excellent; there was nothing significant to add to McCreary's notes on his crime. The victim was a sixteen-year-old girl, German, first generation; the autopsy showed her body was unmarked, her virginity intact. Moving on to Halliwell and Kinder, Halliwell appeared to be clean, but the verdict was still out on Kinder. Even though DCJS had nothing on him, Timberlake's feeling was that Kinder might be going under an alias. He had not been issued a social security card until 1969. Likewise, all three taxation branches—state, city, and federal—had received their first payment from him in that year.

"The feds, too?" Reppa spoke abruptly. "The first time ever?"

"As Kinder, anyhow. And unless the guy was a career graduate student or something, it's unlikely working for Annabelle was his first job. So we have to figure he traveled before under another name and social security number."

"Could we peg him if we had his prints?"

"Maybe, if he has a record under another name."

"And if he's clean?"

"Then DCJS can't help us. We'd have to send to

357

Washington—'' Timberlake began but checked himself. He appeared to consider and then, very sharply, gazed at Reppa. "You think he's our boy, don't you?"

For an alarming second or two Reppa felt he'd been seen through. He stopped himself from saying unconvincingly, "Not really," and instead, sitting back in his chair, said coolly, "By process of elimination. Halliwell, Behrman, and Mald seem out. Halliwell and Behrman because in a million years they couldn't have snagged McCreary and killed him with his own gun. Mald I have other reasons for rejecting."

Timberlake snorted. "Where's it written down that McCreary was blown away by someone you ran across while doing that pardon investigation?"

"Do we have any other candidates? If we do, I'm listening."

Timberlake chose to slide away into a discussion of his talk with the barmaid at the Empire Bar. She insisted she'd never seen the woman who gave her the shopping bag before the other night, but she did recognize a photograph of McCreary. McCreary used to come into the Empire fairly often, she said, usually in the early afternoon with a couple of honchos who worked in the state office building down the street. She hadn't seen much of him, though, for a couple of years now.

"Because he's been stuck behind a desk," Reppa said. "No longer able to take off in the middle of the day while doing field work."

Timberlake said curtly, "There's an even better reason. The barmaid claimed one of the guys he used to hang out with was Josea Greenwood, and Greenwood's no longer seen much either around a Hundred and Twenty-fifth Street."

"Who's Greenwood?"

"You don't remember the brouhaha back in the early seventies after Attica? When the black groups wanted Greenwood put in as a deputy supe up there, but Rockefeller's men were scared shit of him? He was seen as only a cut above Cleaver and Rap Brown. So he got jobbed out of the appointment. But when Rocky finally stepped down, the new regime immediately tried to make points with the black community by finding a spot for Greenwood. The last few years he's been rampantly upwardly mobile. There've even been rumors he might become the next head of Correctional Services."

"Think he could have pulled McCreary's chain somehow on the Behrman-Moffett case?"

Timberlake said smoothly, "The road we're on seems to have a fork. One path leads uptown, the other leads downtown. To avoid stumbling over each other, I recommend maybe we should each take a different route."

It was at this point that Reppa realized Timberlake wanted to disentangle himself from a walk that he thought was headed down a blind alley. Reppa was in no way inclined to try to argue him out of it.

Later that morning, after he had circled Annabelle's block slowly on foot, he settled in a coffee shop diagonally across from her building. It gave him, sitting at the counter, an unobstructed view of the front door for the price of two cups of coffee and a tuna salad sandwich. He was there again early the next morning as soon as the place opened. The counterman pestered him awhile but went away after catching a look at his shield. Still, even when he was left alone, it was not his kind of way to spend time. Patience, Leilah'd counseled. Even the Collier brothers had to eat.

But for the second day in a row no balding men with beards or women wearing long black dresses emerged with a shopping cart or a tiny, monkeylike dog. He began to wonder if they didn't have their food delivered somehow and if Adelaide hadn't been paper-trained.

Late in the afternoon he entered the building, following a tenant on one of the lower floors inside, and took the elevator all the way up to the top, where he stood contemplating the cold metal door, thick as a safe, the locks as solid as could be.

All on the other side of the door was silent.

He wanted a way inside. He wanted, as an alternative, a neighbor who knew something about what went on inside. He got neither. There was no building superintendent with a duplicate set of keys, and none of the other tenants knew Kinder as anything other than Annabelle's secretary, or Annabelle other than by reputation. Two of the older tenants recalled having run into her now and then on the elevator but not for many years. She hadn't spoken. They hadn't dared.

Parked down the street that night, around eleven, long after the coffee shop had closed, he started when Kinder appeared quite suddenly, dogless, bearing down on his car. Twin blades of light seemed to spring out of the rimless glasses.

Had he dozed off while watching the door? It almost seemed that Kinder had popped out of a grate or a manhole. He ducked down.

But Kinder, in sandals and a purple burnoose with the hood up, passed him by, turned down Eighth Avenue, and disappeared. He climbed out of his car with a sense of haste, and with an equal sense of what a fool he'd be made if Kinder had spotted him and was waiting for him when he rounded the corner. But the heavy flow of cars and trucks and buses on the avenue dispersed his fear. Perhaps McCreary had walked into the point of a gun, but not this side of midnight on a major artery.

There was a terrible sense of letdown when he got to the corner and Kinder was nowhere in sight—all that time during the last two days wasted. But then, hurrying down the block, he stopped like a tennis player caught going the wrong direction when he passed a small bodega and saw Kinder, with his profile to the window, calmly pondering an array of dairy products.

He tried to focus on the moment—what did he do now?—but he could only stare at Kinder: the beard and thick glasses, the thin, bony ankles protruding from the bottom of the burnoose. Kinder's hands, the long fingers judiciously pushing aside the front rows of yogurt containers to get to the ones way in back, which were stamped with a later date.

His selection made, Kinder moved on to a consideration of dog food. He held up a can to check the ingredients and then returned it to the shelf and picked up another.

Reppa didn't get the idea until Kinder fell into the line at the cash register. Cans wouldn't work, of course. No telling how many fingers besides Kinder's had handled them. But the principle was there now. He took out a handkerchief. What else, searching his pockets? Keys. Nail clippers. Shield and ID—

Mald. McCreary had tricked Mald into handling his ID card. But McCreary'd been a stranger to Mald, while Kinder had already seen his face and his ID card and was dodging every effort to show him either one again. Still, there were other things in his wallet that were plastic—and he had the nail clippers.

He sprinted back to Annabelle's building.

A few minutes later, crouched behind a parked car, he watched Kinder pause as he went to put his key in the front door lock. In annoyance Kinder seized the jagged

361

strip of plastic that was stuck in the lock, yanked it out—with thumb and forefinger—and tossed it away.

No sooner had he vanished into the building than Reppa jumped out of his hiding place and gathered the strip of plastic carefully in his handkerchief.

A print of Kinder's right index finger (the thumb had produced only a smudged partial) was on its way to DCJS by eleven the next morning. Before the day was out, however, it was the furthest thing from Reppa's mind. In the forefront once more, and for the last time, was Zippy.

At least once each day during the past week he had sat down with himself and decided that he was no longer bound by his pledge to her. How, now that Wilkes and McCreary had been murdered, could there still be any chance that de Spirit was the Behrman-Moffett killer? Only if you believed the events weren't linked, and he could never do that. So, then, he really ought to tell someone about the arrangement she and the ADA handling de Spirit's appeal had cooked up. But who could be trusted to do the right thing with the information? Sorting out which players were on which team was a full-time job in itself. You couldn't go by the uniforms. You for sure couldn't go by the uniforms. Still, he really had to find someone to tell. He really had better. But did it have to be done right now? Wouldn't it just make things all that much more confusing?

Last week, the morning after McCreary's body was found, he'd tried to call Zippy at her office. But her extension was busy, and when the moment came to try again, the momentum was no longer there. He was best off, he decided, leaving well enough alone for the time being. She had made her bed. Disrupting it (he could not deny) would be as much an act of jealousy as of conscience.

And how altruistic, be honest, were his own bedsprings at the moment?

He was embarrassed to have to admit to himself that despite all the statements he had trotted out to explain his motives to others, only Smail had received close to the true one. He wanted, damn it all, to come out of this feeling like a winner. *The* winner, when you got down to brutal honesty. Shaken at first by this realization, he soon felt better about himself than he'd felt in over five years. In a sense something in him, some worm of self-insignificance, had been exorcised.

He would keep Zippy on hold until this was over. Nothing else was possible.

But he hadn't worked out in advance—or perhaps just hadn't seen that such things could not be worked out in advance—what he would do if she called him. At home, no less, as he was setting up the TV trays for dinner. He reached for the phone because Leilah was immersed in her notebook, but her reflexes got her hand there first. For him, thrusting the phone casually in his direction without looking up from her notebook. But there seemed to be a frown in her voice.

"Frank?"

He knew who it was instantly.

"I know this is breaking all the rules, and I swear to you I wouldn't have called you there—"

"What is it?" he broke in, his heart racing.

"De Spirit found out about the deal I made with the ADA. Somebody told him, and I'm afraid. He was just up here trying to get into my building—"

"Where's Cupach?"

"With his kids," she said a little wildly. "He took them up to the country for Memorial Day, and I can't—"

"Then call the police." He was aware of the harshness that had come into his voice.

"No—Frank, it'll all blow up in my face if I bring anyone else in on this. Please. You're the only one I can trust."

"What do you want me to do?"

"Come up here. Just for tonight. Just until Steve—"

"And stay over with you?" Leilah looked at him incredulously.

"Please. You have to."

"I can't, Zippy."

"But *you have to*," she repeated more shrilly. "I know—I know you'd have to do a lot of explaining to Leilah. But please. I can't stay here alone. De Spirit is crazy with anger. I'm too afraid he'll get in the building somehow."

"The only explanation I can give," he said, exchanging a glance with Leilah, who shut her notebook, "is if I tell her everything."

"Then do it!"

"Including what you and the ADA have cooked—"

"*Yes!* Anything! Just get up here! Quick!"

It sounded as if de Spirit were at her door already.

"Are you all right? Are you in any danger right now?"

"Now?" It seemed to confuse her. "No, not if you come up here! Please! Hurry, Frank!"

All right. But it's going to take me some time—"

"*Hurry!*"

Reppa hung up the phone and stared numbly at it.

He felt Leilah touch his arm. "Who's after her, and why do *you* have to go up there?"

"De Spirit. There's no one else she can call on."

"Why not?"

He explained to her.

"That's her problem, Reppa. It's not yours."

"No longer true. I made it mine when I let too much time go by without saying anything about it to anybody."

"Terrible answer. It's yours only if you want it to be yours."

"I can't figure it all out now, Leilah. I just know I have to go."

"What are you going to do? Stay overnight? With her?" The *Leilah* had reached her where all his putting on shoes and getting ready had not. "So that I'll be the one left alone? There are worse goblins out there than de Spirit."

He turned, tugging his belt through his holster. "I'll be back. As soon as I'm sure she's all right. A couple of hours at most."

Leilah looked at him as if he were promising something extraordinary, perhaps even something impossible. "And what if you can't come back?"

"What would stop me?"

"How do I know? You're the one who's been out there making all these new friends." She turned aside when he bent to kiss her, and all he got was her chin. "I've just got you to tell me what they're like."

"It's enough. Trust me. I know which ones are the really bad guys."

"Sure, Reppa, but Wilkes and McCreary weren't sweetness and light personified, and they both seem to be dead. Somehow I don't think it was the Tooth Fairy that got them."

He went out without giving her an answer and drove uptown, knowing he could get there faster in his present mood than any cab. He parked around the corner from Zippy's building. He switched (unaware of what he was doing until he'd done it) his gun from its holster to the tense, trembling hand in the pocket of his jacket. He saw without having to look any further that his fear came from not knowing what he had to fear. Zippy was real to him. Wilkes and McCreary had not been. The panic in her voice was real. He watched the slow, sinuous movements of her body from the enormous distance of a week ago—more nearly two now—and knew that she had never been out of his mind, only at the back of it, like an image that inevitably must assert itself again as soon as the mirror is turned around.

The front door of her building was open, but the stool where the doorman sat was unattended. Smells filmed every surface of the lobby like cheap skin cream. Reppa had to wait for the elevator, and when it arrived, two children and a dog came storming out. With a harried "Hold it!" a woman squeezed in behind him just as the door shut. He pressed 8, she 6. On the way up they both read that the elevator had last been inspected on December 12, 1979. It was five minutes after eight when she got out. "Have a good evening." The car sped off before he could reply.

There was a young black man in a green khaki uniform in the eighth floor hallway, leaning against the wall, head bent over a newspaper. One of the maintenance crew? The head was raised as Reppa stepped out of the elevator and then dropped again immediately.

He was halfway to Zippy's door before he realized that the man was standing beside it. The newspaper rattled. His questioning gaze drew another furtive glance. The face was like none he had ever seen before. Small but with very sharply etched features. Smooth skin, no hint of a beard. Save for the eyes the features could have been a girl's. The lids and sockets were laced with scar tissue, the pupils danced hectically. It made a disturbing contrast. The hand in his jacket pocket chilled.

The eyes had left him no room for doubt: This was Danny de Spirit.

"Waiting for someone?"

A faint shrug.

"Miss Dwersky?"

The pupils stilled for an instant. De Spirit moved off the wall and shoved the newspaper under his arm. Only his hands spoke, the fingers twitching.

"What do you want to see her about?"

De Spirit finally answered. "I'm bothering you here in the hall?"

"You're Danny de Spirit, right?"

De Spirit took a long step backward, then another. The eyes went one direction down the hallway, then the other.

"I'm Frank Reppa." The name seemed to mean nothing to de Spirit. "Parole Officer Reppa. I did your pardon investigation."

De Spirit's eyes returned from their travels and regarded him glancingly.

"I recognized you from your pictures."

De Spirit smiled and after a tense pause said, "You know where Zippy is?"

"Where? What do you mean?"

De Spirit's pupils darted away again. Following them, Reppa saw a white card stuck in her doorjamb, just above the knob. De Spirit stood beside him, inert, as he read:

Danny—
> Back in a minute. Wait.
> Z—

The message was typed. Removing it from the door, Reppa saw it was on the back of one of her business cards.

"How long have you been here?"

367

"Why?"

"Five minutes? Ten? How long?"

"Maybe five." De Spirit's voice grew lazier as Reppa's grew more insistent.

"Did you knock?"

"What for? She ain't home." Reppa started to raise a hand to the door, but stopped when de Spirit added, "She ain't. I already looked."

"Where? *Inside?*"

De Spirit continued to respond indolently to Reppa's mounting anxiety. "Door's open, man."

"And you went in—?"

"Man, why you getting all excited?"

"De Spirit, what the fuck *exactly* are you doing here?"

"See Zippy." De Spirit's face had suddenly become a blank, staring mask. "We got an appointment, like."

"Appointment for what?"

"My case, man. She called me."

"When?"

"At the Y. What's going on? Why you all excited?"

"Stay here. Right here. *Don't move.*"

"Where you going?"

But Reppa had already entered the apartment. As in a theater just before the movie starts, reduced by the sudden dimming of the lights to a long gray cavern, all details had been erased from the twilight foyer he stood in. He looked for a light switch, found none. He ran down a hall. Darkening rooms loomed on either side of him without perspective. At the end of the hall he swerved right. It was the bathroom. His hand brushed against a raised disc on the tile wall, and a light came on.

He could see, down the hall, de Spirit standing in the foyer. De Spirit neither ventured any farther nor retreated, as if he didn't know whether to be curious or frightened.

"Goddammit, de Spirit, get your ass out of here!"

"What're you doing? Man, what's going on?"

"Out!"

De Spirit stood rigid and folded his arms, demanding that he explain. Through a doorway between him and de Spirit but closer to him, Reppa glimpsed a corner of a bed and dangling over the edge of it a bare foot and ankle. He saw, moving toward the doorway, the beginning of a long white leg. He felt, in his stomach, a violent ache.

There was a window in the room. It let in light from the street, and though no more was needed to confirm what his mind had begun seeing the moment he read the message in the door, his hand groped for the wall switch.

De Spirit approached now, warily, from the other direction. Reppa was powerless to stop him. De Spirit drew back with a sound, as if he'd been kicked in the chest. "Oh-h-h . . . shit . . ."

Her blood drenched the center of the bedspread. The pillows were spattered. She lay on her stomach, arms splayed, eyes closed. Nude. Two ragged wounds in her back; one high between her shoulder blades, the other lower and to the left.

There was no weapon. So he could make sure of that, he went closer. He wanted to see the other side of the bed. Still no weapon. But a cream-colored Princess telephone lay on its side on the floor, the receiver off the hook.

He turned slowly around, and de Spirit was backing out of the room, eyes wild.

"Did you . . . ?"

De Spirit made a mute negative gesture.

"They're going to think you did, you know. That's the whole point!"

De Spirit cocked his head and peered at him.

369

"Go—get out of here—take care of yourself, and I'll take care of this!"

For a moment Reppa had the uncanny impression that they looked straight into each other's minds, and then de Spirit spun and ran out of the apartment.

Reppa heard the door shut. Left alone with her, he felt the corners of his eyes warm and at the same time was filled with an equally strong sense of rage. He had to remind himself that she had not been entirely an innocent victim. At the same time she had been entirely out of her depth. And she was now gone. Savagely, numbingly gone. Regardless of how wrongheaded her judgment had been, she hadn't deserved anything anywhere near this.

Without warning he was overtaken by an experience that anyone who has never been an athlete might call hallucinatory. He saw, with cold clarity, what each and every one of his movements would be in the minutes ahead. It was pure reaction to extreme stress, the sort of programming you never got over when you had been trained to look upon your performance under pressure as the ultimate crucible.

The rest of the apartment was almost dark now—three rooms in all besides the bedroom. The living room was the largest and had the most furniture, but it did not have what he was looking for. He found it in a small alcove off the kitchen. Her typewriter. A Royal portable, no cover in sight, on an oak table. He threw a dish towel over the keys, though in his heart he knew no one would find any prints on them except hers.

Then, leaning against the table, he asked himself, *Why? What had been intended to happen?* It was a setup, obviously, but how had it been put together? The killer must have had a pretty fair knowledge of de Spirit. *Back in a minute. Wait.* And an unlocked door to tempt an ex-junkie burglar. De Spirit, it could have been calculated, would arrive some minutes ahead of him. Enough time for the pull of an old habit to take hold. Take a look, Danny. Go ahead. The lady wouldn't have left the door unlocked if she didn't mean for you to go in. De Spirit, gliding around her apartment when he got impatient waiting for her, would have left his prints everywhere and hopelessly incriminated himself. And when he stumbled on her body, it could be calculated with almost absolute certainty, de Spirit would bolt like a scared jackrabbit.

But it hadn't quite happened like that. Perhaps because de Spirit had brought along a newspaper, which helped soak up time while he waited. Perhaps because, after a glance inside the door and twelve years inside a cell, he'd discovered the old habits were gone. And even if it had happened the way the killer planned, there were still some things that didn't click. Where, for one, was the weapon? Wouldn't it have been left behind as the clincher? One of her kitchen knives, say, and a torn pair of panties, to show there'd been a struggle, an attempt at rape? A simple deduction. Just about anyone finding her stabbed and de Spirit on the scene could be expected to make it. A convicted murderer fresh out of prison, invited by his sexy Legal Aid lawyer over to her pad for a case conference; he takes it as an invitation to seduce her, becomes enraged when she resists.

But as it stood now, his own eyes were the only witness that de Spirit had even been in the building. Unless the doorman—

Was it only chance that the stool inside the door had been empty when he arrived? The man away from his post for a minute, answering nature's call? If that was the case, then how had de Spirit, who got there a good while ahead of him, been allowed upstairs, since Zippy, by appearances,

371

wouldn't have been home when the doorman buzzed her apartment? Wouldn't de Spirit, black, a strange face in the building, have been made to wait downstairs or told to come back later?

So. The doorman, it began to seem, hadn't been at his post when de Spirit arrived, either. Where was he all that time? Lured away? Paid to take a walk?

Reppa returned to the bedroom. Moving quickly around the bed, he picked up the telephone receiver in his handkerchief. The dial tone came back a few moments after he depressed the button. He spun the dial with a pen. Nine . . . one . . . one. The woman who answered wanted to know before anything else who he was. Then, when he'd reported the murder, did he live in the building? Had he touched anything? Was he sure she was dead?

Within a minute after he'd hung up, the phone rang. Once—just once—and then it stopped. They were ringing the bells in Riverside Church. Quarter past eight. The phone had rung before the bells, but things, he thought, were still definitely occurring on someone's timetable. The receiver back on the hook, proof that the body had been found. What next? He'd been told by the woman on the phone to get out of there. Leave everything just as it was and go wait down in the lobby for someone to come. The sensible course of action to take. So sensible that he'd have followed it unquestioningly if he hadn't already thought twice. Why wasn't the weapon there?

The bells stopped. Outside the window, any minute now, sirens would begin to wail. Or would they? He couldn't decipher the logic of it yet, but it came nearer. He stepped into the bedroom closet and pulled the door closed behind him, all but a crack.

The apartment was silent for what seemed like a long time, but he'd begun counting to himself, and he'd only gotten to a hundred and four when he heard the front door open. He stood breathless. He couldn't see the bedroom door through the crack, but his one eye took in all of the bed.

He was at a hundred and twelve when the man appeared on the right side of it. His back was to the closet, but Reppa no longer needed to see his face. The full head of iron-gray hair was enough. Then the shoulders and head swung partway around, bringing an arm up over her body. Reppa saw fleetingly that the hand at the end of the arm was gloved. He did not see the gleaming object in it until it dropped to the bed beside her body. It was a brisk movement, all part of one motion, but it stopped as abruptly as if a moving picture had turned into a still.

The hand was rigid. Cupach's gaze locked on the bed, his mouth shut like a trap.

The next moment the hand was yanked away. Cupach's other hand, also gloved, plunged under the bedspread and emerged with something blue. It was flung toward the closet, obscuring Reppa's vision for an instant, and when it fell away, Cupach was no longer there.

One hundred and twenty-three . . . the front door shut. When Reppa reached for the closet door, he was startled to discover his gun in his hand. For an unnerving moment he felt how much it had been in him to use it.

The blue object had been a robe. It lay crumpled on the floor at his feet, ripped across one shoulder. He looked ahead to the bed, and there, beside her body, was a switchblade knife. De Spirit's prints must be on it. But how? And why had Cupach come back to plant it? So risky. Why? Because Cupach must have been afraid to leave it before, afraid either Reppa or de Spirit would find it before the NYPD did. Find it and get rid of it!

It was a struggle not to pick up the knife and take it with

373

him. He felt cold, and his hands were sweating as he wiped off the handle with his handkerchief. Putting it back beside her body, his fingers shook. Not looking at the bed helped, but not much.

He'd just finished replacing the knife when he heard the front door again. From that moment it was a foregone conclusion. He was in up to his neck. He ran into the bathroom and shut the door. Started the sink running, the toilet flushing.

The detective who found him there didn't dispute it when he said he'd gotten sick after finding the body, but he was kept at stubbornly by three of them for a long time before they stopped challenging his version of the events that had brought him to Zippy's apartment. He gave them the card he'd found in the front door. He told them about the missing doorman. He held back nothing about her phone call to him or his encounter with de Spirit. De Spirit, he'd have to trust, would be bright enough when they picked him up to tell his piece of it straight. Her phone call to him not only explained what he was doing there but provided the police with the foundation to put together on their own who had killed her.

If they wanted to.

He said nothing of having hidden in the closet and watched Cupach plant the knife and the robe. He did not mention that he had heard the phone ring once after he'd called them. He foresaw their line of action. They could be relied on to learn very quickly that his interests here were not theirs. Or less finely: If there were even a tiny error here on his part, once they discovered that Cupach had not been Zippy's only bedmate in recent days—and they would— there could be a very concerted and, from what

374

he knew about their methods, very successful effort to snare him for her murder.

But the immediate worry, now that the fury that had carried him for the past quarter hour was wearing off, was that he'd begun to feel afraid again. They came in the door in pairs and threes and fours until there were a dozen of them to his one. Who they all were and where their allegiances lay was beyond him to gauge. He just wanted to get out of there.

Breathing in the air in the apartment—the compound of masculine smoke and sweat and feminine scents and sprays— was painful, the needling sensation in the passages of his nose and throat so sharp that it was almost indistinguishable from tears. But who to speak to? He could see two of them dusting for prints, having taken his. He could hear someone wanting to know who'd put the dish towel over the typewriter keys. He tried to sit down somewhere but found himself in someone's way each place he went. It wasn't that he was forgotten—it was that everyone assumed someone else had him in tow. Looking down at his shirt, he couldn't remember whether he'd been told to hang his shield over the pocket or thought of it on his own. Parole officer. A cub scout among boy scouts. Behind him someone wondered where de Spirit was. Who'd gone to get him? And when he turned around, it was to be asked rhetorically if anybody'd checked whether she had parents or a husband. It all looked and sounded blurred and chaotic and thoroughly disorganized, but it also looked and sounded as if everyone here had something to do except him.

Drifting back into the living room, he was grabbed by the arm, not forcefully but almost as an afterthought, the man who'd done it holding him there while he finished another conversation. Then he was told they'd be taking him over to the 26th in a few minutes for a statement. The 26th covered Riverside Drive and 116th Street? All he needed was to run into Sweet or Graham.

Someone came in waving an unlit cigar and announced they'd found the doorman. Locked in the storage locker in the basement. There was a general sense of excitement among the men, who weren't doing much else just then, about having a new face to talk to.

"Where there's smoke, there's fire," the doorman shouted, entering ahead of two detectives. A born entertainer. "I get a call there's smoke coming from under the door down there. When I get in the locker, somebody shuts it on me. Right away I think, no shit, now anybody can walk in. Where is she, if you want somebody to identify her?" At last, to get rid of him, he was hauled back downstairs.

Reppa had been on edge throughout the whole scene, for the doorman was the same one who had been on duty the last time he was here. ("Looking for an absconder, he says, and now a tenant gets murdered, he's the one finds the body?") But there had been no recognition in the brief look the doorman had given him.

Not a print to be had on the knife, someone said.

"Is it the sticker?" someone else inquired. "Or is it the sticker?"

Reppa reached in his pocket when asked for a match and came out with the broken band from his watch. When had that happened?

In another pocket he found the watch itself. It was seventeen minutes to ten.

They were beginning to talk about taking him over to the 26th again.

He went to the window. A corner of the moon was just beginning to peek out from behind heavy clouds when the phone rang.

376

"Reppa," someone called. "Who's Reppa?"

There was an extension on a glass table in the living room. Under the phone was this week's *Time* with a subscription tag on its cover. Zipporah G. Dwersky. He wondered if he would ever find out what the *G* had stood for.

Dutifully he picked up the receiver and said, "Reppa."

"Thank God," said Leilah.

CHAPTER SIXTEEN

THE INVESTMENT

The assistant area director had pasted some ten or twelve newspaper stories on large slabs of cardboard. They sat on the area director's desk like a giant deck of cards. The uppermost one contained page three from that morning's *News*. Pasted above the lead article was the headline from the front page: DE SPIRIT LEGAL AID LAWYER SLAIN. The article itself had forced the area director to summon the five men who were now with him in his office on the top floor of the parole building. They were, in order of their importance (the area director's order of their importance), Supervising Parole Officer Bowden Delanghe, the chief of the Bureau of Special Services; Parole Officer William Timberlake; Parole Officer Frank Reppa; and the assistant area director and Senior Parole Officer Donald Smail.

"You never should have gone to her place. You should have called the police right away."

"She made me promise not to."

"She also told you de Spirit was threatening her. Yet you told the police you're positive he didn't kill her."

"Would he have been standing outside her door reading a newspaper when I arrived if he had?"

378

"Then what was he doing there? If he didn't kill her, who did?"

Reppa grimly shook his head. To tell them Cupach had killed Zippy would be speculation. To tell them he now believed Cupach had also killed McCreary and Jill Wilkes would still be only a presumption. To tell them he had seen Cupach return to Zippy's bedroom and plant the murder weapon would be suicide.

The area director possessed all the traits that were essential to gain him the top job in the New York office. He was obsequious with secretaries, intransigent with parole officers and senior parole officers, terrified of commissioners and visitors from Albany, ambitious but afraid to risk even the smallest grain of power he'd already earned, cautiously running the affairs of his office in such a way that no errors of judgment could ever be laid on his doorstep. Reppa sensed all this, and he knew the man would rather be lied to by someone below him than placed in a position where he would have to lie to those above him. The area director would thus be careful not to probe his story of last night's events too deeply, would actually welcome any distortions and omissions that would enable him to disclaim responsibility, if at some future time the shit hit the fan, by saying could he help something he hadn't been told?

But Delanghe was another matter. Reppa had to admit that Bowden Delanghe scared him. Slim, immaculate, and deeply tanned though it was only early June, Delanghe understood better than anyone else in the agency, with the possible exception of McCreary, the complex machinery of the criminal justice system. Yet, for all his understanding, he would never rise higher than the head of BSS, a job that gave him far less power than the area director's. Delanghe was too shrewd for the comfort of those above him, too much the bureaucrat to win the admiration of those below him. It was an odd blend. At his desk every morning as soon as the doors of the building were unlocked, Delanghe was often still there in the evening after the last parole officer had finished taking reports. What went on at his desk, though, wasn't the usual paper-pushing and pencil-sharpening of petty officials. Delanghe spent much of his day clipping newspaper articles, studying wanted cards and police bulletins, updating his files on every major crime in the United States since Prohibition was repealed. Mass murders—he could recite the grisly details of them all. Bank robbers had two file drawers entirely to themselves. That most of the information in those drawers was of little use to the Division of Parole was studiously ignored by all of the area directors he had served under, and there had been four.

Reppa had spent the past twenty minutes telling Delanghe and the others why he had gone to Zippy's apartment last night and what (apart from the minutes between his phone call to the police and their arrival) had transpired there, and he could imagine how everyone's mind except Delanghe's was working. The area director had not wanted to hear that one of his own men had found the body of the victim of what promised to be a sensational and highly controversial murder, but on the other hand there was no overwhelming call for him to do anything; after all, no one was suggesting a parolee had murdered her. The course to take for the present was to criticize everything Reppa had done, make it clear that it would go on record that he'd acted on his own accord without the agency's sanction, then call the police commissioner as soon as his office was empty and stoutly demand protection for Reppa so there would be no repetition of the McCreary episode. He wouldn't get it, but that way, regardless of what happened, he'd be on record as having done everything he reasonably could.

Reppa's impression was that Smail and the assistant area director were sitting in dread that they would be called on for their opinions of the position in which his actions last night had placed the agency. Timberlake, meanwhile, was angry that he would not be called on for his opinion.

"What was your exact relationship with this Dwersky woman?" Delanghe said now.

"We became friendly while I was doing de Spirit's pardon investigation."

Reppa waited for the inescapable: "*How* friendly?" Delanghe would have grasped that he had not told all he knew about Zippy and that theirs had been something more than a professional acquaintance. Eventually Delanghe would also try to siphon out of him whether Zippy had said, when she phoned him, why de Spirit was threatening her. The only choice, when Delanghe started on him, was to lie. He knew too much now to stop, but if the wrong person learned what he knew, he would *be* stopped—as finally and as utterly as McCreary had. There was no way of telling which pipelines led to Cupach. He had always fancied himself a maverick and now realized he had no alternative but to become one. He had isolated himself. He was now totally and irrevocably out there alone.

He looked sideways at Delanghe, prepared for the worst, but Delanghe said nothing. His thin, bronzed face was turned expressionlessly to the area director as if in deference to rank: *Here, from your humble servant, is a can of worms—would my master's hand care to open it?*

When the area director spoke, it was slowly, almost hesitantly, and off the point. "Where is de Spirit now?"

"Locked up," the assistant area director murmured when

381

no one else volunteered. "They revoked his bail when they picked him up last night."

The area director grunted. He muttered something that sounded like "Protective custody." When it drew no response, he said, "Certainly we have to wonder whether there's any connection between this thing last night and McCreary." He paused, as if hoping he would be contradicted by Delanghe.

But Delanghe nodded and spoke firmly. "Strong possibility."

"You really think so?"

"If this Dwersky wasn't killed by de Spirit, it was done so it would look like he did it. Reppa and Timberlake here can tell you we've been operating as if McCreary was iced because of his outside horsing around on the Behrman-Moffett case."

"What about the Wilkes woman? Have they decided yet whether she was murdered?"

"Not so they're about to tell us."

"You aren't thinking her death is tied in with McCreary, too?" The area director's voice again seemed to seek contradiction.

"The notes McCreary left indicate he paid her a visit just the day before she died."

"Then *all* these killings could be interrelated somehow . . . ?"

"Out of our ball park." For an instant Delanghe looked directly at Reppa. "We're only concerned with McCreary."

"Then what should we—?" The area director paused, and his eyes anxiously swept four unresponsive pairs of eyes before settling on Delanghe's, which were placidly waiting. "My own thinking is we should continue to function strictly as an adjunct to the police in their investigation of McCreary's murder."

"Precisely."

"But if it develops that his murder is only one part of a much larger investigation . . . ?"

Delanghe shrugged. "Dodgy."

"In the past," the area director offered tentatively, "we've always operated, when there's a conflict, on the basis that a police investigation takes precedence over ours."

"Absolutely," Delanghe said. "Always."

His eyes landed full force on Reppa again. And now, Reppa thought, here it comes. But after a disconcerting interval Delanghe said to the area director, "This is something we can take up between ourselves. No need to keep the others from their work."

Reppa contemplated the tanned face as it turned from his and gazed away at the wall. He knows I'm in this to the gills, he thought, and he wants me to know he knows. And he realized that at some as yet unspecified time but, unless something miraculous occurred, in the very near future, he would be prevented from finding the piece he did not yet have. Cupach may have eliminated Wilkes, McCreary, and Zippy so there could be no revelations that Andrea Behrman and Elizabeth Moffett had not been killed by Danny de Spirit. But if de Spirit hadn't killed them, who had? He remembered Leilah's notion when he first discussed the case with her that they had been killed by two cops whose charms they had resisted in the course of a burglary investigation, and it no longer seemed so wildly absurd. It did not even seem absurd that Cupach might have killed them himself so that he would have a spectacular murder case to unravel.

The person or the act?

When all was said, that was still the first question, and he seemed as far away as ever from answering it.

*　　*　　*

It was impossible to get Cupach, he reluctantly decided, short of assassinating him. Even that would have been palatable if he could have filled his head with something besides his own feelings of impotent rage.

Proof that Cupach had killed anyone? Proof that would stand up against Cupach's denials? Only in Zippy's murder was there a shred of evidence, and even that was tenuous. Told he had been seen by Reppa at the site of the murder, Cupach could be counted on to say he'd come to visit Zippy, been alarmed to find the door of her apartment unlocked, discovered her body, and staggered out shocked and grief-stricken. Knife? He'd planted no knife. Phone calls to Reppa and de Spirit? He'd forced Zippy to make no phone calls. A very simple explanation for all Reppa's accusations against him. Jealousy—that of an underfulfilled man toward his better. A jealousy so overpowering that Reppa had shaded the story of his encounter with de Spirit in de Spirit's favor and then, going further, may even have destroyed evidence in Zippy's bedroom to conceal the fact that de Spirit had killed her. Perhaps—just a suggestion— Reppa ought to be given a lie detector test.

"At least it would show you were telling the truth when you said you saw him plant the knife," Leilah said.

"And when they ask if I wiped it off to get rid of any prints? Tampering with evidence in a murder case is a felony."

"Surely you could find *somebody* in the police department who'd listen to you."

"Right. I could advertise. 'Wanted: one honest, uncorruptible police officer interested in information that could lead to the arrest and conviction for murder of a former detective now bucking for a deputy commissioner's spot.' Somehow I don't think the response would be too great.

384

"All you need is one person in the right place."

"I've got you."

She waved off the flattery. "Someone who would know how to go about putting together a case against him."

"And if I guess wrong in looking for that someone?"

Ordinarily Leilah would have bolstered him with some wisecrack, but any stab at humor now would only have made them both feel more fragmented than they already did. Consequently she had difficulty expressing herself, and it only emerged in a roundabout way that from her point of view his dilemma was nearly insoluble. In fact, she said wistfully, she couldn't even think what more she could have done in his place.

"Unless it was to get the information Muntz has," she added casually.

"How?"

"I can think of ways."

"All of which would cost ten grand. If you're going to suggest I break into Muntz's apartment and toss it, don't. He convinced me that whatever he has, it's being kept elsewhere."

"I'm sure it is, too. What you have to do is come up with the money."

He continued to miss the look she was giving him. It could have been there wasn't enough light. Only a candle at the foot of the bed. But both of them were sitting up for the first time in over five months; both of them, side by side. The pulleys had come down just that afternoon. Molnar was talking about maybe a few steps in a walker soon. It would have been a cause for celebration if there had not been another cause. Zippy had been buried that afternoon, and he had gone to the funeral. Cupach had not.

"The Parole Officers Association is out. Now that Kinder's prints have come back negative from DCJS, they've

385

stopped believing Muntz could have anything that has any bearing on McCreary's murder. And if Cupach killed McCreary, then they're basically right.''

"What does a negative from DCJS mean?"

"He doesn't have a record in New York under Kinder or any other name. Also, he's not wanted by another state."

She watched him stare at the candle awhile. "What are you thinking, Reppa?"

"What it is Muntz has."

"Your guess?"

"Something about Kinder, I'm almost sure of it."

"Is there any way you can find out what he did before he became Annabelle's secretary?"

"I got Timberlake to send his prints to Washington. They'll check everything there. Not only criminal records but whether he's on file with Immigration or wherever."

"While you were at it, why didn't you send Behrman's and Mald's and the rest of them?"

"Timberlake refused to waste the forms and the time he'd have had to take to fill them out. He thinks I'm shooting blanks as it is."

"He's still convinced McCreary's murder has no connection to Behrman-Moffett?"

"Only indirectly. He and Delanghe and the rest of BSS think McCreary was in tight with Josea Greenwood. They know Cupach is up for the open deputy commissioner's spot, and they're trying to find out if there's another faction supporting Greenwood for the job."

"Then that's it—if Cupach and Greenwood are in competition."

He saw her look now, though he did not realize it was a different look. "Some of it at least. McCreary would have been trying to improve Greenwood's chances, and what better way than by exploding the truth about the Behrman-Moffett case.''

"There might have been something in it for McCreary, too. A nice little political plum if Greenwood got the appointment.''

"It would help explain why he was so unconcerned about throwing over his career with Parole.''

Leilah considered something then that he had been backing away from considering. "If BSS has begun thinking McCreary was working for Greenwood against Cupach, they're also going to begin wondering soon if Cupach didn't have something to do with his murder.''

"If they haven't already. But no one's been talking to me much since Zippy was killed.''

"Why not, do you think?''

"There's an inner circle in BSS. Delanghe, Timberlake, and one or two others. When it's something as big as Cupach, just Delanghe himself.''

"Can't you even go to him with what you know?''

"Would you in my place?''

"I'm not even sure that if I were you, I'd be talking to me.''

"You would be. If you knew how much I trusted you.''

"Well, tell me sometime,'' said Leilah, and they sat in silence.

"It would be worth a lot to know what Muntz has,'' she said at last. "If it tells us who killed Andrea and Elizabeth, it could also give us a way to get Cupach.''

"By proving de Spirit is innocent?''

"The man must be on the cusp if he's ready to kill however many people it takes to keep the truth from coming out.''

Reppa clutched her shoulder blade suddenly with his

hand and then looked at it as if he expected it to have picked up an impression.

"I see what you're getting at," he said. "I think."

"What I'm getting at," said Leilah, "is fairly simple. I don't think Cupach knows the truth himself."

It was the following afternoon in Timberlake's office that the sequence of events begun all those weeks ago in the battered apartment on West 123rd Street took on a new aspect that enabled Reppa for the first time to see a thin ray of light at the end of the tunnel. From the moment Timberlake told him word had been received from the FBI that Kinder's prints were on file with them under another name, he could almost hear himself thinking: *All right!* But Timberlake had the information, and he wasn't imparting it until he got something in return. This man Kinder might be wanted for something, after all, and Reppa, well, it looked like Reppa was the logical candidate to talk to someone from the United States Army.

Army? "What about?"

"They're not sure yet. He may be a deserter."

Timberlake reached for his hand and pressed into it a piece of paper that contained a government phone number with about two dozen digits and a name with fifteen letters. An equal division of duties was still paramount in their uneasy partnership, and it was clear Timberlake thought this one would take time but give nothing in return. But that was because he was unfamiliar with Annabelle's family background, so the name on the paper—Alexander Loomis—meant nothing to him.

Reppa went into a glazed stare for a moment and then roused himself and left Timberlake's office. When he was back in his own, the phone rang. To his great surprise it was Leilah, who had never been known to call him at work. He said, "You must be psychic."

"Not usually," she said, "but I guess that means you've heard the news, too."

"About Kinder?"

"Kinder? No. What about Kinder?"

"His prints match those of Annabelle's brother. The army had him down as dead all these years. Now I have to call them and discuss whether they want to go after him for desertion."

"Someone also ought to consider whether to go after him for not supporting his daughter."

"His daughter?"

"Well, somebody has to be Andrea's father."

"Oh, come on. Annabelle was her mother, and she and Alexander are—"

Incest, Leilah cut in dryly to remind him, was only a taboo. It wasn't a physical impossibility.

So he reminded her that the real question now was where Kinder had been all those years between his supposed death and his resurfacing as Annabelle's secretary.

"Good Lord." He heard a sound at the other end, as if Leilah had slapped her forehead. "It was right in front of us, Reppa. Lee could be a nickname for Abilene. And do you know what *Kinder* means in German? *Children*."

"Abilene's children," he said with a frog in his throat.

"That must be what Muntz has. No wonder he thought he could turn a quick few bucks on it when Andrea decided to get married."

"The walls have ears," he said suddenly.

Leilah caught on instantly. "Hello, switchboard. Hello—hello."

* * *

It was on the front page of the *Post* when he went to the Y at lunch. The grand jury had refused to indict de Spirit for Zippy's murder. Meanwhile criminal lawyers all over the city were flocking to Rikers Island to cajole de Spirit into letting them take on the Behrman-Moffett appeal for free. On page three beside the headline story was a separate article announcing that an NYPD investigation was underway to determine if there was any truth to a report that Zippy had been having an affair with a former police detective who was presently being considered for a top-level departmental position. Everything but his name, Reppa thought. By inference it could be only one man, but even the newspapers couldn't dare to risk identifying him.

Riding the train home that afternoon, he tried to rid himself of the feeling that he was going to be hit from behind at any moment. It was a feeling that had been growing for several days. He had the ball but no blockers. For him at this point the wisest move would have been to hand it off. But whom could he give it to?

Leilah was waiting where he had left her that morning and every other morning this spring. But she was beginning to look like a normal woman again. Gore helped her take the brace off twice a day now for an hour at a time, and they still had some forty minutes left before he had to help her put it on again. Her breasts filled the top of the thin cotton shift she wore like flowers he hadn't seen in bloom since last year.

"Now we really have to find out what Muntz has," she announced when he told her the faceless army official he'd spoken to on the phone that afternoon had sounded less than enthusiastic about the prospect of trying to court-martial a soldier for desertion thirty-six years after the fact.

"We pretty well know what he's got. He learned that Abilene Loomis somehow faked his son's death."

"Reason?"

"So Alexander wouldn't have to go overseas and perhaps get killed. Loomis tried to get him exempted as the only son of a minister, but the army wouldn't buy it. The only other option was for Alexander to declare himself a conscientious objector and go to prison."

Leilah's hand reached for a wedge of Jarlsberg, to tide her over while the oven was working on Cornish hens and baked potatoes.

"Living your entire life in hiding is more awful in its way than spending a couple of years in prison," she said. "Yet he's continued to live as Kinder. Even though the time when the army would have been hot to nail him has long since passed."

"He might not have realized that."

"Most men would have tried to find out. He could have gone to a lawyer and had him feel out what the army would do if he turned himself in. Instead he's buried himself away with a nutty sister.

"But not until 1969. For the twenty-five years before that there's no record of him anywhere. At least not in New York State." He looked at Leilah, but she was staring into space. "Where are you?"

"All we know for sure is he didn't do anything he was arrested for, and he didn't pay income tax under the name of Kinder. He could have been living in New York all that time and using still another name."

"And become Kinder in 1969? Why?"

Leilah looked down and licked her fingers in lieu of reaching for the last slice of cheese. "With all we know about Andrea's family, we're still missing the piece that would make the whole mess form an intelligible picture. Ask yourself, and I'll ask myself. What are the biggest questions that we still haven't answered? I mean other than how to prove Cupach is a murderer and the identity of the person in the bedroom that morning with Elizabeth Moffett.''

"I'd start with where and who Alexander Loomis was before he became Kinder. Then I'd want to know if it's possible he really could be Andrea's father. If he is, we've gone a long way toward understanding the relationship between him and Annabelle and why they live as they do.''

"A little incest isn't enough to turn two people into recluses.''

"Not most people, but remember—they're the children of a fundamentalist preacher.''

"Point well taken, Reppa. I sometimes forget that everyone didn't grow up reading Jane Austen.''

"I didn't know she wrote about incest.''

"She didn't, but you knew it was on everyone's mind,'' Leilah said simply. "If I were writing about Annabelle and her brother, I'd have them thinking now that their secret can't be kept much longer unless they change their way of life radically. News of the world must seep into that loft occasionally. They'll know de Spirit is getting a new trial and that if he wins, the case will probably be reopened.''

"That's saying their secret has a direct bearing on what happened to Andrea and Elizabeth.''

"I'll take the bit if you're too shy. For the record: One or the other of them murdered those two girls.''

Reppa's brows went up. "There's still not an ounce of proof.''

"There may never be. The best we may get is some glimmering of why Andrea and Elizabeth were killed. For that we're going to need the answers to two questions that in my mind are as big as the ones about Kinder and Annabelle. Why was Adelaide Loomis so self-sacrificing that she devoted her life to furthering Annabelle's career and raising Andrea as her own daughter? Let's stay with that one for the moment. Ideas?''

His brows were still up, and they stayed up, to ponder. "She could have seen that Annabelle had the potential to become a great artist and wanted to make sure she had every chance to develop it.''

"A rare woman who would do that for her sister. An unbelievable woman.''

"Okay, then maybe Abilene Loomis was behind her decision. He, too, might have seen how talented Annabelle was and commanded Adelaide to help her.''

"A backwoods preacher who'd allow his youngest daughter to run off to New York and become a beatnik artist? This after she'd already borne an illegitimate child, perhaps by his son? Highly improbable. The idea that he'd put his other daughter up to aiding and abetting her is off the credibility map entirely.''

"I'd better check the oven,'' Reppa said in a move to deflate her self-importance. But no epiphanies occurred to him in the kitchen.

Her own ideas on Adelaide weren't so great either, Leilah acknowledged when he'd returned. A near impossible admission for her to have made flat on her back: sitting up meant the loss of omniscience, a corresponding acceptance of fallibility.

The second question they considered over dinner, like an old couple deciding on a movie. Leilah said, having too much hen in her mouth to bother stressing each word for its shock value, "What was Elizabeth Moffett doing living with two girls so vastly different in temperament and style from herself? Clearly they fascinated her somehow,'' she went on before proceeding to an attack on her baked potato, and Reppa had to marvel once again that after all this time of living like her exemplar she still had the lean

393

profile of his own. "Let's presume it was at least subconsciously sexual. Now. Given her insecurity about her own sexuality, she probably did no more than live vicariously through them for a while. In particular, through Andrea. But there came a moment when she could no longer refrain from doing a little experimenting on her own, and the person she chose, again borrowing a page from Andrea, was not your average contributor to the Kinsey Report."

Reppa could not bear her pomposity any longer. "Look, Sturm, she was into bondage—it's as simple as that."

"With someone who had a few doubts about his own sexuality," Leilah replied imperiously. "You might almost conclude that he had a severe problem. But the nature of it still eludes us."

"Yeah, and?"

Leilah sighed over the amount of resistance her hen was putting up to having its leg torn off.

"Can I interest you in a knife?"

She swore vigorously, a word that may never before have been applied to a female bird, and looked away from his eyes. "Reppa?"

"A hatchet?"

"I'm all wired up, and I'm talking all around the point because I don't know how to say it. But you've got to get Muntz to give us what he has."

"He has a request in for something in return."

"Ten thousand dollars isn't so much."

"More than half my year's salary. The governor's never been known to give a state employee an advance."

"What if, uh, I gave it to you?"

Her eyes were still looking in the opposite direction from his. It was just as well.

"If I took out a second mortgage on this building? We could consider it an investment."

394

Reppa, flustered, started in explaining why he never took money from . . .

"It's my future at stake, not just yours, stupid. Never mind that, anyhow. I'm calling my man at the bank in the morning."

"No way," Reppa said. "It's not enough that I'm going to wind up fired, now you want to—"

"*Listen to me, Frank Reppa.* This isn't only you anymore, and if you think it is, I don't know where you've had your head for the last month, but I don't want it on my pillow." She laid her fingers on his wrist and squeezed. He seemed to feel his whole hand below it go numb in an instant and grabbed her wrist in turn. "So we just agree, all right, that there are two people working together here. Like, you might want to call us a doubles team."

Some bobsleds had two people. So did seesaws. He could see how it had been done. The two people whose curiosity and impatience only a month ago had little in common were now wedded to the same purpose like a pair of steel traps, hand to wrist to hand to wrist.

He hadn't considered the logistics. In his experience money had seldom changed hands in larger amounts than a few dollars. Once, in the army, he had carried around $398.48 after winning it in an all-night poker game and been astounded how unprotected he felt.

Muntz wanted half in advance, half on delivery. In cash. Small bills, nothing larger than a twenty. A peculiar demand, but Reppa didn't question it. Muntz could be allowed his idiosyncrasies, if that was what they were, just so long as he got what he wanted. *They* got what they wanted.

Five hundred twenties made a package as wide as an accordion. Stood upright, it kept toppling over. Leilah refused to help him divide it in half when he lugged it home from the bank that Friday morning. Money in the house made her even more nervous than it did him. She suddenly remembered she was Jewish, and in a few more hours it would be sundown.

Lois Cerny met him at the front door of Muntz's place in the same coat, but this afternoon her head was wrapped in a black babushka, as if she were already in mourning. Even the hall of their apartment had a funereal air. Darker than he'd remembered it, and there was a new aroma that made him yearn for the pungent garlic ozone. It was only that the exterminator had been around, but he seemed to smell something more terminal than the passing of a few roaches.

"You mustn't excite him like you did last time," she pleaded.

"I'll try not to."

"You have kinder eyes than his," she said distractedly and left him for her room.

"It's a fool's mate," Muntz announced when Reppa had found him studying his chessboard, "if I take his bishop. So I push my queen's pawn instead. Now, then. His queen's pawn is attacking the square I want for my knight. What a struggle."

"I brought the money."

Reppa seated himself and opened his briefcase. His hands didn't feel like his own. They felt clumsy and at the same time weightless.

"So you did," Muntz said and gave him what could only be described as a semi-incredulous leer.

Grab went the old man's hands. Packets of bills were lifted out and fanned between his thumbs and forefingers. A stream of muttered syllables erupted from the interior of his mouth and dispersed without a single one of them being understood by Reppa. He sounded like a monkey that had been given a crate of bananas. When the count was satisfactory, the mouth dissolved into a weary smile.

"When do I get what you have? And I'd like a receipt."

Muntz looked up and seemed to resent the demand for his attention. "Not likely I'm going to run off to Brazil in this cripple's go-cart."

"I'd still like something in writing."

"My word is gold," said Muntz. "Forty-three years in the life, and I've never shortchanged a client. The money's there, Muntz is there."

But he didn't resist when Reppa put a typed statement in front of him and showed him where to sign.

"Now, when do we make the swap?"

"When I have the merchandise." Muntz clicked his tongue, and it struck Reppa that he seemed eager, now that business had been taken care of, for a last fling with intrigue. "Tonight at dusk. Say eight o'clock."

"Sooner."

"No," said Muntz and added with a curious inflection in his voice, "I only know where it is. My agent will have to get it."

Reppa took another scan of the room and its contents. Desk. Scabrous carpet. Shelves of books that looked as if they hadn't been opened in years. Could Muntz have bamboozled him into believing the goodies were elsewhere when they were here all the time? When he glanced up, he found the old man staring at him.

"No, son. Only Muntz's pawns are exposed. The heavy artillery is impenetrably defended."

"In a safe somewhere?"

Muntz wasn't about to answer. Reppa watched the clouded eyes blink—but weren't they less clouded today?—and made a move to rise.

"Eight o'clock," Muntz repeated.

No one showed him to the door.

The afternoon was very warm. Windows were open everywhere on Second Avenue and curtains, too. Bright sunlight had kindled the windshields of parked cars and suffused the speckles of mica that were ground into the sidewalk. There was the smell of an open hydrant in the air, and the pleasant aroma of pigeons mingling with that of garbage cans drifted in the open window of his car. Over his shoulder the top of the Empire State Building seemed a hundred miles away, an urban backdrop to a rustic village street.

After a time he turned on the radio, let the newspaper fall from in front of his face, and watched the front door of Muntz's building. Everything continued to be very motionless. Under his scrutiny no one had entered the building or left it. The skateboard was still on the stoop, and the glass in the closed door seemed to generate a glare of its own.

Someone will come out soon, he continued to think. With luck everything would fit to his size, and it would be the old woman, easy to follow in her incongruous coat.

He had to wait another half hour before he saw Lois Cerny. It was as if a blind had gone down at first, when the front door opened, replacing the sunlit glass with the dark foyer within. For a moment, seeing the folded wheelchair under her arm, he mistook it for a shopping cart.

She left the wheelchair at the bottom of the steps and went back inside the building. The radio played "Heart of Glass." He had never gotten it integrated that it was the group, not the lead singer, that was named Blondie. A yard away from his head cars sped past on Second Avenue. The clatter of their passage could not distinguish itself in his ears from the song. Across the street the wheelchair stood like an empty orchestra seat in front of two players, a man and a meter maid gesticulating over a parking ticket.

Lois Cerny came out of the building again, this time with Muntz. She carried him in her arms with remarkable ease. A breeze touched the ends of the babushka knotted under her chin as she lowered him into the wheelchair, straightened the blanket over his lap, and gave him a push to start him on his way.

Reppa got the window of his car rolled up and the door locked. By the time the meter had swallowed another of his quarters, Muntz was clear down to Second Street. Without knowing where he was going but certain it could not be far, Reppa followed at what he felt would be a sensible speed, about that of a snail stalking a turtle, until he realized how fast the old man was zipping along. A motor in that thing? Yes, for Muntz's hands—on the arms of the wheelchair, not spinning the wheels—were being used only for steering. They could be going on a much longer journey than to the funeral home on the corner, where he'd first assumed Muntz was headed, to get an envelope that was stored in their safe. He felt a mental tingle, certain now that they must be on their way to a shyster colleague of Muntz's in one of the dismal law offices off Orchard Street.

But no, Muntz turned west on Houston Street and started toward the Bowery. It was the sort of Byzantine promenade where a scraggly old man in a wheelchair could look absolutely in his milieu.

In the intersection of the Bowery and Houston Street some bums waving filthy rags were doing a slow-motion adagio around the windshield of a forlorn TR-4 that had failed to beat the light.

Reppa had begun to feel the old exhilaration. People who have never lived on the Lower East Side will talk about the "pitted-out" feeling. They will tell you the instant they set foot on the Bowery, they become immediately morose, lowered in spirits, depressed. Reppa had always taken a somewhat jaundiced view of these critics of his terrain, but he had to admit that on this occasion he was undoubtedly weird in feeling nostalgic. He had an odd notion that the approach of summer had induced his reaction. This day in June, as he now realized, was the one whose rareness some poet had written about centuries ago.

Muntz had arrived at the intersection of the Bowery and Houston Street. A bum in a beaten felt hat and baggy khakis was shuffling away from the throng around the TR-4 and starting toward the wheelchair to offer his services in the crossing, but Muntz waved him away. The bum kept on coming, oblivious. His one hand grabbed the back of the wheelchair, and his other hand, holding a tattered rag, went to the back of Muntz.

They careened across the intersection, skirting the island in the center of it. Reppa, from his distance more than halfway down the block, thought for a moment that Muntz had turned up the juice in his wheelchair and the bum was being dragged haplessly along behind. But then he saw the bum's legs, loping easily, their gait faintly familiar, and his own legs turned to water.

With a sense of utter helplessness, knowing he was too far away, he started to run.

In front of him the whole scene: the wheelchair sent crashing into the curb at the southeast corner of the Bowery, Muntz flying out of it like a cloth doll, Cupach bending down as if to offer assistance, hands going under the old man's jacket—and then Cupach, seeing him coming, straightening and beginning to run himself, swiftly, peeling down the Bowery and around the corner of Stanton Street before Reppa could get across the intersection. And on the island in the middle of the intersection men with their rags crowding together and looking on blearily.

Muntz lay sprawled, body draped over the curb, legs in the street. Beside him was the rag Cupach had been carrying.

In the place where the rag had been during the crossing, near the center of his back, was a knife.

What followed was like nothing in Reppa's memory since Zinser boy keeled over on the field. A confusion of movements, of voices, none as loud as his own, of screeching car brakes, of a woman somewhere screaming and screaming and screaming. Of himself falling on his knees beside Muntz. Of his voice saying uselessly, "Don't everybody stand there—call an ambulance." And then of his hand feeling vainly for a pulse, sliding up the sleeve of Muntz's jacket, while his other hand went where Cupach's had gone, under the jacket, and felt a hard object in Muntz's shirt pocket. Of a siren near to his ears and a spinning red light. And then his fingers extracting from the shirt pocket something long and metallic.

They came up, two patrolmen, and Reppa felt himself being pulled roughly to his feet. They looked around for a reliable witness once they took in that Muntz's death was not the usual meaningless statistic on the Bowery, but Reppa had moved quickly and far. There was nothing for him any longer on Stanton Street, he realized after he'd taken a glance down it, and he stepped into a bar and sought the rest room.

He wondered, putting cold water on his face, how Cupach had known Muntz was on an errand that could destroy him. All at once he heard again: *Your eyes are kinder than his.* Had Lois Cerny meant Cupach? That Cupach had visited Muntz recently, too? Could Muntz have been trying to play both ends?

And now, somewhere in the jumble of Muntz's apartment, was Leilah's five thousand dollars, and all he had to show for it was a long, flat key. So flat that the shape alone told him what it belonged to.

CHAPTER SEVENTEEN

SCARLET AND GRAY

Reppa opened the door, which had been double-locked, and called, "Leilah?"

They had decided, upon learning that Lois Cerny had found the five thousand dollars, that they would let her keep it and give her the additional five thousand, as pledged, provided the court granted her permission to open Muntz's safe deposit box. But meanwhile they still had two hundred and fifty twenty-dollar bills in a strongbox in the closet. So Gore had been told to double-lock after herself, and he'd started announcing himself when he got home. "Any luck?" Leilah watched him pull the holster off his belt.

"No, it's been over a week now since anybody in the gallery has seen Mald, and today, when I called, the woman I spoke to tried to pump me for information about his whereabouts even before I could begin pumping her."

"Reppa, I've been thinking some more about how you can flush him out."

"If he hasn't already been flushed away."

"Think positive." Leilah laughed brightly—too brightly—leaving Reppa in some doubt as to just how she herself was thinking.

Sitting beside her on the bed, he held out a hand and turned it over. "All right. How do I find him?"

"They must know at the gallery where he lives. At least must have a phone number where he can be reached."

"Which they haven't been able to do now in over a week."

"My point. They're getting as anxious as we are. Tomorrow go in there and tell them you're a cop. They'll be so relieved when they see your shield that they won't notice the difference."

"Impersonating a police officer," he had to haul off and remind her, "is a criminal offense."

"Reppa, in the past week alone, how many criminal offenses have you already committed?"

"But this one crosses the line." He paused, with his eyes on the ceiling, reluctant to admit to something that by this point had begun to seem almost childish. "Pretending I'm a cop—even just pretending—would be like playing for Michigan."

"What?"

Reppa tried to recover. "The cops have been my opposition in this all along. Woody used to say the first day of the season, 'Think Michigan.' After wearing the scarlet and gray, to even think of switching over to maize and blue—"

"How old are you? Thirty-eight and you're *still* listening to your goddam football coach."

"Woody wasn't just a coach. He was special."

"Excuse the sound of my poor little flute in your marching band, but wasn't a certain coach fired about a year ago for taking a punch at one of his own players in the middle of a game?"

"It was a player on the other team," he corrected, though without much conviction.

403

"If you could hear yourself. You sound like someone trying to deny the world is round because a football field is flat."

"Football has rules—a code. Nothing I've been part of since has one."

"Oh, yes, it does, and you've been following it. You just won't admit it."

Her voice was so superior that he wanted to shake her. "What—what've I been following?"

"The call of the wild. The urban wild. Whatever works, works. Whatever works better, works better. Whatever works best, works best. There are no more truths, Reppa, only lies that can hide the absence of them."

Was that what was underneath her wisecracks? Was that *all*? His own face, he felt, was creased desperately with smile lines, and he heard an aggressively hearty sound in his voice. "I still have my principles, Sturm."

"I've seen examples. You and Eliot Ness."

"Sherlock Holmes played a lot of roles, but he never impersonated a police officer."

"Neither did Archie Goodwin. Neither did the Lone Ranger. Want to start on comic strip characters now? Batman and Robin?"

"You have to use something—"

"What were you using when you finagled McCreary into giving you the investigation assignment out of rotation? Who was your model when you started screwing Zippy? Who's been behind your decision to withhold information from the people you're supposedly working with?"

"But you agreed—"

She stiffened, her head tilting back and her jaw firming. "But I don't have any idols, and I don't want to be yours. If you need one, look to yourself. If all you see in yourself is a lot of confusion, join the club. Cheap dues. Just go on paying me rent and keeping me in notebooks, and I'll see to it that you're invited to all the meetings. The Bank Street Irregulars. For the moment I move that we adjourn. I smell steak and onions.''

"A murder investigation?'' the girl behind the information desk said. ''Well, I don't know.''

"Just his address and phone number,'' Reppa said.

"But we've been instructed . . .'' He looked unveeringly at her until she scratched around in the drawer of the desk and came out with a pen. ''Well, there's this phone number, but we haven't been able to reach him at it now for several days ourselves.''

"The address, too, if you don't mind.''

"We do have strict instructions.'' She looked down at the hand that was holding the shield for her consideration like a stolen watch. ''Oh, all right. But he isn't there. I suppose I ought to tell you, we were actually thinking of calling the police if we didn't hear from him in another day or two.''

Reppa waited until she had scribbled the address. ''How do you know he isn't there?''

"The assistant director stopped by last night and again this morning. Mr. Mald hasn't picked up his mail all week, and nobody's seen him.''

As the front door of a modern twelve-story building on West Fifty-seventh Street closed behind Reppa twenty minutes later, the doorman stepped out from behind a potted fern. ''Sir?'' He was paunchy and middle-aged, wearing a green uniform and very shiny black shoes. His craggy features and heavy-lidded eyes reminded Reppa of a custodian in his high school, a Hungarian refugee who'd worked evenings as a movie usher. This, not the uniform, was the reason he felt as if he had been caught sneaking into a theater.

"Officer Reppa," he said. "I'm looking for Carlo Mald."

The doorman made a pass at examining Reppa's shield more closely, and then his manner became suddenly distant, as if, for the moment, he would rather be somewhere else. "I'm afraid Mr. Mald's not in. We haven't seen him in quite a while, in fact."

Reppa moved tentatively toward the elevators. "Mind if I take a look?"

"Sure. Seven F."

The F apartment was at the east end of the hall. There was no name on the door. The bell echoed far away and hollow, as if it were ringing in an abandoned mine. Knocking for several moments brought an old woman's sharply inquisitive face to the door across the hall. It went away abruptly when Reppa got down on his knees and put his nose to the bottom of Mald's door. Smelling only the carpet beneath him, he rose.

"Is there a super around with a key to Mald's place?" he asked when he got back to the lobby.

"We have keys," the doorman said. "But we can't use them unless there's an emergency."

"Would a corpse classify as one?"

"You think Mald died—?"

"I think he had help. Grab the key, and let's go upstairs."

The doorman made a dismal excuse for an apologetic smile and said he couldn't leave his station.

"Then give me the key."

For a moment there was that well-remembered hooded look that he'd gotten once when he'd asked the custodian to let him in the locker room for a forgotten pair of sneakers.

"By the way, where's your partner?"

"I don't have one. I'm not a police officer."

"Noticed," the doorman said dryly.

"I'm a parole officer investigating the murder of a fellow parole officer. Mald may have information for me. Meanwhile he may be dead himself. Here're the options. I get the key and check out Mald's place—quietly. Or I call the police and tell them my suspicions. If Mald's in there dead, the whole place will be swarming for the rest of the day. If it's a false alarm, they'll want to know why they were called. And when I tell them I had to do it because you wouldn't let me in . . . well, they just might feel somebody wasted their time unnecessarily."

The doorman stared at him. He saw the man's indecision: cops weren't his favorite visitors, either. "A parole officer—what's that make you legally?"

"Licensed to carry a gun. Licensed to arrest people." Then, sensing that wasn't quite what the man was waiting to hear, Reppa added, "Nobody's going to skin your ass, take my word, if you let me borrow the key for a few minutes."

"This guy Mald isn't . . . ?" The doorman stopped and made gestures of vacillation. But at last he turned and went through a door at the rear of the lobby. In a moment he came back with one hand in his pocket. When he took it out, his manner was shrewd, knowing. "If he's in there croaked, one favor. My lunch relief comes on in ten minutes. Don't call the cops till after he gets here."

"I'll call you on the intercom, either way."

"I don't want to know either way. I gave you the key because I thought you were a cop, and I believed you because I don't want the cops in here if I can help it."

The doorman had an intelligence only a refugee could

407

fully appreciate. Reppa, a generation removed, neverthe-less knew better than to smile his gratitude.

He remembered as he took the elevator upstairs again that he'd neglected to check in with Leilah.

The key opened the door without a problem, but the chain was on. He stood debating with his hand, which had slipped his gun out of its holster. The butt, held like a club, squeezed through the crack in the door. He raised the barrel and chopped downward. He had forgotten, in his concentration on the door, the old woman across the hall. His first whack at the chain was echoed by a grunt from her, his second by a louder one. But when he turned, she stopped grunting and clucked under her breath. "Crazy in there," she said and went back behind her door when his beating at the chain had bent the socket enough so that the bolt sprang.

He stood in Mald's doorway staring uneasily at the sallow, featureless room that awaited him. It was hard to say what room it was meant to be, because it was empty. No furniture. No carpet. Nothing on the walls. Two windows, but over them the blinds were drawn so tightly they looked like gray, barren canvases. There was a smell Reppa could not identify; beyond that it was no worse than the smell in any room that hadn't gotten air in a long while. Presently he grew aware of another smell trailing faintly from a dim hall to his left. The tree of life.

As soon as he went down the hall, he felt comfortably afloat. Taking a breath, he sensed immediately that he was in danger of becoming airborne if he held it long enough. The room he entered was no less sallow than the one he'd left, but it had a feature. Mald lay on a bare mattress. He was wearing an undershirt and shorts that had the greenish hue of clothes that were approaching a state beyond laundering. They clung to his body like the loose wattles

408

of a flesh that had once belonged to a much heavier man. His toupee still had its metallic sheen, but it was slightly askew, pushed sideways toward one ear like a beret. Beside the mattress, neatly arranged at one end but veering off at the other like the footprints of a palsied mouse, was a long, long row of burned matches.

The impulse to open a window was suddenly a physical necessity as Reppa's knees started to buckle. Seven floors below, the green awning of the building captured and held his gaze. Against the gray oatmeal sidewalk it looked bilious. A woman with bright orange hair walked under it.

He heard a muffled groan behind him. Turning back to the room, he found the gallery owner's fingers scratching at the undershirt. The fingers began to move faster. Mald's eyelids struggled upward, unveiling pupils dull as moles. The gaunt head rose, and the mattress gave a single plaintive *whoosh*. Some dim recognition that he had a visitor came slowly into Mald's eyes. He got precariously into a sitting position. One of his hands disappeared inside his shorts and was out a moment later with a crumpled joint. "Match?" The lead-colored pupils gazed needfully at Reppa.

"You'll have to live without it for a few minutes."

A short laugh escaped from Mald's throat. "Live?"

"Because you're the only one left now who knows the truth."

The last word elicited another bleat. "I?"

"Danny de Spirit didn't kill those two girls. It was Annabelle's brother, wasn't it?"

The person or the act? Something of the answer had to be revealed to him here. But Mald only looked more and more disoriented.

Surprised at his own continuing calm, Reppa said, "Look, I don't care how long I have to wait for your head to clear—we're going to talk."

So saying, he sat down beside the mattress. Mald, feeling the intimacy, reached up with both hands and tried briefly and ineffectually to straighten his toupee. Offering the crumpled joint to Reppa without much hope, he suggested, "Share?"

"Put it away. Your brain's not going anywhere until we've talked."

Mald's frown was more moody than annoyed. "How'd you get in here?"

"The doorman gave me a key. When I told him I was afraid you were in here dead."

The gallery owner hesitated a moment and then mumbled conspiratorially, "I can't be . . . so long as she doesn't know where I am."

"Annabelle, you mean?"

The suddenness with which the name penetrated Mald's haze was startling. He hissed fiercely, "She got Wilkes, but she won't get me. Wilkes didn't know her like I do. Wilkes thought she could force her to make me have a show for those awful new paintings of hers."

"So you're ready to admit now that Annabelle paid you to represent Wilkes."

Mald's mouth was taut. "I didn't care about her money."

"No, probably not," Reppa said, his own mouth tightening at the realization that McCreary had, in his perverse way, given him a whiff of the true scent when he'd shown him that arrest sheet. "More important was her silence. A promise that she'd never reveal to the art world that you'd once served time on a manslaughter rap."

Mald looked as if he wanted to ask how Reppa knew all this but closed his eyes instead. "Oh, that Adelaide . . ."

"What about her?"

"Cold as ice until I got so frustrated one night that I grabbed her and shook her. It freed something in her. In both of us. Before I knew it, I'd told her that I'd once killed a girl. Not thinking that she would, of course, tell Annabelle. They were a pair, those two. Each lived half of her life through the other. Adelaide was out in the world, Annabelle only in her own head. All for her art until she met that girl . . ."

"At Andrea's birthday party," Reppa said, breaking into the reverie.

Mald's eyelids fluttered open. "You seem to have found out everything."

"Not yet. I still don't know why Andrea and Elizabeth were killed."

The gallery owner's eyes, under their drugged glaze, looked as if the mind behind them was sifting through the words and images that had accumulated since Reppa's arrival, trying to distinguish between what he had said and what was only Reppa's speculation. Reppa, for his part, knew his own eyes must look troubled. Somewhere among all of this there was still a loose piece. He was sure of it.

The room was more cheerful than it had been a minute ago; a light breeze came in the window. But then Mald began scratching at himself again, the elongated body writhing on the mattress, and their eyes met in hapless recognition that they were two men who understood too much about each other.

"Tell me what you know about Annabelle's secretary."

"Who?" The word was clipped and irritable.

"The man who answers her phone when you call her. Are you aware that he's also her brother?"

"I never call her. We haven't spoken in years."

"Her brother's been living with her since 1969. Serving not only as her secretary but also probably as her lover."

Mald was looking at him with curiosity. Like everything

else about Mald, it was tinged with fatigue. "Annabelle has no male lovers. Not even brothers."

"Sorry to disillusion you, but she's had at least one. She had a child. Andrea, to be exact."

Mald's face was discouraging. It seemed to be trying not to look surprised. Almost accusingly, the gallery owner said, "Then that explains everything."

"Not to me."

"But of course it does. She was always so protective of the girl. Once she even told me she'd kill me if I ever so much as touched her. In her whispering way, but the message was clear. She meant it—absolutely."

"When did she say this?"

"At Andrea's birthday party. The minute she saw my interest in Andrea."

"Did anybody else hear her say it? Elizabeth Moffett, by chance?"

Mald was squinting at him, squinting and frowning.

"And hearing her threat, Elizabeth dropped her drink, didn't she—dropped her drink and ran out of the room?"

The gallery owner nodded distantly. "With Annabelle right behind her. They were gone a long time, and when they returned . . . well, there was a look on the girl's face."

"What sort of look?"

"Odd. Very odd. She stayed away from Annabelle for the rest of the evening, but she kept sneaking little glances at her. Weird little glances. Andrea and Jill both noticed them, too. They must have seen that Annabelle was also looking and acting rather strange. It was clear there was something going on between her and the girl."

Reppa hesitated while he spliced together the scene Mald was describing and understood now why Halliwell, whose eyes had been looking only for men who might be trying to seduce Andrea, had noticed none of it. "Seeing the pull between them—that's what drove Andrea to leave the party."

"Annabelle," said Mald gravely, "had been her saint. Above everything worldly. Certainly above anything sexual. Her sudden interest in Elizabeth must have come as an equal blow to Jill Wilkes. She'd been rejected, you know, by Annabelle. Very nastily rejected."

"Sexually?"

"It amounted to that. It was a slap in the face, literally, and I don't suppose she ever forgave Annabelle for the incident."

"You saw it?"

"No, but Adelaide did." Mald smiled remotely and looked at the ceiling. His senses returning to him, along with a corresponding appearance of disinterest, he said wearily, "Poor woman. She tried so hard to bring her sister out into the world, but the results were always disastrous. This one evening she invited Annabelle to her place to meet some critics she'd been cultivating, and somehow Wilkes found out about it from Andrea and put her up to getting them invited, too. Wilkes then proceeded to make a pest of herself, cornering Annabelle at every opportunity. Finally she wound up getting slapped and making quite a scene."

"For doing what?"

"No one was quite sure, because it happened in Adelaide's bedroom. Annabelle had gone in there to get away, as she often did at those kinds of gatherings, and Wilkes apparently followed her. It must have been something physical. Almost undoubtedly something physical occurred between them. Or at least Wilkes tried to make it occur. No one had explained to her that Annabelle was not someone you touched. She has the most extraordinary aversion to physical contact of any sort. Once at one of her openings she went so far as to bite a critic who tried to kiss her. So Wilkes got off lightly, really.''

Reppa struggled with his next question. ''This pull between Annabelle and Elizabeth—you made it sound sexual. Are you sure it wasn't something else?''

''Am I sure?'' Mald threw up a deprecating hand, as if to say, *What else is there?* ''With Annabelle the signals were always obscure, but Elizabeth's were very obvious. She was infatuated, and I've seen that look on enough women's faces not to be wrong.'' He paused to smile introspectively and then said, ''Besides, Andrea and Jill, seeing the same thing I did, formed the same judgment. Though while I was secretly amused, their reactions were very different. Andrea seemed horrified, and Jill was— furiously jealous, I would imagine.''

''Yet in the painting I saw in your gallery she seemed to be trying to show in reverse her view of what happened the morning her two roommates were murdered.''

Mald shrugged. ''A warped woman. Her view of everything was reversed.''

''I have a different idea. I think Annabelle acted as a procuress of sorts for her brother, who couldn't meet women on his own because he was in hiding. Jill somehow found out about him, and when he murdered her roommates, she suspected immediately that he'd done it and blackmailed Annabelle into getting you to launch her painting career. His name is Kinder now. At the time of the murders he had another identity. Try to remember, Mald. When you went to Annabelle's loft back in the days when you were representing her, did you ever see evidence that a man might be living with her?''

Mald threw up the same hand and turned it over. ''When

414

who went to Annabelle's loft? I've never been in Annabelle's loft. I know no one who has.''

"What about Adelaide? Did she ever give you the feeling that she might be harboring someone somewhere?"

The answer was a long time in coming. When Mald finally spoke, his voice had to strain to keep its weary and unemotional tones. "Talking to you is pointless. You can't help me. Only the police can, but if I go to them, all they'll care about is that I concealed knowledge about a murderess all these years, and I'll be ruined. Meanwhile here you are railing at me about this mysterious brother of Annabelle's who's in hiding, and the only person in hiding I'm aware of is myself. If Annabelle finds me, she'll kill me.''

"She won't, Mald. You may well be killed, but it won't be by Annabelle.''

"You don't know her." For an instant the web of indifference within the gallery owner broke, and he whined at Reppa. "You didn't hear her that night. That whispery voice. And those eyes. *You should have seen her eyes*. She would have killed me, and she did kill Andrea and Elizabeth—and now she's killing everyone who knows!''

"You're really convinced? You've really thought all these years that she was the killer?''

"There's no doubt." The reply was sullen and despairing.

"Why? Her own daughter, Mald. Why would she kill her own daughter?''

The gallery owner was silent for several moments while he assembled in his mind all that Reppa had told him. "That woman a mother?" he said, unbelieving. "Jesus Christ, some man actually . . . ?''

The sentence was left unfinished as he lapsed backward on the mattress and closed his eyes.

"When Adelaide was alive, did she ever say anything to you about her brother?''

"Stop. I spoke to you because Wilkes insisted you knew too much. I saw that you did and showed you her painting to lead you afield. Now it appears that in doing so I've caught myself. You refuse to see the truth about Annabelle. She has no brother, or anyone else living with her."

"But she does. He's living with her now, and I've met him."

"Are you sure?"

"How could I not be sure?"

"I've shown you." It was a disappointing retreat from something that Mald knew and that he supposed Reppa also knew.

"When? How?"

"In the only way I could." The voice was garbled, Mald's throat constricted by the odd angle at which his head lay on the mattress. He looked, as he began to bring his knees up toward his chin, like a fetus for a race of skeletons.

Reppa started to get to his feet. The pressure in his head had eased, but he felt more disassociated than ever. He wanted to tell Mald it was safe for him to come back out into civilization, that he didn't know anything he could be murdered for—but he had begun to realize that Mald was living now pretty much as he lived most of the time, the only difference being the few hours he spent each day at the gallery.

In rising Reppa laid a hand on the corner of the mattress. The springs gave with only the slightest sound, but the shock of another presence there beside him ran visibly through Mald's body. One eye opened, then the other. Reppa left him lying curled on his side, holding the crumpled joint in his hand and looking sightlessly at it.

CHAPTER EIGHTEEN

JUNE 10, 1980

"Sitting up by yourself!" Gore exclaimed, and it took no special intuition to know that she was going to say next: "You know you supposed to hold on to something."

"I am," said Leilah, coolly clamping the lid on her concern. "My sanity." Then, although she knew she would be refused, she asked for seconds on Gore's stuffed cabbage.

The woman snapped to duty, shaking her finger. "Too much give gas."

"I'm still hungry."

"You eat already enough lunch for two people."

"I'll get it myself," Leilah threatened cheerfully.

She'd actually started to rise when Gore came running over, shouting, "Stay—stay!"

"Do I get seconds?"

"Cheese," Gore told her. "Cheese after cabbage. Good stomach." She only meant to be helpful, but her *good* sounded so goddam maternal.

"Jarlsberg," bargained Leilah, knowing the woman meant cottage.

"Don't have."

"Oh, yes. Just look in the refrigerator." The Eighth Avenue Deli had been delivering to Leilah for years, and all it had taken to get them to continue their service on the sly after her accident was a visit from one of her friends. She was already planning, one eye on the phone, today's haul as soon as she got rid of Gore.

The Jarlsberg arrived, a single meager slice. "Bring the whole thing." Gore hesitated for so long that she started to get out of bed again.

"Talk about spoiled," Gore muttered.

The talk about how rotten she'd been spoiled continued, under Gore's breath, for several minutes. Leilah finally had to ask if the woman wanted to swap places with her, say for about the last five months. The two of them traded a brief look, and then Gore traded a longer one with her brace, which lay next to her under the sheet, an armadillo-shaped mound.

"It hasn't been an hour yet. Well, barely," Leilah admitted when she saw Gore glance at the clock.

"You want cheese?" Gore could drive a bargain, too.

"Oh, Christ," Leilah said, raising her nightgown so Gore could get the monkey suit around her. Then, as Gore was strapping her in, "Too tight."

"No surprise, the way you eat."

"I haven't gained an ounce. Not one single ounce." Neither had she been on a scale lately, of course, but her own eyes were the only proof she needed. She knew her body as a prisoner knows his cell. Now if she could just feel she was alone with it.

Ten minutes later her wish came true. Gore was off to spend the afternoon baby-sitting for her other charge: a four-year-old grandson. The instant she heard Gore's key turn in the lock, she was on the phone. The Jarlsberg had left her thirsty, so a cold quart of beer was the first thing she demanded. Gore would find the empty under the bed the following morning and a few chicken bones besides, but Leilah had long ago convinced her that these were Reppa's doing. God knew, the man needed to be lectured. Leave it to her, Leilah promised each time, to domesticate him.

Now that the Jarlsberg was depleted, everything but the rind, she put the plate on the night table, knife laid neatly across it. The *L* engraved on the handle reminded her that her parents, who'd given her a whole array of monogrammed kitchen paraphernalia on her thirtieth birthday (first initial only, because they still hadn't despaired of their belief that a change of last initial was imminent), would be making their annual pilgrimage to the city in a few weeks. How could she, not having explained Reppa to them, hope to explain both Reppa *and* her accident when they limoed in from the airport, lamenting to each other the whole ride that they had spent so much of their lives in this city when there was Key Biscayne?

She contemplated her notebook in silence: pages of dialogue, of introspection, of massive self- and cosmic analysis—pages that came so fast, many of them, that they were nearly illegible. For every five words she could decipher, two were lost. Her fingers ached to get to the typewriter. The long hours of sitting on her can that she used to complain were inhuman now seemed idyllic.

When the phone rang, she eagerly reached for it, expecting Reppa's voice. Instead she heard a man asking for Reppa. He automatically got what everybody who called in the middle of the day when Reppa was signed out for the field got: "He's in the field." Got even if Reppa happened, as in the old days back last fall, to be right beside her—late getting started on his home visits or, more frequently, home early with his mind on the same thing hers had been on all morning sitting at the typewriter.

She hung up. Then grew immediately uneasy, because

419

she'd realized Reppa's voice was not only expected, it was overdue. The clock said ten after one.

Possibly he'd run into a snag trying to find Mald. In any case he should have checked in with her. Unless, for some reason, he couldn't. This, in her recent experience with Reppa, could mean anything from his sneaking in a few paddleball games somewhere to someone else's having been murdered. She made her usual comforting quip to herself whenever panic lurked: "Better dread than dead."

Besides, Reppa was a winner. Ideally he'd be rich and famous someday, but even if he fell short, she'd be content so long as he was doing something interesting. Though she would have preferred he were Joyce Carol Oates, she'd begun to see that being a parole officer had its merits. And she was also beginning to see that he had the perfect equipment for it: nice instincts for how little he could do in the way of changing the world and how much was out of his control, just about the right balance of credulity and paranoia, a tenacious mind. Not brilliant; tenacious. Meanwhile he needed more respect for himself, but what respectable man didn't? She could help him get it. Pretty much all on his own he'd worked out that Danny de Spirit couldn't have killed those two girls, and she'd been there to give him a shove every now and then in the direction of who had. It meant sitting on her own desire to be first in everything, but now that they were both more or less on the same wavelength, it wouldn't be long before they had it all.

But then what? Where would they go with it? Whom could they trust? Who, ultimately, in this age when yesterday was already ancient history, cared about a twelve-year-old murder? Plenty of people could be made to, of course, if they thought they could somehow rustle the credit for freeing the wrong murderer and nailing the true one, and bet your ass they'd all be in there trying, from the governor on down. Where Reppa saw himself as unhealthily cynical, Leilah saw herself as robustly skeptical. Whatever worked, worked. Whatever didn't, regardless of whose baby it was, went out with the bath water. So she just wrote her stories, which were really all one long story. This is, was, could be, should have been your life, Leilah Sturm.

There were noises at the door, metal scraping against metal. The deliveryman having trouble with his key? Her eyes left the notebook to rest on the clock. It was fast for the deliveryman. Despite her nearly starving condition, he almost always took at least an hour.

She heard the door close. When she didn't hear "Leilah?" she called, "Reppa?"

"Yo."

"Okay?" There was no reply to her question, only footsteps moving rapidly, going straight to the kitchen, as if they knew their way around. The deliveryman, after all? Definitely not Reppa. Reppa would never not have stopped in the bedroom first.

Cupboard doors banged reassuringly, pulling her up just short of calling out again. The deliveryman. Only him. Or was it "only he"? Yes, "he"—you said, "It was he." So there, that kind of grammatical conscientiousness proved she wasn't panicking. Still, when she looked down, she found the phone receiver in her hand. Over the sound of the dial tone she heard herself laughing. Panic? She would have screamed bloody murder if the line had been dead.

"Hello? Hey?"

The kid they had at the deli, she remembered now, always announced himself when he entered. Nothing elaborate, just "Deli." But he never said "Yo." Would they have been so dumb as to send a new kid without instructing him? She dialed, very quickly, the number of the deli. When it was busy, she regretted that she had made this arrangement. More exactly, she regretted that her stubborn metabolism had kept her from ending it.

Her hand strayed to the cord that rang Gore's chimes. Then she remembered Gore had gone to visit her grandson.

The scene went silent. For a second or two nothing moved anywhere in the apartment, and then there were footsteps coming down the hall. She heard her voice once again calling, "Reppa?"

She felt as if she were going to start screaming or throwing things or just explode, but what stopped and held her was knowing none of this would do any good. Movement novels had supplied her with responses to almost all the life-threatening situations modern heroines had to face— abortion, rape, cancer—but this one was out of Mickey Spillane. Burrow under the covers and pray it would be over quickly? She'd be damned if she would.

Her eyes sprang to the night table with uncertainty. Still there? *Yes*. The plate tumbled to the floor as she snatched up the knife. She'd wanted the plate, too, anything and everything to throw, and she started to swing her arm toward the pile of books nearby the bed.

But he was already in the room with a knife of his own, something clear and glistening wrapped around the handle. He wore black rubber gloves, a black turtleneck. She saw shaggy gray hair and a huge face, but its features looked as insubstantial as the blood felt in her veins. It seemed that all the senses had been drained out of her and there was nothing left but a vague, dreamlike reaction to what was happening.

He hurled himself at her. He was immense, but everything about him was out of focus. She wasn't sure whether she was shaking and screaming or silent and rigidly still.

422

His arm came smashing down on top of her chest and pinned her to the mattress. The breath was knocked out of her instantly, but the impact shocked her into movement. She struggled desperately as his other arm rose, and flung herself over on her stomach, clutching her knife in the folds of her nightgown in both hands.

She felt his elbow smack against her spine like a blow from a fist, but more heard the blade of his knife than felt it. It banged into one of the metal reinforcements on her brace, clattered, bounced off. She heard her nightgown tear, a grunt from him when he saw what had stopped the blade. Then he began trying to turn her over, the rubber gloves squeezing her shoulders. She fought until she felt him sprawl on her legs and slide one arm under her. This was it. *Now,* she thought. *Or never.*

As his arm wrestled her up from the mattress she went limp, allowing him to ease her over on her back. She could smell his face, it was so close to hers. He said something but perhaps only to himself. In his mouth the words sounded quiet and without any particular emotion. But when she threw her arms around him and hugged him against her, he said something else that showed surprise. Her knife, with him swarming all over her, had no hope of finding a vital organ, but neither could he get at her as long as her arms were embracing him. So she waited.

For several seconds nothing happened. He had so much more strength than she, but he seemed unable or unwilling to use it. Then she realized what he was doing. He was trying to get some of the sheet wrapped around his face before he started wrestling with her again. It could only mean he was worried that she might scratch him. That some of his skin might get under her fingernails. She watched with unfocused eyes as the sheet went over every-

423

thing but his eyes. Where was his knife? she wondered, seeing both his hands occupied with the sheet.

There still being no vulnerable place to stab him, she dared bring the hand holding her knife out from behind his back, praying that when he lifted himself off her, she would have an instant to lunge at his chest. But his eyes flicked that way and saw it. One of his hands seized hers, the other yanked the sheet away from his face and threw it over her eyes.

She felt, unable to see, his fingers trying to pry the knife out of her hand, and then, when they couldn't, grabbing her wrist and twisting. He was suddenly using both hands to get her knife away, which left her other hand free to fly up and claw at his face. Then, as he tried to push her away, she sprang up at him, so abruptly and with such force that the sheet flew off her face and their chests collided. Pulling back, she saw straight into his eyes for a second. They were rigid with a determination to end this. She did not have to see anymore to know it truly was now or never.

Still, her eyes were held by his in an almost physical connection. "Why . . . ?" she murmured. Cupach said nothing. With one hand he was searching behind him on the bed for his knife. His other hand still had tight hold of her wrist. To Leilah his silence only made him more terrifying. It infuriated her. "Son of a . . ." she hissed, and in place of the last word spat venomously at him.

For a fraction of a second Cupach let go of her wrist and mopped his face, but then he seized her again. He grabbed her throat, both thumbs pressing hard on her windpipe.

Leilah immediately felt her lungs bursting, her head swelling. Her arm was still free and wanting to use the knife, but to move it was impossible. Everything seemed to be rushing toward her throat. Her eyes were open, her lips were moving, but she was unable to make a sound. She felt herself dropping away somewhere. The lower part of her body was surging, and she tried relaxing it, every muscle. Her fingers opened, the knife leaving them. She stopped trying to grab for breath. She went limp again, closed her eyes . . . .

The pressure? What had happened? Her throat wasn't being crushed anymore, but she didn't dare open her eyes yet or breathe. She could feel Cupach's weight, some of it at least, leave her. In spite of herself her eyes fluttered open, and she saw he was again feeling the bed behind him. His knife—he was looking for his knife.

Again she tried to spring up, but she didn't have the strength yet. He easily pushed her down and held her flat while he continued to grope behind him. Her knife was beside her somewhere, it must be right in his view, but he ignored it. She understood then. He had to have his because the handle . . . it had something wrapped around it. The glistening her eye had caught—plastic? So that any prints that were already on it wouldn't be disturbed? And the knife itself? Flashing on Reppa, his description of what he'd seen from Zippy's closet, she had a concurrent flash: The reason he'd gone into the kitchen first was to get one of *her* knives, one that—

Now she knew. Killing her was only half of it.

"It won't work," she heard herself rasp. "He's not living here anymore."

Cupach pulled his head around to look at her.

"When I found out about Zippy, I kicked him out."

She could see his eyes didn't believe her. "He was here this morning."

Said quietly but in a tone that had no doubt in it. *He's been watching*, she realized, *watching us and waiting*. Her answer came quickly. "To pick up some things. He was gone when the woman upstairs came down to take care of me. When she left, I was still alive.'' She gave him a moment to follow the obvious line of thought and then said, ''True, he could have come back after she left and killed me. He still has a key.''

She watched him hold back a smile. When she spoke again, she tried to smile a little herself. ''Only I had the lock changed this morning.''

A gamble that he'd picked the lock or gotten in with a master key of some sort, not a copy of hers. The change in his face told her she'd been right.

''Bitch. No locksmiths came here today.''

''The old woman did it. She's handy. That's why I have her.''

Cupach seemed to freeze for a moment. Then he rose up off her to turn and glance at the bedroom window, as if to gauge whether it could be made to look like someone had gotten in that way. She craned her neck, trying to see how far away her knife was. But she couldn't find it anywhere. Had Cupach knocked it off the bed? Her throat was suddenly very sore, and the brace weighed her down a ton.

In turning to the window, Cupach spied his knife. He swung the rest of the way around and leaned backward to reach it. It freed her arms for a second, and a second was all she needed to ring Gore's chimes.

''What's that?'' he said when he turned back and saw the cord in her hand.

''The woman upstairs. Her signal that I need her.''

Their eyes met. Cupach's showed no concern. *Stupid*—she'd forgotten that he must have seen Gore leave the building. Now he didn't believe anything she'd said.

''Please. You don't have to kill me. Really you don't.''

He answered so calmly it amazed her. His voice terrified her even more than the knife in his hand. "If I don't, what will happen to me?"

For an instant her whole body went numb. Cupach's voice continued, eerily quiet.

"The others know only about de Spirit. That the case against him is falling apart. But you and Reppa know about *me*."

"We're not the only ones."

He shook his head very slowly, almost sadly. "But you are. Only Reppa saw me kill Muntz. Don't lie and say he didn't recognize me because I know he did. As I know that he's aware I killed Zippy."

"And Wilkes and McCreary," she added dully. "You murdered them all."

"No, not murder. Self-defense. It isn't murder when you kill someone who's trying to destroy you and everything you've worked for. It isn't murder when you kill someone who's trying to free a convicted murderer."

"But de Spirit—he didn't kill those two girls. You must know by now—"

"I do know," Cupach said in the same deadly even voice. "I know he was convicted and therefore he's guilty and no one must ever be allowed to say otherwise."

Leilah stared at him, feeling both fear and bewilderment. He wasn't just twisting words; she saw that now. His whole way of looking at things had been twisted. She tried to make her next plea sound spontaneous. "Nothing Reppa and I know would ever stand up in court."

"Neither will de Spirit's murder conviction." He smiled patiently down at her. "Unless."

"Unless what?" she breathed hoarsely.

"People discover that a parole officer doing a pardon investigation got carried away with his cause and decided

427

to get rid of everyone who could disprove his belief that de Spirit was innocent.''

"You can't—no—nobody will believe Reppa killed all those people.''

"But they will believe he killed you. The rest will follow.''

Her head shook wildly. "His fingerprints are on that knife, you think. But they aren't. He never uses those knives—he never even goes near the kitchen.''

"Stop. *Don't you realize I know how you live?*''

Cupach's indignation was all the more fearsome for the fact that his voice was still quiet, controlled.

"You can't,'' she murmured.

"Oh, but I do. What do you think he and Zippy talked about all those afternoons?''

"You. How much better in bed he is than you are.''

She knew what she had to do. Not break him—she couldn't really hope to break him—but she didn't know what else to call it. That voice could not be allowed to go on so calmly.

"More lies.'' He thrust the knife into her face.

Quickly she said, "Zippy was in love with him. She was ready to leave you for him if he'd leave me. But he wouldn't. Because I'm better than she was.''

"Flat on your back all these months.''

"The way most men like it.''

His smile faded. "Trying to distract me?''

"Want a little? Knock off a quickie before you knock me off?''

She started, teasingly, to hike up her nightgown, looking all the while at the broad forehead, the calm and quiet eyes, the pale lips that wouldn't stop smiling but never smiled deeply enough to disturb any other feature on his face. She'd never deliberately appealed to this element in a

428

man before, and now she regretted her inexperience. His face remained indomitable as he slashed at her hands to make them let go of the nightgown. But was that a flicker of interest in his eyes? She couldn't tell. Blood covered her hands. The knuckles on both of them had been gashed by the knife. She raked her fingers over his arms, his shirt. Now his lips stopped smiling, and his eyes very clearly flashed. This was one thing he could not have on him. Stains . . .

The knife soared high over his head. She grabbed his wrist as it plunged downward and with both hands held on with every ounce of strength she had. The blade hung suspended for an instant a few inches above her. Then it began coming downward again, aimed at her left breast, slowly, unstoppably, Cupach's arm too strong for her. She tried to writhe out of the way, thrashing her head from side to side, and succeeded a little, the blade going into her shoulder beside the collarbone. Cupach yanked it out, frustrated, and tried to slide it across her throat. But he couldn't get rid of those hands, they were everywhere. With his other hand, the one he had been using to balance himself on the mattress while sitting upright over her, he slapped at her wrists. His first blow missed, because she was squirming so much, and caught more of the blade than it did of her, nicking the side of his hand.

Hurriedly, he tried to switch the knife to his free hand while she was clinging to the other one. But this was not so easy; the knife, when he went to make the transfer, was as firmly in her grasp now as in his. More in hers suddenly. Leilah felt, under her pressure, the angle of the blade slowly changing, and saw a startled look come over his face, which quickly faded as his mouth opened and his eyes went dull. She forgot about trying to wrestle with his

429

hands and paid more attention to where her own were. When she realized she was seeing only the handle of the knife between them, she could not believe what they had done, and was struck by how small they still looked and felt inside his hands. The blood on them could no longer be entirely her own. She saw his mouth start to form a word as something dark and wet bubbled out of it. He tried again to speak, but the warm liquid began spilling out.

But she could not stop. She kept twisting the handle of the knife, twisting, twisting, until long after she knew it didn't matter anymore. Even then she could not let go. Her hands were trapped under him, crushed between his chest and hers. He had flopped on her, his massive jaw impossibly brushing against her cheek. It smelled so much cleaner than it should have. She could just about reach the phone if she got one of her hands free, but she was afraid that if she did, his bulk would suffocate her. So she lay there and tried to take short, shallow breaths. They hurt terribly, no matter how short she made them. She realized that, besides from her shoulder and hands, she must be bleeding somewhere else. But maybe not. All that stickiness she felt between their chests could have been his. In any case something was definitely broken again. She prayed it was in front this time. She prayed that the fact that it hurt most when she breathed was a good sign.

She prayed for a rib. Even two or three. "Holy," she whispered. "Holy shit, this isn't real." But she couldn't stop thinking: *God, if I just could get to my notebook.*

When Reppa came home and got no answer to his "Leilah?" he ran to the bedroom, where he found her with her eyes closed. They opened after he pulled Cupach's body off her, and she made one of her fetching remarks.

CHAPTER NINETEEN

DITCH PLAINS

New York State law not recognizing common-law marriages, the legal proceedings to decide whether Lois Cerny was entitled to open Muntz's safe deposit box might have dragged on for months had Muntz not been a murder victim. Even then, although there was no next of kin, the judge could well have refused her permission, for Muntz had died without leaving a will. But once the DA's office learned there was a safe deposit box, they grew as anxious as Reppa to examine its contents. Anxiety of a different nature gripped the NYPD the evening they discussed the untoward demise of former city police detective Stephen Cupach with Reppa and Leilah. The two were interviewed separately, Reppa at the 6th Precinct, Leilah in her semiprivate room at St. Vincent's Hospital. No one tried to make a case that Leilah had taped Saran Wrap around the handle of one of her kitchen knives and invited Cupach to lie on top of her and be stabbed, but it was far from universally conceded that Cupach's presence in her Bank Street apartment had anything to do with the recent rash of deaths suffered by people connected with the Behrman-Moffett case. Cupach might have gone wrong somewhere, but *that* wrong? There were some, however, who believed that

Cupach had not only killed Jill Wilkes, John Jacob McCreary, Zipporah Dwersky, and Lowell Muntz but also Andrea Behrman and Elizabeth Moffett. These people (and several were lower echelon cops) were ready to believe anything of Cupach now that he was safely dead and out of the way. Bowden Delanghe, unfortunately, was not one of them.

But dedicated civil servant that Delanghe was, he could also be as unconventional in his style as Reppa was in his, and the two of them were standing there in the Citizens Federal Bank right along with everyone else on the Thursday morning in mid-June when Muntz's safe deposit box was opened. Reppa had assumed Delanghe had gotten permission for them to be there; the bank assumed, after seeing Delanghe's credentials, that *someone* surely had authorized his and Reppa's presence; the representatives from the DA's office and the state income tax department assumed at first that the two of them were bank employees; Lois Cerny, in the new coat she'd bought with part of Leilah's five thousand dollars, assumed she was momentarily going to be the center of attention and was startled when the tax man, and not she, was the first to handle the safe deposit box.

Reppa's observation was that it was small as such boxes go, scarcely thicker than one of Leilah's notebooks. When the lid was raised, out came a bankbook, a .38, and some dozen envelopes similar to the ones he'd seen under Muntz's desk blotter. The tax man seized the bankbook, the assistant DA's hand went for the gun; then they both sat down with the envelopes.

The tax man looked for cash, bankbooks, bonds and other securities. None of the envelopes contained any of these items. He soon lost interest. But the ADA didn't. When he saw the envelopes contained letters, photographs, and personal documents, he started shoveling them into a briefcase.

Then there was a clearing sound from the throat of Bowden Delanghe. He said firmly, "The Behrman package may be our baby also." The ADA paused and looked at the handcrafted leather ID holder in Delanghe's hand. It was no great surprise. Parole's entry in the Behrman-Moffett sweepstakes had become a well-known secret. Still he seemed to debate whether to refuse to show Delanghe the envelope. But then, perhaps because he was sure Delanghe would know the many legal devices for obtaining a look at it sooner or later, he relented.

Delanghe's hand came far enough out of the envelope for Reppa to glimpse the two death certificates in it, but Delanghe didn't give him enough time to see everything he wanted, and he had to ask.

"Could I just—?"

His voice had too much in it. The ADA seemed about to snatch the envelope back. Even the tax man looked up from the form he'd begun filling out. Delanghe, as always, wore no expression, but a speculative glint appeared at the corner of the eye he fixed on Reppa. "Quite a coincidence," he said almost merrily.

"What's that?" the ADA inquired suspiciously.

"Nothing," Reppa said hastily. But he saw Lois Cerny trying to exchange a glance with him, suddenly stirred again by acquisitiveness. Face to face with her and seeing Delanghe engaged in his inscrutable tactics, he could feel nothing but resentment and the beginnings of rage, as though only minutes had intervened since that awful vision yesterday afternoon. Leilah's lean, pale face amid all that red. *If anyone tried to come between them now.* Still, he did owe Lois Cerny at least a nod.

She would get the rest of that ten grand.

*　　*　　*

Delanghe, of course, had seen the nod and would want to know what it meant. His office in the Parole building was no larger than Reppa's and seemed considerably smaller when both of them were sitting in it. The six file cabinets, each as tall as a standing man, were part of what produced the sensation of claustrophobia, but only part of it. Reppa sat close enough to the door to feel it at his back, but he didn't feel it as a route of escape, and for the moment he didn't see another.

He did not know what he expected Delanghe's strategy to be; still, he was surprised when his opening assault focused not on the circumstances surrounding Cupach's death but on what Reppa had been doing yesterday talking to Carlo Mald.

He tried to answer casually. "Well, I thought Mald might know something that could help us."

"Do what?"

Delanghe crinkled his eyebrows to lighten the demand, but Reppa still felt the pupils below them staring at him unwaveringly. "Find McCreary's murderer. But at the time, of course, I didn't know that Cupach—"

"What about Behrman and Muntz?"

"They'd also been contacted by McCreary. Timberlake took one area of McCreary's activities in the days just before he was murdered. I took the other."

"Nobody's questioning your decision to divide the effort. But I'm puzzled by where you seem to have chosen to concentrate all your attention. None of the people you've been chasing around after are what I'd call prime candidates to have blown away a parole officer. But on the other hand, one of them could have—" Delanghe interrupted himself with a laugh, though it was not a sound that tried to convince Reppa he saw a comic side to this, and

434

began beating his fingers on the top of his desk. Shave and a Haircut. "What about those death certificates? Did they tell you anything?"

Reppa shook his head as if confused. "Well, obviously—for one thing—they're fakes."

"*Both* of them?"

"What else?" Reppa said, and said again with a nervous shrug, "What else? The people are still alive."

"Are they?"

Delanghe's pupils, he observed now, were shrunk to pinpoints.

"Well—I've seen and spoken to both of them."

"So you said in the report you did when you finished the pardon investigation. I've read it, you know. I've read—no, not read—*studied* everything you've done since the day you learned the cops were trying to squeeze Jimmy Wallace."

"There's nothing in that report that I didn't believe was the absolute truth."

"At the time you wrote it." Delanghe smiled. "What about now?" Reppa licked his lips. Then he moved restlessly, turning away from those sharp, drill-like eyes.

"Look, Reppa. I've known all along your main interest in this wasn't to help us find McCreary's killer. You were taking up where he left off. For reasons I can't as yet fathom. What were they? And notice I use the *past* tense."

Reppa continued to sit silent. All last night, all the way to the bank this morning, and all the way on the subway ride back to the office with Delanghe, feelings of triumph and failure had alternated in him. Ever since that morning in Jimmy Wallace's bedroom he had found the job of searching his motives a difficult and slightly terrifying one. Although he seemed to know what he wanted—to succeed, get all the way to the end, come out the victor—he had no real idea what that meant or why it was so important to him.

And yet, when at last he spoke, it seemed to him that he had known all along what he would say.

"You want my reasons. First I want yours for wanting mine."

"My reasons?" Delanghe paused for a long moment; then his smile thinned to a bare trace of itself. "Who killed Behrman and Moffett? Do you know, Reppa?"

"Do you?"

It came back so swiftly that the shrunken pupils vanished for a moment behind a blink, but then Delanghe recovered himself and spoke commandingly. "It's not yours, Reppa. You went way beyond your depth as it was on McCreary."

"I also caught his killer. More exactly, my partner did."

Delanghe didn't pretend to see any humor in the remark. Reppa's quick, unsettling glance had made it clear that it was in no way a joke.

"Caught him, yes—but not explained why he tried to kill your girl friend."

"So it would look like I'd done it, and I'd be stopped from nailing him for McCreary's murder."

Delanghe said matter-of-factly, "The cops may have been satisfied with that, but I'm not. There's more to it."

"He may also have been trying to pay me back for screwing up his attempt to fix Zippy Dwersky's murder on de Spirit."

"Still more."

Reppa could not deny it. He wasn't sitting across the desk from a Smail or a Lidsky. Nor, he knew all at once, would he ever be again.

"Cupach was trying to button you, wasn't he, because

436

he was afraid you could turn up proof that de Spirit didn't kill Behrman and Moffett."

Again Reppa didn't deny it. But he knew that his silence told Delanghe nothing new.

"And can you?"

"Proof?" This one could be answered, and answered emphatically. "No."

Delanghe leaned back from the desk, indifferent, as if no longer concerned with what he and Reppa had been discussing. But then he came forward again, smiling ironically, to say, "March 27, 1944. What happened on that day in Elizabethtown, Kentucky?"

"I don't know. I wasn't there."

"Neither was Muntz. But he thought that day was important enough to get copies of those two death certificates. Why?"

"Muntz would have to answer that. I can't speak for him."

"Then let's go to something where you can—and had better—speak for yourself. What about there in the bank with his woman? What was that all about?"

The door pressed sharply against Reppa's back as he said, "It was a private affair."

"It's *our* affair." Delanghe's irony had turned into a kind of stilted reproach. "You're a parole officer," he said stiffly, and his voice hesitated between contempt and rebuke. "You've been acting all along on behalf of this agency. Though I seriously question whether you've been acting in the interests of this agency."

Reppa, hearing the canting tone in which he had been upbraided, felt his own voice grow easier. "Didn't you just tell me that Behrman-Moffett wasn't Parole's concern?"

"One hundred percent not."

437

"What I was doing with Muntz was entirely on my own, then."

"It's impossible ever—" Delanghe stopped. The briefest uncertainty crossed his face before the hooded expression returned. "Do you want to keep on working here?"

All the tensions of the last few days forced themselves in on Reppa suddenly. "I—not unless it's on my terms."

"There's no such thing. There are only *the* terms. They're no one's. They just are. If you're going to meet them, you'll have to start coming across with straight answers."

"For whose benefit?"

Hearing the quiet hostility in Reppa's voice, Delanghe glanced involuntarily at his file cabinets. Still, he managed to say, smoothly enough: "Your own."

"For my own benefit, what I want right now is two weeks vacation."

Delanghe waited several moments. Then he said, "For what reason?"

"Personal. I'll put in a memo to Smail if you want."

Delanghe's face was still an implacable mask. "Do," he said harshly. "And before you go, leave your gun and your shield in the safe upstairs."

"Is that an order?"

"A suggestion. A *strong* suggestion."

"I understand," Reppa said.

"Do you?" said Delanghe. Head erect, face stiff, he again beat on the desk top with his fingers for a moment.

There was a long silence, and Reppa decided at last that Delanghe had finished with him. But when he got up to leave, Delanghe spoke again.

"What you're leaving behind here must seem to you like nothing—and it may in fact *be* nothing—but it is the *only* thing. In this building and in this office, but especially in these file cabinets, is as much purpose as I could find anywhere. And I've made it quite a lot.'' He turned away from Reppa and looked out the window at the back of his office. The light struck his face sharply, highlighting the tanned flesh, so that for the moment he seemed younger. ''If you think you'll find more somewhere else than you have here, God help you. If you think what you're doing has already given you more, no one can help you.'' His glance shifted to the file cabinets. ''Many of the people in there thought the same thing in one way or another. They got the first message: Systems don't work. But they missed the second: Only people within them survive.'' He paused to return his gaze to Reppa, and for the next several moments, with the light behind him, his eyes disappeared in shadows. ''If all this seems too simple to you, then you've missed the third message: The simpler you can keep it, the longer you survive.''

Leilah had her notebooks spread around her on the bed, and one of her friends had loaned her a dictating machine. Though on principle she was opposed to the idea of writers who worked orally (writing, by sheer definition, was a manual art), yesterday had taught her she didn't have forever to get back to her typewriter. But she couldn't start feeding her notebooks into the machine just yet. She was bandaged all over. Her sternum had been padded to protect a hairline fracture, her shoulder was clamped, and there were stitches in her hands. She wasn't in much pain, though. The dreamy cast to her eyes spoke of some powerful sedation.

''They always claim your whole life passes before your eyes,'' she said distantly. ''Not true. All I saw was how much I hadn't gotten in.'' An urgency came into her voice. ''Will you take me to the Opening Day game next year? Will you, Reppa? Regardless?''

439

"Promise."

"No promises." Her hand gripped his, and her dark brown eyes filled with tears. "Promises are made to be kept. I don't want anything you're only doing because you've committed yourself to it."

He suspected she was talking about something more than a Mets game. He asked and awaited her answer with equal parts of disappointment and relief, for he could see ways, now that the goal had been sighted, of letting the ball pass out of his hands.

But Leilah said, "No, Reppa. You can't stop now. There's someone else besides yourself whom you've made a commitment to in this."

"You?"

"And besides me. Think. To whom else do you owe it to finish what you've started?"

"Oh, Christ. Don't say McCreary."

Leilah hesitated a moment and then with a wan smile she obliged him: She did not say McCreary.

The number you have reached, 555-2614, has been disconnected . . .

And when the elevator arrived at the eighth floor, Reppa saw the door had yet another padlock on it. Later, following a winding staircase at the rear of the building, he discovered that there was also a fire door, but the face was steel, and sunk into it like a vertical row of golden Cyclops eyes were three Fox locks. From the roof of the building across the street he could see drawn curtains in all the windows. For a long while he found himself rooted to the spot. It grew dark. No lights went on behind the drawn curtains. Was anyone still in there? He decided it made no difference. Either way he was sure now of his direction.

The birth certificates had shed first daylight on the mind

440

of the Reverend Abilene Loomis, and the death certificates had revealed what was in the corners of it. Meanwhile Reppa's own mind had been illuminated as well. He understood at long last something of the nature of his quarry. The man had committed two monstrous murders, but he had acted for a reason that was not so monstrous. It was, once you comprehended it, pathetically human.

For the moment he was still a parole officer but in name only. Badge and gun locked away in the office safe, he had nothing to vouch for his authority, which had never been very great anyway. Never enough. He had overstepped it day one, when he talked to Wallace's old grade-school teacher. But if he hadn't overstepped it, where would he be now? At ten o'clock on Friday morning, either behind his desk on Fortieth Street or somewhere in the middle of Harlem. Instead he was in the Old Chelsea Post Office complaining. The clerk barely listened; she had heard it so many times before. What she couldn't understand was why, when everybody knew what an inept operation the post office had become, people still bothered filling out temporary change-of-address cards. In minutes, however, she was back at the counter, telling him she couldn't understand why his mail wasn't being forwarded to him, because his card was right here, properly filled out and processed. Were they sure they could read his new address? he asked astringently. Just as tartly the clerk told him it was perfectly legible. Could she be so kind as to make doubly sure? He'd come all the way back here, not having received a stick of mail since leaving.

The answer, with a glance at the card in her hand (which he strained unsuccessfully to see), came tersely. No mistake was possible. His *Montauk* had been clearly printed. "Oh, well," he murmured apologetically, "the

441

mailman out there must not realize yet that I'm on his route.'' To which the clerk, making the most of her opportunity for triumph, retorted, *There* was the mistake— obviously his. He'd forgotten his request that his mail be sent to him care of General Delivery; it was undoubtedly sitting in the Montauk post office right this minute, waiting for him. He clapped a hand to his head. Good God! How stupid could he be! Sorry! "Glad," said the clerk, "to have been of *help*, Mr. Kinder."

It was around one hundred thirty miles from the city, about a three-hour drive. It could be accomplished in two-and-a-half if traffic was light and you held the accelerator steady all the way at a safe five or ten miles over the limit. It took him over four, making tortuous side junkets through Quogue, Westhampton, and Sag Harbor. Even then he doubted he could have lost anyone who was seriously trying to follow him.

Once in Montauk, he spent his first two days at the beach but was unable to get in the water. June was warm in the city, but at the easternmost tip of Long Island the ocean temperature was still prohibitive. He was staying in a place on the Old Montauk Highway called Flo's Escape. The summer rates were not yet in effect. His tacky little room was presently ninety dollars a week; by the end of the month the rate would be nearly triple that. While on the beach, lying in the blazing sun, he formed no particular plans and tried to think very little about why he was here. Sometimes he convinced himself that all of this had already been decided, but always, in the next moment, it seemed to him that he had made no decisions at all. What was clear to him was that neither McCreary nor Cupach would be here now. Possessed as they had been, there had been for them few moments of confusion and uncertainty; from the start they had known their aims and experienced

442

little of his crippling self-inquisition. He could almost envy them, even if they had failed ultimately. For if they had achieved their objectives, at least the reward would have been tangible and distinct. His own reward in this could be no more than further wonder at the strangeness that had come over his life and a recognition that the Bowden Delanghes in this world were not the ones who had the message.

He did not go near the post office until the morning of the third day. In the interim he'd used his car everywhere he went, watching the road behind him constantly in the rearview mirror. While jogging along the beach at the end of the day he would turn swiftly from time to time, but he never saw anyone duck behind a rock. At night, when he turned the lights out in his room and peered through a crack in the blind, the cars parked within range of his window were always empty. To check whether the police in Montauk had been instructed to keep him under surveillance, he walked up to every patrol car he saw and asked directions to some place or other. The reaction to him never differed from the reaction of cops to tourists in every town that was kept afloat by the summer season: a kind of simmering patience. Finally he left a briefcase on the front seat of his car one afternoon while he was at the beach. Returning to the car, he found all the doors still locked (no signs of tampering), and none of the four hairs he'd hidden in the various pockets of the briefcase had been displaced. It convinced him. Unless he was pitted against a super gestapo, he was not being watched. And there was nothing thus far to suggest the competition was anything super.

He was certain of all this the afternoon of his second day in town, but since it was Sunday, he could do nothing until the following morning. The post office was a block from the main highway on the corner of a short side street. He went inside for a few moments to get the lay of it and then returned to his car and pulled into a parking area across the street behind a row of stores that faced the highway. There he sat over an open newspaper, watching the entrance to the post office. Cars drove up and were left idling while their drivers got out to deposit letters in the drop box. Other cars stayed longer, their drivers disappearing into the building and reappearing with envelopes and packages. Many came to get or send their mail on foot. A few came on mopeds. Kinder did not venture to the post office at all on the first day of his watch, nor on the second. Just past noon on Wednesday he came on a bicycle. He had on faded khaki walking shorts, a green T-shirt, sandals, and a floppy straw hat. His eyes today looked at the world through wire sunglasses rather than the thick rimless pair. Not seeing the familiar glasses or the pale, balding head, Reppa might have missed Kinder were it not for the wicker basket attached to the handlebars on the bicycle. Bouncing out of it as soon as Kinder dropped the kickstand was a small black dog he recognized as Adelaide.

Sitting in his car, Reppa studied the entrance to the post office with a calm, unwandering attention. People went in, people came out. Kinder eventually was one of the latter, Adelaide cradled under his arm.

It was a matter now of staying in range without being seen. Kinder would be living along the cliffs somewhere, or he would be in one of the fishermen's shanties. In Montauk Kinder could not but lead him near water. He already had an inkling, practically an instinct, that it would be very near water.

With Adelaide as a passenger the bicycle could not go very fast. So that the dog wouldn't jump out of the basket, Kinder held his straw hat over it as he pedaled away.

444

Reppa waited until the bicycle reached the main highway and turned east before following.

The Montauk Highway, heading toward the Point, was mostly empty, and as he drove along it under the noonday sun, the emptiness hung heavily over him. He was reminded of the road along Lake Erie, not the congested area around Cleveland but the long, lonely stretch just before the Pennsylvania border, which was deserted beyond endurance. He had once craved that kind of desolation but no longer. Now he wanted civilization all around him. He hoped Kinder was not living in the rough, subsisting crazily on wild berries and game. That would mean Kinder had a weapon, a knife or a rifle. He remembered that Kinder, for however short a time, had been in the army.

Staring at the bicycle, never letting it out of his sight but at the same time carefully staying well behind it, Reppa became aware that his shirt was drenched with perspiration and his heart was going at almost double its normal rate. Everything else he was feeling seemed immensely slow and cold. The car wheels under him were barely moving. Behind him, in the side-view mirror, the road glared painfully, catching and reflecting the sunlight like a ribbon of ice. Coming out of a long curve, he realized all at once that the road ahead of him was empty. He accelerated sharply. A hundred yards or so farther on he spied the bicycle again, parked on the shoulder of the road at the top of a steep rise. Kinder was standing with both feet on the ground, a hand pressed to his forehead.

Mopping it while he caught his breath from the climb? Or making a visor so he could stare behind him into the sun?

Later Kinder halted again at the top of another long, rising curve. They had passed several crossroads by now, and for a stretch the highway was lined closely on both

445

sides with heavy foliage. It looked, too, as if there were nothing but wilds ahead of them; but Reppa, having driven this way the previous evening on one of his reconnoitering missions, knew the appearance was deceptive. Still to come, between here and the Point, were a number of small settlements, unexpected parentheses in the dunes and the wilderness.

The bicycle, at a guess, was about two hundred yards away. Kinder seemed in no hurry to go anywhere. Before starting up again he waited for a truck going in the opposite direction to pass him. Reppa, inching along at the foot of the curve, found his view of the bicycle obstructed for several long moments by the truck as it came toward him, hugging the center stripe. Crafty on Kinder's part. Reppa could no longer doubt he had been spotted.

He hit the accelerator. Going uphill, the car gathered speed very slowly. By the time he reached the top of the curve, Kinder had added many more yards to the distance between them, pedaling furiously. As Reppa swooped down out of the curve, he saw the straw hat fly out of the basket and then something tiny and black scrabbling to get out of the road. Spinning the steering wheel violently, he missed it by only inches.

His eyes, glued to the windshield, got a glimpse of Kinder, hunched far forward now on the bicycle seat, sprinting off down a side road at the right of the highway. Seconds later there was a shriek and shudder of machinery under Reppa as he braked hard and turned, all four tires spitting cinders, into the same road. A sign that had flown past him just before he'd hit the brake had time to register now as something more than a blur.

He was entering Ditch Plains.

Patches of small cottages and bungalows. Here and there a kid playing. He noticed these things peripherally and noticed, too, that the road was level and fairly straight—but somehow the bicycle had disappeared. Into one of those cottages or bungalows? If so, he could just about forget it. There were too many. It would take hours to go around to each one. And even if he did, Kinder was hardly going to come to the door when he knocked. But then, smiling to himself, he remembered there were other, better instincts than his that could be trusted in this situation.

He drove back to the highway, got out of his car, and stood waiting. It took a while before he saw it, at first only as a black dot along the side of the road but then gradually taking shape as it moved toward him. He smiled again when it passed him and toddled down the road to Ditch Plains. Before following on foot he checked his pockets for paper, a pen.

The cottage wanted a coat of paint. No one had mowed the grass since the previous summer. It looked, from the road, like a large outhouse. The cottages on either side of it were no more stately, but they seemed to be vacant. Only the dog told him this one wasn't. It sniffed at the door, whined a little. The door was locked, no mat on the stoop outside it, shutters on the windows. Around back was the only sign of life he could find here. A rubber bone. When he put it in front of Adelaide, she rolled over on her back, and he remembered the name had been a mistake.

The message he wrote was brief: *Your choice*. He shoved it under the door and knocked. He walked away for a few minutes. When he returned, Adelaide had dragged the message out from under the door. A new toy. He wrote another message, same two words, and added: *You have an hour to decide*. This paper he wedged in the door, too high up for the dog to leap.

Wondering what he would do if he were Kinder, he

447

went back to his car. It was twenty after one. There wasn't another train out of Montauk until late in the day. No buses. The closest airport was several miles. He sat and looked at the minutes going by on his watch, one by one. The highway was, of course, not the only route of escape. There was the beach. A man running, even on sand, could cover a fair amount of ground in an hour. As could a man swimming. It came to him, sitting there and watching the minutes pass, that he was not going to be altogether unhappy if Kinder fled. He further understood that he was more frightened of Kinder than he'd ever been of Cupach. Beyond his own death and that of someone close to him, he truly feared only two things: confinement and failure. Confinement paralyzed the spirit, and failure rotted it, and Kinder smelled of both. He would always retain pictures of that loft on West Eighteenth Street, but the one he would remember best was the small cell-like room, the narrow cot, sheets trailing limply on the floor.

Then it was past two o'clock. He could stall himself no longer. The cottage, when he drove up to it, looked every bit as uninhabited as it had earlier, but the dog and bone were gone from the yard. As he knocked on the door, his thoughts were on who would answer. *It just better not*, he whispered to himself, *be someone in a long black dress*.

The door opened slowly, and Kinder, slender, pale, and bearded, stood facing him, more or less at attention, his arms to his sides. He still wore the khaki shorts and green T-shirt, but the dark glasses had been changed for the thick rimless pair. Behind them were two very large, very vigilant brown irises. Reppa seemed to see something bright and blue reflected beneath their surfaces when he said, "Alexander Loomis, now known as Abilene's children."

Kinder was beyond words for a moment, but only a

moment. He said with a quiet reverence, "All family members deserve to have something named in their memory."

"Including Annabelle?"

He watched Kinder's eyes fold over.

"Annabelle needs no memorials yet. She'll outlive us all."

"I've seen her death certificate, Loomis. She's been dead for over thirty-six years now."

"Do you believe everything you read?"

It was said so mildly that Reppa was suddenly unsure. "Annabelle died a few weeks after she gave birth to Andrea."

Had the irises shown blue for an instant again? He went on.

"Your father saw a way to get you out of the war. He made a copy of her death certificate and replaced her name on the copy with yours. Same number of letters. Then he substituted *M*, male, for *F*, female, and buried her under your name. By the time the army learned you were dead, they would have had to dig up the body to prove otherwise."

"So they would." The irises regarded him fixedly. "But they would have found only an empty grave." Kinder gave him a few seconds to absorb this and then said, "You see, at the same time my father spared me from being killed in the war, he packed off the family black sheep to New York. Annabelle wasn't his daughter."

For a moment Reppa was so incredulous that he neither moved nor spoke. Then he managed to say, "That grave couldn't be empty."

Kinder continued as if Reppa had not spoken. "It was thrown in his face by my mother just before she died. Annabelle's true father was a gospel singer who had once been a rival of my father's for my mother's hand."

It sounded unbearably stiff, as if it were being offered

449

only under duress. Absent from Kinder's voice was all trace of the mockery that Reppa had heard in everything until now. He said, "Anyone can make a copy of a death certificate and doctor the information on it. Not even a preacher can obtain an original death certificate unless someone's died."

"Not legally perhaps." Kinder shrugged. "But my father was desperate. He wanted to save my life and as an afterthought saw how he could also rid himself of any further responsibility for my half sister. In a way my mother's revelation was a blessing in disguise for Annabelle. Now she was free to leave home and go wherever she wished to pursue her artistic talent."

"And of course it was a blessing for your half sister in still another way. It made things between the two of you only half incest."

Kinder's mouth twitched. There was a resentful silence. "Don't use that word," he whispered then in an ugly tone. "Don't you *ever*."

"Do you deny Annabelle was Andrea's mother and you were her father?"

"You said I had a choice." Kinder started to close the door. "I prefer the police. They're more humane."

"They won't be once they're told that Annabelle's dead and that you took her name and identity and have been posing as her all these years."

"Silly." Kinder nervously turned over a hand to show Reppa's absurdity. "Annabelle's not dead. She's right here."

He opened the door wide, as if inviting Reppa to inspect the cottage. In the insecure light beyond Kinder, Reppa seemed to see a dim form standing in the interior. The heat of the afternoon and the long tense days of tracking Kinder had worked steadily on his faculties, and now, as he

450

blinked at the image, only enough resolution remained for him to murmur: "Take me to her."

"Annabelle came out here for more privacy, but instead she has less. How did you find us?"

"I didn't," Reppa said. "I only found you."

"I wish that were true. Oh, how I wish." In Kinder's voice it sounded grimly ironic. "Will you go if I take you to Annabelle?"

"Not until I've actually spoken to her."

"That may not be possible."

"I won't be surprised."

Kinder answered him faintly, almost under his breath. "But I will be if you aren't."

To Reppa's ears it sounded hollow. He hoped it was hollow. But when Kinder did not take him into the cottage but instead began leading him away from it and toward the bright open sea, he feared that there was still much he had not understood about this man.

They followed a maze of winding paths along the cliff line for more than a mile, Kinder in the lead but not insistently, as if he, too, were unfamiliar with the area. A light mist had begun to roll in from the east. For a while they were able to see the ocean far below and here and there a sunbather, but then the beach narrowed and grew increasingly rocky, and the trees and undergrowth thickened. The terrain along here was very different from the rest of Long Island, which was relatively flat and sandy and open. This was rugged and primeval.

After some twenty minutes of walking Kinder slowed his pace and began to scan the cliff line as though for a landmark. At last he stopped in a half circle of large, jagged rocks, where he stood gazing downward through

451

the mist. His finger rose, then straightened. "Down there," he said.

Following Kinder's direction, Reppa saw only tangles of vines and, on down the cliffside, scrub pines and bushes. "Where?"

"On the beach. She's drawing."

"Naturally. In a place where there's no way I can see for myself if you're telling the truth."

Kinder said with a shrug, "You could go back the way we came, I suppose, and work your way down from the town beach. Perhaps in the mist she won't see you coming in time to . . ." He completed the thought by turning to Reppa and staring dully at him.

Glancing away, Reppa saw, some ten or twelve yards ahead of them, what looked like the mouth of a path. Pointing to it, he said, "Where does that go?"

Kinder shook his head hopelessly. "Nowhere."

"Then how did Annabelle get down there?"

"By walking from the town beach. She chose this spot very carefully our first day here and marked it for me so I'd know where she was in case . . ." Kinder let that thought drop, too, and said, "Since you won't take my word, I suggest you find a way to get down there and see for yourself."

Reppa strode to the path and saw it went down the side of the cliff for about twenty yards before arriving at a shelf of large rocks. Beyond the rocks he could not see, but he estimated they were high enough and far enough down the cliff that standing on them would provide him with at least a partial view of the beach below.

As he started to descend the path, he heard Kinder call to him. When he turned, he saw that Kinder had sat down on a rock and was smiling. "It goes nowhere. Truly."

In his mind's eye the front of Kinder's head jutted out of

a dark doorway, rimless glasses glittering. Turning back to the path, he saw a figure in a long black dress standing before a curtained window. He knew now how it had been done, and he realized the method had been revealed to him when Mald showed him a sample of Annabelle's art. "In the only way I could," Mald had said, and the song he'd been humming as they went down the hallway in the gallery was "Funeral March of a Marionette." Mald had known the bent Annabelle's mind had taken and could have told him Kinder had not left him sitting alone in that bleak, barren office to take care of the elevator and Annabelle had not left him standing for so long in that lifeless, museumlike room so that she could make a grand entrance. But Mald had only known a small part of the secret. For Mald had not quite known Annabelle.

He got to the shelf of rocks. They were not as large as they had appeared from the top of the cliff, and when he stood on the tallest of them and stared down through the trees, he could see only a small strip of beach far below. Near the edge of the surf, between clouds of mist, he seemed to see a black figure seated on a chair.

He looked behind him once more. Kinder was sitting far forward, hands clasping bare, hairless legs, frowning downward at him. He had to choose. If he went down to the beach, Kinder would be gone when he got back. But if he did not go down there, Kinder would claim it was only Reppa's overactive imagination that had convinced him Kinder had used the hour after getting the note to engineer one last deception.

Reppa was motionless for a moment, considering, and when he stepped down from the rock, it was with the recognition that he was not here for justice or retribution. True justice in this instance could only be self-imposed. Men like Kinder, although they went uncaught, did not go unpunished. The whispery voice crying out that twelve years in prison wasn't nearly enough punishment for two murders belonged to a mind that had long ago comprehended that. Annabelle *had* been a prisoner in her own loft. In that sense Reppa had been absolutely right. What he had not understood was that Annabelle was a self-made prisoner. It occurred to him (though he knew he could never prove it) that the day Danny de Spirit had been sentenced to life was also the last day the outside world had seen Annabelle.

Below the rocks the path dwindled quickly to only a faint trail, and he became immersed in dense thickets, prickly bushes. Black flies that beleaguered his face and neck. Poison ivy and sumac. He blundered ahead stubbornly, pushing and shoving through undergrowth, beating aside branches, believing the path could only be a way, however rough, down to the beach. When at last he emerged into the open air again, he found himself standing on a narrow overhang. What seemed a sheer drop faced him. Inching up to peer over the edge, he felt the ground start to give way, heard rocks tumbling beneath him. He pulled back in frustration, aware now that when Kinder had said this spot had been chosen carefully, he'd meant treacherously. The path had been a lure. From here the beach was all but inaccessible.

But when he looked behind him and thought of the climb back to the top of the cliff and the time it would take him, his frustration became perplexity. Drawn by the path, drawn farther by the figure on the beach, he had gone plunging downward as Kinder had intended. And the moment he had been out of Reppa's sight, Kinder had undoubtedly doubled back to the town beach, from where, with his enormous head start, he would simply walk along the sand to the figure, remove it, and then return to the cottage and await the next development. The deception could go on and on, Reppa saw now. For while Annabelle was resigned to being a prisoner, Kinder was determined to remain free, as if one half sought punishment and the other wanted to be the sole agent that decided how and why that punishment was administered.

Should he interfere? He hesitated and stood looking up, as if to avoid seeing the wide open space ahead of him, the tangle of foliage and insects behind him. But then he remembered that in undertaking the pardon investigation he had committed himself, and he began to understand the responsibility of that commitment. The doors that had been locked to McCreary had been no less locked to him. But in his persistence he had been like a gnat who slipped through the screen. And now that he had, he had committed himself to discovering what was there.

Slowly, on his hands and knees, he worked his way along the cliff until he got to ground that felt more secure. When he stood up, he saw he was between two small headlands. To his right, just a few yards away, erosion had gouged a long, sloping trough in the side of the cliff. At the base of it, between the headlands, was a triangle of beach. He had to wait for a break in the mist before he saw it was empty.

The sea was churning, waves crashing over partially submerged rocks, as he came toward it, sliding down the trough, crouched like a skier.

As soon as he reached the sand, he looked west toward the town beach. His eyes could penetrate the mist for only a hundred yards or so, but in that space he saw nothing. No one coming.

He turned and ran toward the headland behind him. The tip of it protruded into the ocean, and to get around it, he had to wade out a ways and then scramble up a pile of wet, slippery rocks. But once he was on top of them, he saw immediately that the figure was still there, seated on a metal folding chair, its back to him, an open sketchbook in its lap. He could feel already, in his fingertips, the plaster shoulder when he seized it.

Nothing moved when he approached. Nothing stirred anywhere. Even the pages of the sketchbook did not flutter. He had not realized until then how quiet and still the air over the beach had gone.

Step by step, his feet crunching in the sand under him, he moved closer to the figure. There was no worry about noise; nothing could hear him. There was no hurry; nothing could stop him.

He put out his hand and touched the shoulder.

He knew it was flesh, solid flesh, even before the figure turned to him. He stared at the person whose reality he had doubted, and his blood froze.

The blue eyes met his, coldly wrathful. Something flashed in the hand at the end of the long black sleeve.

Reppa fumbled for the gun he no longer had, but then he saw he had no need of a weapon. As he stood stunned, silent, and rigid, the palette knife lowered, and the figure turned back to the sketchbook.

A moment later, although he continued to stand frozen, he began to see as if with double vision. As a parole officer and former football coach, he searched for a hidden stratagem. Having been drilled in spite of himself in the ways a writer sees, he sought the psychology behind it. And then it struck him where his mistake had been. Who, besides Kinder, said the town beach was the only route to this spot? Thinking back to the walk with Kinder along the cliff line, he remembered how fortified and unassailable it had looked the last quarter of a mile or so. But up ahead, to the east, was unknown. He shaded his eyes and gazed toward the Point. He saw, rearing out of the mist, another headland, and while he could not see beyond it, he already knew.

When he glanced behind him before starting to walk eastward, the figure in black threw him a bleak, hopeless look, the eyes wide and round and empty under the long, hanging hair.

Within ten minutes he was back. In the time he'd been gone, there had been only one change. The figure now sat with both hands concealed under the black dress. His own hands were held out in front of him. In them were a false beard and a pair of leather sandals. He noticed now that the figure's feet were bare. As he approached, he seemed to see the figure's face twist as though with some inward pain, and when he dropped the beard at the figure's feet, he heard a faint groan. But the figure only continued to sit there, oddly serene.

On the far side of the headland, behind a rock at the bottom of a steep path that his eyes had traced up the cliff before becoming lost in mist and foliage, there had been a white plaster figure. Hollow, light enough to carry under one arm, without clothes or hair, it had the posture of a sitting woman. A slenderish, small-breasted woman. In a gray-black wig and a long black dress it would have been quite indistinguishable from the figure seated before him now . . . slim, hairless ankles, long, gnarled feet, the bones laid close and prominent beneath the face, the eyes large and blue and bottomless.

The hands never did come out from under the dress to form the familiar balance scale, but the voice was once more talking to him in its familiar whispers. He grew conscious of an uneasiness at the back of his mind: a deep uneasiness occasioned by his own voice whispering to him that he was hearing things that no one had ever heard before or would ever hear again.

In talking to him the figure had grown increasingly relaxed within itself. Sitting there, it spoke steadily and quietly and went on staring at him. Past him, more often, at some faraway distance. He forced himself to listen, even after the expression on the figure's face had grown so peaceful and so relaxed that he could no longer look into the blank eyes. He thought several times of interrupting but never did. Tense and nervous as he'd been when he was first in the figure's presence, he was now thoroughly numb.

It was going to be over soon. Most of it was already over.

In a sense Alexander Loomis really had died all those years ago when he had exchanged identities with his half sister, whose fear and groping toward sexual awakening had been as awkward and guilt-infested as his own. Who had once, only once, allowed him to go too far, because neither of them had been quite aware of where he was going. And who had become pregnant and been sent away after they had both taken an oath that they would never reveal his part in it. But he was terrified his father would find out anyway, and more relieved at first than scared when the army took him away from home. While he was in boot camp, Annabelle had the child. But it was a long and difficult delivery, a surgical one, and she returned home very weak. Commanded by the reverend over and over again to tell the name of her child's father, she had finally collapsed and admitted the truth. Alexander knew none of this until he came home on leave before going overseas. By then Annabelle was huddling all day in bed, and his father was shouting that his two children had committed the sin most unforgivable in the eyes of the

458

Lord. Thinking to lighten the stain, Alexander reminded the reverend that Annabelle wasn't really his daughter. But this only made it worse. Now his father decided that Annabelle was the cause of everything evil in the family and ordered her from his home. Annabelle's response was to stop eating, stop doing everything, and just shrivel up in her bed. A few mornings before his leave ended, she started shaking all of a sudden and couldn't stop. In a while she lost consciousness, and by noon she was gone. No sooner had she died than the reverend gathered Alexander and Adelaide together and told them what they must do if the Loomis family was to survive this blasphemy.

So Adelaide went off with Andrea, and Alexander went to the place in the country most remote from Elizabethtown. A place where no one would wonder unduly about a man who dressed and posed as a woman. In the beginning it was only going to be temporary, until the war had been over long enough for the army to lose any curiosity it might have had about him and he'd no longer have to rely on his father and Adelaide to send him money. Afraid to go out of his room, afraid to be spoken to, and especially afraid to be touched by people who thought he was a woman, he hid away within himself most of the time. For something to do he experimented with his talent for making things. As a boy he'd always been whittling and had become quite good with his hands. Now he discovered those hands had a lot of ideas in them. Since he couldn't go out among people, he constructed some of his own. For company. People who looked as lonely and misfit as he felt. But they weren't enough. Sometimes, too desperate to prevent himself, he gave in and became Alexander again for a few hours. It unsettled him more and more each time he tried it, and not just because of the fear that the army might catch up with him and put him in jail. Even worse were the responses he got from other people, particularly women. They were so shrewd in New York, all of them, and they made him so conscious of himself, of his pale, skinny body and his twangy, fumbling voice. It was much easier all around, he learned, to live in New York masquerading as a woman. And very much easier as a woman so odd no one dared bother her.

He would never have tried to do anything with the people he made, but Adelaide kept insisting. He didn't know why she had to follow him to New York. He was doing all right on his own. But then she came and saw ways of making things better—her idea of better—for everybody. Since she couldn't go on forever taking care of him, and his people seemed the only thing he could do on his own, he had to find a way to make a living out of them. She would help. She had an idea, she said, and when she told him what it was, he was amused. It seemed like it could be a fantastic joke on someone. On everyone. But it was never supposed to happen that he'd become famous, and when it did, he was driven even deeper within himself. Now he could never come out of hiding. He really was who he was pretending to be. After a while, though, he began to like it. Everything but not having anyone to share it with. Maybe after Adelaide died and got out of his way, it all could have changed. Changed back. He had the feeling for a while that it was going to, but there was a deeper feeling that he really didn't want it to anymore. If he could find just one person. One person like him, a lot like him. If it could just have been kept to one person . . . .

Reppa noticed that the voice was fading, losing words, beginning to gasp for breath, and he found this new sound unnervingly, even painfully disturbing. The hands had emerged from under the dress and were twisting one another now in the slumping lap. The long, slender body had sagged in the chair, and the eyes were beginning to glaze over. Reppa saw for a brief moment beyond this image that of a man staring into himself, staring backward to see himself as he must have looked standing in front of a chair and gazing down at a body that was bound to it, and gazing then at another body whose eyes had seen his own body for the first time, seen it as it truly was and not as it had been hidden from her all her life. Some of this man must have wanted his true identity to be known to his daughter—perhaps desperately wanted it to be known—but he had not been aware of this desire in himself in time to stop himself from going about it wrong.

Reppa understood, when Loomis began slowly to rise, that there would be no more. From beneath the dress he heard something drop. Then Loomis moved, and when Reppa saw the palette knife lying on the sand, he heard himself groan. With a slight ducking motion of his head Loomis nodded, and the sudden brillance of the round blue eyes made an impression, as they calmly met his own, that would last in him forever.

He stood aside. Loomis turned, trembled slightly, and then began walking slowly away from him. The head was straight, the eyes were fixed on the mist, on the horizon beyond it that could not be seen. The black dress trailed behind, leaving splashes of red that formed, as Reppa's eyes followed it, a long, narrow aisle across the sand.

Then a wave came, and the last few yards of the aisle were washed away. He stared at the dress floating on top of the water, the long hair spreading and shimmering like a net. Then only the hair was left. He saw a few strands of black, some gray, and filmy lines of red radiating slowly outward. In a moment another wave came, and all these colors were gone.

461

EPILOGUE

On an unseasonably cool morning in late August Reppa, having finally gotten around to clearing out his apartment, sat on the front steps of the building on East Ninth Street for one last time. Shortly after leaving Ohio State he had developed the habit of tabulating in his mind for a few minutes every now and then the progress of his former teammates and opponents, and he indulged in this whim of nostalgia now.

Danny de Spirit had briefly become something of a hero when he was released after pleading innocent at a preliminary hearing to the murders of Andrea Behrman and Elizabeth Moffett. Now, however, he was back in custody, under indictment for a series of burglaries on the Upper West Side. His stepbrother, Jimmy Wallace, was faring somewhat better. As a condition of being restored to parole supervision, he'd been ordered at his final violation hearing to enter a residential drug treatment facility. Currently he was at Odyssey House on East Sixth Street, where Reppa had once tried to visit him. But visitors other than parole and probation officers were not allowed, and Reppa at the moment was neither.

Stanley Behrman and Jeff Halliwell were still living, as

best he knew, in their own tenuous and changeless fashion, but something must have happened to Carlo Mald. The gallery had become a repository for art deco, and though Mald's name was still on the door, he himself was never seen there anymore.

About the men and women with whom he'd worked at the Division of Parole, Reppa knew no more than any private citizen whose only information about the criminal justice system came from the media. There had been a furor in the middle of July, when the widow of John Jacob McCreary had sued the state for denying her the life insurance due the spouse and family of a parole officer killed in the line of duty, but the state had recanted before the suit ever got to court. Later in July Bowden Delanghe had taken part in a panel discussion on whether the parole system should be abolished, which had appeared unexpectedly one night on Channel 13.

The stocking behind the door in his bedroom had been disclaimed by Leilah, who'd noticed it ahead of everything else, and he supposed now that it must have belonged, after all, to Zippy.

All the furniture worth salvaging had been removed from upstairs, but that still left most of it. Leilah pretended to a feeling that some sort of ceremony had to be made out of his departure, but he knew she was just uneasy because he'd had nothing to celebrate lately whereas she'd had so much. The eighty-five thousand dollars she'd gotten when the paperback rights for *Sugar and Spice and Everything Nice* were auctioned meant she would not have to go back to John Jay when her medical leave of absence expired. Since the book was partly about Lois Cerny, she'd known what she was doing, apparently. The ten grand really had been an investment.

Reppa's own investment for the moment was in her

career. Until she could get around on her own again, she needed a chauffeur. Also, on occasion, someone to answer a few phone calls and claim she wasn't in. You could say a secretary. When she came up behind him, he felt her cane tap him on the shoulder. Turning, he watched her point it questioningly into the foyer.

"Aren't you going to get your mail?"

"Who's still writing to me at this address?" He inserted his key in the box and removed a long envelope.

It had been there for several days, judging by the postmark. It was from Woody Hayes, who was being courted for the head coaching job at a rival Big Ten school and was looking for assistants. It was going to cause problems.